SILVER UNDER NIGHTFALL

SILVER UNDER NIGHTFALL

RIN CHUPECO

HODDER &
STOUGHTON

First published in Great Britain in 2022 by Hodder & Stoughton
An Hachette UK company

1

Copyright © Rin Chupeco 2022

The right of Rin Chupeco to be identified as the Author of the Work has been
asserted by them in accordance with the Copyright, Designs and Patents Act 1988.

A CIP catalogue record for this title is available from the British Library

Hardback ISBN 978 1 399 71157 9
Trade Paperback ISBN 978 1 399 71158 6
eBook ISBN 978 1 399 71160 9

Printed and bound in Great Britain by Clays Ltd, Elcograf S.p.A.

Hodder & Stoughton policy is to use papers that are natural, renewable
and recyclable products and made from wood grown in sustainable
forests. The logging and manufacturing processes are expected to
conform to the environmental regulations of the country of origin.

Hodder & Stoughton Ltd
Carmelite House
50 Victoria Embankment
London EC4Y 0DZ

www.hodder.co.uk

For Tam—
for pulling me out of the gutter

THE FOREST
OF FANGS

They never tell you it's the girls that are hardest to kill.

He would've liked nothing more than to forget every ball he'd ever been forced to attend, but the mind is a funny bastard, one he'd trained to retain information on the off chance it could save his life. And so he remembered. He remembered *her*.

First-year debutantes tended to flee from him once the introductions were over, which was only a shade politer than those in their second and third years, who needn't bother speaking to him at all. But she was sixteen years old and a willowy little thing, all dolled up in pink lace; stammering and nervous at first, but braver than she let on. She'd stayed and smiled and talked to him like he wasn't a pariah among the aristocracy, like she wasn't risking her reputation over a conversation with him. She had lovely green eyes and smelled like jasmine.

She'd called him *Armiger*; not *Lord* or *Lady*, but a neutral title he felt was more in keeping with who he was. She hadn't mocked him like so many others had.

The bar for empathy was on the ground as far as the nobility was concerned, but when you were used to eating dirt, being thrown a bone felt like kindness.

And so it had hurt, in an unexpected, bewildering way, when he'd received the order to execute her.

Like most of the damned, she was beautiful. She'd always been breathtaking, but death had a curious way of remolding her features, shaping them into an artificial perfection that mere mortals could never reach. He was reminded of his old school lessons; of chameleons who changed their colors for camouflage, of butterflies that mimicked flowers for their own protection.

But Lady Daneira's preternatural beauty was not for her protection. Lady Daneira's beauty was bait.

She stood in the small clearing with moonlight threading through the dark tresses of her hair, braiding it in softer shades of light. Her small, white fingers trembled as she undid the laces of her gown, deliberate in their clumsiness.

"Come to me," she crooned.

He approached her. His eyes were not on her face, nor were they on her now-exposed bodice. They were on her lips, which were stained in a scarlet hue darker than any rouge could achieve. She smiled at him then, and he could almost—almost—see traces of the girl she once was, even as her arms wound themselves around his neck, her breath light against the base of his throat.

"Please," she whispered, and her mouth opened—wide.

She was quick, but he was quicker.

She shoved him away with a screech and stumbled back as blood pooled down her chin. He'd stabbed a wooden stake right through the flesh, exiting at the back of her head. She wrenched the weapon free, leaving an ugly, gaping hole between her upper cheek and lower jaw, injuries she ignored as she flung away the stake and focused on his face, her lips twisting and fangs protruding farther when she realized what he was.

"Reaper," she snarled, and leaped.

She blurred from view, reappeared behind him, then disappeared again as he spun around until she was surrounding him from all sides simultaneously. A neat trick for someone only two weeks dead. He drew out Breaker from where it lay strapped across his back, the thick handle a bludgeon all on its own. His thumb moved across a hidden switch, and concealed twin scythe blades snapped outward at the farthest end like ram horns, curved downward and sharp.

She was too fast, though, and he was still mortal. The problem with carrying something that was essentially five weapons in one was that it weighed the sum of its parts.

Gauging a vampire's movements with human eyes was pointless and often fatal. So he concentrated on his sixteen years of training—sixteen years of getting bled out and stabbed and maimed so badly that his sharpened senses could pinpoint exactly where she was about to attack based on which part of his body was already phantom-aching.

His left side throbbed. He turned to deflect, the steel slamming against fingernails that could tear through bark. She flickered away and came after him from a different direction, only to be frustrated once again.

"Why won't you let me kill you?" she cried out as petulantly as a child. A vessel had been severed somewhere behind her right iris, and from that eye, blood cried down, hardened, and clotted.

He had no energy to spare for talking, and when she came at him a third time, he deflected the blow and mounted his first real offensive. She drew back to avoid the downward slash, Breaker's edge missing her neck by a precious inch. Her wounds were ugly, buttered in a permanent splotch across her face, half of which was drenched in sticky, already congealing blood, but even confronted with this proof of her true nature, he hesitated.

If he'd been smart and staked her through the heart right from the beginning, as he'd done countless times to countless creatures of the night for countless other bounties, the fight would have already been over. *Short, quick, brutal* was the basic tenet of Reaper training.

But he'd never been known for his intelligence. The three days spent hunting down Lady Daneira had been three days of hoping not to find her. That the witnesses were mistaken. That it was some other corpse they'd seen haunting Tennyfair lands. That it wasn't someone he'd known, however brief the acquaintance and however light her jasmine scent.

He could almost hear his father now. *You've always been a softhearted fool, Son. You got that from your mother.*

Lady Daneira was freshly turned, but still a freshly turned novice, even if that made her a thousand times deadlier than the average fighter. She wasn't used to her food fighting back so early in her undead life, and her untethered rage at his rejection left her open to reprisal. In that moment, staring down at her mad, lovely eyes, he accepted that she was lost. Drawing out the battle would be the cruelest thing he could do.

So when she came after him again, he'd steeled his resolve, asked her quietly for forgiveness, and struck from below, altering the angle of his slash to catch her unaware.

He kept Breaker nice and sharp. As far as beheadings went, it was a clean one.

He dropped to his knees afterward, holding her. Her eyes were wide and staring, mouth slightly parted in shock. Her gaze fluttered to his, and in their depths he saw stray bits of humanity returning.

"Armiger Remy," she whispered in newfound recognition. And then, one final time: "Please."

Still cradling her head carefully against his arm, he reached over and picked up the discarded stake. Her eyes followed his movements as he crouched over her fallen body.

"I'm sorry." The words always felt hollow, but he said them every time. She was lucid—they sometimes were, near the end, but never for long.

Now her smile was exactly as he remembered it. "Send me to heaven, Armiger."

And this time, Remy didn't hesitate.

He sat with her awhile. He'd never understood the point of administering final rites, mainly because he was shit at it. But undead or not, the Duke of Tennyfair had been adamant Remy bring his daughter's body back intact so they could inter her on family grounds. Reaper law demanded that he cremate her, but his father had told him to make an exception this time.

Gently, he placed her head against the crook of her arm and breathed a small prayer over the body, as he'd always done and was expected to do, though the words brought him little comfort and even less peace.

Then he rose to his feet.

"I really do not have the bloody time for this," Remy said.

He only had a second to feel a pinch of warning in his right arm, because this attack was swift, more calculated and precise than any of Lady Daneira's attempts. He countered it all the same and blocked another pair of hands right before they could shove through his back and exit his chest with a fistful of vertebrae. His attacker snarled, fangs bared and fingers satisfactorily mangled by the abruptness of Breaker's steel, before retreating when Remy swung his weapon again.

Eight vampires surrounded him; ethereal and inhuman, dressed in dark, albeit expensive, linens and silks—all an unnecessary, *ridiculous* show of intimidation that would surely impress the owls and squirrels who'd come to watch. More glaring than the suits was the condescending, mocking insufferability radiating off them like cheap cologne.

"You got one lucky shot in, Hunter," one of them jeered—a boy who looked no older than he was, with carefully primped hair and a cold smile. He wore his arrogance like a second coat. Remy wanted to punch him. "You won't get another."

"Which of you turned her?" There were no coincidences when vampires were involved. His stomach churned at what they must have done, at what her final hours had been like at their hands, and his blood was up, exhilarated, ready to let. He hadn't wanted to kill Lady Daneira, but now he was itching for a massacre.

"Do you always take that tone with your betters, fresh blood?"

"Only with the ones that piss me off."

The vampire laughed. "And what will you do about it? Who would they believe—a noble, or some commoner who's just slayed a duke's daughter in the woods?"

Remy said nothing. The vampire glided closer, emboldened by his silence and their numbers. "What's one more dead, then? Who's to say that we didn't stumble upon a depraved hunter assaulting a sweet young girl out here and took justice into our own hands? The Summer Lords and the humans are on the verge of an alliance now, aren't they? We've got a moral obligation to report crimes, don't we? And you *did* kill her. Where's the lie in that?"

"Tell me who turned her."

"Does it matter?" another of the vampires asked—an older one with rougher features at odds with his primped clothes, and a full beard. "You make for better entertainment than she ever did. Kill him. Leave his body as a present for the humans. Let them believe the poor little girl eviscerated him as her final act of spite."

A compartment from within the base of Breaker's handle slid free, a thick chain springing out. A straight blade no longer than his forearm but equally as sharp as the scythes' had been soldered onto the end, and Remy swung it in a wide arc. It caught two of the vampires in their stomachs. They hit the ground flailing, hands grasping at suddenly exposed entrails.

The chain made a second pass. Blood sprayed, and they stopped twitching.

"Witch's teats, Naji," one of the others gasped. "Look at that thing! He's not just a hunter, he's the damned Butcher's get!"

That revelation did not cause an immediate retreat, as one might expect. Remy could smell their desperation. There were more problems to be had with the son of *the* infamous Reaper than an unknown hunter trying to make his bones off bounties. Better credibility and a more plausible testimony, for starters.

They leaped for him.

Remy bisected the bearded vampire first, then sank one of his scythe blades straight through his heart for good measure. His opponent crumbled immediately, nothing of him left but ash sweeping through the wind.

He took out one more with the double blades while he jerked at his chain, the knife attached to it gutting a second creature behind him. He used its swinging, looping momentum to slice up a third across their kneecaps, then across their lungs when they dove at him from above. The group's bratty ringleader snarled and persisted despite their losses, avoiding the deadly combination of Reaper blades even as his last companion made a fatal mistake, jerking into the chain's path while he struggled to evade the scythe. The knifechain shucked his skull open, exposing brain and bone shards.

To his credit, the snot-faced kindred was a better fighter than the rest of his stooges. The arrogant boy kept clear of Breaker, but his mounting frustrations were evident at his inability to draw near enough for a fatal strike.

The vampire doubled his speed until he was nearly a blur, invisible to most other humans. Remy switched to a more staggered defense, using his oversized pipe of a weapon like a shield to batter the lightning-quick slashes away, eschewing his own quickness for an economy of movement. Finally, the undead youth leaned harder into his upswing than was needed, and Remy promptly relaxed his arms like he'd given up. At the same time, his fingers dug into the faint, barely discernible grooves on either side of Breaker where twin daggers lay hidden, so perfectly carved into the steel that they might have been part of its design. He yanked them free. Before the vampire could crow about his victory, he had already driven one into his pale white throat.

The youth gargled, blood pouring out of his mouth like a bubbling, stuttering waterfall. He tried to back away, but Remy dogged his steps and trapped him against the nearest tree with the blade.

"*Who turned her?*" Remy's voice was a snarl. He pressed the second dagger against the vampire's chest. He needed to know. He could do little for Lady Daneira now. But he *could* pry the confession out of this fuck-arsed dumbwit, even if Remy had to reach past his overstarched suit and into his chest to yank out the truth.

The smug, malicious confidence the boy had once strapped on like armor had dissolved. He could only jerk his head slightly, garble something incoherently from around the blade still wedged through his vocal cords.

"*Who turned her*, you deceased little prick?"

"We didn't turn her," the boy warbled through a mouthful of red. "We didn't!"

"That's enough bloodshed for today, Reaper."

Remy took his second dagger from the vampire's chest, but kept his first buried in the youth's throat out of principle. Breaker was still a few feet away; too far for a successful lunge. He took a step toward it anyway as he braced for an incoming attack, then added another when none was immediately forthcoming.

He was expecting the newcomer to be yet another dramatic brat. He was only partially correct. The stranger had *dramatic* stapled to him, but it was the kind of dramatic that attached itself, unwanted, like a very glamorous leech, and demanded attention on behalf of its owner whether it was warranted or not.

And the stranger was made to be looked at. He was exceedingly handsome, even by vampiric standards. He was darker than those in the band Remy had just annihilated, with suggestions of kohl about the eyes, and had a strong chin covered by a five-o'clock shadow that would have hinted at a three-day drunken binge on Remy but gave the intruder the respectability of a warlord fresh from battle sitting down for a portrait to commemorate his misdeeds. His hair was long, tied carelessly about the nape of his neck, and somehow still looked impeccably groomed.

Remy hated him already. By contrast, he was bloody. He was dirty. He stank of several days' worth of back roads and petrichor. He smelled like the farthest thing from flowers.

And there was something about the noble—because there was no bloody way in hell that he wasn't one—that set off warning bells in Remy's head the way Lady Daneira and the vampire youths had not.

Had the stranger attacked, Remy would have been dead on the ground by now. Should have been.

The man took in the bodies with neither anger nor surprise. They could have been livestock for all the interest he gave them; he looked bored more than anything else. "I am here to collect my foolish brother," he said, clearly offering no apology. "You can be certain that he will be punished for his role in this."

The youth still impaled against the trunk winced.

"By whom?" Remy was still raw, still seeking an outlet for his rage. Lady Daneira's blood was still on him, still seeping into his clothes. "You? And what punishment *will* you deem worthy, *milord*? A slap on the wrist? A temporary limit on his monthly allowances?"

"That is no concern of yours."

"It is every concern of mine!" Remy shouted. "Your brother was responsible for a girl's murder! For no reason other than his own entertainment!"

"My brother made no such confession. In fact, he protested his innocence quite vehemently." The vampire plucked the dagger out from his sibling's throat, as graceful as such an action could ever be, and tossed it back at Remy, who caught it by the handle. "Come, Naji."

Clutching his neck, the other boy shot an angry, if slightly fearful, look back at Remy, then scrambled to the lord's side.

"You have my word that my brother shall never harm the people of Tennyfair ever again, and my word is—"

Remy dropped his daggers, snatched up Breaker in three quick steps, and charged at him.

The noble avoided his blows, exerting the least possible energy to deflect and keep out of range, and Remy knew mockery when he saw it. He redoubled his efforts, but always seemed half a second too slow, the vampire lord no longer where he expected him to be when his scythe blades swooped down to slash. Remy wished he'd made the time to gulp down another fresh vial of bloodwaker; one dose would not be enough for this fight.

He spun the knifechain, sending it into a deadly, whirring arc above his head.

The vampire grabbed at the links and snapped them with a deft twist. With nothing else to keep it moored, the knife flew on, disappearing swiftly into the darkness.

And then the noble was on him. They hurtled into another tree, Remy taking the full brunt as he slammed hard into the trunk, breath leaving him in one long, drawn-out gasp, blooms of pain popping up everywhere. Thorns and rough bark clawed at his back, but he was in no position to shift free. The man kept him trapped, with nothing but Breaker between them.

The lord's hand was wrapped around one of the scythes' blades. Remy knew it was digging into the man's skin, judging by the flow of blood gushing down his wrist. He knew it must have hurt like hell, because he wore at least one whetstone out on Breaker every month for easier stabbage, had nicked himself on it enough times.

The stranger seemed incapable of pain, but he was more than capable of fury. The dark eyes on him promised a thousand cutting deaths more excruciating than any Remy's scythes could deliver.

This was, quite frankly, a common reflex among vampires whenever Remy was within murdering range. Vampires threatened all sorts of atrocities on him with alarming frequency. But the noble was also looking at him with more than just that—there was a spark of sudden interest in that coal-black gaze, the amber highlights within it making him look all the more arresting. He was staring at Remy like he'd only just realized he was there.

And then the lord smiled with a rapacious, predatory hunger that had nothing to do with Remy's attempt to kill him, and *that* made Remy's hands dampen with sweat.

"I understand that you had to do what was necessary to restrain my brother, even if it meant delivering him serious injury," the lord said, the words whisper-soft and low. "That fight has been settled, with you the victor. But if you wish to continue, it is I you shall be facing next. And *this* battle, my pet, you will not win."

The vampire was far too strong. Far too close. Remy's daggers were on the ground, and he had little room to move his scythes. "There will be no justice until he is punished according to the law," he found himself growling.

"The law? Whose laws, Reaper? Your human laws, which seek to kill my kind with extreme prejudice? What would your version of human punishment be? To have my brother while away his life in your gaols? Stake him? You will gain nothing but our ire, and your lords now do everything to prevent that. What is one woman worth, after all?"

"Her life is worth just as much as a man's, vampire or otherwise."

Their gazes locked. Remy was suddenly too aware of the stranger's startling heat. There was no reason he should ever be this warm.

The vampire took the tip of his chin between his own thumb

and forefinger like his face was a butterfly specimen he'd freshly plucked from air, and Remy froze.

"Was she your lover? Is that why her death causes you such anguish?" The fresh intensity in the lord's eyes had only increased, and it made Remy feel . . . uncomfortable. Vulnerable.

"No," he managed through gritted teeth. "But she didn't deserve this."

The man grinned, exposing long, elegant fangs, white as ivory in the dim light. Remy tensed, his mind seeking out other weapons, other alternatives. The vampire bastard knew this wasn't a fair fight. He had the strength of thirty men, of at least five Remys. He looked capable of punching through the moon if he jumped high enough. All Remy had was a limited drug supply and a cylinder full of spent knives.

"An admirable trait, for a human—death wish notwithstanding." His knuckles pressed deeper against the scythe's edge, taunting. "I have fought this weapon before. I know who your father is. They say you are not completely human. A mooncalf. A cambion."

Remy summoned up his last reserves and hurtled forward. It did shit-all, because he was slammed back again, and now his wrist was imprisoned above his head, a forceful hand pinning it down. The stranger bent toward him, mouth a hair's breadth away from his own.

"There are many things we suffer through that we never deserve, and that is true whether you are dead or living. I will offer what compensation I can to her family, to the best of my ability. Seven deaths to pay for one woman's is a generous offer. I suggest you take it."

He let go, and in the blink of an eye vanished, reappearing on the other side of the forest and calmly straightening his collar. Only then did Remy notice the curved sword at his hip, at the sheer arrogance of the man not having used it at all.

The younger vampire, Naji, at least had the wisdom to remain where he was throughout the fight, though the faint smirk on his face faded when his elder brother shot a dark glance his way.

"This is not over!" Remy yelled after him, rather uselessly given the aftermath, suddenly aware of the cold the vampire had left in his wake.

The lord smiled. You could hammer at the diamonds of those dark eyes for years and never make a dent. "I very much hope not, Pendergast," he said.

He turned and walked away without another look back. Naji scurried after him.

Remy waited until they were truly gone before succumbing to numbness. His legs buckled, and he landed hard on his rear as his feet skidded out underneath him. He'd made it through three consecutive fights and was somehow still breathing. It was understandable to feel weak now.

But he'd lost. He'd never lost before. On top of that, it had been quick.

His eyes flicked toward his scythe blades, still dripping with the vampire lord's blood. Breaker was made almost completely of silver. It must have hurt the noble to touch it, stoic as he seemed. The man had all but opened his own vein, simply to teach him a lesson. Remy did not appreciate it.

But his father would appreciate the additional corpses. Remy had not brought enough sacks to stuff the lot in, though the wagon he'd left waiting near the side road should be enough to bring their bodies away along with Lady Daneira's. One vampire had been ancient enough to be rendered into ashes. It explained the noble's indifference at seeing seven of his own clan slaughtered. The rest had been new converts, not old enough to be ashed—small fry, according to their convoluted undead hierarchy.

Freshly turned vampire bodies sold well in the black markets of Aluria—a novelty item for the extremely wealthy and privileged, sources of experimentation and study for those who dabbled in the sciences. Remy didn't like it, but his disapproval wasn't worth bollocks in Aluria.

The man who had bested him was a Summer Lord. A Third Court vampire. His father was going to kill him.

Remy reached into his pocket for a small bloodwaker vial, unstoppering it and gulping down its contents gratefully, feeling his strength return. A much more intelligent Reaper would have taken the dose before running headlong into a fight.

A much more intelligent Reaper wouldn't have attacked a vampire lord, either. "Why the hell don't I think these things through?" he mumbled into the gloom.

He looked at the remains of the vampires strewn around, and then at the headless body of Lady Daneira, still as peaceful as when he had first laid her out, untouched by the carnage. The blood trickling out of her was darker than that of the other vampires, he noticed. More black than red, with hints of a darker blue to its sheen.

Lady Daneira had not smelled like anything in death. Vampires never do.

But this vampire noble had carried with him the very faintest of fragrances, as unnerving as it was unfamiliar. As keen as Remy's nose was, it was unlike anything he'd ever smelled.

More likely it was a sliver of a scent of a memory, he surmised, of what the vampire lord had been like when he'd still been human.

And, irrationally, the thought pissed Remy off even more.

2

FAMILY

Daylight in the kingdom of Aluria was more of a concept than an observation. The thick gray clouds looming overhead were a near-permanent fixture. Fortunately, the light rain held steady when he arrived at the manor. The only indication that he'd beaten dawn by a couple of hours was the faint lightening of what little sky could be seen. Clouds hogged sunlight in Aluria the way dragons hoarded treasure, and they made Remy's work all the more difficult for it.

The stable hands had long been familiar with his odd hours and the work that entailed; they took the reins from Remy without comment, unhitched his stallion from the cart, and guided the horse away. They ignored the heavy tarp stretched over the wagon that hid the undead from sight; they knew better than to look.

"Dr. Yost has been waiting for you, milord," one of the men, Willoughby, said, unable to keep the fear out of his voice.

Remy couldn't blame him. It took courage to work at the Pendergasts' ancestral home. Triple the wages was still a pittance when they had to serve someone with the Duke of Valenbonne's temper, or when they had to ignore the corpses ferried to and from the manor at unnatural hours.

Quintin Yost was the duke's physician. He'd come with excellent references from Anhelm, Ruthersgard, and Sanburkh—all lords from impeccable bloodlines. The antidotes he'd developed based on his studies of vampires, or so it was mentioned, had helped extend old Anhelm's life for over a decade after his terminal illness had been discovered, and his father had hired the doctor to attend to him exclusively for that very reason. But his unabating eagerness for bodies to dissect had always repulsed Remy.

If Remy had had his way, he would have burned the corpses instead, would have refused so much as an ash for the doctor to take. His only consolation was that Lady Daneira would be safe, properly cremated by her family before her interment.

"Young Jack is here as well," Willoughby continued. "I told him to wait in the kitchens until you've settled things with the doctor."

"Thank you, Willoughby. I'll take it from here." Remy pressed a few coins into his hand and saw the man's mood brighten. "Send my regards to the missus for me."

Dr. Yost did not fit the stereotype of one with an unhealthy interest in the undead. He was ruddy-faced and stocky rather than thin and sallow, jovial in disposition, with a soothing bedside manner. It didn't matter; something about the physician's heartiness felt like an oversell, and it had always made Remy uncomfortable. The man held an umbrella above his head to keep dry, but when he lifted it toward Remy's direction, the latter chose the rain over the man's hospitality and stepped away.

"Well, Lord Pendergast," Dr. Yost said, circling the wagon like a vulture contemplating the choicest of the carrion on display, "seems like we've had a much more substantial haul than expected. How many of these lovelies do we have?"

"Six," Remy said shortly.

The doctor lifted the tarpaulin to peer inside, made disappointed clucking noises. "I suppose the unfortunate lady of tonight's bounty has already been delivered to her family?"

"If you mean to ask if she is safely out of your reach, then yes."

Dr. Yost took no offense to Remy's barb; he never did. "Distasteful as it may sound, young sir, it is a necessary undertaking. I am doing nothing that the fools at the Archives aren't doing themselves, and I have more brains than the lot of them put together. I am learning more with your father's health in mind, and my studies show much promise. Determining how vampire blood bonds on a cellular level, translating that into other methods of rejuvenating the human body . . . with more adipose tissues to extract cytokine from, the antigens should . . ."

But Remy was already slipping away, leaving the physician alone with his latest test subjects.

Jack's was a far more welcoming face. Remy frequently employed youths to keep a close eye on any vampire attacks within the surrounding areas, paying them for the privilege. Jack was his best informant. He told Remy where the vampires were lurking, and then Remy set out to kill them—far less complicated than most of the official reports that came out of Elouve.

"This one's gonna be a little bit different from the usual fare, Armiger," the red-haired youth said soberly. "Old Taggart's boy this time, or what's left of him, just over at Glycespike. Two days ago."

"What's *left* of him?"

"Body parts strewn from there over a two-mile radius they say, nearly all the way to Wyndbrook. Vampires don't eat flesh, do they? Not many animals that could tear someone limb from limb like that. But not an ounce of blood on what they could recover." Jack had been doing this long enough that even he'd been desensitized to the violence. It was easy to be, with the reports of attacks increasing every month.

"They don't, and there aren't any. This is the worst one I've heard of so far." Remy folded his arms and leaned against the doorframe. Seven victims, all within the span of a month. The last four had reportedly been mutilated as well, but not to this extent.

"Seen a lot, haven't you?" Jack asked with the faint, ghoulish curiosity of one who'd never had to experience such tragedies themselves.

"I've seen enough." Remy tossed him a small bag containing half a dozen gold coins and generous handfuls of copper. "Convey my condolences to the Taggarts, and keep me informed of other similar incidents. Tell the villagers to keep away from the borders between the two villages and, by the Light, say nothing of this to my father. I should be able to ride out in less than a fortnight."

The boy caught the money, bowed low, and retreated silently.

It was a new day, but Remy's work was far from over. He'd been awake for nearly twenty-four hours, and while he'd like nothing better than to linger in the bath, where he could scrub his skin raw of the day's excesses before tumbling into bed, he knew his father was expecting him. Nobody kept Edgar Pendergast, Duke of Valenbonne waiting.

Ten minutes before a washstand and wearing a fresh set of clothes was enough to make him presentable. He spent another five cleaning Breaker, collecting the blood into a small vial, as was the family protocol. He'd brought back the knife and chains the vampire noble had snapped off, but reforging them would require another visit to Elke. The woman would not be happy to learn the ease at which the lord had broken the silver after all her hard work on it.

He then placed the blood sample container inside his coat pocket and dragged his feet the full distance between his bedroom and his father's chambers, as if any further delays might annul the visit entirely. It was a habit from childhood he had never completely unlearned.

Despite the darkness of the corridor and the rain still pouring outside, he could see the walls covered in newspaper clippings; all carefully framed, all listing the duke's exploits and the accolades bestowed upon him by the previous Alurian king: DUKE OF VALENBONNE BEHEADS JENGII VAMPIRE from the *Daily Gazette*. DUKE OF VALENBONNE VANQUISHES UNDEAD LEGION from the *Alurian Times*. EDGAR PENDERGAST, DUKE OF VALENBONNE, SAVIOR OF ALURIA from the *Wayward Post*—his father detested tabloid rags, except when they wrote in his favor.

The headlines filled the whole length of the duke's hallway, leaving little room for anything else.

The Duke of Valenbonne himself was still up, sitting in his favorite well-worn armchair by the fireplace. The room was insufferably hot, a good ten degrees warmer than the rest of the manor. The old man's numerous and ongoing ailments played a factor, but Remy had always thought that his father's own incapacity for warmth left him seeking it elsewhere.

His first sight of the duke was a frail, spotted hand at the armrest, pale-skinned, trembling from prolonged rheumatism. Remy's boots made no sound on the plush carpet, but the old man shifted, then grunted to acknowledge his arrival. A cup of tea sat on the table by his elbow, steam still rising from it, and a row of medicine bottles were lined up neatly behind the cup like sentries on night watch.

The duke's pale manservant, Grimesworthy, bowed low to Remy from his usual spot at the corner of the room. He was one of only a handful of servants still working at the manor, and the only hired help to last longer than two months. The man was massive and might have been an oak tree in some previous life, because he looked to have been carved out of bark in this one. Remy was of no exceptional height and resented the way the man loomed over him.

"Tell Cook that I am ready for breakfast," his father told the servant, dismissing him quickly.

The man bowed. Remy had yet to hear him speak since his father had hired him.

"No runny eggs this time. She knows as well as I that my gout flares when they're runny."

Another bow before the giant shuffled out of the room.

The Duke of Valenbonne could no longer walk or stand unaided and had to be wheeled around on the rare occasion he left the manor, yet he insisted on bringing his cane everywhere. It lay across his lap; it gleamed a pure dark mahogany in the firelight, the wood nearly black despite its sheen, with an intricate carving of the Pendergast crest whittled into one end. The cane had been almost as infamous as he once was.

The savior of Aluria was unrecognizable now. His brown hair had faded into thin wispy strings of white that dotted his scalp amid the age spots. His muscular build had shrunk, his handsome features losing the fight against bouts of long illnesses exacerbated by the physical demands he'd placed on his body for decades as a young hunter, all the injuries and fractures he'd accumulated and neglected against his physicians' orders finally coming home to roost.

The blanket across his knees hid the worst of his injuries—a badly twisted leg, even thinner than the rest of him. One of his eyes had clouded over in a strange white film. His doctors had given him just over a year before what remained of his sight in that eye was gone, and only two more before the rest of him followed suit.

Given the pathetic figure he presented at the moment, it felt almost ridiculous, the terror the man could still inspire in Remy—and the guilt.

"You're late," Edgar Pendergast said flatly.

"I had to make arrangements with Tennyfair." The grief-stricken howl the poor man had made at the sight of his daughter still rang in Remy's ears.

"No use dillydallying with the family just because you met their daughter once. Poor chit probably didn't even recognize you. Most of them don't, when they're new to the turning."

"They needed to know that she died quickly."

"If you'd wanted the girl for yourself, you should have spoken up sooner," his father said. "I'm on good terms with Tennyfair— she would have been a tolerable match."

"I wasn't interested in her in that way," Remy said stiffly.

"Oh? You've always been too emotional for your own good, Remington, but not even you would have reacted so strongly to a girl you'd met only the once, and months ago." The glassier-than-normal sheen to the duke's cloudy eye was either a sly glint or further nerve damage. "Or were your past talks with her more . . . *stimulating* than you had both let on?"

"No." He had no desire to explain that he remembered her kindness more than he did their conversation, that it was all he required to fight for someone else's dignity. Lady Daneira had treated him with the respect very few in upper society had ever given him. She had called him *Armiger*. It had mattered.

"I trust, then, that your mission was successful."

"Yes, sir."

"Bloodwork?"

"Yes, sir." Remy reached into his pocket, set the sample on the table.

"Grimesworthy says you brought more corpses than expected. Yost will be pleased. A separate hunt?"

"I believe they were responsible for Lady Daneira's turning."

"Regular riffraff?"

This was the part he'd been dreading. "Nobles."

Valenbonne shifted again, staring back at Remy with his one good eye. "And did you find out the name of their clan before you killed them?"

A deep breath. "One made reference to the Summer Lords."

His father picked up the cup of tea, sipped slowly from it. Then he drew his hand back.

The cup shattered against the wall right beside the fireplace, the sound unexpectedly loud, but years spent living with his father had taught Remy to stop from flinching outwardly.

"Fool boy!" Edgar Pendergast roared. "The Summer Lords? All the bloodsuckers in the world to pick a fight with, and you take on the Summer Lords, the Third Court? Peace negotiations are being finalized even as we speak! If you weaken the council's treaty with that accursed clan, you could compromise the whole of Aluria, you . . . you . . . worthless, incompetent cretin!"

He doubled over, coughing rapidly, flecks of blood and phlegm spraying his lips. Remy leaped forward, taking out his own handkerchief to press against his father's mouth.

"Blue bottle—" the duke wheezed, once he'd regained his voice. "Two pills—"

Remy found the required medication and a glass of water from another side table. His father downed the tablets quickly. Another hissed command, and an oxygen tank was wheeled out from behind his chair. After that it was a matter of Remy waiting, tense and expectant, until finally his father's breathing grew less rapid and he could take in air with smaller effort, puffing in slower measures.

"Fool," he said again, lifting the mask from his face. His voice was calmer, depleted of his previous anger, talking now like the remains of his teacup were not sitting on the floor in plain view to them both, staining the carpet. "Aluria is caught between several vampire factions. As much as it enrages me to be beholden to any of those corpses, we cannot antagonize them. He spared you, didn't he?"

Remy gritted his teeth. "He didn't—"

"You would have killed them all otherwise, because you never think about the consequences. You should have found out more about this renegade clan. This lord's disinclination to fight tells me he is part of the Third Court delegation at the very least, but I doubt you even realized that. What are the possibilities for reprisals?"

"I was promised no retaliation if I spared the remaining survivor."

"And you were fool enough to believe that?"

Remy was silent, staring straight ahead.

"And did this vampire lord give a name?"

"No." But the lord had known his. *Pendergast*, he had said. Remy opened his mouth, but his father silenced him with a glower.

"No. Enough of that. We have other business afoot."

He transferred his glare to the table by his side. The only things within the duke's reach were his medicine bottles and the blood sample, and he would chuck Grimesworthy at Remy before he would chuck any of those. "You always had the brains of an ox. You never ask the right questions. Five lesser clans are attached to the Summer Lords, and they are all just as dangerous as their liege. We have no way of knowing which particular pack you have insulted, but it doesn't matter. Offend one, and you offend them all. Two of the eight vampiric courts have been exterminated, but we cannot afford to look weak in the eyes of the remaining six, no matter what negotiations the Third Court has made with the queen. We must be prudent, lay low, and see what comes of the council's negotiations, though I have little confidence. Hartley and Lopez are buffoons who should never have gone into politics. And as for Astonbury . . ." A wizened lip curled in disgust. "The Summer Lords would have never even made headway into our realm if the boys and I were still in charge."

This wouldn't have happened if the boys and I were still in charge was a diatribe the Duke of Valenbonne liked to bring up more frequently as his health took a nosedive. Valenbonne, Parnon, Lee, Zuriyah, and Kartha—the Golden Five, the elite dukes and marquesses whom ladies swooned over and whom adventurers aspired to be. For years they'd trained novice adepts into worthy Reapers and single-handedly kept Aluria from becoming vampire fodder, even as other kingdoms fell around them. They had exterminated the Second Court. Valenbonne had personally staked its leader.

But Parnon and Kartha were dead now, and the rest were in no better shape than his father.

"Giselle Delacroix will be sponsoring a gala a week from today, in Elouve. Unlike Lady Daneira, you have had more than just one passing conversation with the duchess, and I'm certain they were much more *interesting* than any you've had with the girl. She has written to me, hoping you would accept her invitation."

Remy's face was a mask of solid indifference. Behind that mask was the rest of Remy, screaming into the void.

He did not want to meet with the Duchess of Astonbury. There were things that had made a more lasting impression on him than she had. It was not her beautiful face or the way her mouth kissed his or how her slender hands had felt on him that recalled her to his memory, but the four hundred and ninety-seven tiles on her bedroom ceiling. They were the four hundred and ninety-seven reasons he'd been able to control his panic that first time, focusing on them instead of the weight of her on his body, pretending that she was gasping, moving, doing all of that to someone who was not him.

Time had softened the subsequent trysts, even made them pleasurable. But always, he remembered her ceiling.

"I do not wish to attend any of the woman's parties, no matter how sought after they are." His voice was steady. At ease. Bored.

"Oh? That's a surprise, considering how enamored the duchess and her friends are of you. How long has it been since you'd last seen her—eight months at least? It would be good to renew your friendship."

The last time you told her to pass me among her friends like a stallion put out to stud was because you wanted any information the lord high steward had of the Night Empress's movements—and in the end, he had none to give. It was hard to know what to bottle down first—the brief rush of hysteria or the surge of red-hot anger—but Remy managed to keep both at bay. "I still have other bounties to fulfill."

"The innkeeper who claims there's been a spate of attacks down Havershire? The farmer who says there's a succubus south of Pai Lai? The trivial reports the village boys send you? Those missing children?" His father's lip curled in disgust. "Inconsequential affairs unworthy of a Reaper. Let lesser hunters deal with them. The peasants have no love for cambions. They will chase you out the instant you accomplish your mission and claim that as their gratitude. Save your energy for the ones who matter. The ones in higher positions who can put in a good word for you, to deflect you from further scrutiny. Save your strength to see to Aluria's security, as I have always done."

"I'm not a cambion," Remy grated.

"No, but as far as they're concerned, you may as well be. How many times must I repeat this, you lummox? Your mother was bitten before you were born, boy. She died birthing you, possibly at the cusp of her own turning."

"I am well aware of how she died," Remy said tersely. His left hand moved to his forearm, pressing down against the scar there that traveled from wrist to elbow.

"Then stop acting like you've forgotten! That is enough to convince people that you are a vampire's get, the only one within spitting distance that they can revile and resent for also being the Duke of Valenbonne's son. I have worked hard, invalid as I am, to ingratiate you into the social circles that women like Giselle Delacroix occupy, so that you will continue to enjoy their protections after I'm gone, however ungrateful you are for my efforts. You still have much to overcome with the nobility. Do you really think the peasantry would know any better?" Edgar Pendergast coughed again, a hacking sound that suggested a chest full of more phlegm. "Give me the water."

Remy guided the glass to his lips again, waited till he'd had his fill. But the old man was far from finished. "Why do you think I've been pushing you toward the woman? For all the instructions I've given you about managing your way through the season, you've retained as much etiquette as a wet sock would. Giselle will give you the security you need from censure. She was generous enough to extend this invitation. More important, she will protect you from Astonbury. You will not reject her offer."

Remy closed his eyes. His father pushed him toward the duchess because he hated the Lord High Steward Astonbury. Hell, even the duchess hated the lord high steward, and she was *married* to him. Remy was the vehicle for both their revenge and their spite, and by the time he'd been old enough to understand, he was already trapped. "Yes, sir."

"It is not just the duchess's friendship I want you to renew while you're there. Rumor is that the Third Court is set to make an appearance at this very gala. It would be good to familiarize yourself with the vampires we have supposedly allied ourselves with. Should negotiations fall south and our treaty with them dissolve, it would be valuable to know more of the lords we'll be hunting."

"Vampires at the gala?" Remy was stunned. "Father, surely you can't expect any of the other nobles to—"

"On the contrary. The duchess's ball is the most talked-about event this season *because* of it. I don't doubt that the poor fools believe that the crowds will give them security, along with the Summer Lords' oath that they will not harm any of those in attendance. Did you know there are rumors flying about of vampires within the city, passing themselves off as human?"

Remy didn't react. "Why? Have they found one in Elouve?"

"No. Not yet." Valenbonne grinned, displaying yellowing teeth.

His canines were only just less pointed than those of the creatures he'd been killing all his life. "But I would not be surprised to find the Third Court stooping so low. Investigate any new faces among the nobility. Observe which of the Summer Lords are the most likely to give us problems, and head off any other trouble while you're there. The Third Court vampires have killed more than just a few ancestors of ours, though we have tried to return the favor. Best not see yourself murdered so easily as they were."

"Yes, sir."

"The self-professed vampire king shall be bringing his fiancée as well, as another show of good faith. I'm told she has a delicate condition, this heiress to the Fourth Court."

Remy never knew how his father acquired his information. Most of his friends were dead, his servants feared him, and if his pervasive illnesses didn't chase people away, his winning personality did the job. Dr. Yost, the cadaver fanatic, likely supplied most of the gossip. Even Grimesworthy was a possibility, for all his apparent muteness. He had the personality of an automaton who'd accidentally been brought to life, but Remy always thought he could make quite the capable snitch.

Remy did know about the Fourth Court, a once-powerful cabal known nowadays for its dwindling roster of members. The crone who led the sect was old even among vampires and fragile. Apparently, her daughter took after her in health. He wondered why the head of the Summer Lords, who could have their pick of brides among other, more robust vampire stock, would willingly forge marriage bonds with the sickly heiress of a dying house.

"Two vampire factions as our allies are better than having them as enemies—for now. There is still very little news concerning the Sixth through Eighth Courts, only that they are lying low following the massacres of the Second and Fifth. The Night Empress poses the more dangerous threat. Do you understand me?" Pallid hands curled into themselves, blue veins standing out against sallow skin. His father's voice turned guttural, as enraged as his body would allow. "The Night Empress has *always* been our goal."

Remy knew. He'd been raised and trained to take down the First Court and the demoness that ruled over it. The First Court had killed his mother. The First Court had destroyed his life before he'd even been born.

"You will attend the Delacroixes' ball, Remington. Find schisms we can exploit."

"Yes, sir."

"When was your last dose?"

"Just after my last fight, sir."

"Take another now. I have a fresh supply in my medicine cabinet. You know that you cannot be remiss in taking your medications according to schedule."

It looked rather like blood itself, a bright crimson mixture. The apothecary who had first concocted it for the Reapers called it the *trezirea sângelui*; Alurian hunters found *bloodwaker* easier to remember. It heightened the senses and accelerated one's reflexes, enabling them to hold their own against the strongest vampires. But take more than two or three an hour, and it had the unwanted effect of overtaxing the body well over its limits and scrambling your brain along with it. The Reapers had found Parnon that way, dead from an overdose, bloodied after destroying his rooms in a final fit of madness. It had taken money changing hands and many threats to keep the details of the hero's death out of even the most lurid tabloids.

The mixture was pungent and foul-smelling, like the spiky durian that fruit merchants from Garandha would bring to the markets to sell in the summer. But it also tasted, just a little, like strawberries. It always made Remy feel bloated afterward, like he'd eaten a bigger meal than he'd intended. His father always insisted that he take Dr. Yost's formula rather than the one created by the Archives' scientists in Elouve—as much as Remy hated to admit, the former's concoctions were far more effective than even what the highest-ranked Reapers carried.

He gulped down the thick syrup. His mind cleared, exhaustion fading. His father watched him carefully. "You have all of today to prepare for your travel to Elouve tomorrow," the old man said. "I have sent word to Loxley House to have your rooms at the ready—"

"I intend to stay at Kinaiya Lodge," Remy interrupted. Everything important to him was in Kinaiya, including the fact that his father would not be there.

He received another glower, but even his father knew arguing about Kinaiya Lodge was a wasted effort. "I shall make my own arrangements and follow in a few days."

Remy stood up straighter. "You're leaving Blackstone Manor? But your health—"

"I will die, regardless of it being here or at Loxley. I am still a peer of the realm. I can still assert my right to attend the Queen's Council. Astonbury may stop you from attending his paltry dræfendgemot in my stead, but he will not stop me from learning his secrets. I find the Third Court's offer of an alliance highly suspicious. There is something they need from Aluria that they do not want us to find out. I would stake my whole fortune on it. And Astonbury and his toadies are too much of fools to realize it. Whatever they may say, I serve Aluria first and foremost, Remington, even if it must be from my deathbed." Another cough wracked his body, but the old man shook his head when Remy approached again. "Grimesworthy's taking too long with my breakfast. Find him."

It was a clear dismissal. But when Remy reached the door, his father's voice stopped him. "Boy."

Staring back at his child, the fireplace casting sinister shadows over his face, the Duke of Valenbonne appeared rather like a moving, talking corpse himself. "You look so much like your mother," he finally said, looking slightly repulsed by the observation, and turned away.

3

THE CUT DIRECT

I t was mandatory for all notable peers of the realm to convene in the springtime to Alhmeister House at Gold Street to fulfill the roles their fathers had paid the privilege for, which was to pass lucid, preferably decent, laws to govern the kingdom-states of Aluria.

This peculiar unity had been borne from self-preservation rather than any heartfelt solidarity. Two months of what sun the kingdom had to content itself with could do little against the steady fog and rains that encompassed most of Aluria the rest of the time. Over the last twenty years, fourteen small but independent kingdoms had banded together to form one giant empire of semi-autonomous nations, to mount a better defense against the vampire courts. The royals of the house of Ashrai, the first to come up with the idea, served as Aluria's figureheads, but the body politic was represented well enough at the Queen's Council, where their most important lords converged at the start of each season like the world's best-dressed mob.

Fortunately, Remy's business was at the smaller Reapers' training hall a block away, where he was pinched, poked, prodded, and had his blood drawn by one of its physicians; a mandatory health screening every time he returned to the city. They'd been taking more from him than the usual, packets of his hard-earned, literal lifeblood carted off to who-knew-where. "New protocols," he'd been told; some new rash of infection in Western Aluria that doctors were worried over. He'd wondered if the Reapers had been receiving reports like the ones Jack provided him with. But the Reapers never provided him with any details, no matter how politely he'd asked, and today was no different.

"Astonbury specifically asked for more samples of *your* blood, milord," one of the doctors said cheerfully. Remy was having a hard time listening, because the doctor was uncapping a horrifyingly long needle that she thought she had every right to stick into him. "You've been handling nearly twice the number of bounties this month, and he wants to make sure your physical assessment is sound."

Remy was tempted to tell her that Astonbury took a particularly nasty delight in draining him of blood this way because Remy had yet to come back to Elouve in a body bag like the man wanted, but the metal tip plunged into his arm, and it took all his strength to hold still because he was an adult who wasn't afraid of any needles, even if they were as long as a fucking schoolmarm's ruler.

Twice the bounties and none of the credit. Story of his life.

The bleeding done, he'd stopped to watch a Reaper class in session. The year's novices had gathered to listen while the instructor, Bellote, instructed them on the history of the eight vampire courts that plagued the land.

"The Sixth Court call themselves 'the Court of Cultivation,'" the man roared, slamming his hand against the wooden board he'd stuck various bits of information onto, hoping some of it would get through to his students' heads. Remy noted that the Second and Fifth Courts were still a part of the curriculum despite both having been wiped out years before by his father's regiment and the Third Court, respectively. But resurgences were not an implausible idea, and Bellote was a tough disciplinarian who memorized rulebooks for fun.

"That doesn't matter. They are at their most dangerous when they sham courtesy and respect, and it is best to behead them before they can ever utter a word." That was a defining characteristic of a Bellote lecture. Every reference he made to vampires always ended with a call to kill them.

"The same cannot be said for the Fourth Court, the Court of Tranquility." Another loud smack against the board, causing it to sway. "They are the smallest of those accursed clans, and with luck shall remove themselves from existence without needing any more of our help. It is why tonight will be important, and the reason you are all assuming soldier duty at the Astonbury Manor. A Fourth Court vampire has been invited to the duchess's gala, and you are there to observe her."

One of his pupils had enough guts to raise her hand. "I heard that the leader of the Third Court will also be in attendance."

"Our supposed ally, yes." Bellote allowed himself a sneer. "Regardless of what the queen says, the Summer Lords are the most dangerous of them all. It will do you well to study them both. Commit their faces to memory. The day will come when we shall face them on the battlefield. Court kings and queens are no different from regular vampire swill. Imagine yourselves aiming for their hearts whenever you can, their eyes or their necks if those are within easier reach. Imagine the maneuvers these would require from where you stand guard."

Trust Bellote to turn the most exclusive party of the season into an assassination attempt.

It occurred to Remy then that the teacher had lost half of his students' attention. More faces were turning his way, fascination and delight on their expressions upon recognizing who he was.

"Lord Pendergast," Bellote said frostily, finally catching on.

"Do you require a refresher course on the ways of the vampire courts? Your grasp of both politics and economics when you were a novice was abysmal enough to warrant another lesson."

"Just enthralled by your lectures as always, mate," Remy said hastily, stepping away. "Don't let me stay and hinder the brilliant work you're doing."

So the rest of the Reapers shared the same suspicions his father had, which was unsurprising. The new alliance with the Third Court vampires had been kicking up all sorts of heated discussions, and every noble with any vestige of importance attached to their title had shown up this year, determined to have an opinion.

Their wives, relatives, and entourages, less concerned about the state of the kingdom than they were about the state of their dress, celebrated democracy in action with a series of balls and elaborate galas in Elouve, enough within a single week to fuel the next three months. Gossip served as currency, and if there was anything the peerage had in surplus, it was money and rumormongers.

He saw several of the novices again hours later, nervous and stiff as they patrolled the Delacroix grounds with weapons of silver. The average soldier could only be spared a few arrows and a sword, but the Reapers here protected the lord high steward's wife, and so wielded more expensive fire lances. In the absence of sun, fire was the next most potent weapon against the undead.

Astonbury Manor, as in the richer parts of the city, was awash in light. Balls like these made Remy nervous. Give him a fight every time; he knew the rules there. Stay alive, run the opponent through, confirm that they were dead, keep them that way. But here, you could suffer a thousand cuts from a dowager matron armed with nothing but a paper fan and impeccable genealogy, and they would call it a bloodbath. He had no defenses against the painted smiles and fluttering compliments that turned vicious and condescending once backs were turned.

And because of the secondary reputation that had sprouted up around him in no small thanks to Giselle Delacroix and her friends, conversation was not what many of the widows and unhappily married women of the aristocracy desired from him. But it distracted from his wretched history, steered people into a more familiar hypocrisy that the nobility were more likely to tolerate.

Remy had little impetus to be grateful. The women were using him just as vindictively as he was using them.

Giselle Delacroix, the duchess of Astonbury, greeted him at the foyer herself, all charm and dimples. She was fifteen years his senior and enchantingly beautiful, with large blue eyes and chestnut hair and the fullest lips. Her dress could have paid for at least five thoroughbreds and featured far more jewels than he thought was possible, the largest of which she wore as a sapphire choker around her neck. She made a show of welcoming him by planting kisses on his cheeks, a deliberate move. As the lord high steward's wife, she could dare as much. The Third Court were her guests of honor tonight; a supposed dhampir was mere appetizer in comparison.

As always, Remy was relieved that the duke had renovated part of the Archives' west wing for his quarters and had mostly relinquished the manor to his wife.

"Darling." Her voice sounded like sex and sin, smoky and low. "I was worried you'd turned down my invitation." Her hand stroked his forearm, the action uncomfortably intimate. She wrinkled her nose at the Breaker he still carried across his back. "Must you continue to lug about that contraption of yours?"

"In light of some of your guests, I think it would be prudent." Breaker was developed for effective fighting in almost every conceivable situation: in open spaces, in battlefields, in trapped corners. And never did he feel more trapped than at lavish parties at the height of the fashionable year.

The problem with gossip was that it always fixated on the most controversial person in the room, and Lord Remington Pendergast, Marquess of Aphelion, with his mother's suspicious ancestry and even more suspicious death, his vampiresque birth, his work as a Reaper, and the lord high steward's undisguised hatred of his father and therefore of him, was the stuff scandals were made of. It was obvious in the glances people kept throwing his way, the whispers.

But none had his history. Their births were without incident, born from mothers who were very much alive before and during labor, mothers who had not been born in small island nations of strange witching repute, mothers whom dukes had desired long enough to bring across continents but regretted marrying soon afterward. No vampires had been involved in the process of their siring. There were no rumors surrounding their heritage, of their humanity or lack thereof.

There were many other Reapers in attendance tonight. Those who caught his gaze made a show of turning their backs deliberately on him.

"My husband has news of the Night Empress's whereabouts," Giselle said.

"What has he found?" If he could gain the information now, he would have no reason to stay.

The duchess pressed a finger against his lips. "Patience, love. Harrington delivered the papers only an hour ago, and I've had little time to look through them, amidst all the preparations." She reached out to adjust his cravat. "We could read them later," she said suggestively. "Together."

Giselle insisted that he accompany her to the ballroom floor, to lead with the first dance like a husband ought. Some of the chronically stodgy matrons looked on indignantly but could do little in the face of the duchess's persistence.

His dancing was rusty, but Valenbonne had been adamant about immersing Remy in all manners of etiquette, unlikely as it was that he would ever be accepted enough to put them frequently into practice. He managed quite capably with Giselle's encouragement, even with Breaker heavy behind him, but the eyes that followed them around the room were already passing judgment.

His partner was amused by the silent censure. "I'd hoped they would be kinder to you by now, since my favored guests are the *actual* vampires they believe you to be," she murmured. "Shall I make it a point to call out everyone who would denounce *you*, yet lobby in the same breath to get into Lord Malekh's good graces?"

"I'm not likely to bite them if they are rude to me," Remy said, "but they cannot say the same of the Summer Lords."

Giselle giggled. "Well, I am confident that there will be no biting here tonight." Her hand curled around the back of his neck. "Unless you want me to."

She kept a possessive hold on his arm even after the dance had ended, guiding him toward where her closest group of friends stood, chattering excitedly—all attractive wives of indifferent husbands. Remy fought to keep his breaths measured.

"Will they require permission to enter the foyer, Giselle?" Amica, Duchess of Merka, asked, looking titillated by the very idea. "Oh, wouldn't it be grand to let them wait a little while, as a bit of punishment for trying to invade Maharsha the past year? I haven't seen the sun in close to six months. Surely, what passes here for daylight can't hurt them."

"And you'd risk incurring their wrath by having them linger by the doorstep like footmen?" Lady Carina, a statuesque blonde, chastised her. "And it was the Fifth Court who attempted to conquer Maharsha, not the Third. It was the Third who wiped out the Fifth Court. Why do you think Queen Ophelia was so quick to accept their offer of an alliance?"

"Sunlight wouldn't affect vampires who've been living for hundreds of years," said Lady Grenadia, who fancied herself the scholar of the group. "And Lord Malekh, I am told, meets such requirements. But perhaps his fiancée, with her rumored delicate condition . . ."

"They say the other vampire courts fear her," Lady Beiwu said eagerly. "That she has some strange power that could kill other kindred with just one touch."

"Surely they exaggerate," Lady Grenadia scoffed. "Some of the Ancients do develop strange abilities of their own once they've lived long enough, but surely nothing so blasé as a poisoned hand."

"I am only repeating what I've heard, Jessica, and I heard it from one of the Reapers himself. Lord Scovenge."

"My own father was a Reaper, and he's said nothing of that sort. Scovenge is a liar, my dear."

"They also say that the Fourth Court girl is a half-vampire herself," Lady Carina persisted. "That she was *born*, not turned. A true cambion."

"A rare case, if so," Lady Grenadia confirmed. "More often they're stillbirths. Lord Malvorth wrote quite an interesting treatise on the subject, about the number of stillbirths and miscarriages blamed on vampire sires, and the accusations of husbands on their wives of infidelity because of it. It's an interesting look at the hysteria of—"

"Oh goodness, Grenadia," the Countess Beiwu interrupted, fanning herself briskly. "Let's not talk about something so droll as stillbirths when we can talk about the Third Court king, who they say is quite handsome. And however she was born, his fiancée is also reportedly stunning. No one knows exactly what they look like, save perhaps the Reapers. It's said that when the couple had visited Queen Ophelia last week, no one was allowed to look at their faces."

The ladies shivered in delight.

"That could not *possibly* be accurate," Lady Grenadia insisted. "Queen Ophelia is a progressive woman. She would not allow such regressive ideas in her court, even to appease court vampires."

"Of course not," Giselle said. "They wouldn't be guests of honor here today if that were true. Really, Lady Beiwu, the imagination you have!"

"I'd always fancied the ones from the Second Court myself," Lady Leila murmured. "They wouldn't be out of place at your ball here either, Giselle, I would think. They were well-known for their own galas in Meridian Keep, weren't they? 'The Court of Beauty,' they called themselves."

"My mother attended several of their parties," Amica said dreamily. "I remember being to a few myself, years before I debuted. They were all quite nice to her, and to me. She said that she'd grown close enough to one of them that he'd asked her to be his familiar. There was to be a ceremony and all, like a real wedding. He'd paid court to her better than any man from the ton, she'd said. Of course, Grandfather disapproved. Not sure what business it was of his, though. Mother was a well-respected widow, a grown woman."

"A shame they were all slaughtered for taking an earl's daughter," Lady Carina noted dryly. "Be glad that you escaped it, Amica, or both you and your mother would be haunting graveyards to this day."

"Still," Amica said, sounding wistful. "They were all very handsome."

"Not as handsome, I'm sure, as our very own dhampir," Lady Grenadia said slyly, batting her eyelashes Remy's way. "Nobody can move the way Lord Pendergast can."

"I must take my leave, ladies," Remy said, as calmly and as neutrally as he could, already desperate for an exit. "There are people I've been meaning to talk to." He'd spotted another Reaper angling his way toward him, and that was as good an excuse as he needed.

"Only until midnight." Giselle said it playfully enough, but the steel in her voice left no room for argument. "Return to me then. I would be utterly desolate without your company."

"How unfair of you, Giselle," Lady Beiwu complained. "We haven't seen him in months. What right do you have to claim him first—"

But Remy was already moving away, embracing his few hours' reprieve.

Lord Anthony Castellblanc was also a duke's son, a good three years older than Remy, and the Marquess of Riones besides. His father held lands nearer to the outer domains but retained their titles and wealth even after Castegon was absorbed into Aluria. His grandmother was Tithian like Remy's mother, a fact he happily provided at their first introduction, though that was far back enough in his family history that most didn't remember to discriminate. Remy had a healthy suspicion of other people's company, but Riones had a cheerfully attractive face that went with a cheerfully attractive personality, and it took less effort to accept his friendship than to go about avoiding it. Riones was also an excellent card player, and his popularity at gaming halls and gentlemen's clubs made him a reliable source of information, invaluable given the lord high steward's ongoing vendetta against Remy's family.

"Thought you wouldn't make it," he hollered merrily, clapping Remy on the back. The bearded marquess had far more of a fancy for fashionable wear than the average Reaper; tonight, he was wearing a velvet-trimmed tailcoat more silver than gray. A top hat was perched on his shaved head. "Your father takes up far too much of your time, Pendergast."

"The doctors' prognoses haven't been good."

"All the same, seems fairly selfish to keep you in the country with little else to do, knowing you help him much there." The marquess paused. "Heard you finally found Lady Daneira. I'm sorry. Hoped we were wrong, but . . . damn. Rumor going about that it was a vampire noble who turned her? You think the Third Court's got anything to do with this?"

"You'll have to talk to the Duke of Tennyfair for the answer," Remy said evasively.

"Never thought I'd see the day we'd ally ourselves with vampires. The Third Court's always been brutal. Effective, but brutal. The way they exterminated the Fifth—that was a master class in warfare, much as I hate to admit it. Bellote's teaching an adept course on it, even."

Riones shook his head. "Way some of the older Reapers tell, no one's keen on a direct confrontation with Zidan Malekh, so when he offered the queen an alliance, she was quick to accept. The hunters are objecting, but mainly out of pride. Suspect it's why Astonbury's keen on summoning us all bright and early tomorrow morning." At Remy's confused look, Riones clarified. "If the Third Court shows up tonight, he'll want our impressions of them. Been some rumors at the Florence Club about strange vampires up along the eastern borders, too. Got that information straight from Wallace while winning a few hundred off him at hazard, and he should know. Could be the Night Court vampires you're looking for. Astonbury's got a fresh report on that, too."

"He's summoned all the Reapers?"

"Yes, all the . . ." Riones trailed off, looking embarrassed, horrified. "¡Ay, carajo, Pendergast! I thought he'd asked you, too. Is he still sore about your father? I'd thought they'd buried that hatchet months ago."

It was easy for Riones to dismiss a feud, as someone incapable of holding a grudge for longer than a few seconds. Edgar Pendergast and Matthew Astonbury's enmity was the worst-kept secret among the aristocracy, though no one actually knew why Astonbury and Valenbonne hated each other—only that Astonbury had usurped leadership of the Reapers from Remy's father and all but exiled him from the organization.

"I can approach him." The marquess was legitimately earnest. "It's . . . preposterous to forbid you from joining when you're just as much a Reaper as I am and take on more work than most. Why should he risk the lives of millions over something so trite as a rivalry?"

"You forget," Remy said heavily, because this too was another terribly kept secret, "that I am also involved with his wife." The marquess knew nothing about the specifics that led to his encounters with Giselle, and he wasn't about to tell him now.

"Astonbury and his wife have been estranged for years, long before you came into the picture. He is not the only lord with such marriage arrangements, and he has treated her past consorts amicably enough. He and your father are to blame, not you. I could speak up in your favor, argue your merits. Hell, Pendergast. You've fought more undead than some of the older hunters put together."

"No," Remy said hurriedly. "I appreciate you, Riones. But the bad blood he has against Valenbonne will not be resolved this way. You will only earn his ire, and we will all be much worse for it."

"If it's any consolation—when the Reapers do wage a full-on war against the rest of the courts, they'll have no choice but to include you and Valenbonne in their plans, and to hell with what Astonbury wants. In the meantime, you can swan about these soirees and keep the attention of the most beautiful woman in this room. You're a lucky man." He glanced past Remy, and his smile faded.

Remy spotted the cluster of young girls huddled by the refreshment table—another gaggle of first-year debutantes, judging from their skittish movements and nervous subservience to everyone else. One was steeling herself to walk in their direction. The frozen look on her face was one he was familiar with.

It was his turn to sigh. It happened every year. Different faces, always the same dare.

"I can talk to them," Riones said. "Tell them it isn't their place."

"They'll be treated poorly by the older girls if they don't go through with this. No explanation from you or anyone else will stop that."

The marquess exhaled noisily. "You're a better person than I, Pendergast."

The girl was now rooted to the spot, petrified. The waltz was to begin in the next few minutes. She had very little time left to carry out the venture.

Remy closed the distance. "Good evening," he said, trying to sound as kind and as harmless as he could possibly be while carrying Breaker and nearly ten years' worth of infamy on his shoulders.

It didn't work. The poor girl had all the confidence of a mouse knowing it was about to be devoured.

Remy snuck a quick glance at her friends, who looked just as terrified on her behalf as she was. "You were all dared to dance a waltz with the dhampir, weren't you? And you'd drawn the short straw."

The girl blinked up at him with her large eyes and nodded mutely.

"You are aware that the older girls have been forcing the first-years to play this game for the last five years?"

A blush, and another nod.

"And are you aware that I've been giving the chosen girl this talk every year since?"

A startled look, a quick shake of her head.

"Here's what we're going to do," Remy offered his hand out to her. "We are going to dance, and we are going to enjoy ourselves. You are free to talk to me about anything you'd like. If you are not comfortable with that proposal, then you needn't say a word. I'll do my best to appear enthralled by your attentions so your friends will have little to criticize. And once the dance is over, we can part ways amicably, with no offense taken. Does that seem adequate to you?"

Her smile was nervous before he was even halfway through, but any smile was a good sign. She bobbed her head shyly.

"What's your name?"

"Maya," she finally whispered, so softly he wouldn't have heard it without his hearing enhanced by the bloodwakers.

"All right, Lady Maya. Would you care for a dance?"

It wasn't their fault, Remy thought, as they spun across the room, as he peppered her with questions about herself, who her parents were, how long they were staying in Elouve, when she had officially made her debut. The younglings patterned their behavior after the adults. It wasn't fair to him, and he had the right to be angry that they were taught to be cruel so young. But if this meant that there was one girl who would think kinder of him than she had before, he'd take it.

In a minute or so, the waltz would end. The girl would stammer out her thanks, rush back to where her fellow debutantes lay waiting, and probably bask in their reluctant admiration for carrying out the wager.

What he wasn't expecting was the Duchess of Tennyfair. She was clearly in mourning, black-clad and red-nosed, with a pale face devoid of all makeup. She strode into the center of the room while the dance was still in progress, stopping before him and his dance partner, while the other participants had stopped to stare.

"Why did you kill her?" she cried.

The music stuttered to a halt, silence reigning.

"Why did you kill her?" The woman cried again. "She was my only daughter. She came to my window and told me she was all right, that she was doing well. We would talk until morning, until she had to leave."

Breathe, Remy thought. *Fucking breathe.*

"Lady Maya," he said, as gently as he was able, letting go of his partner's hand. "Thank you for the dance. I think it's about time you returned to your friends."

Lady Maya didn't need to be told a second time. She gathered her skirts and fled.

"Your Grace," Remy began in the same quiet tone.

"She didn't die," the poor mother wept. "She never did. She would climb into my bed and I would hold her, just like I did when she was a child. She only had to leave at sunrise. The Alurian sun could still hurt her. She was always so delicate."

"Your Grace." Riones had come to his rescue. With him was the duchess's husband, stricken and apologetic.

"I am sorry, Lord Pendergast," Tennyfair mumbled. "She hasn't been well."

"Did you murder her, my lord?" the woman cried out. "Surely you wouldn't have taken her from her mother. You are a vampire yourself. Why should you deserve to live when my daughter cannot? Why do you deserve a second chance, while she does not?"

Giselle was gliding up to them, looking only mildly piqued. She was a veteran of crises and would have been right at home in a war room. "Your Grace," she said, compassionate but firm. "I am so very sorry. Would you and His Grace prefer the use of my sitting room?"

"Thank you for your kind offer, Your Grace. Come with me, Nell," Tennyfair said, taking his wife's arm. She gave him no resistance, allowing herself to be guided away from the ballroom floor, the sound of her sobbing bouncing off the walls even after the door closed behind them.

"Are you out of your mind, Your Grace?" Riones hissed, as murmurs took hold. "What possessed you to invite Tennyfair and his wife, given what had just happened to their daughter?"

"I invited them only out of courtesy, with the understanding that their attendance was not required." Giselle finally allowed herself to look discomfited. "But Lady Song herself insisted."

"What? But why would she—"

"My father never told me," Remy said.

The marquess turned to him. "What's that?"

"He never told me that Lady Daneira had been visiting her mother after she'd been turned. Nobody did. Did you know?"

"Of course I didn't. Otherwise—" The other man met his gaze, realization dawning there. "Otherwise—"

"She could have been saved." Remy felt every one of the hundreds of pairs of eyes still watching him. In the wake of this new revelation, they had every right to judge. "She wouldn't have been able to resume her old life, but if she hadn't succumbed to the madness, she could have been saved. Father told me that she had succumbed to the frenzy, that there was no other way but to kill her. And I believed him. The Duchess of Tennyfair was right. I did murder her."

"Reaper law demands that you kill her rather than allow her to remain a vampire, even with her sanity intact."

"With all due respect, Riones, fuck Reaper law."

"Don't let this get to you, Pendergast. Any other Reaper would have made the same decision."

"But it wasn't any of the other Reapers this time, was it? You all rejected her bounty." Remy's voice was clipped, perfectly detached. The air felt thick, and he needed to get away before he drowned. "Excuse me, Riones."

He managed to make it all the way to the manor entrance, affecting a leisurely walk the whole time, his face giving nothing away. A butler stepped hastily aside, giving him more room to pass, and Remy waited until the heavy oak doors closed behind him.

He stepped into the crisp, night air, and then, losing his courage, he began to run.

4

A GARDEN RESPITE

Remy was no fool, and it took him less than half a mile to realize his folly. He hadn't been trained to put up with this shit just to give up because his father had screwed him over for the twelve hundredth time. Remy truly was invested in hunting down the Night Empress and the First Court. He genuinely wanted to exterminate them for the betterment of mankind. More than all that, he wanted to avenge his mother, as any good son should. There was more to this than just his arsehole of a sire. Because if there weren't, he'd keep running, forever if he could.

He needed to stay close to Delacroix grounds, if only to steel himself for what had to be done. He needed to get his hands on Astonbury's most recent report on the First Court vampires, and it didn't matter that he was going to let Giselle put her beautiful, refined hands on him to get it. If his father expected him to kiss Third Court arse like everyone inside was preparing to do, then the old man would have to crawl out of his chair and pucker up himself, because Remy was done. He wasn't going back inside that ballroom tonight. His fuck-the-bloody-fuck-off limits had reached its quota.

He could have saved Lady Daneira.

It was true that letting her live as a vampire went against every Reaper creed he'd ever been taught, but if he was going to be banned from attending official hunter dræfendgemot anyway because the lord high steward had the mental acumen of an un-licked cub and the pettiness to match, then the rules didn't matter. He'd broken them before. He'd broken *this* rule before, with Elke, and had gotten away with it. That he hadn't thought to do it for Lady Daneira made her death all the more devastating. He could have saved her. He knew he could have.

The rain had eased. He changed directions and wound up at the Astonbury gardens instead. Within the lush, expansive green-ery lay a sprawling maze, long considered the most expensively maintained landscape in all of Elouve, and it was hideous. Even here, he could see evidence of Giselle's desire to assert control, to demand and dominate. There was an attempt to pattern the shrubbery after animal silhouettes, which was why vaguely threat-ening dead-eyed rabbits and foxes stared him down as he passed. Some of the trees were unnaturally round. Some of the trees were unnaturally cubed. An unfortunate cherub stood at the center of a small slate-colored fountain at the entrance to the labyrinth, gleefully vomiting copious amounts of water out from its gaping mouth. Remy was certain he'd had nightmares about the statue before.

He walked and walked until he was deep enough within the maze that no one could say to any effect that he was even there, and sat down on the first bench to cross his path.

Only then did he allow his breaths to leave him in wheezing, panicked gasps, hands over his head as he bent down, fighting the waves of nausea.

Could he have saved her? She would have been cast out of the ton despite the Duchess of Tennyfair's tears, despite the ongo-ing cease-fire with the Third Court. They would have hunted her down all over again. The Reapers considered death a better fate than an undead life. Even she, in her final, sober moments, had asked him to put an end to her misery.

Send me to heaven, Armiger. That was his only comfort, that she might have weighed her options in those minutes and decided that this was, after all, the only way.

Anger soon took the place of panic; it was a much more familiar emotion; one he was quicker to welcome. "Fuck you, old man," he muttered under his breath. Even after all this, he couldn't muster the audacity to march home and scream all his frustrations in his father's face, partly because the man was dying, and also because he was not likely to care. But the mishandled foliage was as good a setting to vent as he was ever going to have. And so he noisily sucked in a lung, prepared to let the trees know what the hell his problem was.

" 'Old man'?"

He heard her voice first, her heartbeat second. The former was soft and kind. The latter was unsteady and arrhythmic, rattling against rib cage bone like a dry echo. He sprang to his feet, but there was no one else in sight. His consistent abuse of wakers had given him a nose like a bloodhound; he could smell a light perfume, some mix of roses and cloves. But there was no natural scent of sweat like what humans carried, and his own heart quickened.

Vampire. There was a vampire here.

That didn't explain the irregular heartbeats. Vampires weren't known for having one. Two seconds in between pulses, and then one, and then four; human hearts couldn't maintain intervals like those, either.

He looked up.

A girl stared back down.

She sat on a lower tree branch above him. She was clearly dressed for the ball, and the hem of her gown rode up to reveal smooth, creamy pale skin, the barest hint of thighs. Her sleeves were far too long for what Elouvian fashion expected, and they flowed down either side of her, hiding her hands from sight. It was not the type of dress common in Aluria, though Remy was familiar enough with the styles in the outer kingdoms to recognize them.

A spattering of freckles stretched across her nose, dusting her cheekbones. Her dark hair was curled into long ringlets, caught in the wind as she herself swung back and forth with deliberate slowness, watching him curiously with a silver-gray gaze, lids slightly lifted at the corners. She had eyes of a soft, unvarying hue, the color of mist if it could be smoothed down like icing over cake. They were also sharp and intelligent. She had the unearthly exquisiteness of feature that often comprised a vampire's repertoire.

She looked sympathetic. That was the worst part.

"You're in a tree," Remy finally said, rather unnecessarily.

"Yes."

"Why?"

She flashed him a wide, pretty smile, and he could hear her heart going *thump, ba-da-thump, ba-thump, ba-da-da-da-thump.* "I'd rather not go inside just yet."

He was too tired for this. "You're a vampire."

"And you are very likely a vampire hunter." She shot the Breaker behind him a knowing glance. "Are you going to stake me?"

"Do I have reason to?" She must be part of the contingent of Third Court vampires due to appear at Giselle's party.

"I hope not. You don't look like you'd enjoy it, even if you did."

"The fuck's wrong with your heart?"

"Nǐ hěn cūlǔ," the girl said severely, in what sounded like Qing-yen.

"What?"

"I said, you're very rude."

"Sorry. The fuck's wrong with your heart, madam?"

She laughed. "How did you know?"

"I can hear it."

She studied him. "You have a surprisingly good sense of hearing. Does that come naturally to you, or is it because of the poison you hunters ingest to keep up with us?"

"The latter."

"Those will break you in the long term, you know."

"Helps keep us alive long enough for there to be a long term."

"Fair. Mind if I sit down next to you?"

He nodded, and she let go of the branch, somersaulting in the air and landing lightly beside him despite the bulkiness of her dress. If she was expecting him to jerk away from her sudden closeness, Remy endeavored to disappoint. He'd been right; her sleeves were even longer than she was tall, but she'd folded them up underneath her arms to keep them off the ground.

"You're not frightened," she noted.

"I'm not. Thought becoming a vampire would've fixed your heart."

"I'm a very different kind of vampire. Who's the old man you were angry at?"

Remy frowned. "That's none of your business."

"Undoubtedly. Want to talk about it anyway? I won't tell."

He stared at her again. "I'm a Reaper."

She smiled back. "I already guessed."

"I had to . . . kill someone. As it turns out, based on erroneous information. It might not have been necessary after all, and I was . . . am . . . angry."

"A freshly turned vampire?"

Remy nodded, eyeing her warily.

She didn't seem bothered by the admission. "Good vampire? Bad?"

The question startled him.

"Don't you ever refer to other humans as either good or bad?"

She had a point. "She was kind, before she'd succumbed to the frenzy."

"And you thought she could have survived that."

"Yes."

"Only a third of those turned do. Perhaps you're being unduly hard on yourself, milord."

"Armiger," Remy said, before he could stop himself. "Not milord."

"Armiger. That means 'arms-bearer,' doesn't it? But why choose that?"

"It suits me better." He didn't want to have to explain why. He wasn't sure he knew himself. "It has none of the expectations that *Lord* or *Lady* require, and I . . . like that."

The girl nodded. "Very well, Armiger. I'm sure the majority of vampires you've encountered likely deserve it, but I don't make it a habit to kill every human I come across. I like humans. The general idea of them, at least. I've even struck up a friendship with a select few. There's always a way for us to coexist. That's primarily why I'm here." She cocked her head to one side. "Somehow, I don't think this is the first casual conversation you've ever had with a vampire. You've done this before?"

"You're very perceptive."

"You're not the first human I've dealt with, either. But you're perhaps eighty-five percent kinder than most."

He snorted. "Eighty-five percent? This is the best behavior you're likely to get from me." He was relaxing more than he ought to around her. He couldn't help it.

"You can try harder. Night's still young. For instance, you haven't even once complimented me on my gown even though it took me two hours to shove myself inside it."

Remy took a quick glance at her waist, hugged and perfectly cinched with a corset in keeping with the Alurian fashion, at the elaborate curls in her hair that must have taken hours to arrange and rearrange, only slightly mussed from her adventures on the tree branch.

She was flirting. Strange, given that she was of the species he made a living off killing. But after having to murder one vampire, spending a nonthreatening evening with another was just as good as giving everyone else inside Astonbury Manor the finger. It didn't feel like she was here simply to charm the Alurian nobility. It felt like she could be dressed in rags and barefoot besides, with all the hair shorn off her head and covered in mud, and she would still treat him the same way.

She wanted him to flirt back, but that was just another of the numerous skills he was expected to master and was nonetheless shit at, so he opted for blunt honesty.

"The dress becomes you, but it also encumbers you," he said. "You are in unknown, potentially hostile territory, surrounded by Reapers, yet you chose to make yourself vulnerable because you are placing your trust in them despite their lack of the same in you. And that to me, is much more breathtaking than any gown you could wear."

The girl's breath caught. "Are you at least eighty-five percent as kind to other vampires as you are to me?"

"Despite everything I've seen," Remy said quietly, "and everything I've done, I try my best to see people as people."

"You're quite clever."

"I'm not. Politics goes over my head. I don't even know why the Third Court would want an alliance with us."

"Maybe because we're not the bloodthirsty demons humans think we are. Or because we see people as people, too." She leaned forward. "You know, I'm not on good terms with my sire, either."

"I'd assumed that vampires were always on bad terms with their sires."

"Ah-ha. A prejudice."

It was. "My apologies."

"Do you know what does make me feel better whenever I'm frustrated, though? I climb up the highest tower I can find and scream into the wind."

"I was prepared to do something similar before you showed up."

"You'd need somewhere higher. It's much more satisfying that way. It's like you're yelling at the world, and they can't yell back and drown you out." She looked around. "Still want to do it? I'm the only one within range to hear you."

"What would *you* even shout?"

"Something naughty. Like . . ." She took a deep breath, belted out, "You . . . you lumpless wombat! You . . ." She stopped, because Remy was already laughing. It felt good.

"*Lumpless wombat*? That's what you consider an insult?"

She sulked. "It's a very terrible insult in Qing-yen. It's not my fault Alurian doesn't have the right semantics for it. What would *you* say?"

Remy proceeded, without missing a beat, into a steady stream of profanities. She stared at him, wide-eyed. "I suppose those are good, too," she conceded when he finished.

"Even more satisfying to say. Pick one and shout."

"Ah." He could practically hear her mind cycling through the words, trying to find the least reprehensible of the lot. "Ah . . . twat?"

"Was that a question?"

"Twat." She took a deep breath. "You twat!" She shouted at the trees, "You abominable twat!"

"Fucking arse," Remy encouraged her. "Swag-bellied cockchafer!"

"Fucking ass!" She was pronouncing each word with a slow, delighted relish. "Fucking. Cockchafer!"

"Yeast-infested quimswiller!"

"Yeast-infested quimswiller!"

"Foddle-swapped coxcomb!"

"Foddle-swapped coxcomb!" And then again, at his urging, " . . . scum-sucking . . . cuntrabbit!"

"A *what*?" Remy choked.

She fell back, laughing. "I'm saving that one for a special occasion!"

She turned to him, her face all aglow, eyes dancing with pleasure, and Remy forgot the next vulgarity he was about to encourage her to say.

Light, she really was beautiful.

He wanted to say it was a reflex. That this was the only way he'd ever interacted with a woman, and that he didn't know any better. His mouth paused half a beat away from hers, struggling not to close the distance. Her eyes had grown wide again, studying his. Her smile faded. She didn't lean closer, but she didn't pull away, either.

Beyond their unexpected, easy camaraderie, he knew she liked him. More than that, she wanted him. He was at least experienced in knowing what that looked like on a female. Her lips were so very red.

"I fear," she said softly, "that I am about to enter a complication neither of us is looking for."

"Xiaodan?" The voice rang through the gardens with authority. Before either of them could get in another word, a man blurred into being beside the lady, only to step back because Remy was already attacking, Breaker in his hands, and *trap fucking trap shit shit, this was a fucking trap* running a marathon through his head.

The man was quick to block his attacks, eyes flaring with a dark golden hue, but before long he was lashing out with his own punches, knuckles hitting silver.

There was a grating sound as Remy's scythe blades slid into view. A smart jab with it caught against the man's lapel, slicing it part of the way through.

"Stop!" The girl was between them both before either could mount another assault. Her sleeves had been pulled back again, and one hand was wrapped against the man's wrist, stopping the blow from falling on Remy. The other gripped at the handle of Remy's Breaker, and try as he might, he couldn't budge it an inch. Her eyes were bright with anger, like sparks glinting off silver. Never had anyone who looked so pissed off, still looked so lovely.

"Zidan," she said with a rigid calm that suggested she had done this to the man many times in the past. "Let us not make it a habit of starting fights in the places the humans have invited us to. It will not improve our standing with them."

"If you recall," the man said, "he instigated it."

They were the same dark eyes; once the golden glow in them faded, it left those familiar flecks of yellow. It was the same arrogant tilt to his nose. His hair was no longer loosely tied, instead falling past his shoulders, carefully combed. He was clean-shaven this time, but Remy knew him. "*You,*" he snarled. "*You're* Zidan Malekh?"

The Summer Lord flashed the same mocking grin he'd worn several days ago when he'd fought Remy in the woods. "Reaper."

Zidan Malekh. The vampire noble who led the Third Court. The one who could've killed him in the woods. He itched to whack him with Breaker. He wanted a rematch now that he was rested and furious and pumped with bloodwakers, but the girl's grip on his weapon remained unrelenting. Remy pushed, trying to force her to relinquish her hold. He could see Malekh doing the same on his side.

Breaker was on the ground before he realized it. The woman's hand was now on his face—a light touch, almost affectionate, but Remy could feel the prick of her nails against his cheek and knew she could rip out his whole jawbone if she were in the mood for it.

Her other hand was also on Zidan Malekh's face. She wasn't playing favorites.

"My dears," she said softly.

Remy didn't register that she'd shoved him after that, just felt the impact from the blow. It sent him skidding several feet backward, keeping his balance only out of trained reflex. The vampire lord was more graceful, gliding back instead of stumbling, but he wore the same expression of surprise.

It crossed Remy's mind that, fuck, she was strong. A lot stronger than she looked, even with her wobbly heart and gentle disposition.

"While I know you have ample reason to carve the smile off my fiancé's face with your impressive scythes, Armiger—" the girl began amiably.

"Xiao—" Malekh began to object, but she was quick to cut him off.

"—it would nonetheless set back the burgeoning friendship between the vampires and the humans in Aluria by several months, if not years. Tell me I didn't staple this dress on for nothing, Zidan. It's not like you to have so little control of your temper."

This time Remy did step back, of his own accord. " 'Fiancé,' " he repeated. Zidan Malekh was this woman's fiancé. Which meant that she was—

She smiled apologetically at him. "We never got around to introducing ourselves, did we? I am Song Xiaodan, a daughter of the Fourth Court. Your queen was kind enough to invite us to Aluria, and the Duchess of Astonbury graceful enough to extend that to her ball, though this isn't quite the introduction we intended."

5

MORNING WINE

Remy didn't return to the ballroom that night, as he had no desire to look on while Lady Song Xiaodan, the Fourth Court heiress, dazzled the crowd with her fiancé and Third Court king, Lord Zidan Malekh. She owed Remy nothing. But it was nonetheless a blow to discover that she was to wed the vampire whose clanmates had killed Lady Daneira, the one who had made Remy feel like an untried novice. Irrational as it was, it felt like a betrayal of the friendship she had attempted to strike up with him, and he mourned its premature end.

It didn't matter. Lady Song was free to have a hundred bastard fiancés if she'd like, each a bigger gaping arse than the last, though it would take a lot to surpass the one she already had.

Remy felt like a coward all the same, having chosen to avoid them after their encounter at the gardens. He spent the rest of the night occupied in the Duchess of Astonbury's library instead, reading and sulking at equal intervals. He then took out some of his frustrations on Giselle after he'd been summoned to her bed-chambers, much to the woman's delight. Only afterward, satiated and breathless in bed beside him, did she finally provide the information he'd been waiting for.

"It's classified, of course," she murmured, a finger idly tracing circles on his chest. "Even more so than usual. No one but my husband's innermost circle is remotely aware of this. There are reports of the undead attacking villages along the eastern borders, and more toward the north. But the latter makes it Kerenai territory, far enough in the outer realms that it is officially our neighbor King Hallifax's problem, so Her Majesty has been reluctant to send troops without his express invitation.

"There are more of the same, this time along the borders between Aluria and Qing-ye, but the latter falls under the Fourth Court's domain, or so I'm told. Perhaps that is why Lady Song was invited to Elouve in the first place, for them to discuss matters without overstepping boundaries. There is also something . . . unnatural about these vampires, according to these papers, though I don't quite understand all this scientific babbling. You know how all this talk of blood makes my stomach positively churn, don't you, my love?

"There are rumors that they are perhaps Night Court vampires after all. It's been years since one of the First has been sighted. Apparently, they've gone into hiding—it's said that they are not on good terms with the other vampire clans, which would explain such erratic behavior. Another special friend of mine clerks for my husband. For someone who occupies one of the highest positions in the kingdom, Astonbury can be quite an oblivious man." She giggled. "My contact copied the papers you asked for, without Matthew any the wiser. They're yours for the taking."

"Thank you, Giselle," he'd said, but the woman moved over him with a smile, hand drifting lower.

"Thank me properly again?" she suggested sweetly.

He left before the sky had lightened, though the duchess was rarely up before noon. He took a moment after he'd dressed to regard the beautiful woman sprawled beneath the covers, so lovely that his breath still sometimes caught no matter how many times he'd seen her this way. Their encounters always left him feeling both cheapened and exhilarated, the small bouts of self-revulsion warring with that part of him that felt good at being needed.

But the information he wanted was now hidden carefully away inside his overcoat, and for now, that was all that mattered.

There was no valet or servant attending him at Kinaiya Lodge, which was what he called the small, fairly unassuming bungalow he used to hide from his father's influence whenever he was in Elouve, exactly the way he liked it. It would have been a scandal on its own, a duke's son attending to his own meals and cleaning up after himself like a commoner, and Remy had solved that problem by receiving almost no visitors and keeping his purchase of the residence a secret.

He'd also gone and bought all the empty lots around his house to add to the property so he could keep his privacy intact. Being the son of a duke with a generous monthly allowance had its uses.

He had spent the day before the ball making his bedroom and the adjoining washroom habitable after being away for so long, but after the night's surprises, he'd put in only enough effort that morning to run a long bath and break his fast. The rest of his home could be seen to at a later date. A discreet laundress highly recommended by Elke attended to his washings whenever he was in the capital, but Remy had since learned to cook simple meals and become handy with a broom and dustpan.

His initial reasons for building Kinaiya Lodge had been strictly utilitarian, but he found, to his great mortification, that bits and pieces of himself had snuck their way into the decor. Bookshelves stacked with gentlemen's magazines, ladies' fashions, newsletters by prominent bluestockings, and a cluttered collection of historical books on both Tithe and Alurian history. Watercolor sketches he'd made at idler times. Balls of yarn and small feathered toys for the cats who occasionally wandered into the garden out back, with additional food bowls for those seeking nourishment rather than entertainment. A series of thorny succulents along one wall, the only species of plant capable of surviving extended periods without water and his poor attempts at horticulture.

He had taken the time to clean off more of the dirt that had clung to his mother's portrait. It was always the first thing he did whenever he returned to the lodge.

The rest of the drawing room still had a light layer of dust on it when Elke arrived. The red-haired woman promptly pillaged his larder and returned with his most expensive port after he'd let her in, and listened while Remy told her what had transpired the night before.

"It occurs to me," she said conversationally, watching the faint light sparkle against her wineglass as she swirled the liquid within, "that you have remained unbitten all this time *because* vampires find your blood just as dense as the rest of you."

"And what exactly do you mean by that?"

"The Fourth Court heiress wants to tup you, Remy."

Remy had eschewed wine for coffee, having deemed alcohol too early to indulge in at seven in the morning, even for him. He spat the hot beverage out all the same. "She wants nothing of the sort," he sputtered, wiping his mouth on a napkin. "She's engaged."

"Vampire relationships differ significantly from what humans consider commonplace, love. I should know. And besides, you're one to talk, cavorting with a married woman and her addle-brained friends. Humans can be just as strange and complicated." She cast a critical eye at his tired face, the faint circles underneath his eyes—something a fresh change of clothes and a bath could not disguise. Her voice softened. "Perhaps it's time for you to sever your connections with the duchess. I can't think that this is good for you, no matter how much classified information you can woo out of her."

"Not yet." Remy kept his mouthful of coffee down this time. "She's my only source of information. The Reaper network learns things I can't get anywhere else. Not even from you, for all your resources."

"I'm hurt," Elke purred, hand fluttering against her chest. Nobody deserved to be that pretty only a couple of hours past dawn. Today, she wore an intricate corset and a dress that drew attention to the curve of her hips and her bosom. It was her habit to call on him most mornings whenever he was in town—an odd habit, given her Fifth Court past. "I think I'm a rather good source of information. Have you seen that horrid thing the Marchioness of Steadborne was wearing yesterday, for instance? Peorth's was to have the brocade and furs made for the Duchess of Kenora, but the marchioness paid triple the price to take it from the other woman's hands. It looked like several foxes had decided to die on her all at once."

"I'm not really interested in the Marchioness of Steadborne or her dead foxes."

"You should be. Didn't I tell you that I've been accompanying her husband? It's how I learned of his wife's spurious tastes in fashion and general pettiness."

Remy frowned. The Marquess of Steadborne was one of Astonbury's good friends, and very much involved in the Reaper business. Elke was risking much to be his mistress, no matter how temporary the position was. A vampire trying to pass herself off as human in Elouve was risky enough to begin with. Even if said vampire had made a name for herself as an independent, highly successful jewel merchant with a row of popular shops along Gold Street. "Ever find it ironic that you love Elouve more than I ever had?"

"Elouve is my sanctuary, Remy. Kinaiya Lodge is yours; the city just happens to come with your purchase."

"I'm serious. What would you do if they discover who you are?"

She shrugged. "The only choice I'd have. If I ever have to leave, I'll send you a perfectly carved golden cock with twin sapphire eggs just for you to remember me by, nestled in a delicate mahogany box with such beautiful wrapping paper to make your heart sing."

Remy snorted. He was used to her vulgarisms. They had that in common, too. "Don't change the subject, Elke."

"Well, don't give me that look, then. I'm always careful. Why, the marquess's eldest son is a hunter himself. I bet I can ferret out more of the lord high steward's secrets than the Duchess of Astonbury can provide in the space of a night."

"You don't even like him. You were glad that your arrangements with him were finally ending."

"Arrangements can be renegotiated. And it's not about liking my patrons. It's the influence he can bring to my shops that counts most of all." It was her turn to frown at him. "You're one to talk. You shouldn't let her keep using you like this. You're an excellent hunter, darling, but you're not suited for this other line of work. Your father was in the wrong for forcing you into this when you weren't old enough to know better."

"That's rather odd advice, coming from you."

She grinned at him, baring a perfect set of lovely, ivory fangs. "That this is what I do is exactly why you should listen to me. I can spend the night with a gentleman and think no more about him the next morning. Beautiful gems have kept my attention for far longer. But you, love. You're too kind for this. You'll always leave pieces of your heart behind, whether you want to or not, and to people who deserve it least of all. I owe you my life. Consider this one of the small ways I am trying to repay my debt. Why, you haven't even shown me the papers yet, to see the quality of espionage I'm up against."

Remy had to smile. "So you're not just here to spend time with me?"

"A visit can have more than one rationale behind it. Especially when we've got Third and Fourth Court vampires in the city. But don't think this discussion is over. I'm simply too curious about the reports to delay any longer."

She knew him well enough. "Riones told me about what Astonbury intends to discuss at the Reapers' meeting this morning." Remy set his cup down. "Word has come of vampires attacking villages along the east coast, and they believe it might be First Court kindred."

Elke snorted. "The east coast? King Hallifax is too busy building higher walls around his capital to do anything about it. He would rather let those villages be overrun before admitting that he would require assistance."

"You'd know the situation better than I do." Remy reached into his coat pocket to produce the papers and pushed them toward her. Elke was too kind to say it, but Remy had no head for intrigue—not enough to decipher most of the reports he filched.

She scanned the documents. "It says here that Queen Ophelia has already pledged to quietly send in several regiments of Reapers to Kerenai. No word yet on what she intends to do with the attacks near Qing-ye."

"Won't merchants traveling from Kerenai give us the same warning?"

"There are no longer any merchants coming in from Kerenai. Hallifax has blocked the roads, posted sentries at every major outpost along the way—though I'm not sure that would be much of a deterrence where vampires are involved. But there's something much more troubling."

Elke continued to read, her brow furrowing while he made the most of the silence to scarf up the rest of his eggs and toast. "But surely there must be some mistake!" she finally burst out. "I've never heard of such a thing before. If Etrienne had known this was possible, he would have . . ." She paused and bit her lip.

"Known what was possible?"

"He would have used it himself," Elke said, still staring at the papers in her hand. "He would have transformed the rest of the Fifth Court into abominations under his thrall if he thought it would help him conquer Aluria and the rest of the kingdoms. And he would have experimented on me first of all, as was my privilege as his worthless toy. I was already his mindless little husk to begin with. Imagine if he'd gotten his hands on such a secret, what he could have made me do."

"Elke—"

She waved her hand aimlessly. "I'm all right, love. He can't hurt me anymore, and I'm no longer that helpless thing you found dying on a dirt road. But this—this is horrifying."

"Etrienne would have used what immediately?"

It took Elke a while to explain—the documents had gone into more complicated details than previous ones. The first of the reports had been filed by another Reaper—Rai Takenori, the Duke of Isshei. Remy had met him a few times before, a no-nonsense man who always made certain of the facts before committing himself to speak of them. His account had been straightforward enough.

Corpse identified as one Tal Harveston, seventeen-year-old male from the village of Dalwen, a day and a half's ride from Alurian borders. Reportedly killed and turned into a vampire ten days ago, haunted the area for nearly a week before I'd arrived to kill it on the fourth day of Trisalker. I had personally cremated the body, seen that his ashes were scattered along the ocean, in accordance with Reaper laws. So it came as a surprise to learn that the poor youth had been resurrected through some unknown means and had resumed preying on the villagers within Grenarde, leaving behind bodies drained of blood, just as before. I was granted a small contingent of Reapers to nullify the threat, and even then, it took our combined might to bring down what had previously been an easy kill.

I had not observed anything unusual about the vampire during my first encounter with it—nothing more than what was to be expected with a reaping. When my men and I hunted it down the second time, the corpse's physical appearance had changed drastically. I almost would not have believed it was the same vampire that I had previously slain, had it not been for the similarity of features still recognizable despite the mutations. As ordered by Lord High Steward Astonbury, we delivered the body to Dr. Agenot at the Archives' laboratory for further analysis.

"That," Elke said, "doesn't sound ominous at all, I'm sure."

The next report was from Dr. Agenot himself, a transcript of his findings made verbatim and duly transcribed.

Autopsy performed on subject #1294 on the fourth hour and fifth day of Trisalker. While alive, subject had been previously described as five feet and ten inches tall, one hundred and eighty-five pounds, with black hair, brown eyes, and average features. Subject upon delivery lies at six feet and ten inches tall, three hundred and thirty-five pounds, with black hair and eyes of an indeterminate color.

The left eye has turned red, but not from petechial hemorrhaging. The left side of the face has been severely mutilated, the cheekbone and upper mandible ripped away so that only the lower jawbone remains intact. Current muscle mass does not match previous eyewitness accounts of the subject, including that of Rai Takenori, suggesting some unknown, unnatural mutation. Body decomposition appears to be three times the normal rate of the average corpse, the flesh visibly rotting upon naked observation. Nonetheless, there appears to be at least twenty-three marks on its body, similar to those that could have been made

*with a syringe. As subject had not been known to be sickly, or
to have engaged in any forms of vice, these could be evidence of
some unknown experimentation that may explain the remarkable differences between the subject's first and second slaying.
Subject is—*

   Subject appears to be moving.

The next paragraph resumed as if nothing was out of the or-
dinary, though Remy would have given a lot to learn what had
happened in between those lines.

*Subject has been dispatched for the third time by Reapers sta-
tioned within the Archives. Decomposition has continued
throughout the whole process, and at the same aforementioned
rate. Subject indicated no cognitive faculties or self-awareness
before being subdued. I have extracted as much blood as I could
from the corpse, and a cursory examination indicates pathogens
unknown in both humans and vampires, though there have been
very few samples from the latter to come to a more conclusive
analysis. My theory, however, is that any minute bone fragments
to have survived the cremation may have been enough for the
subject to reconstitute itself; further testing is needed. Subject has
been taken to the vault and remains under heavy guard by hunters as an added precaution. As per Her Majesty's instructions, we
are storing any other corpses of similar infections in the yakhchāl
as advised by Lord Zidan Malekh of the Third Court.*

Remy glared at the document. The infuriating vampire
noble had been meddling in Alurian affairs far longer than he'd
thought.

Underneath the report was a handwritten scrawl. Remy had
filched enough documents from him to recognize Astonbury's
hand.

Fresh reports of similar cases at Kerenai. Extraction in progress.
Bodies at Dalwen also retrieved.

"If Etrienne had known this," Elke said, "he would have replicated the process as soon as he was able. The ability to revive slain vampires . . ."

"And now there may be someone else out there, prepared to cause just as much chaos," Remy added grimly. "This doesn't strike me as a natural evolution."

"I would hope not," Elke said with a small shudder.

"And from what you've told me, it means that they have a mutated vampire imprisoned here in Elouve, at the Archives," Remy said.

"Do you intend to tell your father?"

Remy could. Valenbonne would waste no time denouncing Astonbury for it. That may not be enough to relinquish his position as lord high steward, but it could very well diminish his status, incite distrust.

But he wasn't going to, because he didn't trust his father, either. "No. This doesn't sound like a vampire in an extended frenzy. It doesn't sound like any vampire I've ever encountered before."

"What do you intend to do next?"

"Not a chance I'd be receiving an invitation to join the other Reapers on an expedition to Hallifax's domain. Qing-ye would be another two weeks' ride. But Dalwen is only a few hours away."

"What good would that be? The creature has already been apprehended."

"But it's within several miles of both Wyndbrook and Glycespike. I've received reports of similar attacks there from other informants, and I want to see if those incidents are connected."

"What? And no offer to bring me along?"

Remy glowered at her cheerful, smiling face. "We've talked about this before, Elke. The chances of you being discovered—"

"I enjoy my life in Elouve very much, love, but occasionally I too grow bored at pretending I am fully human, no matter how grateful I should be for the opportunity. I could be the nimblest vampire in all the courts if I put my mind to it. It's why I survived this long, against stronger kindred. And besides," the girl said, casting a frown at Breaker, which was leaning against the wall and never too far from his reach. "It's no use beating around the bush, darling. Let me take a look and see what damage you've done it again."

"The chain's snapped," Remy admitted, turning it over for her perusal. "It's nothing drastic."

"If I had my way, I would have strengthened the links, made it harder for it to break."

"It was designed to snap easily. Most vampires are likely to wrench Breaker out of my hands should they get hold of it, and I'd rather lose the chain than find myself entirely weaponless."

"That may be true, but the apparent ease with which you keep wrecking it is almost impressive. This is the fifth time this year I've had to reforge it for you, and the season's barely started." Elke held the chain up to the dim light and sighed. "Let's see . . . I'll take another bottle of port as payment, plus your promise that I'll be accompanying you to Dalwen at . . . when do you intend to make the trip?"

"This afternoon, if I can."

"So soon? And you expect me to have Breaker good and ready by then?"

"Why are you so insistent on accompanying me?"

Elke gazed down at the table, her fingers tracing the faint imperfections in the wood. "These experimentations. They feel familiar to me in so many terrible ways. I want to know firsthand that nothing about this has Etrienne's signature behind it. I'd like to go for my own peace of mind. To make sure my past stays dead and buried, like the rest of them."

The Fifth Court, the Brilliant Court, had called themselves inventors, but they'd been more notorious for their methods of torture and monstrous experiments. For their leader's obsession with a perfect immortality beyond even a vampire's lifespan. For the tests he would inflict on his own brethren to achieve it. For all their closeness, Elke never gave Remy explicit details about her time in Etrienne's court. And Remy never asked.

"If I throw in another bottle of wine, will that be enough time to get Breaker ready?"

Elke smiled briefly. "Make it an Old Varian, and it's a deal." She looked at him. "You're worried, too, aren't you?" she asked softly, because she'd known him far too long. "It's not like you to rush in with so little information on hand."

Remy looked down at the papers still spread across the table. Twenty-three marks on the body. Attacking even as it decayed. The result of someone's experiment.

"I have a bad feeling about all this, El," he said. "Real bloody bad."

6

MONSTERS IN
THE MIST

A strange melancholy had permeated the village of Dalwen, deeper than the thick fog around them. Tal Harveston had been a popular boy, and the people here took the news of his demise hard, like he had been their own son. With that mourning had come both terror and resentment—fear that it would happen to another of their own, anger that the Reapers had done so little to save Harveston from his fate.

Remy bore it well enough. He was used to hate. He had paid his respects to Harveston's mother, a woman in her early forties who looked like she had aged twenty more. He kept his visit short and offered her some small compensation—the dead boy had been the family breadwinner, and this would be enough to let her live comfortably for a few years. Enough still to set her other two sons up in trade or in an apprenticeship when they came of age.

This wasn't the first time. There were missing children all over Aluria, triple this year than it had been in previous others. He hadn't found all their families yet, but the ones he had he could do nothing much for either, beyond offering his condolences in coin. Not all of them had accepted. Many a grieving parent had thrown it back at his face.

The village had been spared the details of what had happened to Tal Harveston after he'd been taken away by the Reapers, but they knew the monster the Reapers had fought.

The woman accepted the bag of coins. She wouldn't meet his gaze.

The other villagers had been hesitant to talk to him, but the idea of some terrible creature worse than a vampire overcame that reluctance. The other mutilated body, still unidentified, had been found on the main roads between Glycespike and Wyndbrook, just as Jack had told Remy. No one in the neighboring villages traveled through those paths anymore. Not since the body's discovery, and not since the fog had settled around them like a thick, hazy soup. They would have to leave Glycespike eventually, they said—vegetables to deliver, livestock to bring to market in the larger towns. But not just yet. No one wanted to be the next corpse. There were rumors of it being a curse.

Elke disguised herself well. She'd met up with Remy, her face scrubbed free of oils and paints and her bright red hair tucked into a severe bun. Her clothes looked homespun and rough-stained, and it took a closer look to see that she was even a woman. This was not the first time she'd accompanied him on a hunt. Objectively speaking, she probably had more experience with this than Remy did.

Late afternoon resembled nightfall in these parts. Remy could barely see more than twenty feet in front of him, and it was getting cold.

If the villagers were right, then what a fucking horrible night to have a curse.

There was no real strategy here but to wait by the roads to be attacked. He tempted fate by spinning Breaker above his head, the movements sure and practiced, the knifechain whizzing merrily along in a circle. It had always calmed him in his youth, and it was calming him now.

"You look ridiculous," Elke said.

"You know, the people from Tithe tie heavy coconuts around thick bamboo and carry them above their heads as they go from one village to the next. This is a similar exercise."

"That would explain both their and your impressively contoured arms." Elke knew why he did it, knew better than to push. She stretched. "If I'd known it would be this cold, I would have stayed at the village and coaxed a little more fire from the Glycespike inn."

"You're not supposed to feel cold anymore."

"You're right. It's my hair. It's all scraggly and frizzed from the damp, even tied back like this. Being dead doesn't do much for your hair." She had brought a fire lance with her, one she'd forged herself. It was part of her human disguise, but Remy suspected it was also a matter of pride for her, proof she could make better weapons than what the Reapers possessed.

She'd convinced him to bring a second lance along, though that had never been his style. Remy had little patience for them— he liked his battles up close and in-your-face messy. But there was enough in those strange reports that he'd let caution overrule his pride.

"A couple more hours." They'd found shelter near some trees, only a few feet away from the main road. The biggest piece of the body had been found right around here; Remy could still smell the faint metallic scent of it, remnants of blood on the ground too miniscule to see.

There had been no new attacks in the area since Jack had made his report. Either Tal Harveston had been responsible for the last killing, or this second creature was biding its time.

Remy was wagering on the latter. Harveston had left his victims intact. That was almost two weeks ago. Jack reported the attack nearly five days after Harveston had supposedly been taken in. The body should have been discovered long before that.

"You could still find your way back," Remy said. "I'm told the inn's famous for their mulled wine."

"They don't take the time to spice their bottles with blood like you do for me. My hair will survive." Elke stilled. "Remy. Wait."

He'd heard it, too. A faint shuffling noise, grunting. It sounded loud in the otherwise total stillness around him, amplified by the fog. This was no horse and wagon coming their way. It was something larger. A hell of a lot larger.

The smell of blood grew thicker.

This accursed fog was a frequent problem on other hunts, and it was just as much an obstacle now. Remy crept forward steadily, newly forged knifechain in hand, since ranged combat seemed like the better idea at this point. Elke was beside him and keeping pace, just as silent and just as swift. There was another grotesque sound from somewhere closer; a grating, crunching noise, followed by something wet and squelching.

The road before them cleared enough for Remy to see that he'd been wrong after all, except that the horse lay on the road on its side, clearly dead. The cart had been overturned, and something was hunched over it.

It was a nightmare. Its back was turned toward them, and Remy saw the protruding bone sticking out between its shoulder blades, the blood vessels pulsing and running underneath the waxy, near-transparent skin. It had a vaguely human shape— long stumps that could be legs, two more that could be arms if you discounted the three more bursting from the sides of its tumorous upper back, all bulging outward like flayed muscle upon flayed muscle. Its skin was a slime made of flesh and looked ready to slide off at a moment's notice, and he was reminded of Dr. Agenot's report of the Harveston boy's rapid decomposition. It was a massive pockmark of a creature twice his size, and it was blocking the path, a significant radius around it now stained red.

Whoever had been manning the cart was also dead. Their remains were unrecognizable as human, save for a huddle of torn cloth on one side of the wagon. The creature continued to feast.

"Preserve us," Elke breathed from behind him, the closest thing he'd heard a vampire utter to a prayer.

The most pragmatic solution would be to ride hard back to Elouve, summon all the available Reapers there, and return with an army to fight the beast. The most arsed solution would be to remain and take it on their own because it could escape in the interim.

For Remy, who was accustomed to making bad decisions, it was an easy choice to make.

The knifechain was deadly sharp, but not even he had been expecting it to plunge through the back of the nightmare's head, the thickest part of the blade sliding back and anchoring to its forehead. It stopped chewing, and rose on its stumps, turning. Remy had to fight to keep his hold on Breaker firm lest it be pulled out of his grasp, even as he viewed the entire monstrosity for the first time.

There was no face. All Remy could see was a bloated eye staring back at them, an eye that took up space where nose and cheekbones should have been. His knife burrowed out from the center of its forehead, but to no obvious effect.

It had no mouth. But from its chest cavity, teeth half as long as his scythes emerged from a cavernous hole that stretched across it from shoulder blade to shoulder blade; still bloody, still gnawing on the remains of the poor traveler and their horse.

This wasn't a vampire. This was a demon dredged up from the pits of hell.

"Bloody fuck," Remy said.

The horror spat out a glob of squirming fat on the ground and then advanced toward them, chest-mouth curled at them in a terrifying grin.

It was faster than Remy wanted it to be, bearing down on them with its tree-trunk legs. Remy ran in a semicircle around it, yanking hard at his chain before it could further entangle itself around the monster's head. Thankfully it yielded, and the knife was pulled back out with a sickening tear, blue-tinged blood spilling on the ground.

Without either needing to say a word, Remy and Elke split, dodging into opposite directions. Elke was faster and loaded up with firepowder. She reappeared at the monster's left, her lance already leveled at its head as she pulled the trigger.

A cascading stream of fire shot out from the muzzle, Elke handling the hard recoil expertly. It scored a direct hit on its forehead, exactly where Remy had aimed at with his knifechain, and the brute began to burn brightly like a torch, the flames soon swallowing up the rest of its head. The great, staring eye slid shut . . .

And opened again just underneath its torso, right below the wide mouth and its sharp teeth.

Remy shifted his aim. The arms were the immediate threat, and he managed to cut down a limb before the monster could reach him, narrowly avoiding a grab. His scythes cut through another appendage, and he swung low and managed to take out one of its stumps before the monster's weight was on him, pinning him to the ground, Breaker between them. The fire atop its head had been extinguished, leaving blackened carcass and charred, visible bone. Remy could smell its rancid breath up close, the teeth snapping dangerously near his face before he managed to twist Breaker so that his blades bit down into the void that passed for its mouth. It reared back, giving him enough space to move and drive it again right into the beast's shifted eye.

It didn't make a sound; Remy wasn't sure it had the required vocal cords to do so. It simply lunged back, away from him, giving Elke another opportunity to reload and fire another round, this time right at the gaping mouth, the overtly large and ragged teeth. But instead of fire, a fine bolt of lightning shot out from the silver muzzle, and Remy swore he could feel it crackle into his skin, even from several feet away.

The monstrous thing swallowed her shot whole and then staggered, already off-balance from the loss of one leg. Its body was glowing like a hot furnace, Elke's attack tearing through whatever entrails it had left, lighting it up from within. Whatever coarse skin that helped shield it from outside flames didn't from the inside, and Remy could see the blood vessels underneath its flesh turning a fiery red. He relinquished Breaker to grab at the fire lance Elke had provided him, having enough self-preservation to know that he would not want to get up close to the monster again no matter how great his love was for melee combat. And when it turned back his way, he fired.

The fire lance's weakness, even in the ones Elke built, was that it could only deliver one discharge at a time before needing to reload. Its strength was that Elke had modified theirs for double the firepower. The shot practically tore the creature apart, reducing it to a thick soup. It flooded the path before them, more liquid now than solid. It was a whole damn mess to clean up.

"Lightning?" Remy asked weakly in the aftermath. "Your lance has *lightning*?"

"Not quite the type of lightning brought down from the clouds, but very effective, wouldn't you say?" Elke tried not to sound too shaken. "It's all built on rather sound science. Might need a few more modifications, though—it jolted me, just a little. Perhaps more insulation—"

"And what the hell was that?" Remy asked, slowly rising to his feet. He'd been expecting some twisted kind of new rogue vampire. Not something that could barely pass for human, hunting so close to the villages. Rai Takenori was not the kind of man to exaggerate. Remy should have believed his descriptions.

"Are you seriously considering bringing it back to your manor?" Elke asked, appalled when Remy reached into his satchel.

"We need to know where it came from. We need to warn everyone in Elouve. The fog might have helped in keeping it out of sight, but if there are more of these things out there, then we're all in more trouble than we realize." He'd brought more sacks, but he'd also been expecting something a lot more solid to bring back. There was also the impossibly foul odor rising from the remains, which was making his eyes water and his nose threaten to mutiny.

Elke sighed, and then took to reloading her fire lance. "At least the chain's still intact this time. I'd think adding more knives would do better damage beyond just the one you have."

"I was thinking that adding spikes might be a nice option."

"What a dangerously novel idea. Shall we send for more Reapers to scrape what's left of this creature off the roads?"

"I'll mark an area to warn people to go around," Remy said, sounding doubtful over his own plan. He moved past the steaming mass to survey its other victims. The horse had been horribly eviscerated; whoever its rider was, even more so. There was an assortment of vegetables scattered on the ground beside the wagon. The beast had ignored those.

Remy bent over what was left of the man and quietly muttered a short, brief prayer over the remains. "Head back to Glycespike and ask the headsman to send word back to Elouve," he said. "I'll stay and make sure no one disturbs the scene, warn them away if need be."

Elke nodded, not even bothering to protest. She would reach the village faster than he ever could. "I'll be back as soon as I can. In the meantime, you'd better find somewhere safer to keep your vigil. As you said, there could be more of them out there."

It was sound advice, and after Elke had gone, Remy returned to the forest edge to keep watch, taking out a few packets of gunpowder and saltpeter to reload his lance. After that, he took up Breaker and resumed his habit, the chain whirling aimlessly above him, lulling him into a meditative wakefulness. The fog was still as thick as ever, and the cold was starting to get through, but he barely felt the chill.

He stared at the sodden mess that had once been the hulking, inhumanly grotesque creature—no word existed yet to accurately define what the mutated beast was. Now that the danger had passed, he was starting to think about the magnitude of what they had just discovered. Takenori had mentioned a stark difference in the Harveston boy when he'd taken the vampire in a second time, making mention of the boy's increase in size and mass, though his descriptions of it had been so mildly understated compared to the reality Remy found himself looking at now.

Was this the same kind of mutation that the Reapers had encountered? The reports were now over a week old. Had they already located the persons responsible for this new breed? Was this the reason the queen had ordered most of the Reapers to Kerenai?

And if that wasn't already enough to ruin his day, the congealed, soup-like mess on the ground began to move.

It was a faint quiver at first, one he could almost put down to a strange trick of the light through the filter of darkness about him, except that it did so again, with much more force and visible shaking.

Any doubt was put to rest when the thick goo began to clump together of its own accord, slowly building itself back up from the ground, rearranging melted flesh and hardening bone to reconstruct the familiarly horrifying shape of the one-eyed, several-armed, grinning-chest anomaly that he'd thought they'd already killed.

"Fucking hell," Remy groaned, shoving more sulfur and silver shells down his fire lance's barrel.

He'd managed to fire at the monster before it could completely reconstitute itself, up to half a waist and a pair of legs, the unnerving, gaping mouth of death already formed. The blast took out a goodly part of hip bone and thigh, but the rest of its body seemed to absorb the impact, growing over the area like his shot didn't matter.

Heart pounding, Remy switched to his more favored style of fighting—in-your-face combat, though more in-your-stomach, given the current situation. The ungodly eye was back, sliding open to focus on him just as he sliced right through its gaze with the scythe. While it might have built up a quick immunity to the fire lance, the silver in his blade still affected it well enough. Blood sprayed across the air, and Remy rolled to the ground just as another appendage grew directly out of one of its legs, nearly impaling him. It wasn't growing back into the same shape this time, with three legs and more on the way, choosing to stunt its height this time for a better grip on the ground. Its mouth was still the same, though, made of teeth and the shrapnel left behind by his and Elke's fire lances.

He was in trouble. If it was capable of re-forming itself even after being obliterated at its most basic organic level, then nothing he could do would stop it. Remy's only hope was to keep it engaged and prevent it from disappearing into the fog long enough for Elke and other reinforcements to show up.

That was much harder than it sounded. Remy cut off more limbs from beneath the now massive, sphere-like blob, then nearly lost his own leg when it rolled forward without warning, bone-teeth snapping as it tried to take a chunk out of his thigh.

Something blurred into view before him, and the monstrous thing was shoved back without ceremony, a thick cut across its midsection, bisecting its mouth.

Remy sprang to his feet, but Song Xiaodan was already blurring away again, reappearing behind the creature. He could hear her heartbeat from where she stood, even more irregular and rapid than when she had sat with him at the gardens. "Get out of the way," she instructed him grimly, "and close your eyes."

Remy, being a Pendergast, did not get out of the way, nor did he close his eyes. But when the Lady Song began to glow, seemingly without any other light source other than one that appeared to be manifesting from within, he was wise enough to stay out of the blast radius when the monster turned to face her.

Remy didn't quite see what happened next, nor could he explain it. The unearthly light that had bathed Xiaodan streaked out in all directions around her, and for a moment the fog around them seemed to dissolve from the force of that brightness alone. It was as if the sun, rarely seen in Aluria, had taken up lodging inside of her and was unleashing six months' worth of daylight all at once to make up for its previous absence.

It was a fatal sunlight, twentyfold the range of what a fire lance had and a hundred times deadlier. The monster didn't just melt like it had previously; Remy never thought that the act of being visibly evaporated could be so violently forceful, but Xiaodan's light was unrelenting.

In that moment, she was stunning.

Nothing of the beast remained when the light faded, save for the previously drying blue-black blood it had bled onto the ground.

"Hello again," Lady Song said to Remy, somewhat weakly. There was still the hint of a halo about her, like she hadn't completely been able to rein in the rest of the glow yet, and it highlighted the silver in her eyes. She was breathtaking, like a goddess who had condescended to step down from the clouds in answer to his prayer. Remy stared at her, dazed, until she stumbled, and the sounds of her heartbeat returned him back to the moment—beats that were far too quick and far too loud.

The light finally disappeared, like a candle unexpectedly snuffed out, and the cold and fog closed in again. He rushed to Xiaodan's side when she tried to stand, and she only let out a brief sound of complaint when he stood back up with her in his arms.

"The bloody fuck are you doing here?" he asked.

"Same thing as you," she mumbled, exhausted.

Likely she'd gone off without her fiancé knowing, judging by Remy's previous encounter with someone Zidan Malekh considered family. "Don't move." He was relieved to hear her heartbeat slowing, her breaths no longer sounding labored. "What did you do?"

"I brought out the sun, Armiger." Xiaodan sighed against him. "I would have thought that was obvious by now."

And then, before Remy could say anything in rebuttal, she lost consciousness.

7

AWAKE

Lady Song Xiaodan was still fast asleep by the time they'd arrived back at Kinaiya Lodge. Not even Elke had been able to discern where the Fourth Court vampire and her fiancé were staying at in Elouve. Given the current unkempt state of most of Remy's residence, putting her in his bedroom had seemed the ideal choice. Elke kept a large apartment near the Alurian palace, and while that had decidedly more room to spare for unexpected guests, Remy had weighed his options and rejected the risk it would demand. A vampire staying at a popular jeweler's quarters would raise more questions than he was willing to answer.

The many varied experiences Remy had had with vampires hadn't quite prepared him for this. Especially once Xiaodan began to snore.

"I think it's endearing," Elke said. She'd shooed him away long enough to strip Xiaodan and lay her beneath the covers, and Remy hadn't found the proper way to protest that, either. "No—I don't think making soup would be the best course of action for this, love. She might enjoy the taste, but it won't help her heal any faster. Have you got more spiced Old Varian? I could try and force a few drops down her throat if need be."

"You're looking pretty settled beside her," Remy pointed out warily. "Won't anyone miss you?"

"I'd already let everyone know that I'd be traveling the rest of the day before we'd set out this morning. I have no intentions of going anywhere when you've got the daughter of the Fourth Court injured in your house." She hesitated. "Lady Song has been . . . kind to me in the past. I have never known how to repay her."

Remy placed the tray bearing the useless chicken soup he'd made on the side table. "Would it be prying if I asked how?"

The redhead smiled. "No. Much of Zidan Malekh and the Third Court's past is a mystery, even to my clan. Perhaps the older courts would know more than I. But he did take down the Fifth and put Etrienne out of his misery. It was the Fourth's achievement, too. Perhaps she'll tell you herself."

"Is it unusual for a vampire to sleep this long?"

"I rarely do, given how infrequently the sun shines in Elouve. We don't know exhaustion the same way humans do." Gently, Elke pressed two fingers against Lady Song's chest. "I suspect this, together with her strange ability, has everything to do with it."

"You knew that she was capable of . . . whatever the bloody hell that was? I may not be up to speed on Reaper affairs, but even I know they weren't aware of what she could do." There had been whispers, though: Lady Beiwu's earlier talk of a poisoned hand.

"They call her the Sunbringer. I do not know how she came to possess such abilities—the first I'd known of it was after witnessing her fight in the war between the Third and Fifth. She wiped out my clan with it. If I had been slower to move . . ." She shuddered. "Etrienne feared her. A vampire who could manifest the very thing capable of its own destruction—he called it a curse, said she would be better off dead. The Fourth Court's decline was not a coincidence." Elke took her hand away from Xiaodan. "I'm sorry I didn't inform you sooner. It's her story to tell. Not something to share without her permission, even with you."

"No offense taken." Remy gave the soup another half-hearted stir, debated eating it himself, then decided against it. "I'll bring a few bottles out from the cellar, in case she wakes. If you can spare a few more hours with her, I would appreciate it."

"I can. Are you heading out?" Elke's eyes widened. "You intend to go to your father?"

"I might not be welcomed at the Archives. Without a body to present to them, there's little else to show." All Remy had been able to retrieve was a small vial filled with the strange-colored blue blood from the scene. "As much as I despise to say it or give him any credit, Yost might know more."

"What was that thing, Remy?" Elke turned back to Xiaodan. "Who would ever subject their body to that kind of horror?"

"That's exactly what I intend to find out." Remy tucked the vial back into his pocket and cast another look at the sleeping girl. He had so many questions for her, but those would have to wait until he'd gotten more answers out of Yost.

And from his father, because that bastard always kept far more secrets than he ever shared.

DR. YOST, as it turned out, knew more than even Remy had expected. The doctor took the vial from him with vicious delight, like he'd been expecting such a gift. Remy was immediately suspicious. "You've seen this color of blood before," he said.

Yost beamed at him. "Not just seen it—I was hoping you'd find more in the course of your hunts. I've been studying vampire cadavers for a reason." He turned to the Duke of Valenbonne, who was currently in bed and being attended to by the physician.

The older man had developed a mild cold upon arriving at Loxley House and had been confined to his room at Yost's insistence. As always, Grimesworthy occupied one corner of the room, content to remain there until his master summoned him.

"See? The tonic I just prescribed to your father was based on years of research spent isolating and studying a vampire's regenerative abilities. In time, we may even be able to introduce some milder forms of the trezirea sângelui to the public—lesser side effects than the ones the Reapers take, but far more effective for strength and speed."

The duke only grunted. "If your damned quack tinctures were as good as you claim, you old sot, I would be long out of this bed by now."

"There is still your age to take into consideration, Your Grace. I work no miracles, only science. See—your fever is gone in just an hour. But bed rest shall never go out of fashion, I'm afraid." Yost turned his smile back to Remy. "The band of youths you procured for me are unusable for my current project, most unfortunately, though blood specimens of any kind are always valued. You must have noticed how particular I've been about finding more specimens from the northern regions of Aluria."

Remy hadn't really thought about it enough to give a fuck at all, but the doctor continued before he could reply. "Quite a few of these newly turned vampires have been manifesting key mutations native to the area they were first discovered. For the better part of a year, I've been building a classification system to categorize vampires based on their migration behavior and attack patterns."

Yost held the vial out before him, admiring the color. "The most unusual feature of vampire blood is that it does not congeal, while human blood does. Those who have not been turned longer than a year often give much greater insights, given that this is the stage in their new undead life when they are the closest they will ever be to mortal."

"So the bodies I brought to you weren't useless after all?" Remy asked.

"For the little pet project I've been working on, they are, unfortunately. This vial, though—*this* is what's priceless. Vampire blood does not congeal, and yet it is sterile. Rarely does it react to other catalysts, even when combined, the way oil and water don't mix. That is why I have been utterly fascinated by reports of these strange new creatures who can withstand assaults that even vampires cannot. Are they a secondary mutation, or should they be considered a different species altogether? They are different enough that to call them vampires would be misleading. How is it possible for such a nonreactive element to bond on such terrific levels to produce these anomalies? This is only the seventh sample of blue blood I've received over the past month, and it will help me tremendously with my classification. The road between Wyndham and Glycespike, you say? The location is always important."

"You knew about these strange mutations, and you thought to say nothing to the other Reapers about it?" Remy was horrified, furious.

"It was under my instruction, boy," the duke said. The color had returned to Remy's father's cheeks, and he was moving about in bed with lesser difficulty than before. "I am already certain that Astonbury knows, and to make things public would only cause panic and confusion. Let the doctor do his work so that you can do yours. The plan remains the same as it's always been, Remington. Report to me all other unusual vampire activity and continue to keep an eye out for the Third and Fourth Courts. What news have you of Giselle's party? It seems she is now boasting of her close friendships with both Lord Malekh and Lady Song. The latter, or so I've been told, appears quite smitten with you. I've heard a few people who attended the ball comment on her inquisitiveness regarding you."

For a brief moment Remy wondered if his father knew Lady Song happened to be in his bed at the moment, probably still asleep. He scanned the older man's face, but Edgar Pendergast had never been easy to read.

The man would have been pleased to know he'd gotten so close to the Fourth Court heiress in so short a time.

"Lady Song goes against the initial stereotype one has of vampires," Remy said, doing his best to sound bored. "I didn't expect her to be so friendly."

"Perhaps. Those pretending to be difficult seem to be more the type to catch your fancy," his father observed with a knowing smile. Dr. Yost approached him with a syringe at the ready, and the duke held his arm out.

Remy ignored the jest. "Surely we can find more answers if we focus on finding the source of all these new vampire mutations? Amenable or not, the courts have no real reason to trust us at this point, even if they wish to offer us an alliance."

"The Third and Fourth Courts have more to do with the Night Empress than either of us are aware of, my boy." The duke breathed in deeply as Dr. Yost pressed the needle against his waxy skin and pushed down on the plunger. "Both will have information that neither Astonbury nor the queen would be privy to, and we must use that to our advantage. You swore on your mother's grave you would find her killer whatever the cost, boy. Are you reneging on that promise now?"

"Never," Remy said, stung that his father would even question it.

"Then prove yourself to me." His father leaned forward. "Honor her, Remington. Lady Song appears to favor you. Use that to find your mother's murderer, however you must. Why on earth would

I allow Giselle Delacroix and her friends to sink their claws into you, but not a Fourth Court heiress with more influence than the duchess could ever dream of?"

THE FIRST person Remy saw upon returning to Kinaiya Lodge was Xiaodan. She was in the drawing room instead of his bed, awake now. She wore a long dressing gown—one right out of his wardrobe, a luxurious red silk from Situ that he'd splurged for on a whim. It exposed a lot of her neck and legs and looked fetchingly good on her.

It wasn't supposed to look good on her. It wasn't supposed to be worn by anyone but him, and now he couldn't stop staring.

Her dark hair was pulled back from her head in a long ponytail, and the soft gray eyes looking back at him appeared almost embarrassed.

"Hello, Armiger Remy," she said sheepishly. There was a bowl of soup cradled in her hands. "Elke reheated it for me," she explained. "She said you made it."

"I wasn't sure if you were going to drink it."

"It helped. It's very good."

"The port helped more," Elke said. She was already wrapping a traveling cloak around herself.

"Where are you going?" Remy asked, alarmed at the prospect of being left alone with Lady Song.

"I enjoy a lot of freedom in Elouve, but even my servants will start whispering if I'm away too long. Lady Song seems well enough, and since you were considerate enough not to snap off Breaker's chain again, there's very little left here for me to do."

"Lady Whittaker," Xiaodan said, halting slightly. "Before you go, I just want you to know that your secret is safe with me."

"You told her?" Remy asked.

"No," Elke admitted. "She recognized me almost immediately. Thank you, milady. After everything the Fifth Court has done, you are generous in your clemency in regards to me."

"Etrienne Sauveterre was a psychopath who never hesitated to torture and mutilate his enemies and do worse to his own clan," Xiaodan said with unexpectedly surprising heat. "The eradication of that stain on both humankind and kindred is all that mattered. I am sorry we could not do more for the rest of your court."

"I doubt there was much either of you could have done in the end. So many of us had grown used to his cruelty." Elke's eyes were suspiciously shiny. She gestured at a wine bottle on the table, its contents nearly gone. "You'd best finish that and keep your strength up, Lady Song. Remy, I'll call on you tomorrow."

"Does she bite?" Xiaodan asked in the silence after Elke had left him to fend for himself.

"Pardon?"

"Lady Whittaker's consorts. Does she bite her consorts here in Elouve? I believe there is an ongoing ban on being a vampire's familiar, is there not?"

"Elke doesn't. She knows better. And if you tell anyone—"

"I won't." Xiaodan's face was a picture of sincerity. "She said you were visiting your father. Do you report to him after every hunt?"

"Almost always, yes."

"Did you tell him I was here?"

"No."

"Why not?"

"I report to him frequently, but that doesn't mean I have to tell him everything."

"I remember you were angry at him," Xiaodan said, and flushed. She was thinking about the gardens, Remy thought. Their almost-kiss. He looked away, intently focused on the biggest of his succulents.

"I want to apologize for last night at the ball," Xiaodan contin-

ued. "I didn't intend to follow you to Glycespike. And I'm sorry for
not revealing myself sooner."

"Given everything that has happened," Remy said, "you'll have
to forgive me for being suspicious."

"You have every reason to be. I thought it would be better if
you heard the apology as soon as possible, so I could also explain
myself. The creature you encountered—I knew about it and was
searching for it long before last night happened. You had already
killed it by the time I arrived. I thought to keep myself hidden,
until . . . well."

"You knew it was there?"

"I've fought others like it before."

Remy stared at her. She grinned weakly at him. "They're never
the same, physically," she said. "Some have more limbs than others. Some are bigger, or are almost impenetrable to fire, or are capable of remaking themselves, like the one you faced. But always
blue blood. And always humans who mutate before their frenzy
is done. Their bodies transforming into these horrors, sometimes
even after the bodies are cremated. Zidan has created categories
for each mutation we've discovered so far, to better study them.
He'd be the person to ask if you wish to know more."

"I don't want to know." Remy remembered Dr. Yost and his
own macabre classification system and shuddered. "Do you know
who's responsible?"

"No. Not yet. It's one of the reasons Zidan and I have come to
Aluria. There are far more attacks here than there should be. As
if this is where the infections first started." Xiaodan pressed her
hands against her chest. "Did Lady Elke tell you that they call me
the Sunbringer?"

"She didn't want to say much about it without your consent."

"That was very kind of her. Is it Lady Whittaker's habit to go
with you on these hunts?"

"She doesn't hunt with me as often as you imply."

"Are you two close?"

"Yes, but it's not what you're thinking."

"How do you know what I'm thinking?" She was exploring the room, stopping occasionally to examine whatever caught her interest—a fresh bouquet of lilies on a side table, a small painting of a waterfall, a shelf of books. The thin silk clung to her figure, gathering at the back of her thighs and calves. She wasn't wearing much underneath it. Remy cast his glance at the ceiling, asking the Three of the Light for strength.

She frowned slightly when she ran a finger along the mantelpiece. "Where do you keep your clean rags?" she asked, moving to the closet.

"I can't let you clean my—"

"Oh, but I insist. As a thank-you for helping me." She opened the door, located a folded piece of cloth, and began to wipe at the mantel's surface. "I only ask about her because you keep several bottles of wine mixed with blood in your larder. As you don't partake in those, I deduced that she must be here frequently enough for you to keep a store of them."

"She used to be a blacksmith before coming here. I have a small forge for her to use on occasion."

"She used to make the Fifth Court's weapons? Zidan says they were some of the best he'd ever seen. It made them harder to kill." Satisfied, Xiaodan moved to cleaning the table. "No servants? It would be more prudent to have someone come in and clean for you on the days you're not here."

"I bought Kinaiya Lodge specifically to be left alone."

"What benefits would you gain from having no valet?"

"A messy room and peace of mind."

Xiaodan nodded. "You value your privacy over everything else. Is that why there are no women's clothes here?"

Despite your affiliation with the many women of the ton, she seemed to imply. Or maybe that was simply his own guilt and his imagination filling in the blanks. "It is not public knowledge that I own Kinaiya Lodge."

"No one else knows that you live here?"

"That was the intention, yes. Though very little gets past the Reapers. They've left me alone, and that's good enough for me."

"Then why bring me to your secret place? Surely you have other options."

"You don't strike me as the type to gossip to other humans, no matter what friendships you have with them."

"Thank you. I don't. I promise to keep your secret as well as I'll keep Lady Whittaker's." Now that the table was as clean as she could get, Xiaodan resumed her prowling, searching for her next target.

"Isn't your fiancé worried about where you are?"

"Zidan is currently away on other business. Some issues with his younger brother, to be more exact. He'll be back by dawn tomorrow." She hesitated by the bookshelves. "*The Unwritten History of the Island of Tithe*," she said aloud, reading the titles as she walked past them. "*The Undisclosed People. The Witching Isles.* You have many books on Tithian culture. They're not usually what most Alurian historians write about."

"My mother was born there. I know very little about her, and I wanted to learn more about the place she was from."

"And what did you find out?"

"That they're a warm people. Affectionate. But they would much rather be left alone by those from Aluria, though their territories have been claimed by the kingdom. And they practice traditions many Alurians consider beneath them, as heretical to the Light." He had been told very little about his mother, but he knew she had not fared well in Elouve because of their prejudices.

Xiaodan paused before the portrait, gazing up at it. "And this would be her?" she asked softly.

Remy joined her, looking up at the only image he'd ever seen of Ligaya Bascom Pendergast. Not for the first time he wondered what his life would have been like if she'd survived. If she'd had a husband who loved them both. "Yes," he said gruffly.

"She's very beautiful. You look a lot like her."

"So I'm told."

"You're still angry at me, I think. What else do you want me to apologize for?"

"You told Giselle to invite the Duke and Duchess of Tennyfair to her ball. For all I know, you already knew who I was and staged our first encounter. You don't strike me as the type to leave anything to chance."

"And you figured out who I was after talking for only half an hour last night? So you know everything about me now?" Lady Song folded her arms in front of her. "I understand that you're mad, and that you have good reason to be. But I swear that our encounter at the gardens was never planned. I guessed that you were a hunter, but it never crossed my mind that you were the Duke of Valenbonne's son."

"Breaker didn't give me away?" Remy itched for a drink of his own. He quelled the urge and stared hard at his mother's portrait instead, hoping to find strength in her placid, serene gaze. "Didn't your fiancé tell you who I was? Because he sure as hell knew that first night we met."

"As strange as it sounds, I am not old enough a vampire to recognize Breaker. The Pendergast weapons are not something that crops up frequently in conversation among my kindred." Xiaodan sighed then, a long, drawn-out exhale. "Zidan mentioned that he'd had to save his brother from a Reaper but gave me no names. He is attached to his ward and very protective. I only realized the connection afterward, when he'd confessed to knowing who you were. As for the Duke and Duchess of Tennyfair . . ." She turned to face him. "I asked the duke not to burn his daughter's body," she said quietly. "It was important that he didn't."

"But why?"

"I was told last night that it was you who had brought her back to them—another thing I had not been aware of, having failed to make the connection in the gardens. I had told Lady Astonbury that I wanted to meet the poor girl's parents after the ball to explain my reasons personally, but I never expected them to show up at the gala. And while making demands of them in their time of grief may seem callous, I had little choice. We are running out of time as it is."

"Running out of time for what?"

"It all comes back to that creature we fought today. I believe Lady Daneira may have been infected by the same virulent strain that mutated the others. Zidan would know more about this than I would, but I do know that a drawn-out frenzy, followed by brief periods of lucidity, were one of the main symptoms of those affected. It is their second death that triggers their transformations."

Ice ran through Remy's veins. "Are you telling me that my killing her could have caused her mutation?"

"I'm afraid so. It's why I requested to have Lady Daneira transported back to Qing-ye. Zidan keeps a laboratory there. If I'm right, then she would be far enough away from the city should she transform unexpectedly. But her parents wished to give her body to your scientists at the Archives instead. I had hoped to plead my case to them directly, to change their minds." She cocked her head at an angle. "You don't look surprised. Did the lord high steward tell you?"

The stack of papers carefully hidden away in his coat pocket felt as heavy as lead. "In a fashion, yes. But I don't know who's responsible for the strain, either."

"It's another reason why we consider an alliance with Aluria important. Humans and vampires do not always see eye to eye, but this poses an immediate threat to us both. The Third Court is one of the strongest of the vampire kindred still remaining, and even Zidan and the others are at a loss as to who is responsible. Had the Fifth Court still existed, I would have thought Etrienne Sauveterre the culprit."

"How are you so certain that the leader of the Fifth Court is dead?"

Lady Song smiled at him then—bright and friendly and wide. "Because I killed him myself," she said with a slightly vicious air, "and I tend to be rather thorough about these things." She raised her hands slightly and glowed.

Once again, Remy felt his breath catch. The light within her flickered as unsteadily as her heartbeat—not so much that the brightness overcame her features, but enough that it highlighted her beauty, like she was something too strange and profound for his admittedly dingy drawing room. The stuttered rhythm of her heart didn't make her seem any less ethereal. It didn't make her look any less bewitching.

He heard his father's voice, a dry snarl. *Whatever the cost, boy.*

"This is the only known way to completely obliterate these mutations," Xiaodan said. "But it takes far too much out of me each time I use it. I was hoping that the Alurians would find another way to—"

There was a sharp knock at the door. Xiaodan's light faded instantly, and Remy turned, startled. "I don't usually have visitors," he muttered, marching over to open the door. "El, if you've left something—"

A group of grim-faced Reapers stared back at him—Remy recognized most of them as some of the lord high steward's most favored soldiers. The Marquess of Riones had also arrived with the group, lurking at the back with the guiltiest expression on his face. "—this is all a misunderstanding," he was in the middle of saying, though no one was listening. "He could never have done this."

"I didn't realize that you would be using my home for the next dræfendgemot," Remy said cautiously.

One of the hunters cleared his throat—it was the Earl of Feiron, the lord high steward's self-professed right-hand man, though to Remy that was just another fancy word for lackey. The man looked past him at Lady Song, and Remy saw surprise on his face as he struggled to modify his obvious hostility for Remy with some measure of cordiality on her behalf.

Then, inwardly, Remy cursed. Xiaodan was still wearing his dressing gown.

"Let's not draw this out for too long, Lord Pendergast," Lord Feiron said formally, "but we do have some pressing questions. Where were you last night from the time you left Lady Astonbury's ball?"

"I was by the gardens." Feiron was not disposed to like him and his father, and based on his past interactions with the man, Remy found that it was easier just to answer his questions, to get him to leave faster. The earl had the temerity of a bulldog, but none of the amiability.

"Is there anyone who can vouch for you there?"

"I can," Lady Song spoke up. "We spoke in the gardens at some length."

"And afterward, after returning to the manor?"

"I made my way to the library," Remy said, "where I passed the time reading until midnight."

"And did you return home after that?"

"You bloody well know where I was after that, Feiron. You could just ask her yourself."

"Answer the question, Lord Pendergast."

He hated the way Lady Song's gaze was suddenly riveted on him when he responded. "I spent the night with the Duchess of Astonbury and left at dawn."

"And no one in the manor can vouch for the time of your departure?"

"You can ask the second footman—I believe his name is

Burnaby—but otherwise no one else appeared to be awake. Now, I've answered enough questions. What the hell is going on?"

"We have more to ask," Feiron said, persisting in unmitigated arsemanship. "We'll need to bring you in."

"I'm not going anywhere until you tell me why you're all treating me like some criminal. More than you usually do, at least."

Feiron looked perfectly ready to argue that, but Riones spoke up. "Oh, come on, Sante. He deserves to know."

"Deserves to know what?"

"About the murder." Riones looked at him, contrite. "I'm sorry, Remington. It seems someone has gone and murdered the Duke of Astonbury, and you're Feiron's main suspect."

8

THE BLOODY CHAMBER

Remy avoided stepping into the Ministry of the Archives on Gold Street whenever he could. It wasn't just that it was Reaper territory and he'd occasionally been denied entry in the past simply for being a Pendergast. It wasn't because it held stores of classified information he was prevented from accessing. It wasn't even that most of the Reapers had taken their cues from the head of the Archives (former head of the Archives, he silently corrected himself), the Duke of Astonbury, and only remembered him whenever a particular hunt or bounty was too distasteful to sully their hands with.

No, it was that the Archives headquarters really were that fucking terrible to look at. A short, squat building of unflattering proportions, as gray as a graveyard and as uninspiring as a flat-cake. Its only recent addition was the construction of a smaller, conical dome-like structure beside it, which Remy had previously assumed was some kind of crematorium but now realized was the yakhchāl mentioned in the reports he'd read, where the infected corpses were stored instead of burned.

It was an easy error to make, since the Archives itself looked like a bleakly oversized kiln, and it wasn't any better from the inside. On the very rare instances Remy was allowed on the premises, he'd observed how the furnishings had remained drab and musty, designed solely for their functional use. Reapers never stayed for too long within the Archives unless a dræfendgemot was in session. It was a gaol with a better budget, albeit with the same lack of imagination.

And that was fitting somehow, because Remy was now in the Archives as a prisoner as opposed to its most unwanted member.

The clothes he'd worn the night before had been collected and inspected for blood, the hansom he'd taken for the ride back home chased down and interrogated. And even as he responded to their inquiries, subjected himself to the indignity of being handled like a suspect, Remy's mind remained partly in shock. Somebody had murdered the lord high steward. Had actually gone and killed that old rat bastard. Astonbury had more than his share of enemies— Remy's father was only one in a sea of sharks who were either jealous of the man's successes, had been jockeyed out of political favors because of the duke's scheming, or had hoped to usurp his position themselves. But never in Remy's wildest imaginings had he thought anyone would be so bold as to carry out the crime.

Fortunately, he was also innocent of all the charges that were about to land on his head, though that didn't matter one whit to Lord Feiron. Remy had spent two hours in a small holding cell with nothing but rats and a cold bench for company, then made to endure another hour of dogged questioning by the earl. But try as the other man might, Remy's answers never wavered. *Yes, I'd talked to the Fourth Court vampiress after leaving the ball. Yes, I'd tupped the duchess after that. No, I didn't kill the duke because I wanted her for myself.* He'd even fought the Third Court king—again—that night, completing his current trifecta of fuckups rather nicely, but Feiron didn't ask about that, so Remy didn't provide.

"You've grown quite comfortable with the Lady Song in the short time she's been in Elouve," Feiron had said, committing to a new line of attack. "A comfortably domestic arrangement, from what we could see. Was that the reason you killed Astonbury, Pendergast? Did she bewitch you, turn you into her familiar?"

"You know as well as I do, Feiron," Remy said calmly, "that to be any vampire's familiar is punishable by death in Aluria, even with the alliance holding. And you've roughed me up enough to know I don't have any bite marks on me."

"Did Astonbury find out about your relationship?" Feiron pushed on. "Was that why you murdered him? To protect her? Was it your intention to keep your trysts with Lady Song a secret from both him and her own fiancé?"

"Do you really think nothing gets past the Summer Lord without his approval?" Remy didn't bother to stick to the truth at this point—none of them would believe him anyway—and since his gaoler was wasting his time, he would do the same and rile him up further. "For the record, I'm no one's familiar, Feiron, though I suppose I'm her bitch at this point, ready to come at her beck and call." He grinned at his own innuendo. "Haven't you heard the rumors? I'm a lapdog to half the married women of the ton. Last I checked, that's not illegal in Elouve. But you would know that, since everyone knows that you, too, are Astonbury's—"

Remy supposed, upon hindsight, that he did deserve that punch. His head hit the bench hard, stars swimming into his vision, and it was a miracle he didn't bleed from the blow.

"You sound just as dignified as the day you crawled out of your dead mother," the earl said cruelly. "But then, she's not the only Pendergast you've crippled, eh? Hathorn even started a betting pool to see which of Craggart's bounties would be the one to put you out of your misery. Let's not wait for another Elouvian Siege to throw you back into those caves again and see who you'll mutilate next—"

It was Remy's turn to lunge. The man raised his hands, expecting a hit to the face but briefly forgetting that his prisoner's hands were still bound behind his back. Remy managed a hard, direct kick to the man's groin despite the small target he was presented with, and the few moments' satisfaction at seeing the pompous noble clutch at his nethers and wail like he was dying, was worth the lord's men throwing him against the wall and raining more blows down on him in retaliation.

He'd been tossed back into his cell after that and ignored for another three hours.

His face throbbed the worst out of all of it. At least they'd had the decency to untie him after the beating. Remy rubbed at it, glaring at the wooden statues on the wall across from him. Whoever had created the Archives' gaols had been under the impression that installing the Three of the Light here would encourage repentance. All it did was nettle him more.

There was the Mother, of course, her eyes closed and her face serene, a baby cradled in her hands. She was always holding babies of various ages and dispositions, as if to depict her matronly, caregiving nature in the obvious manner. Beside her was the Gatherer, bare-chested and clad only in a heavy loincloth, a sack on his back bulging with bread and fruit. Lastly, the Hunter crouched at one corner, though the usual array of weapons strapped to his sides were missing so as not to give the prisoners further ideas, because none of the people in charge of this gaol actually thought this through.

Hunter, Gatherer, Mother. Three of the Light. Not all of those living in Elouve, much less in Aluria, believed in the Light. Far more effective to also erect the likenesses of the Many-Gifted One, Halfghaer the Mighty, and other deities from the various pantheons worshipped within the kingdom. It would be a fairly crowded room, but it should be good enough to instill the fear of at least three or so gods in the gaoled. Feiron was likely to punch him again for even making such a suggestion. Remy planned on putting the idea forward at their next session.

Fuck. They'd actually gone and *gaoled* him. Dukes' sons were at least afforded house arrest, but they thought too lowly of him even for that. There was no one else in the cell to kick but himself, and so Remy stared at the wall instead, finally processing the day's events. Years doing bounties nobody wanted, years being denied entry into the dræfendgemot, and now this.

They'd started a betting pool on which bounty was going to kill him. That stung worse than the beating Feiron's flunkies had given.

He'd wasted years trying to garner the respect that no one had ever planned on giving him.

The door opened and the earl emerged, his normally wooden face forced into an expression of contriteness, an unnatural look for him and almost certainly an act. Behind him was Lord Dorst Aglaice, another Reaper who worked closely with him and the lord high steward. And with them . . .

Xiaodan looked furious. Zidan Malekh was cold and intimidating as always, but the surprise was that he was here to begin with. The Fourth Court heiress took one look at Remy, sitting snug and comfortable in his cozy prison, and exploded. "I told you to release him hours ago!"

"There were certain papers that required processing before we could," Feiron said, lying bald-facedly through his teeth.

"We are very sorry, milady. So terribly sorry." Lord Aglaice had gotten his coveted position among the late lord high steward's inner circle not from either competence or skill, but because of his ability to sniff out the most influential person in the room to blindly obey. He had clearly singled out Lady Song as the more dominant power over Feiron, and his obsequiousness was almost painful to watch. It was nothing a cheerful defenestration wouldn't solve, and Remy was almost certain it would improve their relationship with the Third and Fourth Courts rather than set it back years.

"I am sorry, milady, but with the Duke of Astonbury . . ." Aglaice was turning red. ". . . Err, indisposed, everything has been thrown into turmoil."

The Marquess of Riones appeared to be the only one who'd accepted their leader's death enough to say it aloud. Even Feiron had couched his interrogation in such a way that one would have thought Astonbury had sustained nothing but minor injuries and would be assuming office again on the morrow.

"It wouldn't have taken hours to free him, no matter how many papers you shuffle from bureaucrat to bureaucrat. I would question your agency's efficiency under your late lord high steward, if all the others under his command are just as inept." Xiaodan was in fine fighting form, and Feiron was wilting, curling into himself like a burning missive. "All this required was a key to his cell, which, as I am currently observing, does not even have a lock to it. Armiger Remington, why must you subject yourselves to these unjust sanctions when you could have just as easily walked out of here on your own?"

"Unfair or not, it's the law." Remy wasn't particularly happy to be freed at the moment. Malekh was eyeing him with an expressionless face that nonetheless gave the impression that he was pronouncing judgment on him for his recent bad decisions. "They had every right to question me. My father's rivalry with the Duke of Astonbury was no secret. I had all the motive they require."

"Your alibi should have been well established when I told them Zidan and I were with you at the gardens, and after Lady Giselle had supplied the rest." A faint grating noise like the gnashing of teeth accompanied the other woman's name, a faint rough burr that stood out against her normally soft dulcet tone. "They're keeping you here out of spite, and because they have no other real suspects."

Xiaodan took hold of the bars separating her from Remy. The metal twisted under her hands, distending so that it created a hole large enough for him to walk through. Her smile throughout her unnecessary destruction of kingdom property remained as sweet as honey. It was both frightening and oddly seductive.

Feiron and Aglaice gaped, a pair of inedible fish who'd been robbed of water.

"Will you open the door now, milord," Xiaodan continued merrily, "or should I emphasize my displeasure some more by ripping it right off its hinges?"

"I've already been accused of being your familiar, milady," Remy said. "Your zeal to see me freed isn't helping my case much."

"A familiar?" Xiaodan brightened. "Have they lifted the ban in Aluria already? A silly restriction, really—when done in moderation, it could be a wonderfully beneficial arrangement. Do they think you're mine and Zidan's?"

Remy's amusement died. "Just yours. Not—why would they think I'm his—"

Still doing his best impression of a sickly carp, Feiron attempted to regain control. "In no way did we intend to cast any aspersions on your character or that of your fiancé's, milady," he said hastily, "no matter what Pendergast implies. He's free to go."

"Not quite what you promised me," Lady Song demurred. "You agreed to let him take part in the investigations into the lord high steward's murder, if he's inclined to."

"What?" Remy asked. "I mean . . . I am very inclined to, unexpected as this is."

"I have other, more competent Reapers," Feiron protested. "I cannot have my investigators biased against the Duke of Astonbury to begin with. As Lord Pendergast himself pointed out, he would have good reasons to sabotage the case."

"Your investigators are already biased *for* the duke. Armiger Remington's presence will serve as a balance. After all," she added cheerfully, tucking her hand underneath Remy's arm, "you agreed to a joint investigation into the matter with the Fourth Court."

"What?" Remy asked again.

Lord Feiron looked even more irate at the thought of Remy joining up with the vampires instead of with the Reapers. "This is highly unconventional, milady. It's never been done before. I don't think the other Reapers would—"

"The other Reapers have not included Armiger Remington in your dræfendgemot for close to four years now." Lady Song didn't need weapons. The ice in her voice could kill. "A highly ranked member of Aluria has never been murdered in so gruesome a manner. There are very few precedents for this to begin with. While we had both agreed to pool our resources, it would make for a better show of unity for your citizens to see a Reaper working with the courts, would it not?"

"Milady—" Lord Feiron was clearly fighting a losing battle, though it couldn't be said that he wasn't willing to go down with his ship, "Lord Pendergast is young still—"

"Armiger Remington, milord. I must insist on that."

"Armiger Remington," the man began again, "is young still, and perhaps not as acquainted with the most recent developments of the case—or of Alurian matters in general, given his, ah, father's estrangement with the lord high steward. Perhaps assigning another hunter would be more—"

"I want Remy, milord." The temperature around them seemed to dip dangerously low by force of Lady Song's stare alone. "My fiancé asserts that Armiger Remington is quite capable in a fight and quick on his feet, with a keen intelligence. And despite his work as a hunter, the good armiger has none of the lingering prejudices against vampires that the human population of Aluria regrettably maintain, and that includes many of those within your ranks. His temperament will suit ours just fine. But I do find it very interesting, milord, that you have not opted to use his talents these last few years, yet suddenly find a pressing need for him elsewhere, so soon after I've indicated my interest."

Lord Feiron surrendered. "Not at all, milady. If Armiger Remington is willing to take part in your investigations, then I will not stand in his way."

Another "What?" escaped from Remy. He was still trying to bull his way through the notion that Malekh had defended him, though the tall son of a bitch remained impassive, his eyes focused on his betrothed, as Lords Feiron and Aglaice hurried out of the room.

"Did that go more or less according to plan, then?" Malekh asked once they were beyond earshot.

"Better than what I expected. Thank you, my love."

"I did very little."

Remy watched her grasp Malekh's hands, feeling like an interloper as they stood gazing at each other. Xiaodan was adoring, her emotions easy to decipher. Even Malekh's normally stoic expression softened considerably as he looked down at her upturned face, warmth in his amber eyes. Whatever the circumstances that had brought about their engagement, it had been for something stronger than a mere political arrangement.

Remy could not explain the sudden rush of envy that ran through him.

Xiaodan bestowed him with a wide, beaming smile, genuine this time. "Congratulations on your new promotion, Armiger Remington. As of this moment, you are now the Fourth Court's official liaison to Aluria, and I could not be more pleased to have you with us."

REMY RESENTED the fact that Zidan Malekh had not said one word to him since he'd been released from his cell. The man had maintained his stony silence while Lady Song happily chattered her way toward the lord high steward's study, where the crime had taken place. He wasn't entirely sure where he stood with the Summer Lord. Remy didn't want to have to thank the other man for helping him out of the gaol. It was simpler, though no doubt more craven, to say nothing instead.

He couldn't stop watching them both. Now that she'd put Feiron in his place, Xiaodan was back to her chipper self, and she'd never been more beautiful. Malekh, too, remained as elegant and commanding as he'd always been, and Remy took that personally. They were *both* stunning. He was merely a hunter who killed their kind—so why the hell were they involving themselves in his affairs?

The whole area had been cordoned off and everyone else evacuated from the premises; only the mild smell of tobacco smoke followed them down the otherwise deserted hallway. On a normal day, Remy knew, the place would be bustling with courtiers, clerks, Reapers on active duty. Now it was as quiet as a tomb.

Lord Feiron, who was up ahead, stopped before the heavy walnut-colored doors leading into the lord high steward's chambers. With a wince, he threw them open.

All at once, a thick, heavy, metallic taste assailed Remy's nostrils, the tang of it filling his mouth. The room positively reeked of it. The thick carpets were stained in crimson spatters, the ivory tiles awash in red. Most of the walls had escaped relatively unscathed, save for the one closest to the lord high steward's writing desk, decorated in a series of splatters marking the Duke of Astonbury's final moments. Some scuffing on the floor, coupled with the absence of blood at certain areas, indicated that this was where the man had lain—though the spaces in between the scarlet streaks looked far too small for a whole human body to take up.

Remy was familiar enough with killing to know that this had been an absolute bloodbath.

"Astonbury was ripped apart," Zidan said, finally speaking up. His jaw was clenched, and as he moved with a deliberateness that suggested he was controlling himself with some great effort, Remy realized that all the blood in the room was having a considerable effect on him. "The death occurred sometime between midnight and two in the morning. Dr. Agenot, the coroner for this investigation, believes that the man was already dead, and that the evisceration was done postmortem. The butler, Wellsmith, said he'd received only one visitor the night before. The duke had dismissed him immediately, so he could say little in the way of a description, save that the stranger wore a cloak and was five foot and seven inches high, with dark skin, black hair, and a long scar on his right forearm."

"Which was why I was a suspect," Remy muttered, staring down at the bloody floor and rubbing at the old aforementioned wound. He hadn't liked Astonbury—not because his father hated him, but because the lord high steward had treated him like he'd been just as guilty as his father—but no one deserved this kind of death.

"The duke never took bloodwakers himself," Feiron volunteered. "Not since he'd stopped active service. Doesn't strike me as the same as what happened to Parnon."

"Parnon," Zidan said thoughtfully, quick to pounce on the new information the man had unwittingly supplied. "So the news that Lord Parnon died of natural causes was false? He succumbed to the effects of your Reapers' trezirea sângelui instead?"

"I can't say any more about that, milord," Feiron said, suddenly aware of what he shouldn't have disclosed, sweating slightly.

"Not even the most potent of your drugs can cause someone to physically tear himself limb from limb like this," Malekh said, and the earl winced at his bluntness. "And anyone under the undue effects of bloodwaker abuse would not have passed here unnoticed for long. This is the work of vampires."

"No vampire can infiltrate this place," the other man protested. "The Archives are constantly under heavy guard, with Reapers on duty around the clock. We have royal soldiers stationed outside. How could a vampire enter the premises without anyone the wiser?"

"If your lord high steward had invited them in, then all your vaunted security wouldn't make much of a difference." Xiaodan had taken a circular route toward them, exploring the rest of the room in much the same way she had done at Kinaiya Lodge. She hesitated by the window. "Do the servants remember this being closed when their master and his visitor entered these chambers?" she asked.

"His butler—Wellsmith, was it?—said that his master preferred to have it open whenever he had company," Lord Feiron confirmed. "Not a very assuming fellow himself, easy to overlook. Kept to himself, just like his master—even the servants didn't pay him much attention, unless he was calling for them on the duke's behalf. He said that he'd brought the duke and his visitor some cigars before leaving them alone for the rest of the evening."

"Was it customary for the lord high steward to spend the night in the Archives? I was told earlier that he had private quarters here."

"Yes, he spends most of his time here, rather than at Astonbury Manor. He and his wife are, err . . . estranged." Feiron shot Remy a sideways look. "And he'd turned the mansion over to her for her personal use while he pursued separate interests elsewhere."

"Wellsmith didn't find it unusual, then, that his master never called for him again that night?" Malekh asked.

"It was common for the lord high steward to see to his visitors himself the later the hour. Many of his callers were informants that dealt with affairs of the Crown, you see, so he thought to keep their identities a secret, even among other members of the staff."

"And there were no other visitors that he remembered?"

"There were a few courtiers early in the evening and a spinster or two who often liked to complain about the state of the city. Not likely suspects."

"The Archives is not what I would have thought of as a good place for a rendezvous," Malekh noted. "Certainly the likelihood of being seen is greater here."

"The lord high steward employs a separate entrance and exit hidden away from the rest of the personnel. It would be riskier to entertain guests at his private residence, where there would be fewer guards about for protection."

"It did little for him. Are there any items missing from the room?"

"None that we know of."

"Cigars, you said." Malekh bent over the remains from a nearby ashtray. "I see three stubs, and one more three-quarters of the way finished. They must have talked for some time."

"From Peragnon's," Remy said, breathing in deeply. "Their most expensive blend."

The noble stared at him. "Do you smoke them yourself, Armiger?" he asked, finally addressing him for the first time, a hint of challenge in his voice.

"My father does. Most of the older gentlemen in the ton do. I'm used to its scent."

"You are standing across the room from me. Human noses have not developed enough for such a strong sense of smell."

Remy met his gaze, refusing to back down. "They say I'm not completely human. A mooncalf. A cambion. Perhaps that's it."

Feiron frowned and looked away. Zidan Malekh said nothing, but Remy could have sworn there was the barest hint of a smile on the man's face.

"There's a latch on the window." Xiaodan undid it and pushed it open. "Doesn't seem like anyone had escaped out this way. As skilled as we are, vampires aren't capable of closing an inner latch from the outside."

"And the room is located four stories up, with no ivy or other means to climb down. Whoever murdered Astonbury left the same way they came in. Which brings us back to the lord high steward's strange visitor, with the penchant for Peragnon cigars." Malekh returned to the bloody wall, staring hard at it. "Why close the window at all?" he muttered, almost to himself. "The most obvious answer is to prevent anyone else from hearing Astonbury cry out. But that leads us to one conclusion."

"A vampire would have simply left through the window," Xiaodan said. "He wouldn't have cared if he'd left it open afterward."

"But no human would have been strong enough to kill Astonbury in this manner," Remy argued, before realization struck. "Unless—"

"You might want to look through your ranks for more suspects, Lord Feiron," Malekh murmured. "It may well be likely that the murderer is either a human with a grudge as immense as his strength—or a human and a vampire working in unison."

"You see, milord?" Xiaodan said calmly. "We three do make a good team, after all."

9

THE VAULT

Remy had heard stories about the basement underneath the Archives. Part laboratory and part mortuary, it also housed some of the most brilliant minds in Aluria. Bloodwakers had been invented within its hallowed corridors, as had fire lances and other useful weapons specifically designed against vampires.

But the reality of the basement was that everything in it stank to the highest of heavens and was murder on Remy's sensitive nose. Not even the semblance of sterility across its polished stone floors and white walls could prevent the smell of death from permeating through. Xiaodan made a face but said nothing about the stench, while Zidan Malekh strode in without hesitation; the place may as well have been a botanical garden, for all the attention he paid it. So Remy sucked up every complaint he was itching to make and endured.

Not even Reapers were granted access to the basement, as a rule, but the policy had been altered after Astonbury's death. Now they guarded the doors leading into the laboratories, with more stationed within, far enough from the breakable equipment to put the scientists at ease. Most of the hunters eyed the covered body laid out on the slab before them like it might rise up when they weren't looking. All things considered, it was a reasonable assumption.

They were also watching him. Some looked outright disapproving. Remy ignored them. The poison Astonbury had inflicted on the Pendergasts' reputation had been extremely effective, but Remy no longer had to answer to him or to them.

The coroner, a florid-faced man who had introduced himself as the same Dr. Agenot of the autopsy reports Remy had filched, was the only doctor they were permitted to meet. He was currently expounding enthusiastically on the specific causes of the Duke of Astonbury's death in far greater detail than Remy wanted (which, ideally, would be limited to where exactly the bastard had first been stabbed so he could imagine twisting his own knife in deeper). The complicated medical terms the doctor was tossing about could have been spoken in an entirely different language for all Remy understood of it.

Xiaodan and Lords Feiron and Aglaice looked equally at a loss, but Zidan, to add to Remy's already ever-present annoyance with the man, appeared fluent in the science-speak, the two corresponding rapidly in complex nomenclature until Lord Feiron finally lost his patience.

"If you would be so kind, Dr. Agenot," he said testily, "to couch your findings in layman's terms for the rest of us to follow."

"Ah yes. My apologies, Lord Feiron. It's not every day that I can discuss such matters in the depth I would like, to someone not of the Alurian medical profession. Lord Malekh here possesses quite an extensive knowledge of human biology considering that he . . . ah." Agenot turned red.

"I was a physician myself once, in a former life," Malekh said, to Remy's surprise and further irritation. "But the others would be interested to hear your findings on the subject's thoracic cavity."

"Yes. As you all know, Aston—the victim," Agenot corrected himself hastily, after a nervous squint at Lord Feiron, "will not be presented to you today, as would have been standard. Mostly because of the, err, general condition of the body, and also out of respect for his ducal rank. What I can tell you right now regarding the, err, victim, is that parts of the body remained intact after the attack, mainly the chest and torso. Cause of death, as far as I could determine, was a wound near the left anterior axillary line that perforated the left lung and entered the atria. Death due to hemorrhagic shock was quick. The rest of the other, ah, observable injuries happened postmortem, as far as I could ascertain."

"Excuse me," Xiaodan said, "and please feel free to correct me if I misheard. Are you telling us that what the Duke of Astonbury really died from was a stab wound through the heart?"

"Yes, and from the size, I would guess that it was a rather large sword that did the damage. Larger than most piercing weapons I've seen in the past."

"Someone went to a great length of trouble for a grudge," Zidan said grimly.

"His zweihänder," Lord Feiron said, with a visible start. "Good God, someone killed him with his own zweihänder! He hasn't used it since his rise to lord high steward—it's been stored at the armory ever since! Aglaice, come with me. Lord Malekh, Lady Song—if you will please excuse us." He dashed out, his subordinate at his heels.

"While they confirm the duke's zweihänder as the murder weapon," Malekh said briskly, "I would like to see your autopsy reports regarding both Tal Harveston and Lady Daneira."

"Lady Daneira's has been completed, at Lord Malekh's request," Dr. Agenot said apologetically. "I am sorry, Lord Pender—"

"Armiger," Xiaodan corrected quietly.

"Armiger Remington. The Duke of Tennyfair gave us his permission, as distasteful as it all is—"

"Couldn't you have found some other way?" Remy asked tightly. "Hasn't she been disrespected enough?"

"No number of autopsies will undo what had already been done to her," Malekh said coldly. "There are strange creatures about, endangering my kindred and your kingdom. If Lady Daneira's mortal remains can provide the clues needed for their destruction, then she will not have died in vain."

"It still isn't right!"

"Perhaps Astonbury's enmity toward your father is not the reason you've been exempted from similar Reaper investigations in the past. This is not a vocation for weak stomachs."

Remy glared at him, fists clenched.

"Remy," Xiaodan said softly, "you have every right to be angry, but it is not Zidan you should be directing your fury against. I want to prevent more deaths like hers. You brought her in. I know you've seen the strange color of her blood yourself. We had to move quickly before she revived on her own. It was a wonder she hadn't bitten her poor mother."

Remy hated it. Hated it but knew none of them had much choice at this point. "At least tell me you're done with her. Do what you have to do quickly, so we can bring her back to her parents."

"I'm sorry, Remy. What's particularly horrific about this is that there is no antidote to reverse its effects. We . . . we can't bring her back to her parents. Once Dr. Agenot has taken every sample he can, we must burn them all to ensure they don't rise again—thoroughly enough that not even the smallest bone fragment survives. That's why Zidan and I are here. Being a sunbringer has its uses."

Remy's mouth thinned. "I see."

"Ideally," Dr. Agenot said apologetically, "we would like to keep the bodies for another two weeks to see if they all go through the Rot."

"The Rot?"

"It describes the process perfectly, and we've been using it to describe these mutations ever since. Once we can determine the triggers, we can prevent their reanimation indefinitely without needing to consign them to the fires. Lord Malekh, we've found that your suggestion of lowering their body temperatures does keep them in a suspended stasis. The yakhchāl blueprints you provided to us months ago have already been put to good use, as you must have seen outside. Its entrance is only accessible from within this laboratory, and we are far enough below ground level that it works rather perfectly for our purpose."

"'Them'?" Malekh repeated. "How many of these infected are you keeping here as of this moment?"

"About twenty-two in total, not including the Harveston lad."

The Summer Lord was angry. His face was unlined of emotion, as always, but Remy could feel fury bleeding out of every pore. "The yakhchāl was intended to be a place for you to conduct your examinations safely, not as an opportunity to collect more corpses. The danger increases with each one you keep."

The doctor shrunk back. "We weren't expecting to get as many as we did, milord. These were Harveston's victims, and there are fears that they, too, may be reanimated. We will not have any specimens to study if we can't keep them here."

"Did Astonbury know?"

"It was his idea, milord."

"Does the queen?"

Here Agenot faltered. "Well—"

"You cannot keep doing this, Doctor," Xiaodan said. "So many things can go wrong."

"It's the only option we have left, unfortunately. I've drawn as many blood samples as I could, and hope that our experiments can unlock their secrets. Astonbury was adamant about preserving the bodies in the likelihood we might need more."

"Twenty-three infected bodies, in a city of over three hundred thousand people. Your lord high steward took a very risky gamble, Doctor."

"I only do what my superiors tell me, milord. If it puts you at rest, only one of the bodies are in the last stages of the Rot, and we've kept that at the vault."

"The what?" Remy asked, recalling mention of it in the doctor's report.

"The vault, mil—err, Armiger. A reinforced room built with all the steel and silver they could spare us—not much, sadly. We barely have enough of the silver for Reaper weapons as it is. The hunters have been guarding it at all hours to ensure no accidents."

"You made a gaol for the undead?"

"It's not an unreasonable safety measure," Malekh said. "I've constructed a similar one myself in the course of my own investigations."

"The only important information I am getting out of this conversation," Xiaodan said, "is that there's an infected vampiric corpse in this vault of yours that you have been unable to kill."

"Correct, milady. That would be the Harveston boy. We believe that he is at the final phase of the Rot. His regenerative abilities are almost impossible to slow down at this point, and I do not believe that even ice would be a deterrent. No matter how many times the Reapers take him down, he reassembles himself in the space of an hour. He's shown no cognitive functions, only regressing further with every metamorphosis into baser animal instincts."

"Well," Remy said. "Sounds like we're fucked, then."

"Quite frankly, we're not sure what to do with it, especially with the lord high steward now, uh, gone. We couldn't kill it, even if we wanted to. The vault was the best option. Ten inches of silver- and steel alloy–enforced walls, with a little peephole you can look through. The duke decided that it was far too dangerous for any of the Reapers to slay it again, and it's too rabid for us to approach."

"Bring us to it," Xiaodan said.

"I don't think so, milady." One of the Reapers in the room spoke up unexpectedly, a dark-haired veteran named Slavitt. "A dozen of our best Reapers could barely bring it down the last time, and it's going to fight its way out if you so much as crack that door open. I don't know who's set to take Astonbury's place, but if they're like him, they'll forbid us from letting anyone near the corpse."

"I have a few skills that not even the best of your Reapers possess, sir."

"But milady—"

"I am not just *milady*, I am Song Xiaodan, heiress presumptive of the Fourth Court. I outranked the Duke of Astonbury, and now I outrank you." The noblewoman had the uncanny ability to sound imperious despite her soft, lilting voice. "I will take responsibility for anything that happens inside, and that is why I ask you and your hunters to remain outside the room, with the doctor."

"You may as well let her," Malekh said, sounding amused, like his fiancée hadn't just decided to put them all in mortal peril. "It's easier to nod and say yes."

Slavitt hesitated only briefly, then slumped against the wall, suddenly boneless. "If you say so, milady."

THE SCIENTISTS weren't taking any chances with the creature. There was an outer room where Agenot and the other Reapers were waiting, then an inner chamber that served as a barricade between them and the mutation. The latter had a window made from heavy glass and was overlaid with bars for bystanders to look in—an extra precaution, Remy supposed, ensuring the protection of those outside. And within *that* room lay the vault, which looked how its name implied. Silver, as Remy knew, could withstand most vampire attacks. Agenot watched them nervously through the pane, flanked by the other hunters, as Remy and the vampires entered the inner chamber.

"I may have to activate the locking mechanism to bar the doors," the doctor warned. "It prevents the subject from escaping, but it will also trap you inside with it. I must stress again that I share Sir Slavitt's protests about all this."

"Thank you for the warning, Doctor," Xiaodan said. "But we've conducted our own examinations of infected corpses in the last couple of months, and we have an advantage you humans do not."

"'We'?" Malekh asked, as a dark eyebrow inched higher up his forehead in amusement.

"Just follow my lead, Zidan," Xiaodan muttered.

"As you wish, beloved."

"And what is that advantage, milady, if I may be so bold?" Agenot asked.

"The Rot can infect humans, but not those who are already vampires." Xiaodan cracked her knuckles. It made a satisfying sound against her slender fingers. "It all boils down to whether I can kill it faster than it can kill me."

The doctor tittered apprehensively. "I admire your confidence, Lady Song."

"It's not just confidence," Remy murmured, recalling the way she had intercepted his and Malekh's fight, the strength of her grip against his jaw, controlled and unwavering. The absolutely blinding brightness of the sun inside her.

Xiaodan shot him a startled look, but he was already approaching the vault itself. The only way to look in was through the small keyhole Agenot had mentioned, large enough to peer through, but not much else. Remy crouched down.

There didn't seem to be anything inside, at first glance. He could make out a smaller space within, stripped bare of furniture.

Even the floor was constructed of some thick metal, another preventive measure to keep whatever was trapped there from digging its way out.

There was a peculiar odor seeping out of the opening, vile and reeking and the worst thing Remy had ever smelled in his entire life—worse than the unwanted fragrance that wafted through the basement unchecked. Something massive was rotting within, and whatever it was had not been human for a very long time.

And then it filled his vision without warning—a putrefied, eyeless face; a lipless open mouth; patchworks of flesh that were decaying in some places yet were regrowing in others, on a flesh-sack of a body that could only be described as human-shaped because it had the requisite two arms, two legs, and a torso. But any humanity left in its face had long since been eaten away, replaced by the stuff horrific phantasms were made of.

Reports had described Tal Harveston as a man of average height and weight, but the thing inside had swollen to at least thrice that description, just as Takenori claimed. Its fangs were long, whittled and sharp as a vampire's, and brown from decay, but they snapped down with shocking strength as it tried to bite at Remy.

"Fucking hell." Remy reared back. It reminded him of the creature he and Elke had encountered at Glycespike.

"The Harveston corpse is a unique case, as you can see," Agenot said. "It's far larger, far stronger, and far quicker than the other common infected—a colossus, as we've termed it. In this form, it has the capability to control others mutated to a certain extent, compel them to attack on its behalf."

Malekh only nodded, like this was nothing he hadn't heard before. Remy, on the other hand, was dumbfounded. "You mean it attempted to control all the other infected corpses in this laboratory?"

The scientist looked sheepish. "There were no casualties, if that worries you. There was only one other body it tried to infect—we had not yet put it under the ice like the others. The Reapers were fairly quick at taking action. It's the reason we're keeping it inside the vault, matter of fact. The silver in the walls appears to be preventing it from doing so again."

"And Her Majesty knows nothing of this? You're compromising the safety of everyone in Elouve!"

"These were all under the lord high steward's orders, Armiger," Agenot said nervously. "I only do as he says."

"May I?" Heedless of the sickening, gnashing sounds from the other side of the steel door, Lady Song bent down and studied the corpse. "It really is regenerating," she said in amazement. "How interesting. But regenerating into what?"

"I'm not sure *interesting* is the appropriate word," Remy grated out. "I thought you'd seen these mutations before."

"Not quite. Zidan tends to be much more cautious about his experiments than your late lord high steward. I've never seen any of the infected at the later stages of this Rot because we make sure that they don't survive this long." Her voice dropped. "The poor boy. It was terrible of Astonbury to let him suffer this way, Doctor, and for such a protracted duration."

"How long has it been in there without any bloodletting?" Malekh asked.

"We've been letting it stew for close to ten days," Slavitt said, answering for Agenot. "And as far as we can tell, it's shown no decrease in its strength or speed."

"Nothing more than a mindless shell at this point," Agenot added, "consumed with only the urge to kill."

"At this rate of regeneration, I'm not surprised. Theoretically, it may even survive without sustenance almost indefinitely." Malekh laid his hand against one of the walls of the vault, where heavy dents had been curved into the steel.

"So they could be immortal this way," Remy said, stunned by the implications. "Almost indestructible, but at the cost of everything else."

"Doctor Agenot," Xiaodan said. "I would like you to open the vault's door at my signal."

Agenot made a shocked, spluttering noise. "Milady, surely you still do not intend to—"

"I very well intend to, Doctor, and in case you're about to oppose me, please understand that this is, yet again, another order. Armiger Remington, please step out of the room and join Dr. Agenot and the other Reapers."

Remy could have protested, could have resented the suggestion that he wasn't strong enough. He wasn't some weak little apprentice noble to be cosseted like he hadn't been fighting vampires for years. If Malekh had issued the command, he would have told the man to stuff that order up him like spit through a roast.

But Xiaodan sounded just a little too . . . eager.

Remy compromised, positioning himself outside between the closed door and the window's edge. If the infected corpse somehow found its way past the vampire couple and broke the door down, he could at least be of some use.

"Zidan," Xiaodan said, "take heed of the time."

Her fiancé folded his arms and leaned back against the door, relaxed, like his intended wasn't about to confront some eldritch terror. "Always."

The woman took a deep breath, then focused on the entryway. "Now, Doctor. Open the vault."

The doctor produced a key from one of his coat pockets, used it to turn a lock among the row of buttons on the wall. With a grating noise, the door to the vault swung outward.

Everything happened far too quickly after that.

The decaying creature waiting within was too Lightdamn fast. All Remy could ascertain for sure was seeing a messy, crimson blur, and then a brief glimpse of a hulking, pus-ridden form barreling out of the vault only to disappear immediately from his sight, and for one dreadful moment he thought that it had gotten out even with all the fail-safes in place.

Lady Song moved. In one rapid, graceful movement, she blinked out, reentered human vision, struck at the air. There was a gurgling noise that sounded like it had emanated from some stomach rather than from the throat.

The monster reappeared in the air Xiaodan had just slashed at, cut cleanly in half and only inches away from the door leading to the outer room where Remy and the others waited.

It stumbled across the inner chamber toward Remy and slammed against part of the window through which he watched, with enough force that even the reinforced frame rattled furiously, going *blurgghssggshekchkkk*.

There were more sickening wet noises as the lower segment of the mutation's body slid down to the floor behind it. Braced against the glass, mouth agape from a loss of muscle, the remains of its face focused sightlessly on Remy—the creature growled. Its tongue moved, its fangs clicking.

Calmly, Xiaodan placed her foot against the fallen creature's back. She grasped its head with one hand, and then wrenched its skull off the rest of its body, detaching a few feet of spine along with it. There was a thump as it finally collapsed on the floor, seizing soundlessly.

"Armiger Remington," she said. "Dr. Agenot. If you would both close your eyes. Sir Slavitt, I advise you and your Reapers to do the same."

Remy could feel the searing heat through the walls, the flash of light even through his closed eyelids. When he finally opened them, the monster was gone, the blue-black spatters on the ground the only traces of it left.

Xiaodan was pale, though at least still upright. Malekh was already at her side. The monster had swept past him, and he hadn't even turned a hair at the danger.

"Light help us," Remy said, staring. Xiaodan had been fast. He would have to down at least ten bloodwakers one after another to keep up with that speed, and his insides would promptly hemorrhage in gratitude right after.

Agenot pulled another switch, and the door opened. Remy rushed in, paused. His instinct had been to comfort her, ascertain that everything was all right. Xiaodan had fainted the last time she'd done this.

Malekh's hand around her shoulders stopped him in his tracks. Of course. She was his fiancée. He fought back the brief spurt of disappointment.

As if sensing what he was thinking, the vampire lord turned to look back at him. Something in his calm gaze made Remy flush and hastily look away.

"Fantastic!" Dr. Agenot was beside himself with awe. "None of the Reapers could even begin to—it was an honor to see such a display of—"

"Thank you, Doctor." Xiaodan had a hand pressed over her heart. Remy could hear her heartbeat, sped up nearly double despite the fight's swiftness, eventually slowing down into a more relaxed, if still irregular, rhythm. "How long did that take me, Zidan?"

"Two point seven seconds."

She grinned. "That fast?"

"That fast."

"I'm very impressive, aren't I?"

"Indubitably."

"I've heard rumors," Slavitt said. He and the other hunters wore faces far too blank to not be fidgeting inwardly. "That anything you touched turned to poison. That you could evaporate into mist. That you could wither vampires and humans alike with one look."

"The last is not untrue," Malekh murmured.

"But what you can actually do is create light. More important, you can kill vampires with it. Kill these mutations." What Slavitt could refrain from showing in his expression, the reverence and awe in his voice revealed.

It didn't stop his hand from grazing the hilt of his fire lance. The other hunters copied his gesture.

"And you're sure it won't re-form itself again, milady?" another Reaper Remy didn't recognize asked cautiously.

If Xiaodan had noticed the shifts in their stance, she was diplomatically ignoring it. "Rest assured that you won't ever have to worry about this particular creature again."

"And all that remains are these blood spatters?" the doctor asked.

"Were you intending to preserve its remains even after everything?"

"I—of course not, milady. But as a man of science, I cannot help but mourn what could have been, had we found a better way to secure the subject without risking our own safety. But in light of the darkness and rain that constantly befalls Aluria, your talent was a welcome sight to see."

"I'm glad to find someone who sees my abilities as more than just a curse, Doctor." Xiaodan sounded almost sad.

"It is a most welcome solution to our problem, milady. Each time the Reapers kill it, the separate parts would liquefy, flow toward each other, and then reconstitute the creature—much like a sea cucumber or certain species of jellyfish. If only we could isolate the blood properties that allow that to happen, perhaps determine the neurological impulses needed to willfully control such transformations. The secret to immortality, without needing to undergo such terrifying metamorphoses."

"And we're not going to find that out today," Xiaodan growled. "The poor Harveston boy is finally at rest. I intend to see the rest of the bodies here disposed of, as well."

"But I was under express orders from the duke not to . . ." Dr.

Agenot paused, as if only just remembering that he had performed an autopsy on the lord high steward only hours earlier.

"We will leave nothing else to chance, Doctor. Let them all be at peace."

"You would need to ask for the queen's consent in the matter of the other infected, milady," Slavitt interrupted respectfully. "Astonbury had convinced Her Majesty that it was important to preserve all experiments within the labs by any means necessary. We cannot go against her orders."

"Does Her Majesty know that your laboratory contains specimens she intends to preserve that can be resurrected at a moment's notice no matter the manner of death inflicted by her Reapers?"

Slowly, Slavitt shook her head. "Astonbury didn't want to worry her. Said he wanted to find the answers first."

"Did you swear an oath to the queen of Aluria or to her steward, sir? I do not think loyalty to the Crown extends to keeping secrets from her person."

Malekh reached into his coat pocket and pulled out a small carrying case containing syringes of varying sizes. He selected a large needle among the selection, crouched down near the largest pool of blood, and drew a sample from it. Then he took out another, one already filled with some strange colorless liquid, and squeezed its contents onto the stain.

The blood thickened and hardened, solidifying into a gel-like cocoon.

"A fast-acting coagulant," Malekh said. "A stimulant to induce rapid arteriosclerosis, force it into a state of crystallization. This should put them in a state of paralysis without worrying about their potential reanimation. Easier to do if ice is a scarcity. This one vial can inoculate the rest of the bodies in your morgue long enough for Xiaodan to incinerate them all at once. Obliterating these creatures takes its toll on my fiancée's health, Doctor. I am glad that you have a healthy appreciation for her abilities, but I would much rather take away the frequency she has to perform such responsibilities whenever I can."

"You induced arteriosclerosis into their system?" Dr. Agenot asked, amazed. "A stroke of genius, sir! Of course—as the virus is carried through their bloodstream, halting their circulation would prevent regeneration at the cellular level. But we've tried accelerating fibrin polymerization before, and we could never expedite it to within seconds as yours has."

"We have other distinct advantages, Doctor, as Lady Song has already mentioned. You are limited to working with human proteins. But it is the regenerative qualities of vampire blood that helps speed up the process. I can provide your laboratory with serum for you to replicate, along with samples I've extracted from Harveston's blood. The medical facilities in Elouve far surpass those that I keep in my own laboratory. Perhaps there will be more to be found here with the equipment at your disposal."

"I thank you, Lord Malekh. Recent blood extractions have been impossible until you came along, though our analysis is not likely to be any different from what you have already discovered."

"Have you isolated the two differing blood types from Harveston? Is it of the same AB sequence?"

"How did you know—ah, you would know, wouldn't you?"

"Mind explaining it for the ones who don't?" Remy huffed.

"Gladly, Armiger," said Agenot. "Harveston possesses the A blood type he was naturally born with, albeit almost unrecognizable as human in its current state, swimming with abnormalities still unknown to us. But we've also discovered an AB type in his blood, and unlike Harveston's, it is unmutated. Every test we've conducted on it so far indicates a human donor. It is the same in every other corpse—their original blood type since birth, and another foreign to their genetic makeup. Always of the same AB blood group."

"I'm not the most educated when it comes to the blood sciences," Xiaodan said, "but isn't it impossible to have two different blood types in one body at once?"

"Improbable, but not quite impossible. A quirk of nature may produce different zygotes and therefore differing types within the same person—we call it chimerism. Organ transplantation can also be another cause, rare as that is. An infected corpse with chimera-like characteristics could be a coincidence. Two is suspect. But when all the corpses that come your way are afflicted with the Rot and also possess those two unique types, and one always of a specific blood group . . ."

"I'm more concerned with *who* this blood type might belong to," Malekh said. "In the meantime, the Reapers are to take all the bodies in your morgue for Xiaodan to destroy."

"I'll talk to the queen herself," Xiaodan added.

Remy continued to gawk at the hardened blood on the floor. The corpse had been nothing but a mindless shell, the doctor had said.

He had said the same thing about Lady Daneira. But the girl had visited her mother while still infected. Something inside her had remembered.

And this colossus had made a dash for *him* rather than for the door. Rather than attack either Xiaodan or Malekh, which it would have done if it was surviving on instinct instead of intelligence. Even cut in half, it had plastered itself against the bars. Without eyes, it had turned its face unerringly toward him.

He didn't know if the door, reinforced as it was, would have been enough to hold it had Xiaodan been any slower to act. And the way Harveston seemed to single him out had made Remy take it all quite personally.

"Fuck," he said again, just because.

10

AN AUDIENCE

Remy had never given the queen of Aluria much thought as a person, though he had spent the better part of his life fighting in her name. With the death of Lord High Steward Astonbury, the Reapers in her court had fallen into disarray, unsure which noble clamoring for the lord high steward's position to obey.

Lord Feiron was the next highest-ranking official to assume the late duke's duties, but Lord Feiron was not the type to inspire confidence or loyalty or any minimum standard of competence. Astonbury's underlings had been handpicked not for meritocracy, but for their inability to scheme independently of the duke. As much as Remy had disliked Matthew Delacroix, the man had had a penchant for managing government secrets and dealing with court intrigues that very few could hope to master. His loss had been bad enough for the queen herself to summon Remy and the vampires to her court to try and make sense of the chaos Astonbury had left behind, preempting Xiaodan's intentions of seeking an audience with her.

Queen Ophelia was not a young woman, and she was handsome rather than beautiful. Her hair had reddish highlights that spoke of some old Kerenai ancestry, but her high cheekbones and dark eyes were Ashrai hallmarks. She had no need for a crown to radiate power. Holding Aluria together was no easy task, but Remy was surprised to see Her Majesty in a fighting habit not unlike those worn by the kingdom's Reapers. The queen usually favored elaborate gowns and heavy veils during her rare public appearances.

"I see that you've uncovered many things surrounding my lord high steward's death, Zidan," she remarked, and Remy was astonished by the familiarity with which she greeted the Summer Lord and the Fourth Court heiress as they approached her throne. "Couldn't you have waited for an official summons from me, rather than intrude on royal business with such impunity?" Harsh as the words sounded, they were underscored by her warm, genial tone, a far cry from the stern one she adopted when holding court.

"It's good to see you again, Ophelia," Malekh murmured.

Xiaodan was far more brazen, rushing forward to catch the older woman in a joyful embrace. The queen laughed and returned the favor, while Remy continued to stare in amazement. Granted, he knew deucedly little of politics, concerning himself with the threat of rogue vampires and little else. He'd seen the political maneuvering his father had to do to maintain his waning influence and had decided that life was too short for such headaches. This did explain how the Alurian-kindred alliance was flourishing even with vocal opposition from some in Her Majesty's court.

He wasn't the only one caught off guard by their friendship. The throne room had been cleared of its courtiers and regular hangers-on, leaving only her trusted officials: Gaspard Lopes, the minister of the interior; Montgomery Bellinger, the queen's general-at-arms; and a dozen of his best soldiers, all tacit enough not to make their own surprise evident beyond a slight, uneasy shift in their stance. Bellinger went so far as to allow a faint curl of a sneer to adorn his upper lip.

None of the queen's men liked the vampires. It showed in their silent stares, the way their fingers never left the triggers of their fire lances. Word of Xiaodan's sunbringing abilities had likely spread. It was obvious in the way Her Majesty was saying nothing about it. All the Reapers and soldiers that manned the entrance to the palace and down the hallway into the throne room had glared at Xiaodan and Malekh like she was an explosion waiting to happen.

"And how are things at Qing-ye, my dear?" Queen Ophelia asked Xiaodan fondly. "Are Candy and Vanilla still as rambunctious as ever?"

For some reason, the question sent the vampire into bouts of laughter. "They are the same as they ever were and shall continue to be, and I am very glad for it. They miss you, too."

"Tell me more about this serum you've developed to aid us in this infectious menace," the queen demanded. "How did you succeed in synthesizing a counteractant when the best minds I could gather in all of Aluria failed?"

"Your own scientists were close to making their own breakthrough. They merely lacked the kindred blood required to speed up the neutralization process." Zidan placed a vial similar in appearance to the one he had used on Harveston on the table before Queen Ophelia. "This should be enough to create several dozen more sedatives for the bodies still lying in stasis in the Archives' laboratory. I have left more canisters with Minister Lopes." Malekh nodded to the minister of the interior, who ducked his head in wordless acknowledgment. "Dr. Agenot is already working on replicating more."

Queen Ophelia pressed her fist against her forehead, a customary sign asking the Light for strength. "And whose vampiric blood did you use for this wonderful cure?"

Malekh chuckled. "That would infringe on doctor-patient confidentiality, Your Majesty. And it's not a cure—not yet. A preventative, at best."

"You have my gratitude all the same, my dear Zidan. It would have taken longer to re-create this on our own." The queen's eyes darkened. "Tell me that this was not a deliberate disease engineered on both our people, milord. That this sickness has natural origins, that there is no attempt by outside forces to turn my kingdom into a hellscape of rabid, uncontrollable undead."

"Or an attempt to turn us against each other, to start a war that neither of us wants or can afford," Malekh said, just as grimly.

"I have children, milord. This is not the legacy I wish to bequeath upon them. Is there no way to reverse the process for those at the earliest stage of the Rot?"

"I am a doctor, Your Majesty, not a miracle worker. The coagulants will harden their blood, immobilizing the flow of the strain, rendering it harmless—and sending the affected into a vegetative state. It cannot reverse their deaths."

"Yet vampires are immune to the disease?"

"Vampires already turned, yes. The mutated can mimic the speed and strength we possess but suffer from a near-permanent frenzy and a loss of mental acuity. To say that they are vampires themselves would be inaccurate—they are merely a horrific parody of us."

"So the only sure prevention is to avoid being bitten." Queen Ophelia sighed and turned to the general. "Sir Bellinger, send word to Dr. Agenot to dispose of every corpse within the Ministry of the Archives. Gather them all at Giantsmound and prepare them for kindling."

"Your Majesty, surely there is another—"

"I want the light burning bright enough to be seen from my palace, milord. I give Lady Song leave to do what she must to prevent their resurrection. I will compensate the victims' families for the trouble we have caused them, but we cannot take any more chances. Incidentally, my dear Xiaodan"—and here the queen's tone turned reproachful—"you never told me you held such vast abilities. I thought only the Ancients were capable of such unique skills? And you not having reached your first century yet."

"It was long after our first meeting, Your Majesty," Xiaodan said, looking exhausted. "You could say it was passed down from my ancestors. I have kept quiet about the extent of it for a reason. There are enough kindred clans out there who believe I do not deserve to live."

"But you revealed it to us. Would that not put you in more danger?"

"As it turns out, only I am capable of eradicating these creatures permanently with it. That danger, at the moment, far surpasses my own."

The queen softened. "Oh, my dear. I am sorry for this, and all the trouble people have done in my name. I have given the Duke of Astonbury far too much leeway in this matter, believing he would make the proper decisions, but I see that my faith in him has been mistaken."

"He weighed the risks against the potential rewards," Malekh said. "Finding a cure would have been a major coup to his career, his place in history secured. It is easy to underestimate the infected, to look upon them as mindless creatures that could be easily outsmarted."

"They're not completely mindless," Remy muttered, forgetting briefly that at least two others in the room had even better preternatural hearing than he.

"Oh?" Malekh's voice now carried a tinge of mockery. "How so?"

Remy bristled. "Because if it was driven solely by its urges, then the corpse in the Archives would have stayed and fought Lady Song. Not attempted to escape. That's not what something completely shorn of its brains would do."

"This must be the Pendergast Reaper," the queen said, acknowledging him for the first time. Awkwardly, Remy bowed. "Remington Pendergast, Marquess of Aphelion. Son of the Duke of Valenbonne. Far more courteous than his father," Queen Ophelia added with a faint twitch to her lips, "though every bit as dedicated to serving us as his sire has always done. He may have a valid point that you must also consider, Zidan. Last I heard, Lord Feiron had him held as a potential suspect."

"He was cleared of all charges and accusations, Your Majesty," Xiaodan piped up. "In fact—and I hope you don't mind my overstepping—but I'd taken the liberty of asking for his assistance in our own investigations. He would be a tremendous asset to us."

"I have heard of his exploits," Queen Ophelia conceded. "It has only just come to my knowledge that Matthew Delacroix's hatred of his father was such that he had actively banned everyone from the Pendergast family from joining the dræfendgemot."

That had been the general assumption, but it felt like a blow to Remy, to hear her confirm it so baldly.

Queen Ophelia looked him full in the face. "We entrusted the lord high steward with Aluria's defense, but I never stopped to consider how his own biases have made this an unjust situation for you, and we wish to make amends for it. Whatever enmity he had for the Duke of Valenbonne, that anger should not have been extended to you simply for sharing his name. Regardless of who succeeds Astonbury, I will ensure your welcome into the royal dræfendgemot if you still desire it."

"You're too kind, Your Majesty," Remy mumbled, feeling more pitied than victorious.

"Absolutely not!" Xiaodan interjected heatedly. "You had your chance, my dear Ophelia, but his talents would be wasted there. He shouldn't be relegated to running errands for high-ranking Reapers with just as little sense for governance as Lord Feiron. Your lord high steward has already turned the nobility against him. His death will not lessen the Reapers' prejudice."

"And what do you propose I do with him instead?" the queen asked.

"Zidan and I intend to leave Elouve shortly to pursue his theories regarding the Rot. Please, give us leave to have Armiger Remington accompany us."

"What?" Remy asked once again.

Her Majesty raised a tawny eyebrow. "And why are you so determined to have him?"

"Because Remy deserved to join Your Majesty's official circle of Reapers," Xiaodan said with an alarming honesty Remy did not necessarily want, "and your lord high steward, Matthew Astonbury, may his soul rest in peace, was being an absolute *twat* about it." She spoke the word with delight, drawing it out on her tongue like she'd never had the opportunity to say it before. "I've dragged enough information from Lord Feiron to know how Astonbury constantly undermined Armiger Remington's successes in the hunts he had undertaken for the Crown, claimed the victory in his stead, and then went out of his way to deny the armiger his accolades."

"Successes?"

"He hunted the vampire who murdered three dozen people north of Enumbra. He took down the coven that nearly depopulated the villages near Wargen. He retrieved Tennyfair's daughter. He staked the only known First Court vampire lurking within Aluria in close to a decade—his first mission, in fact. Need I go on? Because I have nearly ten years' worth of kills to list."

A light breeze would have been capable of bowling Remy over at this point. She had researched his history somehow, known achievements that the Archives had never credited him with.

"An impressive record for one still so young." Queen Ophelia quirked up a brow. "But you seem strangely proud to talk about the different ways he has slain your kindred."

"They were no kindred of mine. Remington isn't the only one feared by his own kind."

"I see your point." The queen leaned back against her throne. "The Enumbran vampire. I remember. Astonbury told me it was

Reapers under his direct command who were responsible for putting it down."

"Lies and spite, Ophelia. Astonbury remained livid at the thought of another Pendergast earning merits within his administration. Everyone has treated Armiger Remington abominably—even Lady Astonbury, who sought to take advantage of him with sexual favors for information he should have been privy to in the first place. Regardless of whom you choose to replace the late duke with, the other Reapers will continue to inflict these injustices upon him."

Xiaodan turned to eye the minister and the other soldiers in the throne room. "As will almost everyone else at court," she added coldly.

Remy, far from being grateful, was beet red. It was one thing to be indiscreet with someone else's wife, but another to announce it to the queen. He wished for the ground to open and swallow him up, but he had never been so lucky.

"Why not ask the Reaper himself?" The queen looked at him with mischief in her gaze, fully aware of his discomfort. "What say you, Armiger Remington? Would you like a dispensation to promote you into the royal dræfendgemot with all the honors you deserve, or would you like to accompany the Third and Fourth Courts on their investigations, on Aluria's behalf?"

The first option was easier to take. Easier to take his place among the other Reapers, regardless of what they thought. Easier to concentrate on the Night Empress, to finally earn access to reports on the First Court without having to compromise himself. Far easier than to embroil himself in the middle of an ongoing plague, and with two vampires besides.

"If it pleases you, Your Majesty," he said. "I'd like to investigate the Rot with the Third and Fourth Courts."

The queen leaned forward. "And may I know the reason for it?"

Remy swallowed, remembering the betting pool, the bounties.

"I believe I can be a greater asset to Aluria with them. And I am grateful for your offer, but I hope for more than the mere tolerance the dræfendgemot will ever afford me in Elouve."

Xiaodan's smile was as bright as the sun. In contrast, Zidan Malekh's scowl was like a thundercloud on the cusp of a terrible storm.

"HOW DO you know Her Majesty so well?" Remy asked after the queen had dismissed them, proud of the evenness in his tone. Malekh had insisted on leaving the following day once Xiaodan had taken care of the Archives' infected. More attacks had been reported along the eastern borders of Aluria near Qing-ye, and the vampire nobles intended to conduct their inquiries there. It was further confirmation of the reports Remy had received earlier.

The hallway they were standing in remained deserted. The usual courtiers and hangers-on who often loafed around the palace were missing, and he suspected that had been on Queen Ophelia's orders. Many in the court were still opposed to her alliance with the vampires, if the reaction of Her Majesty's officials in the throne room had been any indication.

"Ophelia was quite young when we first met her, newly raised to the throne. She stumbled upon Chànggē Shuǐ—my home—by accident one day, and I offered her a place to stay for a few nights. I'd never had human visitors before. She'd never been under a vampire's roof. It was awkward at first." Xiaodan grinned. "She's visited many times since then. Taught me how to serve excellent venison, should I entertain more mortals in the future."

"She arrived at your palace by accident?"

"A matter of a horde of vampires at her heels. They'd slaughtered nearly half her retinue and would have gotten her, too, if I hadn't sensed them near my territory." Xiaodan laughed at the look on his face. "I should have mentioned that earlier. You might enjoy staying at Chàngge Shuǐ too, Remy. No valets. Lots of space for peace of mind. I think it's rather pretty, even for a fortress."

"So we're traveling back to your home at some point during this journey?"

"We live east of Aluria's borders. With all the reports of infections near there, it's the perfect location for us to set up base, assess the situation, and figure out what we should do next. We'll likely take a few detours along the way, based on any fresh reports we receive. The attacks appear to be shifting toward Qing-ye, which worries me. There aren't as many Fourth Court vampires around to secure the territories around it." She hesitated, mournful. "It would be good to go home. I haven't been back in months. Zidan would have more ideas by the time we return—he's always been the brains between us two. I'm just the muscle."

"What does that make me, then?" Remy muttered.

"The bait," Zidan supplied.

Remy rounded on him, glaring, but the noble met him stare for unyielding stare. "As Xiaodan said, we'll be encountering more infected the farther east we go, if even half of those reports can be confirmed. Your mother has never been fond of Reapers, Xiaodan, and she will not be happy to have the Butcher's son in Chàngge Shuǐ. Whatever assistance you believe he can provide, he would be best used as lure."

"Are you saying you don't want him with us, Zidan?" Xiaodan didn't seem as ready to defend Remy to her fiancé the way she'd defended him to the queen. She was smiling, her guard relaxed. "Say the word, and I'll let him go."

"Nobody's letting anyone go from anything," Remy snapped, stung to be relegated to a bartered good once again. "If you're suggesting that I would be nothing more than a liability, or that I won't be up to the task, then at least have the fucking guts to say it to my face."

Amber-flecked eyes turned to him. "You are a liability," Zidan Malekh said, as easily and as calmly as if he'd been discussing the weather. "You are a prized meal, an easy target. You only know enough about court vampires to hunt us, not of our ways. And while you may possess your father's skills, it will be years before you can acquire his experience. So yes, Pendergast. You will be a hindrance to us in more ways than you know. And the only reason you are even here . . ." Malekh's gaze flicked briefly toward Xiaodan. "The only reason you are here, traveling with us," he said, "is because she wishes to protect you."

"I don't need any bloody protection." They were both goddamn bloodyarsed vampires—of course he would be the weakest of their unholy trio. But Remy hadn't survived what other Reaper veterans could not, only to be told by some pompous undead noble who had no idea of the shit he'd been through that he was a burden. "If you didn't want me along, then why didn't you bring that up before Her Majesty?"

"I would never be so improper as to undermine Xiaodan before a foreign power, ally or otherwise. *Even* if my betrothed had neglected to inform me of her decision beforehand."

Xiaodan's answering smile was a mile wide.

"Do I have to fucking fight you again to prove myself?" Remy demanded. "What the hell is it going to take to show you I've got as much right to be here as you?"

"Fight me, you say?" Malekh's sudden spark of interest brought out more of the gold in his eyes. "And what do I get when you inevitably lose this wager?"

"Lady Song?" a new voice called. "Lord Malekh?"

The Duchess of Astonbury was fashionably dressed for mourning. She was clothed all in black, but even the veil across her face couldn't detract from her beauty, or the way she honed in on Remy with an eagerness that had nothing to do with grief. "I was told you both shall be leaving with Remington tomorrow at the queen's orders," she said boldly, "and as I will be busy making the necessary preparations for my husband's funeral . . ." She let out a soft sigh, as if she found these arrangements more cumbersome than anything else. "May I have a few minutes to speak with Remington alone, milord, milady?"

Two pairs of eyes turned to Remy—Zidan's expressionless, Xiaodan's openly wary. "I'll be back with you shortly," he told them, moving several feet away to give himself and the duchess the privacy she asked for.

"I am devastated to hear that you are leaving," Giselle said softly. Her eyes looked suspiciously shiny. Remy knew it had nothing to do with her husband's passing, uncomfortably aware that it was because of him. "And I am even sorrier to hear of Lord Feiron taking you into custody. Had I known, I would have demanded your release sooner. It's a—an insult, my love, knowing what they do about us."

"They were only doing their jobs."

"And doing quite terribly at it." Her hands found his coat lapels. "I am going to miss you. I thought we would have more time together. Spend tonight with me. Let me send you off with final memories to remember me by."

Remy looked down at the Duchess of Astonbury, at the soft glow in her eyes. She really was stunning.

"Do you remember," he said, "the first time I came to your bed?"

The woman's rosy cheeks dimpled. Her voice lowered, a throaty purr. "I could never forget. How shy you were. How you could not keep your eyes away from me when I disrobed." She laid her fingers against the side of his neck. "The look on your face, the rough sounds you made. The pleasure of being your first teacher. I recall them fondly."

Remy's hand reached up to find hers, curling over her fingers. "Do you want to know what I remember in clearest detail from that night?"

"Tell me," Giselle whispered, gliding closer.

"That the subject was five foot nine inches in height, approximately two-twenty pounds and of a stocky build, with blue eyes and brown hair. Believed to have been turned near the forests between Laithe and Sandsbourne, responsible for the deaths of five cows, seven horses, and two children. A broken star on the back of his right hand, as confirmed by two eyewitness accounts—a mark of those beholden to the Night Court."

Giselle frowned, puzzled by the unexpected shift in conversation.

"That was the first report you ever brought me. The only known sighting of a First Court vampire in the last ten years. I read it so many times after you'd fallen asleep, and I can still recall it word for word. The next day, I rode out and took that vampire down— my first kill as a Reaper, after all the months spent on the register, months spent being denied my own bounties. They docked me my two months' pay because they had not authorized me to carry that hunt out, and every other bounty they shoved my way after that were always the ones they refused to handle themselves. But finally—finally—I was a Reaper, hunting as one. You made that possible for me. And I will always be grateful to you for that."

Gently, Remy pulled her hand from his neck. "But I can't do this with you anymore, Giselle. I'm sorry."

"Your minutes are up," Xiaodan said, popping up from behind Lady Giselle without warning. The latter gasped aloud. "There will be much to plan for the journey ahead, and we will be requiring the rest of his time for it, Your Grace. And while I am not as well-versed on human etiquette as I suppose I should be, I do know that it is considered highly disrespectful for you to be inviting anyone to your bed so soon after your husband's murder, even if you and Astonbury were living separately."

The duchess's mouth fell open.

"Have a good day, Lady Astonbury." Xiaodan didn't quite drag

Remy away, but a subtle push against his arm was all it took to propel him back down the hallway, Malekh close behind.

"How did you find out about . . . about . . ?" Remy's ears were steaming. It wasn't a secret. Given how confidently she stated matters before Queen Ophelia, she had more than overheard his earlier admission to Feiron at Kinaiya Lodge.

"I didn't intend to," Xiaodan said calmly, "but it was hard not to hear what people in this city speak of so freely. In our brief acquaintance, you struck me as someone far too kindhearted to turn her down yourself, despite all the years she abused you. They kept you longer in the gaols than my patience allowed for, and finding a way to release you sooner meant learning everything I could of you that was relevant to this case. I'm sorry I had to intrude on your privacy."

"Abuse? But she wasn't—" And here, Remy took another pause. "It wasn't—it's not—"

"How old were you when the affair started, Remy?"

"I—" He'd treated it as a simple matter of exchanging favors, like bearing equal responsibility had meant he'd never been taken advantage of. But that was his excuse now, as a twenty-three-year-old who'd grown cynical over the years. Xiaodan was treating him like he was still the scared fifteen-year-old he'd been when the affair had started. And maybe that was the point. "Young," he finally said. "Perhaps it was younger than I should have—"

"Younger than *she* should have," Xiaodan said sympathetically, and suddenly, Remy knew Malekh had been right earlier when he'd said that Xiaodan had intended to protect Remy. Only it wasn't other vampires that she'd been thinking of.

The Fourth Court heiress's face was a study in calm, but her balled fists continued to give her away. "I apologize," she said again. "But you must tell me the truth. Would you still be with her if she wasn't supplying you with the intelligence reports you needed for the Night Empress's whereabouts?"

The answer required no thought at all. "No."

"Good. That's all I needed to hear." Xiaodan turned to Malekh next. "And you. If you dislike the thought of Remy joining us, it would be best if you speak now or forever hold your peace."

"I said he would be a liability—"

"That's not the question, Zidan."

Their gazes locked, clashed. It was Malekh who gave in, almost sounding bored when he replied, "He can do whatever he wants, and I shall make no protest."

A sudden tumult by the palace entrance caught their attention. Remy knew it was bad upon sighting the Marquess of Riones, the man all bloody as hell, with scores and tears in his usually impeccably expensive shirt and coat. His sword was out, dripping red onto the pavement. Behind him people fled past, heading west like stampeding cattle toward the city square, herded along by several more Reapers.

"Protect the queen, do you hear me?" Riones was shouting. "I want every Reaper on active and reserve duty guarding every inch of the palace! Let no one inside or out until we've cleared the Archives!"

"The Archives?" Remy yelled at him. "What's happening, Riones? What of the Archives?"

"Where have you been, Pendergast? The Archives is being overrun!" came the chilling reply. "Tell the guards to round up as many citizens as they can and head toward the barracks! We've got the Rot in the city, and I don't know how long we can hold them off!"

Remy's insides felt like lead. "How?"

"It's those damned corpses Astonbury wanted kept in that oversized ice room of his! They've reawakened, and they're out for our blood!"

11

MINISTRY ATTACK

Xiaodan needed no further details. She was gone from view long before the Reaper was done finishing his sentence.

"Go to Her Majesty, milord," Malekh told Riones tersely. "I've entrusted her with the serum needed to combat these infections. We'll be needing them sooner than we thought." And then he too, disappeared.

With a loud curse, Remy dug into his pocket, discovered a bloodwaker, and downed its contents swiftly.

"What are you doing, Pendergast?" Riones demanded.

"Going after them." He nodded at the man's coat. "Any of that yours?"

"Thankfully, no. We were hauling bodies out of Agenot's ice bunker under Her Majesty's orders. One of the bastards stood up without warning and tore Kibold's throat out."

"Didn't Agenot inject them with the Third Court noble's serum?"

"Agenot told us nothing for nuts. All he said to do was load the corpses up into the waiting wagons. We got most of the scientists out, but there's a few more bunkered down inside. Oswald ordered us out to sound the warning, but he and Maxwell and

Pyalia're still in there. The speed of those pendejos—not even vampires could move so—"

"Oswald Craggart?"

"Yes. Friend of yours?"

"No." Craggart was the Reaper responsible for dumping him with all the bounties no one else wanted to take on, hoping one would be enough to kill him. Didn't stop Remy from taking them, though. "Any soldiers surrounding the Archives?"

"We've sealed all the exits as best we could, but that means nothing if those things break through. Don't tell me you're going in with them, Pendergast! Let the vampires sort out the—"

"They didn't do this, Riones. This is all on Astonbury and Agenot, and the vampires, of all people, are trying to help us. Oswald's sent me on far too many of these shit-arsed hunts. He won't want me to stop now when it's his gonads that are on the line." It was said with more confidence than Remy actually felt. "Secure the premises, find as many other Reapers as you can spare to bolster the defenses at the Archives' barricade. If whatever's inside is set loose on the populace, it's over."

"Pendergast—"

"It wasn't Craggart's intention to make me the most experienced Reaper on hand to be dealing with this damned lot, but that's how things stand. Blast it, Riones. Let me do my job so you can do yours."

Riones slumped, accepting the inevitable. "Get them out quick, Pendergast, and stay careful. We're losing hunters as it is."

Xiaodan was scanning the building for other signs of life when he finally caught up. Malekh was ordering the royal guards already in the vicinity to step away.

The building itself stood, silent and empty, with no signs of anyone else inside.

"How many more humans?" Malekh barked at another soldier.

"A few of the doctors and two Reapers, I think," came the

terrified reply. "Also Sir Oswald, but we don't know what's happened to—"

A window shattered on the first floor, sending shrapnel their way. From behind the broken glass several creatures leaped out, so severely mutilated that it was impossible to believe they had ever been human. The first to clamber forth was gray and massive, with the hunched shoulders and massive chest of a brute, and nearly shed of all its skin, revealing muscle filaments and blood vessels. Just like Harveston, the infection had caused its body to swell to grotesque proportions, but its fangs were larger, protruding halfway down its torso to further highlight its monstrous nature.

More creatures came tearing out, all with varying, distorted degrees of the same skinless shapes, all possessing the same asymmetry of aberration, and Remy realized with horror that tatters of black cloth remained on at least one of them; even in its shredded state, there was no mistaking the dark clothes the Reapers favored.

Malekh drew out his curved sword and disappeared briefly to stab at the nearest mutation. There was a wretched, sickly sound as the blade plunged into the creature's mouth and a deft twist as the noble's hand sliced its face in half, leaving only the lower mandible connected to the rest of its form.

"Keep your distance!" Remy ordered the other guards, snapping out Breaker's twin scythes. The knifechain tumbled into his hand, and Remy looped it through the air, curving it down to strike at another rampaging monster through its chest, pivoting to attack with his scythes in one measured swipe that promptly took its head off.

But the mutations were already targeting the other soldiers. An unfortunate guard screamed as he went down, the sound cutting off when one of the creature's teeth tore through his throat. "Keep your distance!" Remy hollered again, planting himself between the rest of the men and the creatures closing in. He spun the chain around himself, the cylinder in his hands blurring into a spinning arc above his head, a rhythm he'd mastered since he'd been but a novice, until he'd created a personal, nearly impervious shield about his person. An infected drew near and promptly lost three limbs. Its scream was abruptly cut off when Remy's flying blades found their mark with another flick of his hand, ripping swiftly through its throat before gutting its stomach.

Several lunged for his knifechain at the same time, slowing down the momentum of his swing even as they ignored the limbs Breaker lopped off. Remy was forced to keep turning constantly as the attacks came from all directions, cutting swathes through the creatures even as they closed in on him.

Xiaodan reappeared behind one of the infected attacking Remy, hand already raised and angled away, a cutting gesture. Remy didn't see the attack, but he did see the creature falling apart, gobs of flesh and meat spattering the ground.

The vampiress was gone again, blurring into view beside a second mutation, crosshatching it into segments within seconds. In another ten, she had done the same to the rest of the creatures before Remy could do more.

Smiling, Malekh cut down the last of the infected standing. "You needn't worry about her," the noble said calmly. "You'd need more saving than she does."

Remy already had his knives out; it was almost a shame he couldn't stab his ally, too. "These were all the bodies at the lab?"

"It would appear so. Someone knew that the bodies were to be transported today, took steps before Riones and the other Reapers could get to them."

"They already got to some of the Reapers." Remy stood over one of the creatures he'd killed, staring down at the familiar, ripped clothing. Now he recognized its partial features, disfigured as it was, and the one remaining blue eye. "Maxwell Scorenge," he said. Not the first time he'd had to identify a fellow Reaper by their remains, but it never got easier. "He was helping Riones transport the bodies. Just how quickly does the infection spread?"

"Far quicker than it should. Even quicker than I feared, Lord Riones."

The marquess had returned to the scene, his face ashen as he took in the dead, decomposing bodies strewn about them. Several men were dragging a heavy case behind him. "That's Scorenge," he choked out. "Mierda. What happened in there?"

"Is that my serum?" Malekh asked him, nodding to the chest.

"Yes, but how—"

"Take all the men you can spare and throw these bodies into a pile. Find the nearest apothecary and procure as many syringes from them as you can. Inject the serum into every body you can find—one part mixture to two parts water—one cc should be more than enough for each. You'll know you've succeeded when you see a thick cocoon-like layer form over their skin. Cart them into Giantsmound, as Her Majesty ordered, and keep them under guard there. We will incinerate every last piece of flesh from these remains, and we shall do it outside the city. Elouve has been compromised enough as it is. Do you understand, Riones?"

"Yes," the other man said. "If it'll keep any more of them from rising, I'll do it. You heard him!" He roared at the other, terrified soldiers. "Take yourselves to Madame Sophia's and bring back all the needles she can provide us!"

"I smell something bad," Xiaodan said.

"I believe that goes without saying," Remy grunted, watching the soldiers run.

"No. It's not just the Rot. I smell vampire."

"Vampires don't smell like anything."

"Not to humans, no."

"Are you telling me there may be vampires inside the Archives along with those already infected?"

"After the war between my court and the Fifth, I heard rumors that some of Etrienne's men not young enough to be ashed were sent back to Elouve for study." Malekh's smile was cold. "Astonbury issued a statement denying it then. He'd always struck me as someone who thought he was cleverer than he really was. The morgue he maintains appears to have more than just the infected in storage. Agenot was keeping things from us."

He stood. "I want eyes on every inch of the building, Riones. Anything so much as twitches, I want it taken down. How many personnel still inside?"

"There must be at least four more scientists in there," Riones said crisply, "and two more Reapers unaccounted for, excluding Scorenge."

"We must flush them out before they escape into the populace. Xiaodan and I will head in to hunt for survivors."

"I'm going with you," Remy interjected.

"You are human," the noble said dismissively.

"If you think I can't handle a building full of mutated bastards, then you should have complained more when Xiaodan invited me along," Remy said. "If I'm bait, as you say, then there's no better time to put me to good use than here. And if I do wind up getting myself eaten by one of these horrors, then you can wash your hands of me. Cheerfully cremate my remains, if you'd like. Pour your little augmented coagulant whatsit on my bones and give me a rousing send-off at daybreak. But if I stomp on inside and prove I can take on any infected and vampires within, then you owe me. Even if the vampire arse I beat winds up being yours."

It took counting five of his own heartbeats before Zidan's mouth tilted up, albeit not in any amused, genial way, briefly exposing a good amount of fang. It took another five before the noble turned away. "The three of us shall be entering the Ministry," he said to Riones. "If we do not return in the next two hours, you are to set the whole building on fire."

"Lord Malekh!" the lord protested.

"Even that may not completely stop its spread. The alternative is three hundred thousand in the city exposed to the Rot. Her Majesty will know what to do next."

"Now that that's settled . . ." Xiaodan strode toward the main entrance. Before anyone could stop her, she had wrenched the doors open, splintering the frame in her eagerness, and stepped inside.

Malekh sighed. "My fiancée grows impatient. The queen is your priority, Riones. We'll do the rest."

THE DOOR to the laboratory stood wide open, this time with no Dr. Agenot to welcome them in.

Beyond it was a slaughterhouse.

Many of the bodies strewn about within had not undergone the rapid decay that so marked the Rot mutations, but none of them were . . . intact, for lack of a better word. Staring at the grisly remains, Remy could barely fight off a wave of nausea. He hoped they'd all been dead before they'd been ripped apart, half-consumed, and then further decimated.

He spotted Agenot's body. The doctor was staring mutely at the wall, mouth parted in an expression of surprise. Remy was glad to see no fear on the man's face—mayhap there had been no pain for him. The rest of the doctor's lower body lay propped against the wall he was gaping lifelessly at, a bloody track on the ground connecting both.

"Light," Remy said.

"I can still smell them," Xiaodan whispered.

Malekh was prowling the room, ignoring the other sprawled bodies there in favor of inspecting the equipment. "I can't find it," he said.

"The rest of Agenot's body? It's right here. It's all bloody here." Remy had found two more assistants. What he thought were two, anyway. There was far too much blood to be just the one, but too few limbs to be more than that.

Malekh ignored him. "Agenot looked to have been re-creating my serum when the attack occurred. But the vials are missing."

"Perhaps he stored it somewhere else beforehand," Xiaodan suggested.

"Maybe." Malekh didn't sound convinced.

"Could have shattered during the fight," Remy grunted. He counted at least three more people in the room, in no better shape. "Oh, fuck."

"What's wrong?" Xiaodan asked.

"Found the other Reapers." Pyalia had clearly bled out, her throat horribly mangled. Oswald Craggart, on the other hand, sat with his back to the wall, mouth still twisted in rage. His fire lance, unused, lay beside him.

"I'm sorry. Were they friends of yours?"

"Not really. But they weren't mauled like the others." Remy used Breaker to push Craggart's coat to one side, revealing a deep wound on his chest. "I don't think it's the infected that got to them. These look to have been made with weapons."

"This should lead to the yakhchāl." Malekh nodded toward another door near Craggart's prone form. That it was also open did not inspire confidence.

"May as well," Remy said, already moving toward it. He had some knowledge of architecture—enough to know that the Archives was a hideous-looking piece of shit, objectively speaking—but wasn't familiar with how the cone-like structure could lower temperatures enough to keep items within it frozen. The more pressing business was that he could detect no amount of cold whatsoever coming from within the room, which he presumed was a bad sign.

Unexpectedly, his chest throbbed.

Remy turned just in time.

His instincts were the main reason the creature hadn't already opened up his chest. Instead, there was only a clanging sound as its claws hit cylinder, Remy planting the weapon between himself and his attacker in the nick of time. It was another infected, as swollen and as massive and as dirtbag-ugly as its fellows. Remy shoved it hard, and the creature stumbled back.

Malekh was on it, his saber flashing. The creature's head slid noisily off its shoulders, and the rest of its body followed its slide down toward the ground with a nasty squish.

"I didn't need your help," Remy said.

"I'm sure you didn't." Malekh was already whipping out another syringe—how many of these things was the coxswab hiding in his coat?—pushing the needle into the creature's body. "Stay close," he said as he stood back up and strode into the yakhchāl. Remy stabbed at the new corpse at his feet unnecessarily with his scythe, then followed a few feet behind.

The room was larger than he expected. There was little to differentiate it from the standard morgue, with a similar iron table at the center for autopsies and large human-sized cabinets where the bodies lay stored, stacked atop one another. But the floor was wet, and there were small blocks of ice puddling in the corners. Dr. Agenot said that the room was always kept cold. The melting ice around them and the fact that Remy was sweating meant the location had been compromised.

Malekh slid the nearest cabinet open. It was empty. "The doctor said there would be about two dozen corpses in here. Though given everything, I'm inclined to believe he lied about that as well."

Remy tugged another open—nothing inside there, either. "We fought about twenty of those bastards outside," he said, "minus the one that attacked me in the lab, which means there are at least four or five more that are unaccounted for. Not including any Fifth

Court bodies Astonbury might have stolen, if he did." He opened another and stared at the corpse laid out within, teeth bared to reveal its vampiric nature, but otherwise lifeless. "Three or four now," he amended.

There were two more corpses still in stasis inside the yakhchāl, bringing their count down to another two still missing. Remy's heart sank; Lady Daneira's body had not been among them.

"Astonbury, you old fool," Malekh hissed quietly as he yanked open the last of the storage compartments. Peering inside, Remy detected another corpse, this time much more considerably mummified than the others, as if it had been residing there for much longer.

"This is Arnoso Steinbeck," his companion said. "A Fifth Court vampire. I know this because I killed him myself during the war. Astonbury *did* bring in dead Fifth Court vampires to Elouve. This one is safely dead, at least."

Closing the door behind them after Malekh had given the fresh corpses their necessary shots, they resumed their search.

"Zidan," Xiaodan said softly. "Do you smell that?"

Remy didn't, but Malekh's brow furrowed. "Yes. Vampire."

"It could be a trap. An attempt to lure us farther in. It's coming from here." Xiaodan stepped through another doorway. Malekh headed in after her. Remy was poised to follow, but a scraping noise caught his attention.

It was coming from the vault that had once held Tal Harveston's corpse prisoner.

The window had been shattered, pieces of it scattered among the levers and switches, but the steel door inside was firmly shut.

A woman stood before it, clawing in vain at the wall. "Urgghh," she moaned. "Rnnghaa."

Remy knew who she was before she turned to face him. His heart twisted painfully. "Lady Daneira."

He almost didn't recognize her. Something had caused her

face to melt away, leaving nothing but empty eye sockets and a layer of tissue and what he could only assume was fat resembling gelatinized soup. But her hair, her one vanity, was still as thick and as lustrous as ever, settling around a head that sat neatly on her shoulders like he hadn't sliced it off at their last encounter.

Everything else about her was repulsive. Similar to Harveston, parts of her were in the later stages of decomposition, in a perpetual cycle of decay and regeneration where bits of her looked ready to slough off on their own, the rest healing just enough to keep her mostly intact.

"Nghaaa," she gurgled, raising her arms to him.

He should have moved by now, finished what he'd started from what felt like a lifetime ago. But Remy remained rooted to the spot, paralyzed as she approached him, unable to look away.

She rushed at him without warning, even faster than when she was newly turned. Remy's reflexes finally kicked in.

Breaker sliced into her. Her wounds made no spatter, her body simply falling over with a wet, squelching sound.

Remy backed out of the room—and ducked a sword that had been hurtling toward his head. He blocked the next blow with Breaker's base, and then whipped the knifechain into a sweeping arc before him to keep the new attacker out of reach.

His new opponent didn't look like any of the other infected. He looked remarkably human, with all the expected body parts where they were supposed to be, and free of any discernible decay. He was golden-haired and blue-eyed, about six inches of height over Remy, with milky-white skin and strong, handsome features. Only his fangs gave him away—they were long and sharp.

"Another Reaper," the vampire laughed, eyes alight with malicious glee. "Another prize for me."

"Who in the bloody hell are you?"

"I was hoping to find Malekh, but you'll do for now. You must be his newest plaything—he always did have an itch for the brunettes." The vampire swooped closer, but Remy's chain kept him at bay. "Oh, and you can fight, too! Wouldn't it—"

The knifechain wrapped around the man's waist; one jerk was enough to snap it free. "— be grand—"

The vampire disappeared from view, rematerialized behind Remy. "—if I were to—"

Remy turned and yanked Breaker up just in time; his assailant's fangs probed for flesh and hit nothing but weapon.

"—leave a pretty mark on you for him to find?" With almost no effort, the vampire dragged Breaker to the side, leaving his throat exposed.

Remy was going to lose. The fangs were inches away from his neck. All the vampire needed to do was shove Breaker two more inches to the right, and nothing would have stopped him. The man smiled, sensing victory, and yanked the scythe away with a triumphant snarl.

Remy released his hold on Breaker, kicked at the knifechain that lay on the ground at his feet. It leaped up, wrapped around his foot. He kicked out and it unraveled again, struck at the vampire's face when the latter shot forward.

The fair-haired bloodsucker reappeared several feet away, hands clasped against one eye. "You little bitch!" he hissed. "I'm going to make sure you die slowly."

"You will do no such thing, Vasilik." Remy didn't see how Malekh had found his way between him and the other vampire, and he would die before showing his relief. "Sanchin swore he saw you perish at Etrienne's lair."

"Sanchin knows little of so many things, as do you." Vasilik grinned around the trickle of blood still streaming down his face. "Many things can escape notice if you don't look hard enough. And you never looked hard enough for me, did you, Zidan?" He blurred from view once again. Malekh took off after him without another word.

"Leave them be," Xiaodan said from behind Remy, sounding weary, and he jumped. "My apologies. I didn't mean to startle you. We took care of the rest. The Archives are secured."

"That vampire—Basilisk or whatever—he didn't have the Rot." Remy crouched down to retrieve his broken chain, heart still pounding. "There could be more like him lying in wait."

"There's no one else here. His scent was the only one I could detect, though he'd used that as a ploy to come after you first." She was holding something in her left hand—a badly bent pair of eyeglasses, the wire frames twisted and both lenses missing. She held it out for him to see. "Found it stuck to one of the mutations inside. It looked so odd on a creature that was no longer . . ." Xiaodan's smile bloomed with relief. "I'm glad you're all right. Vasilik used to be a member of the Third Court. Zidan's former . . ."

She shrugged and sighed. "He switched his allegiance to the Fifth to spite Zidan, but it seems he didn't die in battle as we thought. And while he is more than capable of bearing long grudges, Malekh says he doesn't have the necessary scientific knowledge to engineer a plague of this scale. I don't know if he's working in league with someone else or simply exploiting the situation. But it's clear Vasilik knows enough about the infection to join in the chaos. Likely he was the one to have started all this, perhaps sabotaged the ice."

"He killed Craggart and Pyalia. That much I can tell."

Xiaodan held out a small container of clear, shimmering liquid in her other hand. "This was what Agenot was working on," she said. "It looks like he discovered something before the attack came. Stored it inside one of his lockboxes before he fled, which may have cost him his life. Malekh has no idea what it is yet, but if Agenot chose to save it instead of himself, then it may be something important. I hope it is. I don't think Aluria can take much more of this."

"I hope it is, too," Remy said, mind still spinning at how close the new vampire had come to tearing his throat out. He looked at the carnage around them, at how close the creatures had come to getting loose in the city. "Because I'm not sure I can take much more of this, either."

12

CLEANSING

The deaths at the Ministry of the Archives had left Xiaodan even more adamant about returning to Chànggē Shuǐ as soon as possible, but not before making a few stipulations.

"First," she said to the now-humbled Feiron, who realized very quickly that, as the highest-ranking person after Astonbury, he would most likely be blamed for the current situation, "you will allow me to obliterate the infected bodies immediately—allow, of course, meaning that I have commanded you to do so and you will obey. Gather as many Reapers as you are permitted to, to stand guard until I have accomplished my mission. I do not foresee any objections on their end. Giantsmound will be far enough away from the city and from anywhere else you consider human habitation."

"We will still need Her Majesty's permission for the other—"

"Her Majesty has given me special permission to issue orders on her behalf for this particular event. Seek her out yourself if you doubt me. And, my Lord Feiron—" Xiaodan leaned forward, smiling. "If I so much as hear one sheaf of paper being pushed around as an excuse to delay the process, you will have more to answer to than just Her Majesty and her wrath. You shall have to answer to me, and I will not be so forgiving."

Lord Feiron visibly swallowed, the knob in his throat bobbing like a fishing lure. "I understand, Your Ma—uh, Lady Song."

As pleased as Remy was to see Lord Feiron so thoroughly put in his place, he had a few pressing concerns. First, though he would not be shedding tears over Astonbury's passing, the man had nonetheless managed to keep the Archives and the bureaucracy within it running smoothly. Feiron had proven himself woefully inept to take up command, and Remy wasn't keen on the idea of leaving Elouve to accompany the two vampires to parts unknown while things in the city collapsed in his absence. Not that he had ever stayed long in Elouve to influence anything beyond which married woman's bed to occupy at night, and at times not even then, but Vasilik's infiltration had left him worried all the same.

The one person in charge of Elouve who actually knew what they were doing was Queen Ophelia, who promised to appoint someone worthier than Feiron for the job. "I've also taken the liberty of asking the other scientists to focus on fast-tracking the serum you kindly provided for us," she told Malekh. "Every research they've conducted so far, including the ones Dr. Agenot had been working on, shall be copied by my scribes and made available to you the morning before you depart. Perhaps you can make better sense of it, or find the means to improve upon them."

"I will send word of any breakthroughs I might find, Your Majesty," the noble promised. "Although what would aid me tremendously in my own research would be the blood-splicing equipment Agenot used, the one that helped him expound on my discovery. My own laboratory is in sore need of an upgrade, and it would be beneficial to have one for my own."

"Is it so very important?"

"Very much so, Your Majesty. It will allow me to trace blood to a specific person rather than merely to a specific blood type. Agenot, for instance, has taken samples from Astonbury's study. We can use it to determine within a reasonable degree of certainty whose blood it was at the scene. I hope to do the same to the samples from these infected bodies."

"The medical apparatuses that you ask for are classified, my dear Lord Malekh, as I'm sure you already know," the queen said severely. Then she sighed. "But I suppose we can afford to spare one for you. You saved my people from an outbreak that could have taken more lives than it already has."

"Thank you, Your Majesty. I would also like to provide the hunters with the information I have collected regarding the various mutations we have encountered so far, with suggestions as to the best forms of defense against them."

"You have a very good fiancé, Xiaodan," the queen said approvingly. "Were he human and unclaimed, I would have married him off to one of my daughters by now."

"Very fortunate, then, that he is neither of those," Xiaodan responded glibly.

The queen's wandering eyes rested on Remy. "I'm sure there are others who have served Aluria nobly who would be just as qualified for such an honor."

"I'm sure you will find many of those even beyond this throne room." Xiaodan's reply was much more acidic in tone this time, but Queen Ophelia only laughed, looking oddly pleased with herself. All of it was lost on Remy, who was only beginning to understand the extent of what he'd just signed up for.

THE ARCHIVES building was being properly fumigated, as the official decree had been worded, and the Reapers were sweeping every floor of the building to smoke out anything else, vampire, infected, or otherwise, that might still be lurking within. The morgue was duly cleaned and emptied of all of its undead, per Xiaodan's command. Oswald Craggart, Lei Pyalia, and Harry Kibold's bodies had been taken out first and placed solemnly in separate wagons; the queen had already announced her intentions to host a state funeral for them. But Maxwell Scorenge's lay alongside the other infected, unable to enjoy the same honors.

Remy sat by a corner and watched the black-clothed hunters stream in and out of the Ministry, trying not to let exhaustion get to him. He should be feeling regret. He should be feeling guilt at killing Lady Daneira all over again—whether or not he'd been given the choice was no longer important. He couldn't imagine what the Tennyfairs must be feeling, and could only hope for their sakes that this would be her last resurrection. It helped to remember that whatever it was he had encountered at the vault had no longer been her, just a husk that something else had occupied.

It was a good day to be a newsboy. A few had set up shop half a block away from the Archives, waving broadsheets at the crowd that had gathered to watch the grisly cleanup. The papers were selling fast; and for good reason, with headlines like THE SUN VAMPIRE: ATROCITY OR IRONY? and KINDRED IN THE CITY: AN EXCLUSIVE INTERVIEW WITH LADY XIAODAN SONG from the *Wayward Post* that Remy knew to be horseshit. That didn't matter to the public. The truth rarely did.

Elke was looking particularly attractive that day, dressed in a billowing blue skirt and a matching corset, a parasol resting on the slope of one shoulder. She sat down beside him as he continued to watch the Archives' spring cleaning, rearranging her skirts to make herself more comfortable. "So I hear that Vasilik Preobrazhensky is still alive," she began conversationally. Remy considered it a good thing that she said his name with no trace of fear, given the wanted vampire's affiliation with the Fifth Court.

"Malekh gave chase, but he couldn't catch him."

"Vasilik was always like that," Elke said. "Always wanting the credit, never thinking about the consequences. I'm not surprised that he would show himself and brag, when he would have been better off staying hidden. He always resented being subservient to Etrienne. The Fifth Court welcomed him, but his stigma for forsaking the Third remained. Etrienne never fully trusted him. You were never to betray your Court for any reason, no matter the provocation, he always said. Most kindred think the same, consider it anathema. Vasilik knew that and worked hard to be twice as cruel. If he's out there and believes you to be a close associate of Lord Malekh and Lady Song . . ."

"There's already a bullseye on my arse however you spin it," Remy said. "I pissed him off back there. He seems exactly the type to hold a grudge."

"It's more than that. Vasilik was a high noble of the Third Court before he was expelled. He and Lord Malekh have history. I know little of the details, but I know that Vasilik enjoyed targeting anyone Lord Malekh associated with by the time he'd joined the Fifth. That includes Lady Song." She paused. "Do you really intend to go with them? I understand your reasons to, but . . ."

"If I don't," Remy said, "then I'll be no closer to the truth. You're one of the very few reasons I'd choose to stay. I'm too strange for the dræfendgemot, too scandal-ridden to ever truly be a part of them. Already there are fresh rumors about me. That Feiron arrested me is no secret, nor that the vampires had spoken up on my behalf. If anything, they'll be all the more convinced that I'm exactly the dhampir they always believed me to be. I'm right, aren't I? You've always been on top of the gossip, even if you try to spare me from hearing it."

Elke looked helpless. It was all the confirmation he needed.

"Whoever Her Majesty decides should replace Astonbury, I doubt I'd find a real place in their new administration. I'd be right back where I started—scrounging for information with pillow talk, relying on desperate villagers and merchants for information. Ironically enough, the court vampires have none of those prejudices."

"I could go with you."

Remy snorted. "That'll only put a target on *your* back in Aluria. Besides, you love it here. All the men and women dancing in attendance on you, all the wine you can drink."

"The butchers do reserve the best of their bloodiest kidneys for me," Elke agreed. She sighed heavily.

"I need you here," said Remy. "Be my eyes and ears while I'm gone, like you always have."

Elke smiled wryly. "Why must you always insist on putting yourself in danger while doing your best to persuade me out of it?"

He had to grin. "Because it doesn't make sense to put us both in trouble when I can do it perfectly fine all on my own. You know where Lady Song's home is? At the eastern borders along Aluria?"

She nodded. "I've been there once before, back when all Eight Courts still honored their alliances. There were more Fourth Court vampires then. I suppose it would look very different now."

"That's where we're headed. If anything else happens in Elouve, send word to me there." He hesitated. "I haven't spoken to my father about this yet. He's set on staying in Elouve indefinitely— he would, with Astonbury gone. If his health takes a turn for the worse, send word as quickly as you can."

"I shall go to you myself. Will you return if something does happen to him?"

Remy paused, longer this time. "I don't know. It's not like there's much I can do. I dislike Yost, but as a doctor, he's worth the exorbitant fees my father pays him."

Elke sighed again. "Are you sure about this, Remy? Once you get yourself fully involved in Court business, there'll be no turning back."

Remy watched as the main doors of the Archives opened and grim-looking Reapers emerged, carrying the last of the body bags. "There was no turning back for me since the day I returned to Elouve," he said.

The funeral of Lord Matthew Delacroix, the late duke of Astonbury, took place a few hours later. Remy chose not to attend.

THE BODIES burned quickly enough, but Remy supposed there was a reason they called her the Sunbringer. Even the two deceased Fifth Court vampires they'd found were consigned to her flames, their fangs and frozen expressions the closest thing to human among the lot. By the time the light faded from Xiaodan, and Remy had rubbed the glare from his eyes, the corpses were gone, with nothing to show for themselves but mounds of ash that the swift winds took care of, blowing them across the plains into obsoleteness. As Remy watched the breeze carry off what had been left of Lady Daneira, he finally felt part of the burden lift from him, however slight.

Xiaodan swayed slightly on her feet but refused to fall when she had an audience, a crowd still wary and hostile around the edges. She climbed back into the carriage that had brought her to Giantsmound with her head held high, face serene. Malekh wasn't with her, which was unusual.

She never looked Remy's way, but it didn't matter. "He's her familiar, they say," one of the Reapers behind him muttered. "Heard how she defended him to the queen?"

"The sun inside of her should have burned her to a crisp. We'd have one less fangblood to worry over."

"The Third Court king didn't say a word, it's told. Maybe he doesn't care. Maybe he's fucking him, too."

Remy turned around, furious, but the Reapers had melted back into their clusters, and none of them would look him in the face.

"That burning was something, wasn't it?" Riones asked, oblivious. Remy had seen fear and suspicion take the place of the other hunters' initial astonishment, but the marquess was as sincere as always, a toss-up between curious and impressed. "Surely she couldn't be popular among her other kindred given the ability she has."

"She isn't," Remy confirmed. "I believe her clan was ostracized for it."

"A shame," Riones said. "Though if I were a vampire, she'd worry me, too. We could use something like that ourselves. Fire lances can only do so much, and even then, it takes an awful long time for them to reload."

"So does she, Riones." Remy watched the carriage roll back to the city, leaving them behind. "So does she."

THERE HAD always been preachers in Elouve. In a city ruled by gold and genteel decadence, most of the citizens were ripe for guilt. A few of the more outspoken sermoners were of the hellfire-and-brimstone variety, but they've always avoided Gold Street and its mansions, knowing full well that their admonitions would be little appreciated there.

One pastor dared to defy convention that day. He stood before Alhmeister House on a makeshift pulpit, one hand carrying a heavy tome while the other was extended into the air above him, as if granting benediction. He wore a simple white robe and the plain triangular cap that proclaimed one a self-professed servant of the Light. The crowd gathering around him lent credence to his blistering tirades.

"We have turned our back against the Light!" he boomed in a voice designed to be heard well past the upper floors of the parliament house. "And now the Great Mother, the Kindly One, the Just and the Merciful—it is for *our* sins that she has sent this plague upon us, as punishment for our selfishness! Only after we have cleansed ourselves in spirit and repent can she seek to lift this aberration from us, but even then, it is not enough! We must call on the queen herself to rid her kingdom of those who conspire against the Light, who seek to corrupt our souls with their vile vices! Away with these lavish feasts and galas, away with the greedy rich who dance in their mansions and laugh while we starve in the streets! It is *they* who tempt this plague upon us, and it is *we* who suffer the consequences! Not even the Duke of Astonbury was exempt from the Light's retribution! Who else shall the corruption take before it is too late, before we are forever exiled from the Three's grace? Will it be you? Will it be you? Or—you! Sir! It shall be you!"

Remy had taken a step back, but the man's keen eyes had singled him out. The preacher's voice rose several octaves, hovering into near shrieks. "You, the familiar who has taken into himself a vampire's lust! You, whose unholy nature has brought upon us this wretched curse! You foul dhampir! Fornicator of the undead! Despicable demon! I send thee away! Cast no shadows upon Elouve! Purify yourself before the Light, lest the rope and the fires of damnation take you!"

"Shut that mouth, heretic!" one of the Reapers shouted at him.

"He's right, though," another said, an Astonbury lackey named Hathorn, who shot a disgusted look Remy's way. "How the cambion caught Her Majesty's attention, I can't—"

But the sermoner's audience was surging forward. "Warlock!" Someone within the mob shrieked, latching on to the man's hatred. "Vampire's get!"

"I hope you don't mind if I don't follow you inside, Riones,"

Remy said tersely. He was used to being mocked. He was used to being whispered about. But never so openly before.

His newest status as vampire lust vessel aside, he felt an odd twinge of relief. He had not wanted to enter today's dræfendge-mot. The queen's blessing had sated his desire to be acknowledged as a Reaper—everything else would smack of performativity. Only Riones truly liked him. The rest would continue to believe every-thing the priest was already spewing about him, even though it was the doomsayer they were removing from the premises.

As it turned out, the marquess already had things planned, directing him toward the side of the building. "There is a hansom that we use around the back. Take it and bring it around later once we've settled matters here. They've been getting a little too sure of themselves lately, these preachers. They've been noisier since the first of the infections started doing the rounds, but after As-tonbury's death . . . Not much headway there, by the way, far as I know. The other servants didn't see anything amiss that night. Half the time, they don't even notice Wellsmith. Astonbury didn't like to make his comings and goings known, even to his colleagues."

The carriage came within view. Riones shoved a satchel into his hands. "I wanted to wait until we were inside, but I figure you can look at these now. You're not likely to miss much—Feiron's probably going to deliver an hour-long lecture on why all this wasn't his fault. I'd almost prefer the doomsayer sermon."

"Riones, what—"

"The queen herself instructed me to deliver this to you per-sonally. It contains all the known intelligence we've received of the First Court vampires over the years. It's not much, sadly—half a dozen reports. No one's really focused much on the Night Em-press and her allies, so she thought you'd be good for presenting your findings at the next dræfendgemot. They say you'll be leaving Elouve tomorrow with the vampires, so I'll likely do so on your behalf—"

"I'll have it ready by then." Remy was grinning. "You're a good friend, Riones. I'd feel better if they put you in charge of everything before I leave."

"Only doing what I was ordered to do, Pendergast," Riones said heartily. "Now, get out of here. Might have to punch a priest if things get too heated, and I'd likely have to spend the rest of the day doing ablution for it."

13

INVESTIGATIONS

Remy was in a much dourer mood by the time he returned to Kinaiya Lodge. Elke waited for him, nearly unrecognizable from her usual dress with her blacksmith's apron and her hair carefully coiled up under a foreman's cap.

"You are not to say a word," she said placidly, handing him a cup of strong coffee when he looked to argue. "I'm here because I have need of your forge, for both your benefit and mine. Perhaps we can have a quiet dinner together later." She spotted the satchel. "Your first official day as part of the dræfendgemot, and I see they've already given you most of the work."

"Are you aware of the preachers going about the city, shouting sermons to anyone who'll listen?"

"One nearly caused a riot a few weeks ago. I believe that was when word of the mutations first spread about. They claimed that Astonbury had been responsible, said he'd been carting in corpses for dark rituals. As you can imagine, the lord high steward put a stop to it quickly." She frowned. "Did something happen?"

He decided not to alarm her. "Best you get people to keep an eye on them. They may know more about what's happening than they let on." A drop of truth in a goblet of lies. The preachers had made the rest of it up, but they'd known about Astonbury's corpses, somehow. "The forge is yours. Right now, I need to get to work." The bag felt heavy in his hands.

"You'd best give me the clothes you intend to bring along while you're at it," Elke said. "Heap them up on your bed."

"I'm not asking you to wash them for—"

"Of course not, you beautiful dunce. If I'll be fine-tuning your weapons, I may as well make some modification to your garb. Oh, don't look at me like that. I won't be hammering steel into your well-trimmed coats. I've always said that you rely far too much on Breaker. Knives saved you inside the Archives. Spread them out a little more, keep them closer to your skin. All I'll be requiring is a needle and some strong thread."

Finally, Remy cracked a smile. "You really are worried, aren't you?"

"Of course I am. Incidentally, before you bury your sweet head into those reports, I'll be taking Breaker. Time to iron out what dents I can find before you go and mess it up further."

IT WAS the knock on the door hours later that broke Remy's concentration. He squinted out the window; it had been gray and foggy when he'd first begun his reading, and it was still gray and foggy, but now with even less light to see through. The tiny clock on his dresser proclaimed it to be an hour after dinner should have been taken.

It shouldn't have taken this long, but he was pleased at what he'd accomplished so far. He'd marked off areas in the map where sightings had been reported, used it to determine other vulnerable places, villages that needed better protection. Elke had offered to help—he would have been done hours ago if she had—but

Remy had been stubborn about doing it on his own. He couldn't rely on her forever.

"Remy," Elke's voice came through the door, slightly uncertain. "You have visitors."

She didn't need to tell him the specifics, because Remy already knew it would be Xiaodan before he'd stepped foot outside his room. That Malekh was with her was the surprise, the noble eyeing his admittedly semi-dusty surroundings with a faint whiff of disapproval. The man had breezed through the Archives' mortuary with no issues despite the revolting smell and even more revolting lack of ventilation, and yet chose to find fault with his lodge. The easy answer was that Malekh was still, in his very passive-aggressive way, trying to goad him into irritability. Unfortunately, it was working.

Xiaodan was on the sofa, a cup of coffee already in her hands. She took no sips from it, only looking intent on using the beverage to warm her hands. She smiled at him, looking worn out as she always did after burning things to a crisp, but otherwise still alert. She was unsettlingly attractive as always, dressed in a simple green qipao that showed far too much leg and heavy riding boots that stopped at her knees.

Malekh had declined his sitting privileges. He remained motionless at one corner, though his eyes were everywhere, taking in the lodge's furnishings. He was wrapped in black from the neck down to his footwear, but despite the shapeless mass he presented, somehow still looked elegant.

"I thought I'd let you know how the investigation into Astonbury's murder has been going," Xiaodan began pleasantly. "Among a few other things that Zidan feels you ought to know before tomorrow."

Remy's eyes shot toward Malekh, who, apparently oblivious to what his fiancée had just said, was inspecting his walls with a faintly condescending air.

"Before we begin, I trust that what I'm about to say next does not leave this room?" Xiaodan raised an eyebrow at Elke.

Elke sat up straighter. "I understand that you have many reasons to doubt me, Lady Song. Anyone from the Fifth Court deserves such suspicion. But Remy saved me. I escaped the massacre you and your fiancé wrought at our keep. I spent the next several years half-dying everywhere I went and would have eventually perished had Remy not taken me in."

"You knowingly helped a vampire?" Xiaodan asked, startled.

"I wasn't very bright as a youth, either," Remy said. "Children like to take in strays, but even then, I wanted to be different. She'd been in no shape to attack me, even if she wanted to."

"He found me shelter," Elke continued, "sent to the butcher for all the cow's blood I could drink—it no doubt contributed to the rumors that he was a cambion himself in later years. He's like a younger brother to me. I will protect him with my life if necessary."

The women traded glances. Xiaodan nodded. "As to the murder, well . . . they've run out of suspects, so I insisted they question the witnesses again. Did you know that the butler has been missing since yesterday?"

"Butler?" Remy asked, temporarily at a loss.

"Astonbury's valet, Wellsmith. No one's seen him since the day before last. It's the general belief that he's fled to the countryside, fearful that he would be blamed for his master's death. My specific belief, on the other hand, is that he was paid to leave without anyone else knowing—or that he's been killed to prevent him from saying what he did know."

Remy swung his sights from Malekh back to her, like the world's fastest pendulum. "What makes you think he even knows anything?"

"He's the only person we've found who could swear to the suspect's description. Didn't you find anything wrong with his account of that night?"

Remy shook his head.

Little puffs of air accompanied Xiaodan's laughter. "He described you perfectly. Dark skin, average height, black eyes—down to the scar on his arm, like yours. There aren't all that many dark-skinned, black-haired young men of average height and Tithian ancestry in the city to begin with, but to have another one with the exact same wound? Wellsmith went out of his way to implicate you."

"But I've never even met him."

"Someone could have paid him to lie," Malekh said from the shadows. "Wellsmith had served Astonbury for many years, long before the duke assumed the high stewardship. I thought it might be blackmail, but as far as I can see, the valet led a fairly blameless life. Then I realized that while we were so intent on finding the man Wellsmith had described, we were quite lapse at describing Wellsmith instead."

Xiaodan smacked the table with glee. Remy, slower to the challenge, stared blankly at them.

"The staff at the Archives all described Wellsmith the same way," Malekh explained. "Thin, lanky build, pale, a forgettable face, spectacles. Even Feiron admitted that he found him easy to overlook."

Remy finally understood. "Are you saying Wellsmith himself was an impostor?"

"The investigators certainly didn't know him by face, and he'd distanced himself enough from the rest of the staff that the other servants would never look at him twice." Xiaodan dug into her pocket and, with a victorious air, produced the familiar wrecked pair of glasses she had taken off one of the creatures in the Archives. "I kept a tally of bodies within the laboratory. Twenty-four in total, including the ones they tried to hide from us." She paused again, eyes dancing. "I burned twenty-five bodies today. The servants may have ignored Wellsmith for the most part, but they did recognize his spectacles."

"So he was already dead in the mortuary," Remy echoed, mind ablaze by this new development. "For how long?"

"Far more than several days. All while someone claiming to be Wellsmith had been answering Feiron's questions," Malekh said. "The swelling can cover a lot of the decomposition on the infected, but there's only so many days' worth of decay you can ignore. By the time Astonbury's murder was discovered, his valet had been dead for even longer. If Feiron still thinks he'll be getting the late duke's position, he'll have a difficult time trying to explain how he questioned one of the murderers and then let him go. Someone knew enough about the Archives to store Wellsmith's body there."

"That is sound investigative work," Elke said.

"All Zidan's fault, I'm afraid. My fiancé fancies himself a detective. He's even rather good at it." Xiaodan looked pleased, grinning at Remy like she was expecting him to applaud her on Malekh's behalf. Elke took the bait and clapped cheerfully.

"It's the most logical conclusion," the lord said, with little trace of modesty. "It explains most things about the case, though not all of it. Who impersonated the butler? And why? Who stands to benefit from Astonbury's death?"

"My father, for one," Remy said laconically. "Although, as they've been feuding long before I was born, I don't see why he would suddenly choose to kill him off now. He's too sickly to take advantage of it. And not many people in Elouve would be willing to risk murder for a Pendergast."

"Something to cross off his list before he dies, if he's as petty as you say?" Xiaodan frowned. "Do you know of any allies Lord Pendergast might have had within the Archives?"

"I'm not exactly privy to my father's secrets, but I doubt that. There are factions within the Archives that would like to see Astonbury gone, but my father's more despised than the lord high steward in certain circles. As far as most are concerned, he's a

relic with little influence in Alurian politics. The Marquess of Riones would be able to tell you about that more than I can."

"And why is he despised?" Malekh asked suddenly. "Was it because of his past conduct as a Reaper, or is it because they, too,
doubt your parentage?"

"Some believe me to be of vampire stock," Remy said shortly,
not prepared to extend the same patience to the noble as he had
done Xiaodan. "But you seem knowledgeable enough about my
family that you didn't need to ask that."

Malekh looked like he was about to say something else—but
then, surprisingly, retreated. His eyes stole back toward the portrait of Remy's mother. He frowned at something he saw there but
otherwise remained silent.

"Astonbury's zweihänder is missing," Elke said, because of
course she would know that somehow. "They've spent nearly
two days searching. It was brought out to polish only once every
month or so," and here her lip curled in disgust at such lapses in
maintenance, "but no one can swear as to who held it last."

"It would be a rather large weapon to carry away," Xiaodan
noted. "And that would explain the need for one of the conspirators to escape through the window. Whatever secret exits there
are in the Archives, it would be harder to hide the presence of
such a sword from anyone passing them on the street. It's likely
a human and a vampire working together, isn't it? One to leave
undetected, the other familiar enough with the Archives and Astonbury's arrangements to plan this and cover up their partner's
departure."

"Even if you find out who's responsible for the duke's murder,
do you think helping Aluria will change their minds about this
alliance?" Remy crossed the room to stand before his mother's
painting, trying to shove down his anger. "Astonbury was at least
willing to work with you, even if it was for his own gain. Many of
those who opposed him adopted anti-vampire stances in protest.

The duke's successor will not likely treat you as kindly. Perhaps Feiron's right—that you should find someone else to work with."

"Someone," Malekh asked shrewdly, "without the circumstances of their birth hanging over them that may jeopardize our work? Is that guilt I hear, Pendergast?"

Remy couldn't answer.

"Armiger," Xiaodan said. "I want peace with the humans just as much as you do. I meant what I said in Ophelia's throne room. I believe you're the best Aluria has to offer. I would not sabotage a treaty that would benefit your kingdom and mine on a whim."

"What do you need me for, then, beyond a symbolic partnership?"

"We know little of Alurian customs, of Alurian sentiments," Malekh said, surprising him once again. "We have, as you pointed out, a far more extensive knowledge of you and your family than we have let on. You are a known face among many villages, a far more welcome sight than you've been in Elouve. You have hunted these creatures to help them, and they know it. It would be easier to move about the region having you with us than without."

"I thought you didn't want me along," Remy muttered.

"I never said that I didn't want you."

Remy stared at him, then looked away. "They tolerate me. There is a difference between that and being welcomed."

"But he's right, Remy," Elke spoke up softly. "You know the way Alurian villages work. They do not. It would be easier to travel if you're with them."

Remy glared at her because he'd expected Elke, of all people, to at least take his side. "What would you need to visit the Alurian villages for anyway?" he asked. "I thought you both intended to ride straight for Qing-ye."

"I did mention that we might take a few detours," Xiaodan reminded him. "We keep informants in certain Alurian towns. We have investigated all that we can regarding Astonbury's murder, and given present Elouvian sentiments, it would be prudent to withdraw and wait for public anger to die down. The Marquess of Riones should be in a better position to find out more about the case. I've just heard that he's been promoted to lead investigator in Astonbury's murder. I think we can trust him."

She cleared her throat meaningfully. "I know I put you in a terrible position at Her Majesty's court," she said. "And that you might have been under some pressure there to accept my offer and save face. But here, we have laid down our cards and shown you our intentions, our plans. If you truly have no desire to travel with us, Remy, then only say the word, and we will leave you tomorrow as friends."

Remy mulled over this new information, touched by her words. Even now, she was offering him a chance to bow out gracefully, to recuse himself from an undertaking of a much farther-reaching conspiracy than he could imagine.

His gaze flitted back to Malekh, who was still watching him. There was no mistaking Xiaodan's wistfulness; she wanted him to accompany them. He could not say the same of her fiancé. Any journey with him along would not be a harmonious experience.

"I'll go where you both go," he found himself saying, feeling strangely at peace with the words.

14

GOODBYE

"Have I ever told you about the time I staked the vampire Aughessy, boy?" Edgar Pendergast asked conversationally.

His father had expected Remy's arrival. Grimesworthy was already there, as foul-faced as ever. He led Remy into his father's private chamber, where the fireplace was roaring, the duke at his usual place in the armchair next to it, looking at the flames as Dr. Yost attended to him.

"I was only thirty-three summers," the old man said. "We'd been planning the attack for months. We'd whittled down their members following the Battle of Sorgrost, after we'd taken out his second-in-command and the hundred vampires under him. Loathsome little fellow, that Nader—Narber? No, Narshall—had been. Wouldn't have seen why Kurdashev picked him if not for the viciousness. The woman, though. Hallenshea, was it now? She was their true strategist. She should have been in charge."

He chuckled. "Still had their own prejudices about women that not even a natural death could overcome, eh, Remington? Didn't help them much. Scargrave cut Narshall's head off quick enough, and I'd done the same to the Hallenshea woman in short order. Pretty, for a vampire. Real shame. But the loss left them wide open for a full-scale attack at Meridian Keep. Poor fool thought he could lick his wounds; didn't expect us to hammer him that same night with fresh troops.

"Wonderful sight, to see it burn. They still have the scythe blade I used to stake him with, proudly displayed down by the Ernswaoll museum near the market quarters. Made my name with those Second Court vampires. First Aughessy, then Kurdashev much later, when he came and abducted the Lady Marissa. People don't forget who saved them. That's what I hold on to, boy. People don't forget.

"Would have attacked them sooner, you know. Lady Marissa was not the only lady who'd been kidnapped, only the last. I implored them to take action long before her abduction, but the previous deaths had been lower-class girls who were beneath the Reapers' notice. Fools who never listen. Sought to rescue them myself, but by then it was too late. The Second Court paid their fathers off, and Astonbury was willing to sweep it all under the rug. That's all the difference between him and me, Remington," his father added, with no trace of either irony or hypocrisy. "I may have my own ambitions, but I fight for all Alurians."

"Your second dose today, Your Grace," Dr. Yost reminded him, pressing against the duke's mottled forearm for a vein.

The old duke let him without comment this time. Against the firelight, he didn't look quite as sick as before. "And now you've chosen to ally yourself with two vampires," he said, as the physician withdrew. "Heading back to Meridian Keep, decades later, for any new signs of the First Court."

Remy stayed silent. He was still looking down at the newspaper his father had spread before him, where the tabloid headlines screamed BLUE-BLOODED FAMILIAR OR VAMPIRE INFATUATION? in block print. A caricature of someone who was probably Remy was kneeling on the ground, planting kisses at the feet of a comically fanged vampire with long black hair who was spraying her surroundings with fire.

His father likely had spies within the Archives now that Astonbury was gone, but Remy wasn't sure to what extent the old man knew about the queen's offer, about his decision to leave with the court vampires.

"The demimonde is frothing gleefully at the mouth at the thought of the Valenbonne heir running around with Third and Fourth Court derelicts." Edgar Pendergast gestured to the newspaper, in a much better mood than what Remy had expected of him. "Forget this, boy. Let them believe what they want to believe. We have the Night Court reports, like we wanted."

"Not even the Archives can confirm any recent attacks," Remy said. "All I can find are eyewitness claims of the distinct mark on their forearms during two of those attacks."

"A tattoo of a broken star. The mark of the First. It is no easy feat to carve a vampire, Remington. Only Ancient blood can ink those permanent designs on their accursed flesh. It is, or so I am told, an excruciating process. If a vampire bears that seal on his body, then they are one of the Night Empress's soldiers."

The duke shifted in his seat and smiled. "The extent of these attacks is what strikes me as puzzling. Far too scattered. A trail of them down south, a cluster toward the east, some more sightings west into Pai Lai, and then migratory patterns into the north. If these attacks are being caused by First Court vampires, then it is suspicious. They cannot be everywhere at once without alerting the Reapers. But they are few enough and done at infrequent intervals as not to incite panic. I have identified some of the vampires you killed for Lady Daneira's sake, Remington. Many have been missing from villages along eastern Aluria for the better part of two years."

Remy straightened. "But why turn them?"

"To shore up numbers for some new nest within the kingdom, perhaps? If you add these cases with the other vampire attacks in Aluria, they do not stand out. And yet . . ."

He nodded, satisfied. "Of course. Perhaps they are test cases. A means to probe Elouve and the Reapers for any chinks in our armor, to ascertain the weakest parts to attack. We did that in Sorgrost, too. My own maneuver. Sent regiments in all directions to see where they responded the weakest. Rather flattered to see them imitating the best."

"I leave with Lady Song and Lord Malekh tomorrow," Remy said, already prepared for the forthcoming argument. "The Third and Fourth Court will have far more knowledge of the Night Empress than all the reports Astonbury or his successor could ever put together."

His father didn't speak for several minutes, staring contentedly into the fire instead. Yost had already retreated to the medicine cabinet to fiddle with more bottles there.

"Astonbury was interred today," Edgar Pendergast said, the smug satisfaction emanating off him like heat. His shoulders shook in laughter. "The old bastard's dead. He was so convinced he'd outlive me. Would send me the eulogy he'd planned for my wake every few months in the mail. Who's sending their bereaved condolences now? Hiding secrets from Her Majesty, eh? All those bodies in the basement. Who's to bet he had something to do with this blasted Rot? Have you seen that, Yost? These mutated bastards, running all over the city?"

"I would be very much interested in gaining access to the Archives' experiments on them, Your Grace," Yost said. "It would be useful to see their notes."

"I'd wish Astonbury alive again just so I could see him face Queen Ophelia's wrath, see the cunt stand trial," the duke said, not paying his doctor any attention. "I'd bury him afterward myself, if I got to see him lose his head first."

Remy stared at him, but nothing seemed to douse his father's good mood. The old man lifted a hand as if to dismiss him.

"Zidan Malekh. A Third Court vampire. He would know who I am. We've had a few run-ins in the past, but our paths had never crossed long enough to make either of us a bigger danger to the other. Wiped out the Fifth Court, didn't he? Doing the work for us. Perhaps the only reason the alliance has pushed through parliament. And yet, quite odd that he would let a Pendergast, of all people, travel with him. Did he tell you anything of himself, lad?"

Slowly, warily, Remy shook his head.

"Grimesworthy," his father ordered, and from whatever shadows that had swallowed him up, the valet reappeared, a folder in his hands.

"They haven't given you everything, of course," the duke said. "Not even the queen's blessing would convince Astonbury's sycophants to give up their most precious secrets. But with the chaos following Astonbury's demise, I have found it easier to convince people to part with information. Two, three pages—but brevity, I believe, is a rare gift. You might want to read it before you make any rash decisions, boy."

"There is nothing here that will change my mind," Remy said stubbornly.

The elder Pendergast shrugged. "Leave with the fangbloods if you wish, then. Without Astonbury and his very charming wife's access to his study, you will be useless here in Elouve. By all means, travel with the vampires. But remember in the end who you truly work for."

"I fight for Aluria," Remy said.

"That's what those yearning to be heroes always say at the start," his father said. "Not so often at the end. A very attractive couple, the Lady Song and her protector. Headstrong in her ways, from what I have heard. A bit like Giselle, don't you think? She looks the type to enjoy a good tumble every now and then."

"She isn't Giselle," Remy seethed.

"You can't tell me you were never attracted to the duchess, boy. I see the lie on your face. But the Lady Song, yes. You feel more strongly for her than you did Astonbury's wife. It's easy enough to figure you out. She bailed you from the gaols, too, didn't she? Defended you to the queen? Lord Malekh seems quite lax when it comes to his betrothed's whims, which works in our favor."

He creaked himself forward. "We do not just fight for Aluria, Remington. We *defend* Aluria, first and foremost. I gave her the best of my years, and I will continue to defend her until my dying breath, even if I must do it from this confounded bed. Aluria gave us everything. Without her, we are nothing. No filthy vampire will deter me from this path, however sympathetic they are to the cause. If you claim to fight for Aluria as you say, then you shall resolve yourself to do the same, to not let some pretty kindred face turn your head."

"I won't," Remy responded angrily. "I *won't*."

His father smiled coldly. "Read the report, Remington. And if you still think you ought to leave Elouve, well . . . my blessing may not go as far as the queen's, but you may have it all the same. Remember Aluria. Remember your mother's honor, and mine, and all that you owe."

"NOBODY TOLD me Fourth Court vampires were this persistent," Remy said, rather weary at this point.

Xiaodan turned to face him. She had chosen not to enter Kinaiya Lodge this time, instead loitering outside by the trees, away from everyone else's view.

"I thought to keep hiding," she said, "and not let you know I was here at all. But after everything that's happened, I thought you deserved some honesty, at least."

"That's the only thing I haven't gotten today, so it would be a welcome change." He wanted to throw himself into bed and sleep for the next two weeks, but he couldn't. He'd be leaving with her and Malekh on the morrow, and for the first time in a long while, he'd be doing so of his own volition, no matter what his father tried to imply. "And what else will you be requiring of me tonight?"

"Nothing, this time. I'm only here to wish you good night."

"Truly?"

"And also, not coincidentally, to keep watch over you, in case anything else should occur."

Remy stilled. "'Anything else'?"

"We assumed Vasilik was dead. While we believe he is no longer in Elouve, I would not make further presumptions about the status of other old enemies, and am instead taking a more proactive approach to watch over you tonight."

"I'm no one compared to either you or Malekh. Why protect me?" She was the notorious heiress of a venerable vampire court. She would have been pampered like the princess she undoubtedly was. Remy would not have imagined anyone befitting her station to stand guard like a common soldier over him.

"Because you've spent far too long fighting for other people, and it's time someone extended you the same courtesies. Zidan and I are the reasons you've been targeted. Consider this our thanks for accompanying us tomorrow, even if I've strong-armed you into accepting."

"I wanted to come with you. I didn't need much convincing." He hesitated. "If you're hell-bent on doing this, then at least come inside where it's more comfortable."

Gray eyes watched him, and within those clear depths, Remy thought he could detect a sudden flash of interest, followed quickly by remorse. "I think not," Xiaodan said. "This place has always been your bedrock, far enough from anyone who ever wanted to take advantage of you. I have already trespassed twice. Perhaps I will deserve the invitation next time."

"You already do." He stepped closer. He couldn't help it. The weather had taken pity on them tonight, the rains easing up so that only a light fog remained, even if the chill persisted. But Xiaodan hadn't bothered with a coat, wearing a simple wrap that exposed shoulders both pale and lovely. "Where is Malekh?" he asked.

"Hunting down more clues. I should apologize for his behavior over the last couple of days."

"Why should you have to?" Remy asked sourly. "He should be more attentive to you."

She grinned, impish, then glided closer. "Do you have a problem with my fiancé, Armiger Remington?"

Of course he did. She knew that. Remy had never had a healthy relationship with a woman in his life, if one could discount Elke. Intimacy beyond anything physical often eluded him. But he knew, beyond any shadow of a doubt, that she liked him beyond mere protectiveness. And, fool as Remy was, he wasn't rejecting that. Wasn't sure he wanted to.

And Malekh. The man made him nervous. He didn't like the way the lord watched him at times. It stirred up odd emotions that he didn't want to dwell over.

"I don't like that he's your fiancé," he said honestly. She was so close. He could see another quick streak of desire across her face, a blaze in the gloom. The attraction between them that had been so apparent at the Astonbury gardens still smoldered. And he . . . they'd always called him a libertine. When she'd explored his history, she would have known of his affairs beyond just Giselle. All he needed to do was bend his head to hers and change everything forever.

"I would like it better," he said quietly, "if you at least stayed inside."

But already she was stepping back, sensing the danger in the offer. Her expression remained serene, if a touch regretful. "I will remain outside. It will give me all the time to think with a clearer head—about us, and the journey ahead. Good night, Armiger Remington."

She made no sound when she melted back into the surrounding trees. Remy waited until the irregular sounds of her heartbeat faded away before heading in.

Alone in his room, he drew out the slim folder his father had presented to him, drew out the scribbled note his father had written on the last page in a shaky, infirmed script, and stared at it for a long time.

THE FAREWELLS the next day were not too protracted. Remy had no one to say goodbye to, save for Elke and Riones. The former had shown up at his doorstep early that morning, armed with new modifications.

"There are far more pockets in here than I am used to having," Remy said, testing out the new hiding spots she had sewn for him, where he could comfortably secret away half a dozen daggers if he had a mind to.

"Alternatives for Breaker." Elke had brought him another fire lance. Grinning, she twisted the barrel sideways, revealing the double chamber within, already packed with firepowder. "You'll still only get one shot off this, but you've seen what it can do." The woman's smile faded slightly. "It's one thing to hunt vampires, Remy. It's another to hunt *with* them. Perhaps I worry more than I should, and I wouldn't want to be dismissive of your own skills, because you're a damn good hunter, but I can't help it. Stay safe, and send word to me as soon as you can."

What else could he say to that? Remy laughed and hugged her tightly. "I will."

Anthony Castellblanc, the Marquess of Riones, had also arrived to see him off. "Do you really think that?" he asked, stunned. "You believe the Night Court is planning an assault on Elouve?"

"My father thinks so, and he's rarely wrong about these matters. Someone is trying to test how quickly we respond, and you wouldn't do that if you weren't planning a full-on assault on the city, searching for the weak spots. I think it's best if you tell Her Majesty to shore up the city's defenses."

"Thank you, Remington. The strategies the Duke of Valenbonne employed during the Elouvian Siege may prove useful once again if this is—" Riones immediately quieted. "Ah, my apologies, Pendergast. Running my mouth off again. Just remembered you were a part of that."

"I never even think of it anymore," Remy lied. "Show the queen my report. Pretend you wrote it, in case Feiron and the others complain."

"Like hell I will. I'll tell them you'd found it all out, and they can choke on it if they want." Riones chuckled. "Have always wanted to tell them that to their faces. They're falling quickly out of Her Majesty's esteem, and thank the Light it's finally happening."

"Anthony, thank you for always looking out for me."

"You're not the only one they consider an outsider. Castegon's been a part of Aluria for nearly a decade now, yet you would think I'd come from some backwater region that puts their breeches on the bottom side up, the way they act sometimes. You were kind enough to me when I was new to Elouve. You saved me that time in Gorngareft, when we were fighting off that coven. Ought to look out for each other, yeah? Get back to Elouve in one piece, Remington."

After that, there was only one last place to visit.

He'd asked Lady Song and Lord Malekh to meet him there. For several minutes, the couple kept a respectful distance, giving him time to pay his respects.

"I would have thought that the nobles of some higher standing in Elouve would have their own family crypts," Xiaodan observed quietly, her voice low as if not to disturb the sleep of the dead around them.

"Higher standing is the key reason my father didn't bother with hers." Remy wasn't always in the city, but he visited his mother's grave religiously, always without his father's consent. It was a peaceful enough place, and he paid the gravekeeper plenty of money to keep the weeds free around her modest tombstone. *Ligaya Bascom Pendergast*, it read in flowing script across the smooth marker, and then *Beloved Wife and Mother*, though only one of those had ever been true.

"Her name means 'joy' in the Tithian language," he said. "I never met her, but I like to think she was that."

"Was your father against you leaving with us?" Xiaodan asked.

"On the contrary, he was practically eager to see me off."

Malekh, too, had stepped toward the grave. He stared down at it with his usual stern expression.

"Did she pass away from some illness?" Xiaodan asked.

"Didn't anyone tell you when you investigated my past?"

"I heard of some mystery surrounding her. Everyone seemed reluctant to talk, but they do view you with suspicion because of it. It wasn't relevant to Astonbury's murder, so I decided not to pursue it until I could talk to you myself. Was it a strange sickness?"

"If only." Remy bent down to brush off a thin layer of dust on the top of the headstone. "She was killed by a vampire—one of the Night Court."

"But that doesn't explain why they would treat you with—"

"One of their vampires was also allegedly her lover. She bore a sigil of their court on her shoulder when she died—their mark of possession." Remy heard Xiaodan's intake of breath and ignored it. "Some believed she was taken against her will. My father thinks otherwise. There was a reason he no longer treated her as a wife at the end. And after years of living with him, I can understand why she would want to turn to someone else. Even kindred. That's why I need to know more about what happened to her. To see her honor restored."

Malekh remained silent. A shame, Remy thought, that this was one of the rare instances where he chose to be.

Ask Lord Zidan Malekh, his father's note had said, *a sire and former high noble of the First Court. Ask Lord Zidan Malekh, former consort to the Night King, and once his Lord Executioner. He once killed under the Night King's name. He could do so again.*

Seduce the Lady Song if you need to. And Malekh, too, if you must. Remember your vows.

And Remy did.

He rose from where he'd knelt and turned to them. "Let's go."

15

TRADERS

It took only thirty-five minutes after leaving Elouve's city gates for Remy to begin complaining.

This was all absolutely, objectively Malekh's fault. Remy had been misled into believing that the journey would be undertaken with horses, perhaps with some other more luxurious transport if Xiaodan preferred a more comfortable means of travel. He had not been prepared for the two monstrosities that were currently whinnying and pawing their hooves before him.

They were horses. Or rather, they *used* to be horses. They were now skeletons with skin stretched tautly over them and had neither muscle nor fat to pad what should have lain between. They were coal black from mane to tail, their eyes a glowing red. Despite their emaciated features, they were massive in height, and Remy would not have relished the idea of encountering any one of these creatures in some lonely wood.

One of the horses had only three legs. From the way it was prancing about, the shortage was not an issue.

Xiaodan fussed over the demon horses like they were the fashionable lapdogs favored by some of the noblewomen in the capital, rather than the terrifying wraiths that they were. The devil steeds were also hitched to the carriage they were to use for their journey.

"I suppose Zidan and I could reach Chànggē Shuǐ on foot in the space of a day, instead of the weeks it would take humans on horses," Xiaodan said. "But I'm not quite recovered yet, and Ophelia did gift Zidan some new medical apparatuses. They're delicate and too cumbersome to carry on our own."

"You misunderstand me," Remy said. "That's not the part that I find most worrying. The bloody hell are those?"

"Zidan calls them helhests. I call them Peanut and Cookie."

"Peanut," Remy repeated, feeling a little detached from the situation for a moment. "And Cookie."

"They're the swiftest things on four legs—and three—in all the kingdoms. They'd be even faster if they weren't dragging us along. We could reach Qing-ye in a week's time if we rode straight through with the carriage. But we'll head to Ankersaud first, then go east, so it may take longer."

Had these helhests been stabled inside the capital, it would likely have caused an international incident. Remy should have been suspicious when Xiaodan had admitted that the mounts they were to ride were stabled outside of Elouve, at some isolated farmstead tucked away five miles out. The woman who owned the place, a *human* woman named Mari, assured Remy that the horses were fairly docile, and that Lord Malekh had purchased some sheep or pig from her to serve as the horses' meal during their stay.

"And they're not forcing you to do this?" Remy persisted, because a sheep's price didn't seem like it was worth the headache of stabling demons.

"The lord and the lady saved me a time or two in the past," Mari said cheerfully. "And why, they're good horses, if you look past their appearances. Quite fond of their lumps of sugar, though

Lord Malekh was adamant about not feeding them more than two a day."

"It's not—it's unusual to find someone living so close to Elouve helping Court nobles."

The woman stared at him, confused. "But you're doing the same thing, aren't you, Armiger? Helping them, I mean."

Remy supposed she had a point.

One of the hell horses neighed at him, revealing a pair of perfectly formed fangs as it did.

"I think he likes you," Xiaodan said with every show of sincerity. "They're gentle, you know."

"How did you even find these creatures?" Remy choked.

"It was all Zidan's doing."

"He bit them?" It was bad enough turning humans, but if Malekh was going about forcing innocent horses into undead mounts, that was a line Remy didn't even know could be drawn, much less crossed.

Xiaodan burst into laughter. "Most mammals rarely survive any bloodletting from us. Inoculating them with a weaker strain of our blood was the best option we could think of. Zidan invented something to boost their immunity, to give them a limited version of our strengths. They're powerful enough to withstand hours of direct sunlight, and they're twenty times stronger than your average wild horse. They do require some blood every now and then for sustenance, but the rest isn't all that different from caring for regular steeds. I'm afraid the stallion you brought won't quite be able to keep up with them. Perhaps you could leave it with Miss Mari? It might raise more questions if you bring it back to Elouve."

Remy hesitated, looking over at his horse.

Malekh smirked. "Considering that we've let you accompany us, helhests are manageable in comparison."

Maybe it was the shock of realizing actual vampire horses were possible, or maybe because Remy had been in a bad enough mood all morning that he was itching for a fight. Malekh had certainly been ready to accommodate on the latter, so he didn't see why he shouldn't take the undead arsewit up on his offer. Remy was already moving, fists raised, and was pleased to see the vampire meeting him halfway when Xiaodan glided firmly in between them again, crossing her arms and sending her most intimidating scowl their way.

"We will have none of this again," she said firmly. "We haven't even started, and you're already at loggerheads with each other. If this is what the rest of our travels shall be like, I will be very displeased. Remy, it would do you a world of good if you stop both jumping to conclusions and assuming the worst of Zidan. Zidan, explaining would have been easier than antagonizing him."

"An explanation?" Remy asked. "What possible reason could there be to turn two helpless animals into the undead?"

"Because they were already dying." One of the helhests whinnied happily into Xiaodan's palm. "They'd been crippled and abused, bound for the slaughterhouse. I rescued them like the soft fool that I am, but they were in bad enough shape that they would've been doomed to a life of suffering anyway, until Zidan proposed an alternative."

"You mean he just happened to have some vampire potion lying about that—"

"It was a restorative originally intended for Xiaodan's heart," Malekh broke in. "I modified it for the horses to take in smaller doses. As it was synthesized using vampire blood, the effects are as you see them now. It's not a serum I would offer to anyone, man or beast, had it not been a final option. They were in pain, and Xiaodan refused to let them be any longer."

From their point of view, they'd have considered that better than death. Remy would have been inclined to put the horses out of their misery, as painlessly as possible—but the funny thing about vampires was that they didn't see being undead as a curse.

"Now do you understand?" Xiaodan pleaded. "And will you both behave until we get to Ankersaud? I'd rather not have to stop every hour or so just to yell at you two to get along."

Remy and Malekh glanced at each other—an unspoken, grudging agreement. "I can leave my horse with Miss Mari," Remy relented. "But you do know that people more unsavory than I am would kill to get their hands on such a serum."

"Only I know the process of creating it," Malekh said, the arrogant git. "And I would carry it to my eventual grave before I would ever teach a human its secrets."

"Miracle of miracles," Remy said sourly, "we're finally in accord. Still would have appreciated a bloody heads-up beforehand. Some humans would consider this a dealbreaker."

Xiaodan folded her hands behind her back, looked him straight in the eye and said, with a disarming sort of embarrassment, "I didn't realize it was something you would feel so strongly about. I'll do better next time."

"Next time?"

From behind her, Malekh smirked again, because the bastard had guessed at what his reaction to the helhests would be even if she hadn't, and Remy was back to wishing he could have stuck Breaker into him before Xiaodan had intervened.

He had little time to think for at least an hour after that, gripping tightly at the armrest beside him. Outside the carriage, scenery fled past, far too swiftly to appreciate whatever view they might have offered, because holy hell of a fucking Light, these helhests were *fast*.

He must have said it out loud—shouted it, probably, because the clatter of the carriage wheels (no doubt modified to keep the whole coach from rattling apart) and the whistling of the wind was far too loud to attempt a normal conversation—because Xiaodan let out a rather pleased cackle and yelled back, "I know, aren't they grand?" at him. The beasts continued their inhuman pace at breakneck speed, and then there was even less talk after that. Malekh had taken up the reins outside the carriage. Xiaodan simply settled into her seat and entered some odd fugue state of suspended animation, asleep yet somehow not asleep, while it was all Remy could do not to be jolted about in his seat, one foot already braced against the wall of the carriage to avoid pitching forward.

By the time the carriage slowed to a stop near a village, he was almost certain vital gray matter had leaked out his head through his ears, and that he'd dropped the rest of his wits some thirty miles back. Remy staggered out of the coach and spent a few minutes trying to regain his sense of balance and gravity, which mostly consisted of clinging to the nearest tree trunk until the urge to throw up had passed, trying to ascertain if his senses were still about or if he'd somehow lost them during the ride, too.

"Light," he croaked, once he'd gotten his tongue to work.

"It can take a while to get used to them," Xiaodan said apologetically.

"Not certain I want to." The equine anomalies responsible for his predicament were standing placidly off to the side, pretending to graze. Remy spotted the telltale smokestacks from a distance, confirming that there was a good-sized town up ahead, though they'd been prudent enough to disembark some distance away before they could be seen. Two vampires were enough to make anyone nervous, even without throwing their blood-drinking skeletal undead horses into the mix.

He tried to work out where they were. "Is this Halrayett?"

"No." Malekh had emerged from his side of the carriage. He was tying both undead stallions to one of the trees, though Remy doubted there was anyone around willing to go near the beasts, much less steal them. "This is the village of Ankersaud."

"That's not right. Halrayett is the closest village to the capital. We won't be reaching Ankersaud for another six hours, at least."

Xiaodan was laughing again. "Peanut and Cookie wouldn't

have scared you this whole time only for us to have barely made our way out of Elouve at this point."

"I wasn't frightened. That's not the same as wanting to hurl—" And then he froze. "That's impossible. It hasn't even been an hour since we'd—"

No. Not impossible. Not if the fucking demon horses from hell were pulling your carriage at a speed faster than lightning could shoot up your piss stream.

"They're called *helhests*," Xiaodan insisted, because apparently Remy let out the long stream of curses aloud again.

THEY WERE right. (Remy really, *really* didn't like it when they were right, especially Malekh.) Halrayett was a small village with a five-room inn and stable, with more cows and sheep than there were people. This was a bigger town than that, one of the kingdom's more visible northern outposts. No one familiar with Alurian geography could mistake one for the other, and the small wooden sign that said WELCOME TO ANKERSAUD hanging right above the gates was the first obvious clue.

"The helhests will be fine outside town," Malekh said briskly. "Mari fed them well, so they won't be hungry for another few days. Our contacts in Ankersaud should give us a quick summary of how things stand at the eastern border. We'll spend another hour or so for any supplies you think we'll need, Xiaodan, and then we'll ride out again."

Remy decided to stop thinking about estimating distances via human logic, because none of it mattered anymore, and instead followed the pair into town. Peanut and Cookie nickered merrily and watched them go.

Remy didn't often stop at Ankersaud, preferring smaller hamlets and villages to spend the night. Ankersaud was popular enough to attract visitors from outside even Aluria, and both Xiaodan and Malekh seemed comfortable with the crowd as they weaved in and out of the busy streets, Remy close behind. They looked human enough not to stand out; that they were obviously nobility was much more difficult to hide. People hurriedly stepped out of their way, some even bobbing their heads awkwardly with a murmured "sir" or "madam" as they walked past. Remy concentrated on Xiaodan's willowy figure as she glided through the throng, but occasionally he betrayed himself, his gaze straying to Malekh before he realized what he was doing.

It wasn't fair for them both to be this attractive, he thought sourly; one was his ideal woman if she wasn't spoken for, the other a Lightdamned shitpouch even if he *was* the best-looking man Remy had ever seen.

A brave street urchin attempted to pick Malekh's pocket at one point; the vampire latched on to the boy's wrist before his fingers could even graze the inner seam, hauling the thief up easily with one hand so they were at eye level. The waif gulped visibly, but Malekh simply reached into his other pocket, produced several pieces of copper, and transferred them to the street rat's tattered coat.

"Pay more attention to whom you attempt to rob," he said calmly. "This should be more than enough for you and your friends. Now, be off with you." A firm nudge sent the young boy disappearing into the crowd.

"Isn't he something else?" Xiaodan asked admiringly, watching her betrothed turn to another band of raggedy-looking children watching nearby who promptly dispersed from the force of his stare alone.

"He shouldn't be playing with his food, is all I see here," Remy muttered, earning a chuckle from her.

Their destination turned out to be Ankersaud's central market, another reason for the town's popularity. The place was a natural stopover for merchants arriving from the kingdom of Pai Lai that lay farther northwest, and everything appeared to be on sale here, from rarer crops like mangosteen and ginseng, to bolts of cloth dyed from prized mollusks native only to the region, to even the closely guarded yakkan fur and meat the Pai Laians farmed zealously on the Zarensha Steppes. Most of the stalls were draped in colorful fabrics designed to catch the eye, with rows upon rows of their wares arranged before them for customers to peruse. Hawkers announced the importance of their goods, beseeching passersby to linger and browse.

Malekh stopped before one of the gaudiest stalls—a confusing clash of colors was Remy's initial impression, with tartans of orange, pink, and bright green hanging down its sides like curtains, embellished by gems so large they were clearly fakes littering the shelves and tables. The items on display were of the splashy kind that one might expect of souvenirs with no real value: stuffed cane toad decors, straw dolls wearing ridiculous hats, ceramic pots with poorly painted petunias on them, a drinking goblet that was for some reason shaped like a fish. Remy had no idea how the shop managed to stay in business, given the exorbitant prices it was asking for.

Sitting in front of the stall was an old man with a scowl and a crooked squint, stocky build wrapped in a shapeless white robe, as bare of accessories as his shop was drowning in them. He had a heavy cigar clamped between his teeth and gave a grunt in greeting when he spotted Malekh, but otherwise said nothing else.

The vampire noble crouched down, squatting beside the geezer. "Is Eugenie here?"

The old man took a heavy drag, nodded, and jerked a thumb toward the shop's interior.

"Do we have customers, Paolo?" From within, an oyster-shell-encrusted drape was pulled back, and the woman that came bustling out was more in keeping with what Remy expected the stall's proprietor to be. There were far too many ringlets in the lady's hair and an improbably enormous hat made of some faux animal skin set jauntily on her head at a rakish angle. She wore a thick layer of rouge on her face and kohl slathered at her eyes, her face underneath papered white from powder. Her dress appeared to have the feathers of every known bird in existence sewn into the cloth, making her resemble an overdressed raptor herself.

"Why, Lord Malekh!" she called out, hands fluttering to her mouth. "And Lady Song! What an absolute dream! I presume that you were pleased with the last trinket you purchased from me? And all the trouble tracking it down when it left Cassamides!"

"It was invaluable, Eugenie. Fanciful work, as always. It's one of the reasons we're back."

"Seeking more of my wares, then? Shall you stay longer for tea and crumpets? I just put on a fresh pot to brew, and it should be ready in three!" The woman gestured at them to hurry inside, and Remy heard the metallic clank of overhead hinges as the old man pulled the curtains closed behind them. It occurred to him then, that the walls of the small store were thicker than those of the other stalls. Anyone seeking to eavesdrop would find it difficult, especially with the old man outside serving as a guard.

"I'm afraid we're in a hurry, Eugenie, as usual," Malekh said politely, "so we'll have nothing else but our standard, and anything you might have heard of Langsford and Priyahn."

"Ooh, a rather interesting choice today, milord. Priyahn in particular is said to be crawling with more of this so-called Rot, though things are quieter at Langsford—oh!" She interrupted herself, looking at Remy. She looked shocked for a brief second, eyes flitting between him and Malekh, before her expression melted into one of delight. "And who might you be, you delicious little thing?"

"Ah." All the etiquette ingrained in Remy had not prepared him for this. "My name is Remington Pendergast. I'm traveling with Lady Song and—"

"Oh, but you're absolutely adorable!" A flock of colorful feathers descended upon him, and Remy found his cheeks being pinched like he was a five-year-old. "How scrumptious! I rarely see milord and milady travel with a companion, and a Pendergast, to boot! A hunter with vampires, who would've thought? My dear Lady Song, putting your alliance into practice!"

"You know who I am?" he asked.

"I wouldn't be in this business if I didn't know who the Pendergasts were, my dear. You were pointed out to me once before—you were quite young then, perhaps only thirteen summers. I'm so sorry you had to go through that. No one should have had to. It wasn't right of your father, and I was glad to hear of you flourishing even after everything he brought down on you."

"I didn't realize people outside of the capital knew about it." Remy was uncomfortably aware of the two pairs of eyes now trained on his back. Xiaodan would certainly be curious. And Malekh—he never really knew what Malekh thought.

Lady Song had researched his Reaper work yet had deliberately chosen not to look into his past. She didn't know about what had happened to him during the Elouvian Siege. She could have, if she'd looked back past his record as a bounty hunter. That she hadn't was . . . oddly comforting.

"Oh, they don't. The few who know have been paid not to talk about it. Your human court took great pains to hide it from even the regular Elouvians. I know that neither Valenbonne nor Astonbury—may his soul be like fireflies at rest, whatever his sins were—speak much of it. Neither did King Beluske when he was alive. But it is my job to root out truth from falsehood—the latter, no doubt, gave rise to the belief that you are one of us. The esteemed lord and lady with you wouldn't be visiting me if I wasn't in the business to know, now, would they?"

"'One of us'?" Remy echoed blankly, slow to catch on.

Eugenie grinned. Her fangs weren't quite as pronounced as others he'd seen, but they were long enough to show that she, too, was kindred. "Alas, I am but a simple trader. Paolo and I try to survive as best we could, though we look forward to an alliance with the humans. That would be very good for us."

"Eugenie," Malekh said.

"Of course, of course. Mustn't always talk shop." Eugenie circled her trove of wares, finally selecting the fish goblet. "This would make a wonderful gift, milord," she announced. "A one-of-a-kind item that you will no longer find hereabouts, crafted by some of the very best artisans from Longhi. At two thousand marks, it is practically a steal!"

"Two thousand?" Remy sputtered, staring at the hideous tankard.

Malekh didn't even quibble over the price. "A considerable sum, Eugenie. A little more than what you usually have on offer."

"Ah, but milord, you will be interested in the history surrounding this little nugget." Eugenie leaned forward, looking serious now. "The news has already started to spread, and I do not doubt it shall reach Elouve before long. The village of Brushfen is gone, milord."

"Gone? What do you mean?"

"Razed to the ground, ashes by the time dawn and help arrived. And before that—tales of horror. Accounts from what few survivors there were, of a horde of vampires that came rampaging through, crazed for blood. I took them in just an hour ago, tried my best to keep things quiet for their sakes, but already people are talking."

"No," Xiaodan said hoarsely. "A full coven? How?"

"The stories sound unbelievable, but each account I've heard so far corroborates the others. At least two dozen vampires, none suffering the frenzy. A calculated attack, and then the fires to hide their feeding."

"Impossible." Malekh said sharply. "There cannot be a vampire nest of that size within Aluria without Her Majesty or I knowing."

"Your brother might know something," Remy said.

Something close to anger crossed the noble's face. "What do you imply, Pendergast?"

"The pack he ran with. Eight of them, all causing trouble near Elouve. They could have been part of this secret nest."

"They're delinquents who boasted more than they should have and paid the price for it. They lied about killing Lady Daneira. Naji can be foolish sometimes, but not enough to associate himself with murderers."

"Those delinquents were dead set on killing me. That's about as murderous as one can get. Maybe if you questioned your brother instead of making excuses constantly for his behavior, you'd know more."

Malekh was slowly flexing his hand, like he was warming up to wrap it around Remy's throat. Fury radiated off the man like heat through thin ice.

"Zidan," Xiaodan said firmly. "You may be right, Remy. Naji's at Chànggē Shuǐ, and we'll have all the time to question him again once we return. Won't we?"

Malekh's fingers unclenched. "I want more details from him, yes. It is true that he is not entirely innocent in all this."

"Until then, we must focus our search here. Eugenie, have there been any whispers of a secret nest in northern Aluria before?"

"If there is, even I am unaware of it. There has never been so much as a sighting in the past. The most likely possibility is that they are new to the area, milord, perhaps traveled here from the southeastern lands."

"Southeast," Xiaodan said, stricken. "That would be Qing-ye, then. Fourth Court territory. My territory."

"I am sorry, milady. My witnesses swore that this particular coven fled quickly, at the first glimpse of dawn. A new clan of the freshly turned, it seems."

"If they still fear the sunlight despite the heavy fog, then that is likely."

"Can your witnesses offer up a description of any of the attackers?" Remy asked.

"Yes. One says that a vampire with short red hair and dark eyes proclaimed himself the leader of that particular pack just as the massacre began. It was he who gave the orders, shouted that the killing and the feeding be done before dawn. I can bring you to the survivors, if you wish." Eugenie looked sad. "Only three of them, milord—a lad who was lucky enough to flee unseen before the bloodshed, and two children who hid under a pile of dead bodies and escaped detection. I did my best to be gentle with them, but they are not in good shape to be questioned. They've only just arrived at my safehouse. I hoped to give them privacy for a little longer."

"I don't intend to interrogate them," Xiaodan said. "But I would like to see them all the same."

"Paolo," Eugenie called toward the shop's entrance. The curtains twitched with an annoyed grunt in affirmation. "Take her ladyship to the hideaway."

"Everything you require is here," she added, holding out the fish goblet for Malekh to take. "I've added something extra for you, for always being such a lovely customer. An artist's rendition of those responsible for Brushfen—a cruder depiction than usual. The young boys are not ready to be giving much detail, but the lad was a goldmine. He'd recognized a few of them from the night before, you see. Said they were asking him for directions to Keshlei, which had struck him as odd because they were in the wrong area for it. At least one had a peculiar tattoo striking enough to recognize—I'd rather not say it out loud, even here.

"I've sent a few scouts to the villages closest to Brushfen, should the nest attack there next. You can reach Brushfen itself quicker by going through the Wurkenbacht woods, though I must warn you that there have been fresh reports of creatures lurking within the forest, and that most travelers steer clear. I shall send word of any new developments. For an additional price, of course."

"You are an absolute treasure, Eugenie."

The feathered woman beamed with pride. "Just catch them that's responsible, Lord Malekh. Rumors of impending vampire attacks can be good for business. But *successful* ones, quite the opposite."

"So they're both vampires?" Remy asked, after Eugenie had temporarily disappeared to the back of the stall to wrap up Malekh's purchase. With Elke as the one exception, he'd never met any other kindred who'd fit in so well with the rest of the human population that no one appeared to be the wiser for it.

"Eugenie is. Paolo is not." At Remy's questioning look, Malekh shrugged. "She's offered to turn him many times, but he always refuses her. He claims that the lifestyle isn't for him."

"He's a familiar, then."

"I suppose so."

"Familiars are illegal in Aluria."

"I'm certain they shall take that into consideration."

"Aren't they worried about discovery?"

"Most of the traders here are nomads. In a few weeks, she and Paolo will be gone. Don't let Eugenie's cheerful demeanor fool you. She is a savvy businesswoman, but she will kill without remorse if she needs to, if anything endangers her or Paolo. She is wise enough to learn her customers' secrets to prevent them from exposing hers."

"Does that mean she has something over you?"

"She knows I am as good as my word."

Remy despised the way Malekh could answer a question without actually answering it. "She isn't compelling her familiar to stay by her side by force?"

"You humans have a corrupted version of what a familiar is. Their relationship has always been consensual, as it should be."

"That's not what we've been told in stories."

"I have heard of domestic arrangements in Aluria where men would beat their wives and the rest simply look away. Are you telling me, then, that one such example of poor behavior by humans is enough to denounce the rest for the same thing? There is more to vampires than just the feed."

Remy wasn't ready to acknowledge his point. "If you say it's consensual, then I'll believe you."

"You, believing me, Pendergast?" The sudden smile on Malekh's face was disconcerting. For once, it was not his usual acrid grimace of pessimism. It looked almost genuine. "There is nothing in these lands that Eugenie doesn't know. They travel Aluria and beyond, move to where the rumors are thickest."

"They're not from the Third Court?"

"Some choose to remain unaffiliated with any court. It is a much more peaceful existence. But Eugenie is as eager to push for human and vampire coexistence as Xiaodan and I, which is why she gives me information at good rates." Malekh picked up a cane toad to inspect. He looked fairly ridiculous holding it.

"Suits you," Remy said.

"I can purchase one for you."

"I'd rather fall on my scythes."

Eugenie returned with his goblet, wrapped up in paper and twine that she laid carefully on the table before them, and then *another* replica of it that she set on the shelf as its replacement.

"I thought you said it was a one-of-a-kind souvenir," Remy said.

"But it is, milord." Eugenie winked at him. "Trust me, I've sold hundreds of these."

"Mal—Lord Malekh said you know almost everything that

happens within Aluria. How much would you charge for news of the Night Cou—"

"Ah ah ah," Eugenie drawled, cutting him off. "We don't do any such business in this place. We only sell unique novelties to enhance your living quarters, from the immodestly rich to the working class. Would you like a cane toad, perhaps? It always looks handsome atop mantelpieces, I've found."

"No, thank you," Remy said, repressing a small shudder at the sight of the stuffed frog. "I want everything you have of the First Court and the whereabouts of the Night Empress, in particular."

"No," Malekh snapped, before Eugenie could answer him. "You know they will kill him, Eugenie."

"I can make my own decisions," Remy snapped.

"Not where the Night Court is concerned."

"Because you were once of the Night Court? Because you once killed for them? Or do you still do so?"

Malekh's face was suddenly bereft of emotion, wiped off his face like a clean slate. But his nostrils flared, and his eyes . . . the sudden rage there, the pain.

Without another word, he turned and stalked out of Eugenie's tent.

"Oh dear," Eugenie said. "Oh dearie, dearie me. You shouldn't have said that."

"Why not?" Remy asked, taken aback by the man's reaction.

"Lady Song never told you? Malekh was once a member of the First Court, yes. But he did not come to it willingly. He was born in Agathyrsi, you know. At the height of their power, the Night King made their most frequent raids there, taking and turning slaves for their amusement."

"I—" Remy stared at the stall's exit. "I didn't know," he said weakly. His father likely hadn't, either. He shouldn't have relied solely on Edgar Pendergast's assertions. Malekh always seemed so confident, so damn *sure* all the time that it hadn't registered with him that the man could have been just as much a victim as his mother. "But wasn't he a high-ranking—"

"That doesn't mean much if survival is your only motivation, and Lord Malekh is quite good at surviving. The Eight Courts have their own varied personalities, but none so frightening or dangerous as the First. It's not something he'd be fond of reminiscing over, I'm sure. I can do you no help in the matter, either. For all my sources, the Night Empress's location continues to elude me. Very few of my confidants are willing to risk their lives to attract her notice."

Remy swallowed. "I need to know, Lady Eugenie."

Eugenie smiled kindly, worriedly. "First, the price to pay for such information would be hefty. Silver has been banned in Aluria for financial transactions, being the most expensive ore to find. The amount of silver that Breaker is made of would serve nicely for half my fee, but I suspect you would not be willing to part with it for anything I have to say.

"Second, I truly do have nothing to say. The only incident I'd ever heard linked to the Night Court was your mother's death—and your own killing of one when you were new to the hunter's cloak. Malekh is right to be worried about you. Perhaps that is the reason he and Xiaodan want you close by. Apologize, my dear. Make it up to him. I'm sure you'll find a way."

"—with a Valenbonne?" Remy heard the tail end of Paolo's speech when he emerged from the tent. "You have done that family a great injustice, and him most of—"

The old man broke off when he spotted Remy, showed no inclination to apologize for talking about him, and only grunted. Malekh was staring down at the goblet in his hands, brow creased.

"Malekh," Remy began, uncertain of where to start. "I'm sorry. I didn't know about—"

"The Ancients of the First Court were not known for commanding loyalty," Zidan said abruptly. "They were known for forcing subservience. Vampires who have lived long enough often develop abilities beyond what humans know. The elders of the First Court could compel others to do their bidding, even against their will. Under their thrall, you could cut your own throat and die singing their praises with your last breath. All the easier to kill in their name."

"Zidan, I—"

"Do you want more explicit details of my time at the Night Court, Pendergast, or are you able to read between the lines and glean from them the things I don't say? Go on. Ask me your questions. What other crimes do you intend to lay at my door that I have not dwelt upon myself at every moment of my existence?"

Remy swallowed. "I have none to ask. I didn't mean to—"

"We're wasting time," the noble said, cutting him off again. He no longer appeared angry, his eyes once again carefully muted ambers, his words low and quiet. "If we are to leave for the north before night comes, we'd best fetch Xiaodan now."

"I—"

"We are going," the vampire said, with such deadly finality that Remy, for once, shut up of his own accord.

"Just because he's one of the undead," Paolo grunted as they watched the noble leave, "doesn't mean he hasn't got demons ten times as old as you haunting his head, either."

"I just want to know why my mother died," Remy said.

"Your mother's gone, child. But you're not. Your life isn't any less important than hers." And then the old man tucked himself back into the corner of the stall, slammed his eyes shut, and grunted again to signal he was done with the conversation.

By the time Remy caught up to Zidan, he had already found Xiaodan sitting in front of a nondescript house some distance from the central plaza. A young boy was sitting in her lap, his eyes closed. She was rocking him back and forth, humming quick snatches of song. "His name is Osren," she said softly, so as not to wake him. "Their house collapsed on him, but his mother's body protected him from the worst of it." She paused.

"His mother's body," she repeated, sounding choked. "When the news breaks throughout Elouve, everything we've done would have been all for nothing. Resentment and fear will rise again. We need to find out who's responsible for this, Zidan. We cannot return until we have rooted out this vampire nest and destroy it before they can harm another village."

"As you wish, my love."

"Good." Xiaodan looked at Remy. "I know this wasn't part of what we promised, but we can't ignore this incident. They could strike again."

"You don't need to ask." Remy looked down at the sleeping child. "We'll avenge them, if nothing else."

16

COLOSSUS

Xiaodan arranged for all three survivors to be housed and fed and their living arrangements paid for. She left money in trust to Eugenie so the children would be cared for for the rest of their lives, with enough to apprentice them to the trades of their choice when they were older. It was a generous endowment, but Remy understood Xiaodan's guilt. He'd done the same thing with the Harvestons and with many other families.

"A prominent tattoo on the forearm, marked with the letter *V*," Malekh said with disgust as he read the rest of Eugenie's report, which had been hidden inside a secret compartment at the base of the hideous goblet. "Vasilik. An attempt to redesign the Fifth Court sigil with his followers. We should know more once we reach Brushfen."

The fastest way, as Lady Eugenie had said, was through the forests of Wurkenbacht. Even the helhests slowed to an uneasy canter upon entering the woods. Eugenie had cautioned them against a nighttime journey, but once trapped within the thicket, the lack of daylight made little difference—not even the sun would improve their dismal surroundings. Everything looked damp and diseased. The trees might have appeared evergreen and leafy from two miles away, but up close, the brown miasma radiating off them grew more visible, as if the previous greenery had been camouflage or bait, or both. A rotting scent—a combination of petrichor and shit—prevailed against the fog, as if something had died of dysentery all around them.

Something eyelike and red winked at Remy from the gloom before dissolving back into darkness.

"This is a trap," Malekh said from his carriage perch.

"Do tell." Remy kept guard from his open window, but nothing else stirred in the dim.

"We've been watched from the moment we entered the woods. I can hear them."

Remy hadn't heard anything. He'd been too busy waiting to see how many more eyeballs the forest could sprout, and if there would be accompanying teeth to go with them. But the faint skittering noises among the branches overhead became as loud as warning bells as soon as the man had mentioned it.

"There is something hunting here. Stop for a moment, Zidan."

The carriage grounded to a halt, and Xiaodan pointed at something hanging from a nearby tree.

It was half of a deer carcass. Nearly all its skin had been flayed, and the blood slowly dripping down indicated it had been a fresh kill.

Slowly, Remy drew out Breaker. "Why isn't anything attacking us?"

"Perhaps we should ask." There was a sound outside of something metallic being unsheathed. Then of something being thrown, a whirring hiss of agitated air. A solid *thunk*.

The creature crashed heavily down on the ground beside the coach. It was large and feathered, but it was not a bird. Underneath the plumage there was no meat, only bone. It had no beak, but it had a mouth, which it used to snap at Remy, its neck extending forward like some demented jack-in-the-box.

Its teeth caught on the chain, and it would have yanked him out of the carriage if Xiaodan hadn't the presence of mind to latch on to him and drag him back. Remy frantically drove Breaker several times into the monster's face, but the creature refused to let go, still clinging stubbornly.

Remy shoved a boot into its jawbone, but it continued to cling to the side of the carriage. He stuck Breaker through the window and slid his scythes out, the blades driving into the sides of its head, cleaving its skull in two. Its grip finally slackened, its body disappearing underneath the carriage wheels as the coach jarred back into speed.

Remy risked his own neck to look out the window, but Xiaodan pulled him back in just as several more creatures, long-limbed and seemingly made entirely of thick vertebrae wrapped in thin glutinous membranes, leaped over the headless form and gave chase. Their flesh was transparent—wide eyeballs and perpetually grinning jaws stretched over sunken faces, bits of brain and other unmentionables floating in watery skulls. Perfectly normal things to be gaining ground on you in the dead of the woods.

At the head of the pack was a mutation larger than the rest of the herd. It had the same unnatural arms and hunched, apelike countenance as those it led, but with more meat to its shape and furred in some areas.

"Another colossus, I presume," Malekh said.

The massive beast roared. Taking that as a command, the creatures around it redoubled their efforts. In another few minutes, they would reach the carriage and the trio would be overwhelmed.

"You could have waited for them to say hello," Remy shouted at Malekh.

"Likely an ambush was planned for us up ahead. I'd rather nip that in the bud while we still have the opportunity."

"Didn't you say these arses couldn't think for themselves?" Remy aimed his fire lance at the closest mutation and fired. The impact knocked it off its feet and set it ablaze, sending it careening into two more creatures keeping pace behind it. Elke hadn't given him the one that could shoot lightning, more's the pity.

"They can't." Malekh abandoned the reins to stab his sword at another flying horror, flinging it over the side. "Someone must be directing them."

"Don't know about you, but they don't seem like the type to take orders."

"Easy enough to herd animals our way without them needing to use their brains. Or what remains of them."

The helhests were no longer galloping at a preternatural speed, so Remy hauled himself halfway out the window, knifechain spinning in his hand. It wrapped itself around the nearest creature's elbow, and a quick jerk of the links severed its forearm. His next throw caught another between its eyes, ripping spongy tissue out through the back of its head.

"Save your strength," he heard Malekh say when Xiaodan braced a boot against the windowsill.

"Can't I just have a *little* bit of slaughter? I'm sure they won't notice."

"Xiaodan."

She let out a small snort of protest but acquiesced. "Give me your lance, Armiger, and your firepowder jar."

The ease at which she loaded the barrel and locked the mechanism back into place was suspicious to Remy. The calm way she aimed the lance, fired, and took out two at once without blinking at both the extra force and the added recoil from Elke's modifications, even more so. "I've relieved people a time or two of their lances," the noblewoman explained cheerfully, lining up another shot. "When you've got poor health and other limitations, you learn to turn anything you can get your hands on into a weapon. That's what Alegra always says."

Remy would dearly like to ask who the hell Alegra was, but a hard crash on the roof told him another winged demon had landed, and that Malekh was engaging it in a fistfight.

"Heel!" the noble shouted. The horses whinnied but slowed to a stop.

"What in the bloody Light are you doing?" Remy yelled up at him.

"I have a theory." Several more thuds in rapid succession. Something rolled off the carriage roof to land in several pieces on the mossy floor.

"This is not the blasted time for your damned theories!"

Malekh ignored him. "Keep them busy." He jumped down, tore past the shambling monsters and right at their pack leader.

"What in the fuck are you—"

The grinning titan thrust out its great arms and knocked Malekh into a tree, and for a moment, Remy's heart nearly stopped. But the vampire twisted nimbly in the air, landed sideways against the trunk, and launched himself forward again. The mutation staggered back, a fist-sized hole in its chest, but righted itself back up and swung a second time.

Xiaodan was having the time of her life. Her last two shots liquefied two beasts, but she soon abandoned the lance to switch to close-quarter fighting when more had drawn up beside the carriage. She spun and kicked upward with her boot. It caught one mutation in the chin and kept going through it to drive her heel up into its brain. Remy kept distance with his attackers, falling back on Breaker's chains to keep him out of reach, occasionally catching some unaware with a blade through their sternum.

Malekh righted his sword and attacked again. It sliced through the colossus's temples like thin paper, but still the monster continued lashing out.

Some of the creatures that had already gone down were ris- ing back up again, crawling forward and ignoring the rest of their body parts scattered about. "How long are we supposed to be keeping them busy?" Remy snarled.

"Can you not last a minute without shutting up, Pender- gast?" Malekh reappeared several feet away from his opponent, eyes raking over its hideous form. He blurred back into the fight again—but this time, his sword sank to the hilt into the beast's shaggy shoulder.

It collapsed. So did the rest of the group, falling silently to the ground without another sound. One creature about to leap onto Remy's scythes died midair before he could stab at it.

"As I suspected," Malekh said, satisfied, picking himself up and dusting imaginary lint off his shoulder. "The dominant mutation that controls the herd has its own weak points. Know the proper place to strike, and you can immobilize the rest."

"Are you mad?" Remy shouted. "By the Light's arse, you didn't know any of that when you chose to throw yourself at it!"

He could have sworn that the Summer Lord looked surprised. "I know what I'm doing."

"Well, congratu-bloody-fucking-lations to you, but I didn't! Being a vampire as old as sin doesn't mean you couldn't be torn limb from limb if—"

He realized he was still yelling. He stopped abruptly, aware of both vampires now watching him: Xiaodan with a soft smile on her face, and Malekh bereft of any expression at all.

"Forget it," Remy muttered. "You're bloody unbreakable, and I'm a fool for thinking otherwise." He focused on the corpses in- stead, relaxed when nothing moved for the better part of a min- ute. "That wasn't what happened at the Archives. They weren't immobilized this way."

"The bodies at the Archives were of a different, simpler strain. The Rot is believed to have originated somewhere in the north-east, so any new evolutions would reach Western Aluria last. This colossus is a much more primitive version. Easier to kill, not as evolved as others we've previously faced."

Remy watched him take out another syringe. "You're going to get more fucking blood out of this?"

"I've had the opportunity to study only one other colossus with similar markers. It's prudent to collect any samples I can."

"How many of those needles do you still have secreted up your arse?"

"When I mentioned shutting up, Pendergast, it was not intended as a suggestion."

"The poor things," Xiaodan said. "Were they villagers, too, Zidan?"

"It's difficult to say. There weren't any reports of missing villagers in Ankersaud. But after the attack at Brushfen . . . I would hope that these were animals, not people."

Xiaodan annihilated the bodies, and they continued on their way. "Up north was once Second Court territory," she said as the horses trotted at a much more tolerable pace, should anything else lie in wait for them ahead. "Such a waste."

"They don't deserve pity," Remy muttered, keeping a watchful eye on the rest of the world outside the carriage. "The Second Court kidnapped girls from all over Aluria."

"Is that what the humans believe?" Malekh's voice drifted back at them, dry. He was sitting on the carriage perch outside, keeping the horses steady, keeping guard. "Do you not think that dashing young vampire nobles drunk on their own egos would not appeal to pretty girls?"

"The Lady Marissa never went willingly. She was kidnapped by Kurdashev."

"What?" Xiaodan was startled. "No. She eloped with Kurdashev. The Second Court leader was many things, but he was adamant that their human paramours come willingly. He did not want to gain Aluria's ire after that terrible business with your Lady Annalisa, but they came after him and his court all the same."

"Lady Annalisa? I am not familiar with her situation."

"Lady Annalisa was a minor baron's fourth daughter. Forty years before, one of the more depraved youths of the Second Court, a reprobate named Giornovo, took the baroness's daughter, tortured, and killed her for his enjoyment. And even then, that malformed baron calling himself her father was more concerned with haggling for the compensation her death emboldened him to demand, than what was left of his poor child's corpse."

"Impossible." Remy was hoarse. "Surely I would have heard of this. Surely they would have defended Lady Annalisa, had they—"

But they had known. Of course they had. *Lady Marissa was not the only lady who'd been kidnapped*, his father had told him. *I implored them to take action long before her abduction, but the previous deaths had been lower-class girls who were beneath the Reapers' notice.*

"The right things for the wrong reasons," Malekh said. "A shared habit among you mortals."

"Zidan did kill Giornovo," Xiaodan offered helpfully.

"He boasted of finding more women to desecrate," Malekh said. "He hunted on Third Court lands. I had every right, even though the other courts did not think so." His voice dipped, barely audible above the sounds of the helhests' hooves. "I do not approve of murder, humans or otherwise."

That rankled at Remy. Bold of the man to declare such distaste when his father's own notes had called him the *former consort to the Night King, and once his Lord Executioner*. He had retreated from questioning Malekh after his attempt at Ankersaud, deciding it foolish while he was traveling with them into parts unknown, while at the mercy of their confounded helhests and carriage. Eugenie's more sympathetic retelling both confirmed *and* complicated matters.

"It strikes me," Malekh added, "that you know very little of what you are supposed to hunt."

"Why don't you enlighten me with your wisdom, then." Remy was trying to be cautious, despite his irritation. He knew enough about trauma not to force anyone else to have to relive it. "Do the other courts even know of Xiaodan's abilities?"

"It is not a secret," Xiaodan confirmed quietly. "Many members of the Fourth Court left because of it. Not many wanted to be associated with the Sunbringer."

"Xiaodan, I didn't mean to—"

"No. It is a reality I have had to learn to accept, and you will need to know this if you are traveling with us. Every court has its own prerequisites, its own rules for acceptance. The Sixth Court appeals to those seeking an immortality of mind rather than just of the body, through meditation and pacifism. The Seventh Court has a military bent, while the Eighth seeks to bring back the allure and glitter of the older courts."

Xiaodan leaned back against her seat. "Zidan's court accepts all who ask, offers them sanctuary. The others do not approve. They are equally as contemptuous that he would saddle himself with a young vampiress who could bring out the sun and endanger his own existence, much less everyone else's."

"They call my clan 'the Court of Wanderers, the Restless Court'—an insult," Malekh added, not sounding offended at all. "They do not approve of our nomadic tendencies."

"That doesn't sound like enough to deserve such ridicule."

"The Third Court is ridiculed because *I* am the Third Court king. It was I who broke the Night Court."

"What?" Remy resisted the urge to climb out the window and onto the ledge beside Malekh just so he could stare the man in the face.

"I killed the Night King," Malekh said, voice devoid of both vindication and sorrow. The horses shifted into an easy trot; they were nearly out of the forest, and the vampire lord's words were a quiet presence, the only other sound. "I, and Lilith, the Fourth Court queen who ruled then. Isn't this what you wanted to know, Pendergast? All those centuries as his sword, and I left his court for nothing but a conscience grown years too late. He sent killers after me. I slew them all. Only Lilith was willing to fight with me, and she paid with her life. The other courts thrived after his death, but the Night King's loss proved their weakness, and they despise me for it."

The utter lack of emotion from Malekh on what was clearly a painful story was worrying. Remy could see it in Xiaodan's expression, the way her hand gripped the sill and her whole body tensed forward as if she was going to fling herself out the window to comfort the man outside carrying the reins in his hands and the rest of the world on his shoulders.

The horses stopped, attuned to their master's mood. The wheels creaked to a halt.

"I told you back at Ankersaud," Remy said, feeling guilty. "You don't need to tell me anything."

Malekh's voice lowered, heavy in the places that should have been filled with grief. "The remnants of his court, wherever they may be, still wish ill to all who stand with me. You bristle at being called bait, but it is what you are. Left to your own devices you will seek them out, and they will murder you and send pieces of your corpse back to us to gloat. You chafe at being called weak, but that simply does not matter to me. We intend to protect you. Whatever your hatred of me, I will not see you harmed."

"I don't hate you," Remy said. "I think you're a fucking prick, but I don't—I don't—"

He didn't *loathe* Zidan Malekh. At least, not when the man said flattering bullshit like this.

"I can take care of myself," he added quickly, not wanting to make things awkward. "I don't intend to leave either of you just to slake my vengeance, even if the opportunity arises. I'm not so foolish as to take on the Night Empress or any of her high nobles on my own, if that should rest you easy. I suppose that I am . . . grateful . . . that you and Xiaodan are concerned for my well-being, even if I may not always agree."

A pause, and then the helhests began moving again, up to nearly the same breakneck speed as before.

"There is no gratitude necessary." Malekh no longer sounded so stoic, if only because he now sounded irritable. "The less of a liability you are, the better this journey will be."

Remy extended his longest finger in the noble's direction, un-caring whether Malekh was oblivious to the gesture, but Xiaodan was giggling and relaxing back in her seat, no longer tense and waiting, like some unspoken danger had passed.

They passed at least one unlucky victim en route to Brushfen. The carriage lay on its side, smashed into bits with its wheels either broken or missing. A man was stretched out on the ground, staring aimlessly at the trees with his throat and chest slashed open.

"Drained of blood," Malekh observed grimly. "A vampire, not the Rot. We're getting close."

RUINS

Malekh had insisted upon seeing the carnage at Brushfen for himself, hoping to find some further evidence
among the ashes. Once out of Wurkenbacht, they had
reached the ruined village just as the clouds above them darkened, the first sign that night was approaching.

Remy would not have known that he was standing on a village if not for the debris and the half-burnt sign that had once
suggested it was a thriving community. Now there was little left
behind but broken piles of wood and the strong smell of charred
smoke.

Malekh wasted no time sifting through what remained, using
his immense strength to fling piles of bricks and wood away. Remy
saw with some revulsion and pity that the fires had not completely
burned all the bodies; some were nearly unrecognizable as human,
while others lay intact.

Xiaodan crouched down beside one of the latter and sighed.
"Drained of blood," she said.

"And the fires appear to have been lit in haste. They were
careless, which corroborates the witnesses' statements that they

wished to leave before sunrise." Malekh continued his grisly survey as Xiaodan carefully carried out some of the bodies, laying them on the ground in a line. Remy found long canvases of cloth that had mostly escaped the flames—wagon coverings, from the looks of them—and placed them over the corpses.

"I'm told that it is the Reapers who conduct last rites in situations such as these," Xiaodan said.

"Yes, but I've never been good at it." Remy stood over the bodies anyway, his mind going over the words he'd been taught, formulaic more than it was heartfelt, but it was the last thing he could do for them. "Bless the Gatherer for the lives we've led," he prayed, "and bless the Mother for the souls we're given. Bless the Hunter for the lives we've lost, and bless the Light that our sins be forgiven."

It felt inadequate somehow, and so he continued, this time with a song. His voice was not of the quality that people would travel miles to hear, but he could manage a decent melody.

"When the good Mother lights heaven's way, you'll be safe here.
When the good Mother takes you from
distant shores, you'll be safe here.
When the good Mother guides you to
your rest, you'll be safe here.
When the good Mother gathers you home,
know that you'll be safe here."

"That was beautiful," Xiaodan said quietly after he was done. "Though I confess it's not what I'd expected of a Reaper's training. It doesn't sound like a litany from the Light's standard dogma."

A reluctant laugh found its way out of him. "It's not. It talks about a different mother that is not of the Three. A goddess the Tithians worship. It's something that my own mother sang to me when I was heavy in her womb."

"But didn't she . . . ?"

"My nanny taught me the song almost as soon as I could talk. She'd heard my mother singing it enough times, apparently. Thought knowing it would help me feel closer to her. And it did."

Xiaodan was looking uncomfortably grave, so Remy added awkwardly, "It's just a song."

When Malekh returned, his expression was insufferable, which meant he'd found something. He was dragging a body behind him. "There were approximately one hundred and fifty residents who lived in Brushfen," he said, "many still unaccounted for. Only thirty-two corpses that I can count, the rest likely lost in the blaze. They put up a good fight, took down at least one vampire."

Malekh tossed the aforementioned undead corpse their way; it landed noisily on the ground. There was no mistaking the fangs, the youth. "He has no sigils on him, though that's not necessarily proof."

Remy took another look. "He has a large birthmark on the side of his neck," he said. "I've gone through reports of missing boys all over Aluria in the last two years. One described a boy nine-and-ten summers, with a birthmark like this one." He shouldn't have been surprised. He'd heard of missing youths returning as resurrected vampires, the short span of time they'd disappeared enough to strip away their humanity for something crueler.

Malekh frowned. "It would explain the sloppiness of this assault, if most of these vampires were new and untried."

"Surely the coven your brother dallied with could have been part of this?" Remy asked.

"More than one coven can hunt in the same area."

"Or," Remy pushed, because he never knew when to stop himself, "you're doing your best to absolve your brother of any wrongdoing and letting that cloud your judgment."

He didn't actually see Malekh take a step toward him. The

noble had been standing several feet away, and then was within breathing distance in the blink of an eye. "Leave Naji out of this," Malekh said.

"How many others did they terrorize before Lady Daneira?" Remy challenged him. "How many more of their ilk are roaming around Aluria at this very moment? Because you sure as hell didn't care if it was just a human victim you could dismiss as insignificant. What if these were renegade Third Court vampires?"

"If Third Court vampires are responsible for this massacre," Malekh said, "then I will personally take the heads off each and every one of them myself, the way I would have with the pack my brother had fallen in with, had you not done so first. I have never considered human life trivial. Not Lady Daneira's or anyone else's."

"You told Xiaodan I would be useless here. With the sole exception of the Marquess of Riones—and occasionally my father, should the mood suit him—the Reapers never protected me for shit. I said I'd survive at the Archives, and I did."

"That is true." A sudden, infuriatingly attractive grin lifted one corner of Malekh's mouth. "I have every faith in your ability to hold your own *now*, Pendergast. You are a capable warrior, for a human. It is everything else about you that I find taxing."

Remy wasn't expecting Malekh to agree with him. He'd been expecting another prolonged argument, not a compliment from the vampire lord of all people, even a backhanded one. It shouldn't have made him burn hot from head to toe, like someone had set off a flare inside him.

"I suggest making camp nearby to rest for the night. Should morning come with no word from Eugenie, we can choose to make haste toward Chànggē Shuǐ or consider other options."

Xiaodan didn't yell at either of them as she was oft to do whenever one started a pissing match with the other. But she was staring after Malekh as he walked away to continue his investigations.

The smile on her face worried Remy for some reason, so much more than anything Malekh had said.

NEITHER XIAODAN nor Malekh expressed any desire to eat, so Remy kept dinner simple: bread, cheese, a slab of smoked sausage. A campfire was out of the question—it would make them easy targets. The quick luncheon he'd grabbed at the inn in Ankersaud felt like days ago, but with the burnt village for scenery, Remy didn't have much of an appetite anyway.

He watched Malekh extract several folds of paper from within the large fish goblet to reread again. One was a map the noble laid out on the ground, with large *X*s marked in red to indicate the sites of previous vampire attacks—smaller in scale than Brushfen, but presenting a similar pattern.

"A vampire coven is haunting Northumber and Darosen," he said, tracing a path along the parchment with his finger. "Brushfen is within their radius; it cannot be a coincidence. The earliest reports were isolated cases, with only one or two travelers killed. They have since been targeting more people with every assault. Brushfen may well be a sign that they are ready to begin preying on larger villages and towns."

"We need to flush the nest out before we return to Chànggē Shuǐ," Xiaodan said. "We have to."

Malekh laid down another parchment, this time a sketch of a man with red hair and a penetrating gaze, with a scar over his right cheek, and a square jaw. "One of the survivors reported seeing him before the attack on Brushfen, leading the Brushfen attack."

"I've never seen him before," Xiaodan said, studying the face. "But his features are easy enough to recognize. Let me read through the rest later. "

"Haven't seen either of you eat anything today," Remy said in between bites. Vampires could go on extended periods without feeding, but he wasn't sure what their limits were. Elke didn't believe in fasting and often took her blood together with her wine in small portions over the course of a day, but she was the only vampire he was close enough with to associate any eating habits to.

"Zidan usually hunts," Xiaodan said. "There's always something to eat in the woods. I usually take my fill of Zidan."

Vampires didn't usually rely on other vampires for their nutrition. Remy paused mid-chew. "Why?"

Xiaodan tapped at her chest. "I can drink blood elsewhere, but Zidan's has certain properties that allow me to gain back my strength faster than animal or human nourishment can."

"So he gives himself . . . what, health pills?" Remy couldn't muster the required imagination beyond picturing Xiaodan wrapped around Malekh's neck, delectable mouth feasting on the perfect flesh there, or why the thought of it unnerved him in distinctly uncomfortable ways. "And you drink that like he's some afternoon tea?"

"A combination of blood thickeners and modified hemoglobins is a far cry from pastries and biscuits," Malekh said, unfastening his collar. Remy's eyes were immediately drawn to the movement, taking in the curve of his neck, a hint of tanned collarbone, before forcing himself to look away.

"Xiaodan's condition forces her to process blood at a rate twice as fast as the average vampire's," the noble continued, thankfully unaware. "The blood cycles back into her system quicker, letting her extract more of the sustenance she requires. Her feeding triggers a faster regeneration on my end, increasing my strength in turn. It is a mutually beneficial relationship."

Mutually beneficial parasites. What a romantic notion. "It explains why you're together," Remy said, then realized the unintended insult. "It explains *a* reason you're together," he clarified, shoving more bread into himself.

Xiaodan laughed. "Curious?"

He'd stuffed his mouth full so as not to get in more trouble, but that didn't stop Remy from nodding.

"How about a trade? I'll answer any questions you may have, in exchange for answering one of mine."

Completely reasonable. Another nod.

"All right. Zidan and I met . . . oh, about thirty or so years ago. He had been turned for nearly nine hundred years by then."

Remy nearly choked on his meal. He'd known that Malekh was old even by vampire standards, but nine hundred bloody years? Astonbury would have given up his right testicle for any information about the Third Court ruler, and his fiancée was tossing out information like it was nothing.

"And I am the natural-born daughter of Queen Yingyue, queen of the Court of Tranquility. That would make me about forty years old, though cambions tend to stop physically aging in our twenties or thereabouts."

"*You're* a cambion?" All the shit he got from Malekh over being one, and his *fiancée* was the dhampir? The cuntsack didn't even look apologetic; he merely tilted his head and closed his eyes, listening to Xiaodan talk.

"My father was human. The Third and Fourth Courts were always the closest allied among the other factions, and Zidan would often travel to our castle to discuss kindred matters with my mother."

"And it was a wonder we could talk much business, with you constantly underfoot." There was a rare unrestrained affection in Malekh's voice, which he made no effort to hide. He sat close to Xiaodan, and his hand found hers, stroking absently at the back of it.

"It took him a while to notice me. He was rude on the occasions he did visit. I declared war on him for that." Xiaodan's smile faded. "Mother isn't as strong as she once was. That's always been a problem with vampires who live several hundred lifetimes over—sometimes you just get so . . . overwhelmed by living that you can spend eternities simply waiting to die."

Sorrow laced her voice. "Mother lost her consort, my father, many years ago, and she still mourns. I was the only child she ever had, and by the time I was old enough, the Fourth Court had fallen into ruins because of her neglect."

"He was her familiar?" Remy asked.

"Ever been one yourself?" Malekh asked, raising an eyebrow.

"I would rather stab my own heart and bleed out than submit myself to a vampire."

"There is more to a familiar than just being a vampire's pet." Malekh smiled slowly. "Although that is not necessarily a terrible thing to be, if one prefers both."

"Yes," Xiaodan said, a pretty blush suffusing her features.

A change of subject was in order. "So how did Malekh wind up meddling in Fourth Court affairs?"

Xiaodan sighed. "Without a firm hand from Mother, we made for easy targets. Zidan did his best to convince her to take a more aggressive position, to stop the forays of the Second and Fifth Courts from taking slices of our territory, but to no avail.

"The inevitable happened, of course. The Fifth Court decided we were ripe for the taking, and they were nearly right. It was only with Zidan and the Third Court's assistance that we survived. The Summer Lords took out all of the Fifth, along with several Second Court vampires aiding Etrienne Sauveterre."

"Including Declan Aughessy, the Second Court king," Remy said. "Aughessy attempted to invade Northern Aluria afterward and claim it for his own. Father and many other Reapers traveled to his castle to kill him before he could succeed. Then Orestes Kurdashev took over, but the Reapers annihilated them again years later, this time for good."

"Edgar Pendergast didn't kill Declan Aughessy," Zidan said. "Xiaodan did."

Remy's mouth fell open.

"Zidan," Xiaodan protested.

"If we are to travel with him, then surely he ought to know the truth about his sire's exploits."

Remy couldn't help it. He burst into laughter. "My pardon," he guffawed, wiping at his eyes with a sleeve. "I wasn't laughing at you, Xiaodan. I was laughing at my father's bloated sense of self-importance. He really does believe that he killed Aughessy. How did he come to think that?"

"We fought the Second Court just as Aluria had declared war on them," Malekh said. "The Reapers arrived in the midst of our battle, the court already in disarray. Aughessy was fast on his way to dying when your father found him."

"I intended to let him suffer longer," Xiaodan said, quieter now. "If anything, your father was much more merciful."

Malekh squeezed her hand. "She killed Etrienne Sauveterre, as well, though his death left some lasting effects on her."

"Your heart," Remy said, realizing.

"He damn well nearly killed me, is what happened," Xiaodan said. "It roused Mother enough from her stupor to do the best and the worst thing she could have done to save my life."

"And what's that?"

Xiaodan placed her hand over her chest, and Remy could hear it go *ba-thump bada-bada-thump bada-thump*. "She gave me a new heart," she said. "One that she'd been keeping under lock and key for centuries."

That didn't make sense. "Are you speaking metaphorically?"

Xiaodan grinned, wagged a finger at him. "One question of yours for one of mine, and I've already been far too lenient. My turn. What did Eugenie mean when she referred to you surviving something when you were only thirteen?"

It was getting cold. They really should have risked a fire. "Ask me a different question," Remy said roughly.

"What? I was—"

"Ask me a different question." He didn't want to talk about it.

He didn't even want to think about it, but it was too late; the past was back in his brain, rotting through. "Have Eugenie tell you if you're that curious, but I won't. If there's nothing else, I'm going to take a piss."

"Let him go," Remy heard Malekh tell Xiaodan as he stomped off. "It's about time for your feeding."

It only took a few minutes for Remy to do his business and shove his breeches back up, though the restlessness persisted. He found a small stream and lingered there, washing what he could of himself without taking his clothes off, and the gurgling of running water helped ease his mind, if only just a little.

He didn't want to think about it. He couldn't even remember most of what had happened, almost like it hadn't happened to him at all and he was only recalling, very dimly for the most part, but in quick bursts of bright graphic details in others, a story that someone else had told him. A hazy fog had settled over those memories, colder and thicker than anything even mist-shrouded Aluria could manifest. He was better off not remembering.

He didn't want to remember the bits he did recall. Like the sound of his screaming, high-pitched and warbly. The feel of the heavy Breaker above him as he whipped it at faster, dizzying speeds, knowing that if he slowed down even once, that they would fall on him and he would die.

"Stop being such a fucking git," Remy said aloud. "Fuck. Fuck it."

He returned to where the others were.

It was a mistake.

Xiaodan sat on Malekh's lap, legs wrapped around his waist. Her mouth was pressed against the side of the man's neck. Her eyes were closed, her face euphoric. She was moaning softly, writhing, moving back and forth against her lover.

Malekh's collar was now completely unbuttoned; his perfect, muscular neck exposed. His head was thrown back, his breathing low and even. His hands were gripping Xiaodan's backside, slowly lifting her up and down against him, in a rhythm that Remy all too quickly understood. Neither had undressed, but it didn't matter. He watched the way their bodies curved hungrily toward each other; sensual, intimate.

He should have turned back around. He should have idled longer at the stream; he would have avoided seeing them in this painful, lovely way if he had. And yet he couldn't leave. Remy's breaths left him in short, spastic gasps, unconsciously following their rhythm like he was a participant rather than an unwanted voyeur. There was a strange beauty to their forms, the arresting way they fit together, and it left him with a slow burning, a yearning for something he could not find the words for.

They cared for each other. Deeply, irrevocably, completely. He had never had that for his own.

He watched Xiaodan's soft red lips move higher up Malekh's neck. He wondered what they felt like, then felt ashamed, because she had spurned his dismal adulterous attempts in Elouve and had been nothing but devoted to Malekh. And how Malekh looked as he—

Malekh's eyes slid open, now nearly golden in their entirety. Though Remy stood in the shadows, they fastened immediately on him like the man knew he was there and never looked away even as Xiaodan moaned and shuddered in his arms. There was a hunger in the vampire's gaze, bold and unapologetic as he sat, letting Remy watch them.

Something curved at the Summer Lord's mouth, too fierce to be a smile. He leaned forward and whispered something against Xiaodan's hair, the words so soft that Remy could not hear.

The beautiful girl in Malekh's arms trembled, her lips leaving his neck briefly. "Yes," she groaned, eager and filled with need. "Yes. I want him, too."

18

BLUFF

The pigeon bearing Eugenie's letter arrived at dawn, just as they were readying to leave. The man with the red hair had been spotted again, the secrets-trader had written, this time at the village of Zelenka, over twenty miles east of Brushfen.

This suited their plans just fine, Xiaodan said. Zelenka lay en route to Chànggē Shuǐ, so they would not deviate much from their planned path.

Remy was thankful that the carriage was speeding too quickly to encourage much talk. Xiaodan was staring down at her hands, fingers nervously twisting at one of her long sleeves. She hadn't stopped blushing since they'd left Brushfen; for a vampire, it was an impressive feat. In contrast, Malekh was relaxed—too relaxed. There was no one leading the helhests outside, but Peanut and Cookie seemed to know where they were going, which was more than could be said of Remy. He concentrated on the rushing scenery outside his window, choosing the faint bouts of nausea over having to look at his companions.

Because he couldn't. It was too easy to remember the way Xiaodan's mouth traveled down Malekh's neck, the way the man's head had reclined back to give her better access. The peaceful expression on his face that Remy had never seen him wear before.

Remy didn't want to remember the way they looked last night, at the unexpectedly sensual way they were caught by what bits of moonlight had trespassed through the fog, and the way it made his own chest tighten, like he was mourning a loss he'd never known till now.

Halfway into their journey to Zelenka, Xiaodan finally spoke. Still pink-cheeked, still fussing with her dress, still not looking up from her lap, she said, "I really would like to apologize. For . . . what you saw. I should've had Zidan's blood in Elouve, before we started, but we were so busy with our preparations and his investigations that it had slipped my mind."

She'd spent her last night at the capital guarding Kinaiya Lodge, fearful of any reprisals from Vasilik. It made Remy feel even guiltier.

"Even so," Xiaodan continued, "there was no good reason to be so . . . forthright, out in the open, knowing we all have little expectation of privacy. You left so quickly last night, and I couldn't quite think of a way to apologize this morning."

She thought he'd left because he was embarrassed. Remy let it pass without explaining himself because that would mean confessing that he'd left because he'd been so fucking aroused. "There's nothing to be sorry for. You're both engaged. I should be more mindful."

"I hope this doesn't change anything?" Xiaodan asked anxiously.

"Of course not. Don't think anything else of it. I won't." He was lying through his goddamn teeth. It had changed everything between them. He had left quickly because he couldn't stay. Not after she'd told Malekh that she had wanted him, too.

He'd mustered enough strength to retreat back into the woods before he could do the unthinkable and take her up on her offer, but hadn't enough willpower for much else, because once he was out of sight and some ways away, he had grimly loosened his breeches a second time and attended to himself, more determined to get it out of his system rather than from any eagerness to finish. He had found no particular satisfaction from this solo act.

Oversexed, he thought. *I've been bloody oversexed for so long that anyone I find even remotely attractive gets me off quick. Fuck Giselle. No. That's what started this whole damn mess in the first place.*

He'd already taken his dose of bloodwakers, and everything was looking exceptionally vivid today, Xiaodan's lips especially soft and inviting in the morning light. And her scent. Vampires shouldn't have had any, so it was no business of hers to smell so light and sweet from her side of the carriage. It was fucking him up, just a little. Maybe something stronger to drink in Zelenka or whatever village they wound up at next; he didn't care which one, as long as there were people about with ale strong enough to dull his senses.

He couldn't look at Malekh, either. The man had seen him. Even worse, Malekh had *liked* that he'd seen them. Probably smiled at him to fuck with his head.

The Summer Lord was currently leaning back against his seat. His eyes were closed, but that tilted smile was there once again, mocking and certain. Without meaning to, Remy's eyes drifted lower toward the man's neck, smooth and unmarked by Xiaodan's teeth. His scent was familiar, the same from when they'd first fought.

Uninvited came the thought of what the vampire might taste like. What if it had been *his* mouth against the man's skin? Remy wondered if the lord was always as gentle a lover as he was with Xiaodan, or if he was ever rougher—

Remy jerked his attention back toward the window, scowling. *Stop thinking. Stop fucking thinking.*

Zelenka clearly knew what had happened to Brushfen. Remy could see the large wooden stakes they'd erected on the ground surrounding the village, a warning to visitors against drawing nearer.

"It would be best to shelter the helhests here and travel the rest of the way on foot," Malekh said. "Let's not give them more reasons to be wary."

"The problem will be passing ourselves off successfully as human," Xiaodan said worriedly. "What do you think, Remy?"

Only then did Remy finally look; at Xiaodan, whose deceptively plain qipao could not hide its expensive satin and elaborate stitchwork, and then at Malekh, who could wear burlap sacks and still be incapable of hiding his noble, arrogant bearing. He sighed.

They secured both the helhests and the carriage inside the woods, keeping them out of sight, and walked the rest of the way. Remy could see a great number of men and women were gathered by Brushfen's gates—far too many guards for a village their size.

"Halt!" one of the men shouted, spotting them approaching. "State your business! Otherwise, be off with you!"

"We are travelers hoping to stay the night," Xiaodan called back in her meekest voice. "Has something happened?"

"There's been vampires attacking all up the northwest, with a whole village razed to the ground. Everyone from here to Southport are arming themselves. We're taking those same precautions." The man eyed her suspiciously. "You don't look like you're from around here, miss."

"I come from Sanchiri, farther east. My companions and I are traveling there."

"Sanchiri?" one of the women asked suspiciously. "That's in Qing-ye territory. They say whole towns up there welcome vampires as their overlords."

"My fiancée's mother lives in Sanchiri," Malekh said pleasantly. "The court vampires in Qing-ye have dwindled enough that they are no longer a threat. It seems to me that it is far more dangerous to be traveling in Aluria now than to the east."

"True. But our village is closed to strangers as of the moment."

"They look suspicious," the woman insisted. "Where are their horses? Their wagons? They look far too coiffed to have gone all this way by walking, what with that gentleman over there with his fancy clothes. Who's to say they're not spies for those vampires that burned down Brushfen? Didn't the mayor warn of suspicious strangers about, asking questions?"

The looks directed their way became much more hostile.

"I think it would be best to leave," Malekh said quietly.

"If what you say is true, then we should find other accommodations," Xiaodan said politely.

"Wait!" The shout came from behind the row of watchmen. An older man marched out, squinting at Remy. "I recognize you!" he roared. "You're that cambion pretending to be a Reaper! The duke's bastard, with the vampire blood! The Pendergast get!"

"Are you fucking jesting with me," Remy said, disbelieving. "You're singling me out as the vampire among us thr—"

There was a cacophony of clicks as a dozen pair of crossbows were trained Remy's way, arrows already nocked.

"We aren't interested in what you say is truth, and what you say is lies, sir," the first man said. "We'd cut you down where you stand if we didn't think there'd be reprisals coming from Her Majesty's Reapers, so we're giving out warnings first. You have five minutes to skitter out of sight before my men's arrows find your throat, and if you're wanting to keep your neck intact, you'd best stay far away from here."

"THE NERVE of them," Xiaodan fumed after they had regrouped half a mile later. "You've hunted vampires to keep them safe, and they dare call *you* the threat?"

"It's happened before," Remy said with all the resignation of one who'd been through it enough times to believe otherwise. "They're right to be afraid. That they're being overly cautious is good."

"I still have half a mind to march back there and give them what-for—"

"That would be counterproductive," Malekh reminded her calmly. "Pendergast is right. Their fears will help protect them."

"But what are we to do if we are not welcome in Zelenka?" Xiaodan demanded. "How certain was Eugenie about her sources? What if some other village comes under threat?"

"She is not one to act upon information until she is certain of its authenticity. If she believes Zelenka is next, then we shall wait for tonight. It would do you well to recuperate in the meantime. You've been using the sun's gift too often in Elouve for my liking, and you got very little rest last night."

Remy was fairly certain that Malekh hadn't intended to insinuate anything by that last remark, but Xiaodan turned red all the same. "I could use some shut-eye," she allowed reluctantly. Then she frowned. "Do *not* kill each other while I'm asleep."

"I'm sure Pendergast and I can put this free time to good use," Malekh said, still deadpan. "There is a wager that needs settling."

"'Wager'?" Remy asked. "What the hell are you—ah, fuck." He'd told the vampire that he was going to survive the attack at the Archives, even turned it into a bet with the noble owing him a favor if he did. He hadn't expected Malekh to remember, much less honor his defiance.

"Well," Xiaodan huffed, "I expect you both on better terms when I wake."

Malekh kept his gaze on the coach after she retired, looking back at Remy only after he'd made certain she was truly asleep, her heartbeats evening out. "I told her you wouldn't be up to our standards when it came down to a fight. She said if I was wrong, I ought to give you the training you should have had, as compensation. That is, of course, if you can last a round with me."

The Summer Lord was goading him; that much was obvious. But Remy would take him up on the offer anyway, eager for a rematch. "On the contrary," he said. "It would be my pleasure to beat the fucking hell out of you."

The nobleman didn't even bother drawing out his sword, his stance more relaxed than expectant. "Come at me whenever you're ready, then. Let's not be all day about it."

No preparations, no warm-ups, not even rules. That was fine by Remy, who wasted no time taking hold of Breaker and promptly charging the lord.

There was a razor-honed, controlled grimness to Malekh's fighting—a strange contrast to Remy's, since he was often more furious than finessed. The noble's movements were as precise as a mathematical calculation. He flowed from one position to the next, knew exactly where he should be to counter every thrust and parry, and followed up with well-placed sweeps and blows that would have sent a lesser man to his knees in seconds.

And nine hundred years of fighting meant he would have learned to perfect those techniques, mastered the million and a half combinations for attacking and counterattacking. That scientific mind of his could no doubt see the blows just before they happened and could economize the best course of action to counter them. It had been the most noticeable thing Remy had seen whenever he saw the man fight—how Malekh would exert only exactly enough strength and speed to win, never showing off with unnecessary posturing.

On the other hand, Remy never pretended to be the smartest in the room; he wasn't one to crunch numbers and probabilities. He didn't have the skills to calculate the force he would need to take another man's head off. His greatest strength had always been his instinct. His other strength, possibly the only strength in a fight against Malekh, was that his moves were unpredictable enough to give anyone pause.

He focused on the immediate space around him, letting Breaker absorb the punches rather than leaping to the offensive because, Light's fuck, this vampire was as fast as ever. And still it felt like Malekh was holding himself back. Remy had fared poorly during their first fight, but he was matching the noble nearly blow for blow in this one.

"Stop that!" he snarled.

"Stop what?" Malekh's fist landed with a thud against Breaker's base, seeking an opening that Remy was unwilling to give.

"Stop bloody going easy on me!" Remy knew he'd guessed right when the man's eyes flickered, pausing for half a moment before Malekh aimed for his kneecaps. He caught the attempt with the flat side of his scythe, but the lord avoided his retaliatory slash. "You were faster than this back when I was whaling on your brother."

Malekh blurred and reappeared several feet away, out of reach. The tension in his jaw could snap off Remy's knifechain. "You're attempting to goad me into losing my temper. You would go out of your way to injure yourself simply out of pride?"

"You wanted me to prove myself back in Elouve. Now you're concerned for my safety. Fucking pick one, and make sure you pick the right one to bitch about." Remy ran to close the distance, chain whirring in his hands, and for the first time, the vampire was on the defensive. If it could be called that. Malekh merely weaved in between Remy's blows, avoiding them with ease, but did not take advantage to mount an offensive.

"Xiaodan doesn't want you incapacitated."

His admission only enraged Remy. "I don't need her concern, either. Why the fuck did you even agree to have me here if you both intend to treat me like I'm some goddamn child, like you do with Naji—"

And then Malekh was looming up in his vision, having somehow gotten past Breaker without Remy being aware of it. Suddenly it was Malekh in between him and his double scythes, face against his.

"The problem, Pendergast, is that neither Xiaodan nor I look at you as a child," Malekh whispered; guttural, coldly furious, and, Remy realized, stunned, thick with desire. "I saw you. I could smell your lust from where we sat. She thought you might join us. She is feeling your rejection most keenly."

"'Rejection'?" Remy echoed in surprise. His overinflated, unwanted reputation with unavailable women had much to answer for, because he was just learning he was far less experienced than he'd thought. He'd assumed he was being *respectful* of their needs, relieving his urges out in the woods away from them like a proper noble. "I didn't—it was a private moment—I left not because I was—was that why she was apologizing?"

"Xiaodan understands what passed between you and the duchess, how unsatisfying you found the relationship. Last night she was only thinking of the pleasure, her own desires. She feels guilty for propositioning you the way Lady Astonbury did. She does not want you to think of her in the same manner you think of the duchess."

Xiaodan was most emphatically not like the duchess. Giselle had never once attempted to seduce him by sucking on another man's neck. "I don't think of her at all like I do the duchess."

"We've argued over you many times." Malekh's hands were warm. They were wrapped around Remy's neck, light enough not to injure, but it hurt all the same. He didn't know how to defend himself against this. "She believes that any overtures toward you would make her no different from the other woman. I disagree."

One of Malekh's hands drifted higher so he could grasp the side of Remy's jaw tightly, forcing his head up to meet his own dark, heavy-lidded gaze. "I said you would be open to *both* our advances if we'd expressed our interest much more clearly."

He leaned in closer. "And Xiaodan is not awake at the moment to stop me."

Malekh didn't despise him.

Fuck.

"I'm not interested in you." Remy could feel the warmth of Malekh's breath against his neck and heard the man take a slow, long inhale, like he could physically sniff out his lies.

"Is that so." A knee moved between his thighs. "Then why are you as hard as the weapon you're so fond of carrying?"

"I concede," Remy rasped. He was sagging, Malekh the only reason he was still upright. "I forfeit this fucking fight. Let me go."

"I know what you did in the woods, Pendergast. I know what you were thinking."

The shudder that went through him was like a lightning bolt. "You're already with her. Why would you both . . . ?"

"Neither Xiaodan nor I had intentions of pursuing anyone else while we remain committed to each other. She has always been honest with me, and I with her. And when we both realized the hunter she'd been enchanted with in Elouve was the same one I'd fought . . ."

Remy could feel Malekh's mouth against his ear, the vibrations as his lips formed words against his skin. "Tell me you don't want this, Pendergast. Tell me you wouldn't want Xiaodan here with me, either. All three of us."

A part of him wanted Malekh to close the distance. To reenact all the dishonorable thoughts of him that Remy had harbored in the carriage. Another part wanted to knock him out cold.

The tip of a tongue stroked a line up his neck, and the latter part won out.

Malekh reappeared three feet from his right, smiling so smugly that it made Remy's fist hurt, even though he'd swung and missed.

"You cannot use my brother to get what you want," the vampire said, now back to his bored, slightly contemptuous self. "If you don't want me to go easy on you, then I shall accede to your wishes."

Remy charged at him, and this time the vampire was true to his word. In one swift movement, Breaker was torn from his grasp, and Remy landed hard on the ground, ears ringing from the cuff Malekh had delivered right across the fleshy part of his shoulder—any harder, and he would have dislocated it.

He was back on his feet despite the pain, rolling quickly to snatch his weapon back up and facing the vampire noble again.

Malekh's eyes were no longer bright from lust. "You think no one can anticipate your moves," he said. "But even random attacks require a follow-through, which you do not capitalize on. Remember that when you try to hit me again."

"Fuck you," Remy said.

"Perhaps one day, Pendergast. Now, shut up and strike me."

Remy hadn't wanted to feel disappointed. His neck still tingled, knowing how close he'd gotten to being marked there, how close he'd come to letting the man do it. How much of it had been an act? How much had been revenge for insulting his brother—Remy's fault for constantly needling the man there, granted—and how much had been the truth? Because Malekh was closed off to him once again, his eyes impossible to read.

Xiaodan was still sleeping. The noble had always been softer when it came to his fiancée, and it didn't feel like he would lie about anything concerning her, even if he was a prick the rest of the time.

Remy didn't want to think. He was angry, even though the vampire was doing exactly what he had asked him to do. Anger was good. Anger helped him focus on the fight and not what had just passed.

"Don't mind if I do," he said, then raised Breaker and charged again.

19

A VILLAGE DEFENSE

All things considered, Remy was still in good shape by the time night swooped in: fingers and toes in working order, nothing hurting that he wouldn't survive from.

Malekh hadn't held back. Remy had enjoyed it. The man made for good practice; he was faster than anyone Remy had ever faced, and his one consolation was that he'd kept Malekh from beating him too badly, even if he couldn't mount any real offensive. The noble hadn't been impressed, merely goaded him to hit harder. Likely the bastard would stake himself rather than give Remy any satisfaction.

Malekh had said nothing else about his proposal. As if he'd never had Remy trapped for the second time in two weeks, mouth hot against his throat. Remy rubbed at his neck and flushed. The asshole had used his tongue, for fuck's sake. The man probably went about fucking anything with two legs and a pulse just for the sport of it. The absence of the latter might not even be a deal-breaker.

Remy supposed Xiaodan was aware of her fiancé's proclivities— that she would choose to stay with him beggared all belief. She deserved better.

No. No, she didn't. Malekh might be a shitsack, but he loved Xiaodan.

He'd kept quiet after Xiaodan had woken. Even after she'd narrowed her eyes at them both and demanded a look at his bruises. After a cursory inspection of his injuries and some more grumbling, Xiaodan let it go.

"Are you sure you're all right?" Her breath left her in soft, quick pants, though no changes in her heartbeats suggested exhaustion. Her eyes were bright. Relief he was still in one piece, Remy thought.

"I'll be fine. Nothing I couldn't handle."

A quick, derisive snort from Malekh.

The conversation, thankfully, shifted to Zelenka. "We'll have to keep guard over the village without them the wiser," Xiaodan said. "They've relied solely on the fortification of their stakes and barricades, but that won't stop stronger vampires from getting past them. Their bonfires are well-placed, but they're not experienced fighters. Just one vampire getting through their defenses could do serious damage."

"And what do you propose we do?" Zidan sat on the carriage perch beside Xiaodan with a hand over hers, and Remy had to quell the urge to shout at him for being such a fucking hypocrite, because only a few hours ago, the lord had his goddamn hands on *him*. Instead, he concentrated on his Breaker, on the loops he was making with it in the air above him.

"Best to stay here and keep watch, be on guard for any movement around Zelenka before the villagers themselves notice. They may not even stage an assault tonight, but something tells me otherwise." Her nose twitched. "There's something in the air. I can smell it."

"The attack will likely come from the forests," Malekh said thoughtfully. "I'll move the helhests farther out. The fog's thicker, and no one will notice them grazing there."

Xiaodan hopped off the perch and turned to Remy as Malekh led Peanut and Cookie away. "You should still be resting," she said severely.

"This helps calm me."

"It looks exhausting."

"I'm used to it. This was the first thing I learned to do from my father. Said that if I didn't get used to the weight early on, I'd never be able to use it the way it ought to be used."

"Are you hoping to ease your mind for what's ahead, or is this because of Zidan?"

Remy stopped so abruptly that his knifechain swung without his guidance, and he just managed to deflect the blade before it could stab him in the hand. "What?"

"I could smell him on you." Xiaodan's gray eyes were gleaming again. "Stronger than he should be. I was worried about your sparring practice with him, but now I'm glad for . . . other reasons."

"You're not angry?"

"No. I . . . Zidan and I talked. It's more complicated than you think."

A million questions raced through Remy's mind, chief among them being *What the fuck?* and *Do I really want to know and get myself involved?*, though his mind stopped short of answering the latter.

Xiaodan had ducked her head slightly. Her breathing had grown rapid, her eyes taking on a slightly glazed look.

"Are you all right, Xiaodan?"

Her head snapped up. "No! I mean, yes. If Zidan bothers you again, please let me know immediately. I'll speak to him."

The idea of looking weak to Malekh by having Xiaodan talk to him in Remy's stead was unforgivable. "There's no need for you to intervene. He can do whatever the hell he wants. I can take it."

"Oh," Xiaodan said, somewhat faintly. "Oh."

They had a quick dinner—or rather, Remy had dinner while

Xiaodan and Malekh refrained from pawing at each other again, much to his relief—then waited some more. They talked very little. Both his vampire companions meditated quietly while Remy cleaned Breaker's blades, scoured it with a new whetstone, and wallowed in his thoughts. Whatever faith both nobles had placed in Eugenie's sources, he hoped the trader was right.

It was Xiaodan who spotted the first of the attackers. She hissed something low under her breath, then was simply no longer where she'd been sitting. Malekh had risen to his feet, looking grim. "Ready yourself, Pendergast," he said. "It's worse than we thought."

Despite their numbers, the pack of undead had drawn far too close to the village for comfort and avoided detection from those standing guard. The gates were closed, but three villagers were standing within the dubious safety of the fires' light, each armed with a sword and a burning torch. That was their first mistake, Remy knew—it marked them as targets at a height that was an easy leap for most vampires. Remy could make out a shadow as it bypassed the stakes and barricades the villagers had worked hard on and leaped for one of the unsuspecting men stationed by the gates.

Xiaodan was quicker. She snatched the vampire out of the air, throwing him down with such force that one of the barricades splintered where they landed. The kindred gurgled; one of the sharp poles had been driven into his chest, keeping him stuck as he flailed, gasping in pain.

Shouts of alarm sounded from within the village. Remy could see more people gathering atop the gates, aiming crossbows.

The attacking vampires abandoned all attempts at silence. With loud, whooping howls, they slammed into the wooden gates. Several more turned to Xiaodan, who stood at the center of the field with her arms crossed, glaring at the incoming mob like that would be sufficient for them to leave. The ones unlucky

enough to take her up on the challenge were immediately dis-
emboweled, as Xiaodan blurred from one opponent to the next,
using nothing but her hands to tear them into shreds like their
bodies were paper.

The vampires aiming for the village entrance had Malekh
to contend with. The noble drew out his saber, its curved blade
gleaming in the dim light, and waited. He gave no ground, even
as the coven converged on him, and lashed out, cutting all within
reach. There was a poetry to his motions, his weapon flashing like
beats to a rhythm, as kindred fell before him.

There were far more vampires than Remy had expected. Xiaodan and Malekh together had taken down perhaps a dozen and
a half, but there were just as many now racing toward Zelenka's
gates, and still more pouring out from the nearby woods. He
found a position of his own somewhere in between his two companions and sent Breaker's knifechain spinning in an arc above his
head. As the vampire mob neared, he increased its arc, creating
a zone where his blade could cut indiscriminately, spraying blood
and other entrails all as black as the surrounding darkness while
it sliced through bodies.

There was a scream from somewhere behind him. Two vampires had gotten through the barricade, and the villagers on top
of the wall were in a panic, flailing uselessly with their pitch-
forks. Remy took down the nearest mutations around him, then
made a running leap for the wall, still swinging his chain. The
links wrapped around one of the vampire's legs, and a hard yank
sent it falling back to the ground. The other lunged for him, and
Remy braced himself, only for the monster to be abruptly cleaved
in two in midair. Malekh blurred briefly into view—fucking
show-off—gutted a third mutation, and blurred back out again.

The vampires around Malekh and Xiaodan seemed faster,
more inclined to strike. This second wave visibly hesitated as they
approached him, and it made all his work that much easier. Remy

dealt quickly with the monster he'd dragged down from the wall, sliced through another vampire, skewered several more.

There was a loud thud as something heavy hit the ground beside him. It was an arrow, stuck into the dirt, and Remy swore aloud. The villagers were firing into the pack, uncaring who they hit. He altered the knifechain's trajectory at an angle so it could swing in a circle over his head, warding off any other projectiles he might not see in the gloom, but leaving him open to the vampires' attacks. He angled Breaker downward so that his twin scythes were at waist level and, when something tried to come at him from behind, sidestepped the swipe and used his blades to cut the vampire in two from the groin up. He spun around to feint at another, all while keeping the knifechain whirring above.

Xiaodan was relentless, flowing from one vampire to the next and decimating them all effortlessly, her nails already on the next target before her previous victim's body had finished sliding to the ground. Malekh was all arms and blade, never relinquishing ground, even in the face of the swarm. The Fourth Court vampiress was too quick for any of the arrows from Zelenka to score a hit, but several found their way to the Third Court king, who, without glancing their way, reached out toward the sky with his other hand to snatch the projectiles out of midair, occasionally using one to stab a vampire within range.

Most of the creatures converged on Malekh. Remy rushed to his side, eviscerating the nearest two as the pack started to close in. The vampire lord said nothing, merely inclined his head in acknowledgment as they stood back-to-back, fighting through the pack.

The horde thinned out soon enough, until only a handful were left; Xiaodan made quick work of the remaining undead until only the three of them remained standing in a sea of mutilated torsos, heads, and limbs.

Panting, Remy surveyed the carnage around them and held

back a quick shudder of revulsion. If this was the same army of vampires that had swept through Brushfen only a couple of nights before, it was no surprise they'd been able to annihilate the village in only a few hours.

But the size of this particular nest was troubling enough on its own. Neither Astonbury nor Queen Ophelia had had an inkling of any active vampire packs within Aluria of this size. Giselle was wily enough to take a sample of nearly every document that passed through her husband's desk, and this would have been a priority. Aluria was already compromised if this many vampires were hidden within its territories.

He glanced down at the nearest corpse that he'd butchered and frowned. The vampire's clothes were in tatters, but not from Breaker. Its clothes were streaked through with dried, rather than recent, blood. They were similar in fashion to those he would have assumed traveling merchants wore, or of villagers when they—

Shock gripped him, then horror. These *were* the villagers. The ones missing from Brushfen. Why so many bodies were unaccounted for.

He didn't realize he'd said it aloud until Malekh responded quietly, "There's nothing you can do for them, Pendergast," in a way that made Remy suspect he'd already known. "The blood pooling the grass beneath them does not run red. They've been infected by the Rot and are in its very early stages."

Blue-black blood, just like the other mutations. "All of them? Are you saying they might rise again like at Elouve?"

Malekh grabbed him by the shoulders without warning. Startled, Remy attempted to shove him away.

"Stop struggling, Pendergast. I'm inspecting you."

"Why—you're looking to see if I've been infected?"

"How smart you are, Pendergast." The sarcasm was strong in Malekh's harsh voice, his abruptness. "What would I do without such insight?"

"I wasn't bitten. You have no need to be concerned—"

"But I do." Malekh's hand was on the side of Remy's face again, turning it so he could continue with his examination. "I worked you too hard during our sparring. If there were any lapses in your fighting just now, then I am to blame, am I not?"

Remy didn't know why the words hurt but knew why they angered him. "Quit the bloody act. Stop telling me that conversation didn't mean anything, then turn around and pretend you're worried for my sake."

He tried to shove Malekh away. The lord caught his hand, turning it so his palm faced upward, and looked down at the shallow cut on Remy's finger where the knifechain had nicked it, just a little. The lord raised his gaze up to meet his.

"You are an infuriating human who constantly tries my patience," Malekh said, "but I've never pretended."

And slowly, without breaking eye contact, the man pressed his fingers against the small wound, tongue briefly flicking out, and Remy's breaths spilled out of him in soft, jittery waves.

"I am not invulnerable, but neither are you. You cannot be angry at me for putting myself in danger, then dismiss my concerns when you do the same." Malekh pressed his finger against the tip one last time and let go. He was perfectly composed as ever as he walked over to Xiaodan. Remy, on the other hand, was trembling, staring down at his hand like he'd grown a third thumb.

Xiaodan gestured at the corpses. "If they had entered the village, they would've infected the people inside. This was a deliberate attack to spread the Rot. But this . . . this seems different from what Eugenie's report said."

"Yes," Malekh agreed, frowning. "She said the attack on Brushfen was a coordinated feeding. This mob was comprised of fifteen or so vampires, and the rest their mutated victims. If they can *control* the mutations like weapons, then whoever's in charge may know the secrets to the Rot's creation."

Xiaodan's hands tightened on the hem of her qipao. "Those poor people. Were they all from Brushfen?"

"It would appear so. None of the ones I fought turned to ash, though that doesn't prove much. We killed a few coven vampires as well, but I doubt that these were all of them."

Forcing away the persistent memories of Malekh's mouth against his skin, Remy risked a glance behind him. The villagers had ceased firing arrows when the number of infected had visibly decreased, but they were still milling about the gates, no doubt discussing what to do about the three of them. Remy saw a few raise their crossbows as if to resume firing where they'd left off, but noisy arguments broke out immediately, and the weapons were lowered again.

"Maybe we ought to discuss this somewhere else," he said, still feeling nervous, exhilarated—and irritated that Malekh had so easily reverted back to his collected, dispassionate self. "I can't dodge arrows as well as the two of you."

A fresh ruckus erupted among the torch-wielding crowd. Remy's ears were sharp enough to pick up the word "vampire" amid the shouts. He had a bad feeling. "I think we may have missed out on some of those undead, because it sounds like a few of them did manage to make their way inside the city."

He was running toward the gates before the others could say another word, re-strapping Breaker to his back so that he was free to wave his arms, hoping the villagers would take it as a sign that he meant no harm.

"Let us in!" he hollered. "Open the gates! If there are any inside, then you have to fucking let us in!"

Some of the men stared blankly at him. Others raised their bows again.

"We've just beaten up corpses for all you absolute gits," Remy yelled again, "and I'd really appreciate some fucking reciprocation!"

"Who's to say you aren't one of them, too?" someone yelled back.

"My name is Remington Pendergast! I'm a Reaper!"

"Are you constantly this loud?" Malekh had caught up to him. "We can simply leap over the walls, if gaining access to the village is what you're concerned with."

"Yes, but then we'll have to fight through a mob of terrified villagers. It's one thing to see you fighting on their behalf, and still another entirely to have you right in their midst, knowing you're one of what they're trying to keep out. They know what a Reaper is. It's the kind of authority that they're familiar with."

The gates swung open.

"See?"

The men and women were still holding their crossbows aloft, but none of them seemed inclined to fire immediately at the three. "What's happened?" Remy barked, trying to remember what his father had sounded like in his prime so he could mimic the thundering voice that resounded through the manor and sent him hiding as a youth.

"Got a vampire inside the mayor's house," one of the men said, looking about ready to shit his own pants at the thought. "We've got it surrounded, but we don't know what's happened to him and his family."

Scared as they were, they kept pace with Remy as he ran, pointing him toward a crowd already gathered, the smell of smoke from the burning torches they held thick in the air.

"They're as good as dead, Jona," another man was arguing when they arrived. "The chances of the rest of us surviving are better if we set fire to the place."

"You'd put his wife and daughters in danger all to save your skin, you coward?" another roared at him. "You can hear 'em screaming! They're still alive in there!"

"Do not under any circumstances toss that bloody torch into

the house," Remy grated out, when it looked like the man was prepared to do so despite the opposition, "or I will personally see you
hanged, black-throated, at the gallows."

"And who the bloody hell are you?"

"Remington Pendergast, son of Edgar Pendergast, Duke of
Valenbonne." A faint ripple of gasps through the crowd—the
Valenbonne name, fortunately, still held some power. "Let me
inside."

"You fool," Malekh said. "There's no telling what you'll find."

"Then you'd best follow me and see for yourself."

But Xiaodan had already taken the initiative. A swift whirlwind
of sleeves and silk, and the now open doorway leading into the
house stood before them, the only indication she'd gone through.
Malekh rushed past the crowd to enter; Remy sighed.

They followed the sounds of weeping into the drawing room,
where a family sat huddled together—the mayor's, he surmised. A
man who was most certainly not of their kin was seated languidly
on an armchair, one leg crossed over the other. The flames still
burning from the fireplace cast a cheerful glow across his features,
the whiteness of the scar on his cheek standing out, as did his
flame-colored hair and the carved *V* on his forearm announcing
his affiliation. He was grinning out his fangs, holding a glass of
white wine loosely in one grip. The other was fastened around
the throat of a terrified-looking man half-crouched, half-kneeling
beside him.

"Took you long enough," the stranger said.

"You've been busy," Xiaodan said evenly. "We've heard stories of you running about, choosing villages ripe for the picking.
Rather dishonorable, to be using the victims from your last raid
to attack the next."

"Not entirely my idea. I work with someone far cleverer than
either of us, Lady Song. Someone who's been itching for revenge
for a very long time." The man turned to regard Malekh next. "You

don't look like much," he said dismissively. "I don't even know what he saw in you."

"Set the human down," Malekh said, "and we'll have all the time in the world to discuss what Vasilik did or didn't see in me."

The red-haired vampire appeared to consider it. "I'd like to keep him here a little longer," he said. "There are three of you, you see, but this little bloodling gives me the advantage. Who knows? Perhaps I'll get hungry during the negotiations." His grip tightened, and the mayor whimpered. "Vasilik sent me here because he would like to strike a bargain with you."

"This is a strange way to win my favors."

"You are not in a position to make such demands," the man snapped. "Vasilik knows the secrets of the blue-blooded plague spreading among the humans, and he knows it imperils your vaunted alliance with Aluria. Our terms are simple. Cede Chànggē Shuǐ and the Qing-ye territories over to him, and we will spare the bloodlings. The mutations will no longer be your concern."

"He cannot cede Chànggē Shuǐ and Qing-ye," Xiaodan said, eyes narrowing. "Song Yingyue owns Chànggē Shuǐ and its territories."

"Your mother?" The vampire grinned. "Our coven grows every day, and the lands we occupy aren't large enough to suit. You and your old bat of a queen own a crumbling fortress and lands far too vast for the two of you to eke out the rest of your existence in. The Fourth Court is a derelict of better times that shall never return, you spoiled brat. Qing-ye is wasted on the Songs."

"You will have to pry my home out of both our cold, dead hands to take it, sir," Xiaodan said with all the pleasant assurance of a mongoose about to take off a snake's head. "If you sincerely believe we are so old and decrepit, then you would have had no trouble invading our lands without resorting to any of this. And yet you chose to drag innocent villages into your schemes. What good will Qing-ye even do you? It is the last place any vampire would want to set up court. The sun would kill you long before you reached Chànggē Shuǐ—"

And then her eyes widened. "I answered my own question, didn't I? Your vaunted coven isn't strong enough to take on the other courts, so you've decided to pick the one clan you consider the weakest among them."

"That means you are already squatting on Qing-ye land," Malekh said. "And Chànggē Shuǐ was the closest to conquer. It would explain why most of the attacks have stemmed from the east."

The vampire was silent, eyes darting nervously from Malekh to Xiaodan.

"I'm right, then," Malekh said with satisfaction.

"The Fourth Court has declined since, but Lord Vasilik respects the power that your mother once wielded, Song Xiaodan. He gives you the option to relinquish your position, to let your clan fade peacefully into obscurity without further bloodshed, and to turn your palace over to a stronger court with a greater destiny. Is that not the more honorable thing to do?"

"How about we start by releasing these people as a show of good faith," Remy said. "Isn't *that* the more honorable thing to do as well?"

The vampire fixed his dark gaze on him. "And you must be Lord Malekh's newest toy," he mocked. "A bloodling *and* a Reaper. Or is it a death wish on your part, Zidan, to fuck hunters?"

"Like hell he is," Remy said, but no one paid him any attention.

"Perhaps Vasilik would know, since he made no complaints about it in the past," Malekh responded, more at ease than Remy would have thought. "It seems to me that his tastes have deteriorated considerably since then."

The vampire's eyes flashed. "Vasilik loves me. He only used you to further his own ends. He would never have stayed so long with kindred so sickeningly attracted to these fragile humans. In a year your betrothed and her court will be as good as dust. We will rise up in their place as the new Fifth Court."

"You will do no such thing," Malekh said coldly. "Vasilik switched his allegiances to spite me. The Fifth Court is dead. If I must stamp it out again as I did the first time, then I will."

"With a Fourth Court vampire nursing a sickly heart, and your Reaper toy? Your clanmates aren't here, Malekh. You are alone and defenseless in Aluria, and I doubt Yingyue would rouse from her stupor to defend her own daughter, much less you and your human lover."

"I would really fucking appreciate it if someone actually corrected him on that," Remy said.

"If you believe us weak," Malekh said, "you wouldn't be clutching the human's throat like it's the only lifeline you have left. If he dies, so will you."

"I am here because Vasilik is magnanimous enough to offer you what he could have taken by force."

"No. You are here because you had expected to deliver another village into Vasilik's hands. Not only have you failed, you've also lost part of your coven and the Brushfen villagers you turned with the Rot. Whatever falsehoods Vasilik has told you about me, I know him well enough. Vasilik never strikes a bargain unless trickery is involved. You are bargaining with us because he will kill you once he learns of this."

"I—" The confident mask the vampire had been skillfully putting up finally slipped. "I—"

His grip on the mayor loosened, and Remy moved. His scythes swiped down, cutting off the vampire's arm and sending both it and the dazed victim it was keeping hostage tumbling to the carpet. But the red-haired man reacted swiftly and seized Remy by the throat with his other hand, sending Breaker to the floor with a heavy crash.

"And is he expendable as well, Malekh?" the vampire asked triumphantly. "Would your precious alliance with the humans survive if they find one of their Reapers dead and mutilated like so much livestock?"

"You're placing far more importance to me than what is actually the case," Remy said—or as best he could with the sharp nails digging into his neck, threatening to cut off his breathing.

"Pendergast," Malekh said. "Shut up."

"Pendergast?" The vampire brightened. "The Butcher himself? Even better. Would they forgive you if you caused the death of their most prized hunter?"

Remy tried hard not to gag as he was lifted off the floor. He could feel the prick of fangs as they came to rest against the base of his neck.

"Wait," Xiaodan said, when Zidan began to move.

"Yes, wait," the vampire mocked. "Vasilik would laugh to see you so domesticated by the Sunbringer bitch. Perhaps he might also claim the Third Court, to—"

The words ended in a gurgle.

"Take it from someone who talks too much," Remy gasped, after he'd stuck into the man's chest the two knives he'd squirreled away inside his sleeves, thanks to Elke. "You bloody talk too much."

The man collapsed. So did Remy, who fell to the floor, bleeding.

20

THE SPRINGS

s Remy had predicted, the villagers were unapologetic, ungrateful, and very glad to see them go. The mayor was perhaps the only one who was truly appreciative, for he had insisted on seeing them well stocked with supplies before they were off. The arrival of the helhests only worsened the situation, and it was with relief from both sides when Malekh finally goaded the horses into a canter, and the village of Zelenka was lost to their field of vision.

Remy kept tugging at the gauze bandages wrapped around his neck. The village healer who'd tended to him was a young woman who had put her needle to good use. It was not a deep wound, Remy was told, though it had looked much more alarming than he had realized. In time it would heal, the scar eventually scabbing itself out of existence.

"Of course," Remy had mumbled then, to no one in particular, really, because they'd gotten him drunk on some strong ale swill masquerading as medicine, and his mind was refreshingly numb from pain. "I know how to avoid a fucking vampire bite. I'm not a goddamn novice. He scratched me with his hell-blasted fingers, is all," he'd continued to ramble until, finally, he'd fallen asleep, with the woman still sewing him up.

His head was much clearer now, though the speeding scenery was once again doing him no favors. Malekh had taken the reins outside though he'd claimed that his undead steeds required no supervision when en route to Qing-ye, which suited Remy just fine. The stitches were already itching despite the salve the woman had applied to it. He'd presented her with a small bag of coins as a thank-you, and also as an apology for his deranged chatter the night before. The woman had clasped them to her chest and smiled bashfully at him. That made two people in Zelenka who liked him.

"Don't scratch at it," Xiaodan said, though her eyes were closed. "You'll wind up tearing it open again, and my sewing skills are worse than Elisabet's."

"Elisabet?"

"The girl who cared for you last night. You didn't even ask her name?"

"After everything that happened, her name was the last thing on my mind."

"She would be disappointed to hear that."

Remy shot a suspicious glance her way, but Xiaodan's eyes remained firmly shut, and she said little else for the duration of the journey.

Remy wasn't sure where they were headed next, if it was straight to Qing-ye or somewhere else. Xiaodan and Malekh had planned it without his input, due to him being unconscious for most of the night, morning, and the better part of the afternoon the next day. But by the time dusk had fallen once more, they'd stopped at what looked to be an inn—and a fairly odd place for it to be, out here in the middle of nowhere.

"I own it," Xiaodan said happily, climbing out of the carriage. "We're finally past the Alurian borders and on my lands. This is only one of many we've built over the decades."

"Aren't you worried about intruders?" Remy asked. It was a pleasant thought, to spend another night of travel with a roof over their heads, but he wasn't sure about the state of the furniture inside.

"There isn't much to take, and that's by design. Most have been bolted down, all made of a forged metal preventing rust."

Remy wasn't listening, because he'd detected a large waft of steam rising out from the right side of the inn. "Is this by any chance connected to a hot spring?"

"We have a bathhouse built in to pipe hot water through, if you wish to give it a try. The rooms themselves were built beside it, for easier access."

"I would very damn well much wish to give it a try."

"For the last time, Pendergast," Malekh said as he settled the helhests in, "stop talking. Your throat's still healing."

Remy rolled his eyes and made a motion as if to cover his mouth, only to flip the noble a rude gesture instead. He then strode toward the main doors, pushing them open and ignoring Xiaodan's startled call for him to wait.

From inside came a fierce growl.

"Fuck."

Xiaodan stepped in front of him, chuckling.

"You're safe, Remy. You just surprised them."

"Them?"

Two large black dogs came loping out, with the same coal-black skin and fiery eyes as the helhests'.

"Do you two constantly travel around, turning every dying an-imal into your fucking creature of the night?" Remy exploded, and then put a hand over his bandages because, hell, that *did* hurt.

"I told you to be careful. And yes, I do try." Xiaodan bent down. The dogs encircled her, licking at her hands—behaving like two overgrown pups instead of the demon hounds they resembled. "This one is Candy, and this one is Vanilla."

"Candy, Vanilla. Right."

"If you're worried about what they feed on while no one else is here, then don't. We're only several days' ride from the palace, and half a day with Cookie and Peanut—Alegra and my kinspeople come here frequently to feed them."

"Great," Remy whispered, barely able to form the words as he rubbed the part of his neck that the bandages hadn't covered. Only a day's ride from Chànggē Shuǐ. He had never left Aluria before. "Thought we were going to stamp out the fledging Fifth Court nest first?" He paused. "What happened to that vampire, anyway? He's dead, right?" He'd been meaning to ask ever since Malekh had wordlessly returned his daggers to him that afternoon, gleaming and polished and devoid of blood.

"If you hadn't killed him yet with your knives, then Malekh certainly did when he cut off his head," Xiaodan said. "I burned his body alongside the infected and the rest of his coven. The mayor believes he might have been one of the missing boys reported in their area, one who was thought dead for years. It's safe to assume at this point that Vasilik was responsible for turning him, too." Her gaze hardened. "He brainwashed them into thinking he cared. It's a . . . a *twatty* thing to do."

"Xiaodan," Remy said wearily, "that is not how you use that word."

"We have an idea of where their lair might be," Malekh said, swinging down from the carriage, graceful even in the simple movement. "The only other place in western Qing-ye that can afford them protection from the sun would be the Dà Lán."

"Dà Lán?"

"It's one of the most beautiful places in Qin-ye," Xiaodan said eagerly. "They're hiding out in my lands. I intend to find them, and this is the most obvious spot they would be. But we should stop at the fortress first." She paused. "I hope my mother can assist us," she added sadly, "though I doubt it."

Remy was tempted to ask more questions, but from the shut-

tered look on her face and the way Malekh cleared his throat as he
stepped inside the building, it was a conversation for another day.

The furnishings inside were as sparse as Xiaodan had indicated, though they were more than adequate. The rooms were
lined up along one side of a narrow corridor, each enough to
fit a bed, a table, and a dresser, though there were dividers that
could be pushed aside to combine two or more sections whenever needed. A second panel of wall could be slid back, leading
outside. Xiaodan demonstrated with one, and Remy spotted the
hot springs only eight or nine steps away. The water was still a
dazzling blue, made distinct despite the growing darkness by the
smooth white stones underneath, and it was clear enough for him
to see through to the bottom and shallow enough for him to stand
in. Steam rose from its surface, curling in the air toward him as if
in invitation. "Yes," he said fervently to himself.

"I'm placing the mayor's food packs in your care for tonight,"
Xiaodan said. "We should reach Chànggē Shuǐ early tomorrow
morning. I'm sorry we can't stay longer for your recovery."

"It's only a scratch," Remy said, not really listening. He wanted
to crawl into the heat and stay there forever.

Xiaodan laughed lightly, then left for her own room. The dogs
followed her and Zidan inside, wagging their tails happily.

Remy wolfed down a small pork ration from one of the packs.
He was hungry, but it hurt to swallow. The hot springs were a
much more seductive lure.

He'd only ever been to Barrowhill for shit like this. He'd
hunted a vampire terrorizing a few hamlets in the area and wound
up lingering there for two days, up to his eyeballs in the blessed
warmth. This was much better; the accommodations at Barrowhill had been stellar but packed with far too many people to have
the privacy he'd craved, the whispers that still circled him there.

He sank down, steeping his battered body in the heated waters. He groaned aloud, and then decided to stop thinking.

His bliss lasted for close to two hours.

Remy's head was pleasantly buzzing, and he almost didn't hear the sounds of someone else entering the water. He opened his eyes. Sat up straighter.

Xiaodan lowered herself into the spring, clad in a flimsy chemise that was nothing more than thin straps across her shoulders, a scrap of golden cloth that hugged at her breasts and reached down only as far as her thighs. Her long hair floated about her like a dark cloud. Remy stared, entranced by the sight.

"You're not supposed to stay in for this long," Xiaodan scolded. She waded noisily over to where he sat, and Remy was suddenly aware that while she'd tried to cover up her bits for his benefit, he hadn't thought to do the same when he'd first hopped in. He shoved his hands down.

Xiaodan didn't even notice. She frowned over him, hand braced against one hip. The other held a fresh roll of bandages and ointments that the young woman—Elisabet, was it?—had likely given her. "At least let me take off the bandages. The steam can't be good for it."

"I feel perfectly fine," Remy croaked, with a fresh hoarseness that had nothing to do with his wound. He'd be damned if he'd climb out now and let her see him on full display.

He was hoping she would blush and make her excuses, then leave him long enough to regain both his breeches and his pride. But her smile was broad and her eyes bright with both mischief and interest. "You don't have to feel embarrassed, you know. I've seen naked people before. But we really do need to change the linens, lest they make your wound worse."

"I'm sure as hell not getting out while you're here."

She only laughed her little bright laugh, then moved closer. "Don't worry. I won't look. Just tilt your head up so I can see your neck better."

Remy stared up at the dark clouds above, scowling, while she got rid of the bandages. He felt her pressing her fingers lightly against the base of his throat. "Does this hurt?" she asked.

Remy shook his head, and she repeated the question, traveling up until she touched a spot that made him flinch. "Your stitches are holding. Elisabet said it looks worse than it actually is. Half an inch deeper, though, she told me, and you could have bled out."

"Guess I'm lucky," Remy mumbled.

"I still haven't had time to get mad at you for putting yourself at risk."

"It was either me or the mayor, and I figured I had a better chance of surviving than he did."

He made no other comment while she shifted her stance, peered closer. She was kneeling by his side, head bent toward him. Her hair brushed against his chest. He would see inside her chemise if he looked down, he knew. The cloth couldn't hide the roundness of her breasts, the tops of it paler than the rest of her.

He kept his gaze skyward.

"Elisabet really did a good job with this," he heard her say. "I wouldn't have been able to sew them so small and so neatly."

"I'll thank her again if I ever pass through," Remy muttered.

"She likes you, you know."

"I gave her nearly a year's worth of wages. Of course she likes me."

"That's not what I meant, and I think you know it." Soft fingers grazed at his shoulders, and despite the water's heat, Remy couldn't stop his sudden shiver, that quick spurt of desire. "Why must you always put yourself down? You are one of the bravest, albeit also one of the most foolish people I know, human or vampire. You saved the mayor and nearly killed yourself in the process. You keep exposing yourself to danger for people who don't care, who wouldn't be willing to do the same."

"I'm not the hero you keep implying I am."

Her hand wandered, tracing a path down his chest. "You saved Lady Daneira. And you've felt guilty about it ever since, when none of it was ever your fault. When no one else was willing to save her."

She was so close. It would be easy to raise his hands, wrap them around her waist with little difficulty. He could guide her to straddle him, let her feel him underneath the water, as hard as the stones they sat on.

He wagered that she could ride him just as well as she'd ridden Malekh. She could cry out, tell him to his face that she did want him.

"So you know about that, too," he said instead, his hands unflinchingly still.

"I read the reports, yes. None of the Reapers wanted to hunt Lord Tennyfair's daughter. It was one thing to stake a commoner, a villager they'd never met. No one wanted to be responsible for the death of a turned noblewoman, especially the daughter of a well-respected duke. The stigma would have followed them for the rest of their lives, no matter how justified their reasons to kill her were. But you accepted."

"She'd always been kind to me."

"Why do you keep turning someone else's compassion into a favor that you owe, instead of accepting that you are worthy of it?" Xiaodan's eyes were a mesmerizing gray, the color of natural moonstone. "Zidan told me about what he said to you when you were both sparring."

"He was baiting me." It came out half-heartedly—Remy no longer believed that.

"That's not true." He felt something oily and slick applied to his wound. He heard rustling as she set the soiled linen aside on the stone ground behind his head. "Zidan always had the better brains of the two of us, but he can be willfully obtuse in other matters. He's used to people chasing him, you see. He's at a loss when he realizes it's he who needs to do the chasing. He always expresses it poorly. He did that when he was pursuing me."

Tell me you don't want this, Pendergast. Tell me you wouldn't want Xiaodan here with me, either. Malekh had said that, then taken the words back just as quickly. "Not sure what you mean."

"Zidan has always been honest, brutally so at times. He was up-front with Vasilik about the nature of their relationship, and it goaded Vasilik into pushing himself harder, to prove that he could be more valuable to him. It was ugly enough for him to defect to the Fifth Court for revenge."

Remy closed his eyes again. "Tough shit for him. Don't see what that has to do with me."

Xiaodan hummed. "I thought that, too, for a while. But he's not one to be easily annoyed. And he's always pissed when it comes to you. It's a good sign."

"How so?"

"Because I once pissed him off the same way. I can be stubborn, as can he. And so can you, as a matter of fact."

Remy kept his eyes shut, not wanting to follow the path that Xiaodan was taking.

"May I show you something?" He felt Xiaodan take his hand. His fingers twitched when he felt warm, soft skin, then hesitated when she guided him to a series of bumps and raised flesh, coarser than the rest of her had felt.

He forced himself to open his eyes, staring at the long, ugly scar that streaked down Xiaodan's chest like a lightning bolt, still well hidden within her scanty clothing. It was ridged and ugly and painful-looking. Remy had sustained many a grievous wound himself, even bore some of those marks to this day, but none this deep and long.

"The Fifth Court attacked my home. We'd been too weak, our numbers too low, and I nearly died. This is the proof. Only the Third Court came to our aid. And now I *would* rather perish than see Vasilik claim the lands I fought so hard to keep with Zidan."

Remy's fingers moved of their own accord, tracing the ley lines of her scar down the valley between her breasts. "You're strong to have survived something like this."

Her own fingers lingered at some of his scars, white against his dark skin, from the longer raised gashes along his shoulder down to the streaks by his waist. Then her hand ran down the marks on his back. "You have yours, too. We're not so different."

"I've never had anything as bad as yours."

"I was very lucky."

"You say I belittle myself constantly, but I think you do the same."

Xiaodan smiled at him and moved closer. "What I am, is confident about what I want," she whispered. "Almost dying taught me that time is precious, that I should seize what I want before it's too late. And I want . . ."

Remy's own heart pounded rapidly as she bent, her long hair sweeping the sides of his face like a curtain. He could stay here in this spring, he thought, wrapped in her heat, and look at her like this forever.

But then she hesitated. "I shouldn't," Xiaodan whispered, and started to withdraw.

He was used to aggressive women. Women who weren't shy about what they desired from him. And Xiaodan had done more for him in a few weeks than Giselle had in the five years he'd known her, the only demand she'd made in exchange being for his own benefit. And seeing her now, denying so sweetly what they both needed—

He owed her so much more than to hesitate.

It was natural for Remy to take both her hands in his own, halting her attempts to move away, and instead pull her forward toward him.

He had spent much of the journey wondering what she would taste like. Entire nights aching for the chance.

Her mouth parted. She was even better than he'd imagined.

Xiaodan felt like woodsmoke and mist, like the warmth that rose from the embers of a well-tended fireplace. He urged her over him, no longer hiding his arousal, and she moaned softly when he rocked his hips forward. His fingers, hungry for more, caressed her inner thighs, pushed the thin fabric of her shift aside. Her hands were braced on his shoulders. All it would take was for her to lower herself onto him. All it would take was for him to knife up into her.

"Wait," Xiaodan whispered. "Not now. Not yet."

"Yes, you can," Remy grated, spreading her thighs farther apart, causing her to move down, just a little, her breath catching as he slowly breached her.

"You misunderstand me." The hands on his shoulders tightened, stopping her descent. "I want this as much as you do. But there are conditions."

"He wouldn't need to know." But even as he said the words, Remy wanted to take them back. His past affairs had made it almost second nature to say.

Xiaodan looked down at him, her eyes an enigma. "Is that what you really want me to do? To say nothing to him?"

"No. I . . . I don't know."

"Do you hate him? Is he a—"

"No!" The word burst from him, surprisingly painful. "It's just that I—I've never had anything like this. Everyone always wants something from me. And I—I—"

"And you don't know if we might do the same to you." Xiaodan didn't look angry at his admission, only sad. "I want you, Remy. But not even you would have emboldened me to go this far. I've always intended to remain loyal to Zidan, whatever my feelings. I would never have chosen to act on my urges, if not for him."

The words made him feel bitter. Of course he couldn't compete against a Third Court king.

And then he took pause. "'If not for him'?" he echoed, cautious.

"My fiancé had made a similar offer to you—an offer you declined to take seriously. He's been sulking ever since."

Remy swallowed hard. "I thought—I assumed he'd only meant to provoke—"

"We are *both* attracted to you, Remington Pendergast." She ground herself slowly on him. "And you're attracted to both of us. While it is easier for you to admit that with me, it's been harder for you to do the same with my betrothed. His prickly personality is to blame, no doubt—your penchant for aggravating him, just as much. I intend to be a faithful wife. And it means that everything I have, I willingly share with him. As he shall with me."

The words, the implication behind them, took his breath away. "I—do you mean to say that I—"

She sank down hard on him with no warning, sheathing him to the hilt inside of her. He could not stifle the loud, desperate groan he made at the searing fire, the gripping tightness of her.

"I didn't tell you the whole truth at Elouve. When I said that I wanted to guard Kinaiya Lodge, it wasn't just because of Zidan's old enemies possibly seeking reprisals. It was also because I didn't want you to seek out the Duchess of Astonbury again. We'd already decided that the next bed you tumbled into would be ours, if you were willing. But I'm growing impatient, waiting for you two to reach a consensus."

Tight, aching, fire. Remy groaned again.

"Those are my conditions," Xiaodan whispered into his ear. "I love Zidan, and he loves me. From the very depths of my soul, I know it. But we are leaders of our own court, and we are more accustomed to—I suppose you can call it submission, in others than with each other." She had the temerity to let out a giggle when he grew even harder despite himself, couldn't stop the agonized gasp he let out. "I wondered if you might like the idea. Zidan thought so. Make no mistake, Armiger. I would be happy with him, even if we'd never met you. But I think we can be more than just happy *with* you. But we won't force you into something you're not prepared for. I never want you to regret anything with Zidan and me."

And then—Light, fuck the Light, fucking *fuck* the Light—she raised herself off him, as frustrated over her abrupt withdrawal as he was, and yet unyieldingly deliberate about it.

"Good night, Remington," Xiaodan said.

And then she left.

21

THE EASTERN PALACE

Xiaodan had frequently called Chànggē Shuǐ a fortress, and it was an apt choice of words. From afar, it resembled a crown of knives, the points facing upward like sharp blades. It was curiously elegant, made of a shiny black material that Remy didn't realize was some kind of obsidian rock until they'd drawn closer.

It was not the castle itself that had first commanded his attention, but the majestically cascading waterfall behind it. The fortress sat on a small island surrounded by a wide, natural lake that doubled as a moat. Water flowed down toward it from a wide rocky cliff behind it, many tens of thousands of feet high. It circled Chànggē Shuǐ and then moved on, or so Xiaodan said, to the rivers and lakes spanning the east.

The cliffs themselves extended to nearly the whole horizon before them, far too high for Remy to make out what lay atop it. Chànggē Shuǐ looked like something out of a grand fairytale. That the landscape served as a natural defense against invaders was an added bonus, and he saw now how the Fourth Court had been able to defend their realm even with their fewer numbers.

Remy had never been to Qing-ye before, and nothing about the place was what he'd expected. Something about the weather patterns here allowed pockets of sunlight—actual real, dazzling sunlight, unobscured by rolling storms and thick fog—to stream down from frequent breaks in the clouds, lasting anywhere from a quarter to half an hour before disappearing, only to reappear in a different spot nearby. The whole of the plains were bathed in uncontrollable glows of light. It was a good, unpredictable obstacle against vampires too young to withstand the sun. Many would be picked off long before they even reached Chànggē Shuǐ.

Remy was not used to so much light. The sudden beams were blinding to him, and he was human.

"So this was why Vasilik wanted your territory," Remy said once he'd picked his jaw up off the carriage floor.

"And the Fifth Court before him," Xiaodan confirmed.

"That fortress. How did you get so much bloody obsidian in one place?"

"When you've had centuries to build, it's easy if you know where to look." Xiaodan couldn't keep her eyes away from her home as it loomed nearer, eagerness rolling off her in waves. "We haven't had enough people to fix it up the way I'd want. But you won't be uncomfortable there."

"If you say so." Remy was trying to keep his expression neutral. She had shown up outside the inn the next morning and cheerfully rambled on about Chànggē Shuǐ, her mother, and some of her clanmates as they careened down the road at the breakneck speed Remy was unfortunately getting used to.

He hadn't slept much the night before. Her proposition had kept him awake until the early hours of the morning, and then he'd dreamt about drowning in the middle of a mass of writhing bodies, every face resembling either Xiaodan's or Malekh's. He'd woken up hard again, then frantically scrubbed himself clean at the hot springs lest either of his companions smell lust on him a second time.

His throat was feeling better than the previous day, the stitches holding up nicely. Remy wrapped a fresh set of bandages around his neck, then decided to let it heal for the rest of the journey by, not coincidentally, saying very little.

Xiaodan didn't push him, and for that he was glad. It seemed like she was determined to give him the space he needed, but even her attempts to leave him alone couldn't stop him from being aware of her presence.

He couldn't stop thinking about last night. About her proposal, about Malekh, about the dynamics of involving him in this strange, heady entanglement.

He was horrified that the thought excited him.

He shifted his concerns to the floor of the carriage. Xiaodan had decided that the dogs were to accompany them back, which meant there were two very large undead mastiffs reclined by his feet, rumbling contentedly. They were used to him by now, one even nuzzling lazily at his boot on occasion. He supposed they could be considered adorable, if you ignored the lolling massive eyes and giant teeth and brimstone-scented drool.

Surely no one would go out of their way to proposition him like this without expecting something in return. Xiaodan—if she was to be believed—clearly wanted intimacy from him. It certainly couldn't be his fighting abilities; he'd wound up with more injuries than he should have.

He was used to paying for favors with sex. It felt odd not to be, and it was especially humiliating to have faced rejection when he had, for the first time in his life, offered it of his own accord. It had hurt his pride.

Was it also submission they wanted? Not obeying commands as a liege might expect from their subordinates, but from—

His stomach clenched at the thought, and he was ashamed that it was not from revulsion.

He focused on staring out the window, because Malekh's eyes

had been on him throughout the ride. Remy wasn't entirely certain if the noble knew what had happened at the springs, if Xiaodan had been as honest with him as she said she was and admitted their indiscretions.

But Malekh had said nothing, content only to watch Remy.

Remy would have normally told him to go to hell, but it was difficult not to feel guilty after his tryst with Xiaodan. Ignoring him was the safer choice.

Xiaodan had said that Malekh wanted him, too. That was what had been at the forefront of his fevered, sleepless mind—thoughts of him and Malekh and Xiaodan—when he'd bent over naked at the hot spring that morning and, with a loud groan, proceeded to defile the nearby stones with the consequences of his disgusting imagination.

Yes. Far better not to look at either of them until they arrived at their destination.

The gates of Chànggē Shuǐ opened, seemingly of their own accord, to allow them inside, which gave Remy the distraction he needed.

Chànggē Shuǐ wasn't a fortress; it was a city. A whole village lay within those knifelike walls, outfitted for luxury. He saw sloped roofs where monstrous sculptures of impossibly shaped lions and curved dragons stood guard, their shine golden whenever the sun's light touched upon their stone hides. The houses surrounding the courtyard were clustered into sections, some walls inlaid with bright pearl and smooth oyster shells, gleaming brightly.

The same could not be said for the structures beyond the immediate circle. Several were in clear disrepair, others on their way to the same condition. Only a handful of residences had been maintained for habitation, he observed, the rest fallen into disuse. There were very few members of the Fourth Court left, and it showed.

Peanut and Cookie wheeled the carriage over to a woman waiting for them. Remy doubted that this was Xiaodan's mother.

The stranger was taller than him, almost Malekh's height, despite the noble being many inches over six feet. She was dark-skinned, toned and muscular, with curls to her short black hair, and she wore a lighter variation of battle armor that was mainly chest chain mail and vambraces.

"Milady," she said, her tone reproachful as Xiaodan hopped out of their coach, the dogs leaping after her, "I thought you'd intended to stay in Elouve longer. I would have appreciated an earlier warning."

"I am sorry, Alegra. A few problems have arisen that need taking care of, including sightings of a new unauthorized coven in our territory. How is Mother?"

"Same as when you left. She still fades in and out several times a day, and we're never sure how long her trances last. I would have also appreciated you sending word," she added with a sigh when Remy stepped out, "that you'd planned on bringing guests. Shall I prepare a room for him, or do you intend to consume him before supper? Good afternoon, Lord Zidan."

"Ah," Remy said, because he'd been waiting for Alegra to crack a smile or let on that it was a joke at his expense, but the woman's features remained inscrutably deadpan.

"This is Armiger Remington Pendergast, Alegra," Xiaodan said, "and yes, I would appreciate a room made for him, as he'll be staying here awhile. He's to help us investigate the unwanted nest." She sobered. "Alegra, Vasilik might well be behind this."

"Him again?" Alegra growled. "I told you he was too much of a slippery bastard to have fallen in the war with the Fifth Court, Xiaodan. The sooner we can flush him out, the better off the world will be. I will inform your mother that you and Lord Zidan have arrived and also prepare clean quarters for the meat."

"Should I be worried?" Remy asked, watching the stone-faced woman depart.

"Pay no attention to Alegra." Xiaodan laughed. "She's fond of jesting when we bring new people to the castle. She once told Queen Ophelia that she could tell the difference between royal and common blood with just a taste."

"Oh," Remy said. "Well then. Glad that cleared things up."

His drollness was lost on her as well. "We'll bring you to Mother. I . . ." She sighed. "I don't know if she'll be coherent, but you'll know how things stand in Chànggē Shuǐ once you meet her. We all occupy the eastern palace, but the rest of the city has been shuttered indefinitely. You'll have to remove your boots before entering, though. Malira likes her floors sparkling."

The inside of the eastern palace was surprisingly well lit; long, thin candles and torchlight fixtures glowed from every corner. Remy had expected grim-faced portraits of ancestors, cobwebs, and grotesquely ancient furniture against fading tapestries, but instead found well-worn armchairs, bright gleaming tables and mantelpieces, and clean polished floors. Blackstone Manor looked much more forbidding than this.

The vampires who lived here were a different story. There were far fewer of them than Remy had thought, even after Xiaodan had told him about the state of the Fourth Court. He could count perhaps eight in all; they were standing to attention as the group entered the great hall, watching them. More specifically, watching *him*.

Remy felt himself tense up as he walked past their stares, wondering if they might be tempted to attack him, even with Xiaodan nearby. Many of their gazes lingered at the bandages on his neck, as if contemplating finishing what someone else had already started.

"They're loyal to Xiaodan," Malekh murmured. Remy wasn't sure why the Third Court ruler was going out of his way to be helpful, but walking with the noble by his side did seem to defuse some of the tension, the other vampires taking in the ease in which the lord was conversing with him. Some of the wary, slightly hostile looks had receded, speculation taking their place. "It is not that you are human, so much as they recognized your weapon."

"My father isn't the fucking bogeyman you all keep making him out to be."

"Your father killed a good many vampires in his prime, some of them friends and family to those present. They've lived long enough to remember some of your ancestors, as well. They have a right to be wary."

"I—" Remy hesitated. He didn't want to be grateful to Malekh, but he didn't want to apologize, either. "Malekh. I'm not . . . I know that we—there's something I must—"

"Are you trying to thank me, Pendergast?" Malekh didn't quite smirk, but he came close. "Or do you plan to offer to me what you had of my betrothed last night, as recompense?"

Remy contemplated falling onto his own daggers. "You know?"

"Was it your intention to keep it a secret?"

"No! I had no intentions of hiding anything—"

"Your interest in her is not what's disrespectful to me. But what she wants from you is not repayment or an exchange of favors, Armiger, as other women have demanded of you. If you aren't interested in more than that, then at least have the decency to turn her down properly so she can give up her pursuit."

Remy took a deep breath. "You weren't lying when you said you wanted to—to—"

"Yes. I had expected you to be accustomed to that, given what we'd heard in Elouve."

"Not like this." The words came in a rush. "Giselle and the rest of them . . . always wanted something in return. If you or Xiaodan ever—I can't—"

He'd learned to close himself off even in his most intimate moments with the Duchess of Astonbury and with the others. But not with Xiaodan and Malekh. He couldn't.

"We expect nothing from you, Pendergast. We are not like the Elouvians." Malekh leaned in, his mouth inches away from Remy's ear. This close, he was suddenly aware of how close they looked to everyone else watching. The noble's voice was thick with promise. "This is not a kindred custom. This is something Xiaodan and I have decided to act upon, something we agreed to."

There must have been something strange about the air in the palace, because it was leaving Remy's lungs in rapid, shallow bursts. He swallowed. "You're telling me to turn Xiaodan down if I'm not interested in her for more than sex. You haven't said what I'm supposed to do about you."

At that, Malekh really did grin. "Xiaodan seeks more than just a physical connection, and she recognizes the same need in you. I have not always required this with my previous lovers. I want you, Pendergast. In the past, I would have never said no to a fuck, no matter how meaningless you might think it is."

This time, the heat Remy felt was entirely his own, pooling down near his groin. "You'd betray your own fiancée?"

"You misunderstand again. I've never looked at anyone else, human or vampire, since I've been with Xiaodan. But we are both prepared to make an exception. Are you afraid?"

They were being guided toward the upper floors, finally stopping before one of the larger rooms. This was not a conversation to have before meeting the mother of someone you were, as the noble had pointed out, lusting after, so Remy reverted back to his bad habits and muttered a low "fuck you" to Malekh just before the doors opened.

Queen Yingyue was not what Remy had pictured, either. He had imagined an old woman, some kind of grand dame with an overpowering presence regardless of any supposed infirmities she might have had. But Queen Yingyue was a young girl, one who looked no older than he did—no older even than Xiaodan, for that matter. Her hair was as dark as her daughter's, long enough that they swept the ground behind her while she reclined in an arm-chair, one easily several sizes too large for her willowy frame. Her hands were small and dainty, smooth and unlined with age—and were in the process of tearing a piece of paper into shreds.

Her graceful head lifted, and Remy found himself staring into brown eyes similar to Xiaodan's, if not for their color. She was heartbreakingly beautiful. But her gaze looked back at him, blank and unseeing.

A figure rose beside her—Naji, Malekh's brother. The lad was dressed far more sensibly now, in a short robe with little to adorn it with. The youth scowled when he spotted Remy, a hand instinctively lifting toward his neck in remembrance, though the skin there was now unmarred.

"Mother," Xiaodan greeted, coming forward to kneel before the throne, her hands raising to clasp the other woman's. "I brought Zidan, and someone new for you to meet."

The soft brown eyes flickered to her daughter's face, and the fog within their depths lifted momentarily. "My child," the woman whispered lovingly. "Have you been away long? Have you gone and quarreled with Zidan again?"

"Zidan and I have been friends for a while now, Mother," Xiaodan reminded her gently. "Do you remember our engagement?"

"You know you shouldn't be bothering him when he's immersed in his experiments at that laboratory of his, my dear," the Fourth Court queen admonished, not listening. "He still feels guilty about the Fifth Court. And you were quite foolish, running off to face Etrienne all by yourself. Chàngge Shuǐ is impenetrable. You know the man will do anything to claim our city."

"I know, Mother. But I'm all better now."

"He worked day and night to save you, you know. Sat by your bedside for days without rest. And when Alegra managed to coax him away, he returned to his laboratory, trying to find a way to keep your heartbeats steady. You were quite foolish, running off to face Etrienne all by yourself. Chànggē Shuǐ is impenetrable—"

Her face changed, suddenly furious and hideous in her rage. "What did you do, Xiaodan? You were not meant to have her heart. We were not meant to bring down the sun. They will kill us! They will kill us!"

She flung herself at Xiaodan with a snarl. Malekh stepped between them, and Queen Yingyue clutched at his coat, still yowling, clawing at the threads.

"There is still time," she panted, trying to reach around Malekh for Xiaodan, her hand opening and closing like talons, grasping toward Xiaodan's scarred chest. "We must bring it back and beg for repentance, lest we burn. Xiaodan!" Her voice rose, a high-pitched screech. "Please!"

Xiaodan didn't move. She only stared back at her mother, heartbroken.

"We have no choice, my love. No, I didn't want to lose you—you, my flesh and blood, the only thing I have left to remember Shethar by." The hand dropped, and the queen sat back, blinking, no longer aggressive. "Shethar would sing to me in the evenings," she said calmly, "and we would row across the Dà Lán on warm nights when there would be nothing else in the world but the two of us. He would—"

A spasm of pain crossed her face. Xiaodan took her mother into her arms with sure, practiced movements. Remy started forward, but Malekh shook his head. "The danger has passed. She always calms once she talks of her husband."

"I miss him," the queen wept. "I miss him so much. Where has he gone? Is he still in the castle? I should look for him." She started to rise, but Xiaodan held her fast.

"Mother," she said softly, sweetly, urgently. "Let's take a nap. I'm sure Father will be here soon. He would want you to rest."

"I am tired," the woman said faintly. A pause and her eyes closed, head lolling back.

Xiaodan rose to her feet, carrying the smaller woman like she was no heavier than a feather. "No changes at all since we left, Alegra?" she asked sadly.

"I'm afraid not, milady," the woman responded from where she'd been keeping watch by the door.

"I'm sorry you had to see that," Xiaodan said to Remy. "But we thought it was necessary for you to know about her condition, if you are to stay here with us."

"No apologies required," Remy said. "I've seen this enough times with other humans. There's not much you can do but ensure their comfort. I wasn't aware that vampires had similar conditions."

"Most vampires don't live long enough to be of Yingyue's age," Malekh said crisply, taking the now-sleeping queen from Xiaodan's hands.

"She doesn't look like she could be older than I am."

"She's six hundred years old."

"Well, shit."

"What's he doing here?" Naji asked, staring hard at Remy.

"Nice to see you've recovered from your injuries," Remy said with false cheer.

"Naji," Malekh said. "Pendergast is a guest. I trust that you will behave yourself while he's here."

His brother only glared at Remy before stomping off.

"Forgive him," Xiaodan said. "He's been looking after Mother since he arrived. He's only been kindred for five years, and immaturity hasn't quite left him yet."

"Five years? I thought he was Malekh's younger brother."

"Adopted younger brother," Malekh said. "I killed all my biological siblings some hundreds of years ago."

"Right. As one does."

"She believes we are still in the aftermath of the Fifth Court war, after Sauveterre was killed," Xiaodan said sadly as Malekh laid the woman down on the bed. Her hand stole back to her chest. "Right after I nearly died," she added, much more quietly. "She has no memories of anything past that. She still believes Father's alive." She smiled faintly. "And she keeps forgetting about our engagement. She thinks Malekh and I are still at each other's throats."

"Were you really?"

"Frequently enough that everyone else in the castle was resigned to hearing our spats every day. I mentioned it last night . . ." Xiaodan allowed herself to blush faintly. "I refuse to give up on her yet. She remembers some of Zidan's more recent experiments, always talks about how worried she is that someone might steal his inventions."

"She built the palace laboratory for me," Malekh confirmed. "Some of the tonics I've made have helped with her short-term memories, but it's been difficult."

"Zidan would wed his laboratory if he could," Xiaodan said, regaining some of her cheerfulness. "As it is, he'll have to settle for me. She'll sleep for a bit now. I would have liked to tell her about my plans to root out the nest at her beloved Dà Lán, but it appears that will have to wait. She despises Vasilik. Zidan, shall we show Remy your laboratory? Or should we wait until we've cleaned it up first?"

"I already swept the place clean this morning, milady," Alegra said. "I will also prepare the gurney and the necessary tools. Shall I wrap the operating room in old canvas again so we can mop the blood up more quickly afterward?"

"Xiaodan," Remy said. "Please tell her to stop doing that."

22

A SECOND HEART

Malekh's laboratory put the Archives' lab to shame. Remy had never seen so many rows of gleaming apparatuses and vials in one place. It was all irritatingly neat and tidy, exactly as he'd expected.

"Alegra and Malira attend to the equipment whenever I'm not in Chànggē Shuǐ," Malekh said, "and they're even more fastidious at keeping the place organized than I am."

The blood-splicing doohickey the man had requested from Queen Ophelia had been summarily lugged in—a huge clunk of machinery with more knobs and levers than Remy knew what to do with in a lifetime. Once it was safely in place beside the rest of its mechanical brethren, Malekh pushed down on a button, and something within it hummed to life.

"This can sequence certain genomes using only a drop of blood." Malekh's eyes were bright and eager, more animated than Remy had ever seen. Unsurprising that machinery would be the impetus. "It could shave days off my work."

"And that would be our cue to leave," Xiaodan said, tugging at Remy's sleeve. "I interrupted him once while he was at his experiments—admittedly a petty attempt to get him to pay attention to me. I don't recommend it."

"So we do nothing but wait while he monkeys about here, shooting his milt off?" Remy asked.

"I rather think," Malekh said with a deliberate drawl, "that I should be finished with my *monkeying* tonight. All the time in the world for me to work you hard after that. Xiaodan can join, too, if she'd like."

Remy turned scarlet. Surely he didn't mean—

Oh, but he most certainly did. Remy had very nearly forgotten that this was a vampire's castle, that everyone but him were vampires, and that they all knew he hunted them as a hobby. None of them would stop Malekh if he wanted to . . . to . . .

"Your jokes aren't appreciated," he said sourly, even as he felt himself stiffen at the thought.

"He never jests," Xiaodan said, eyes aglow.

But the man had already turned his back on them, and Xiaodan giggled and drew Remy out of the room without further explanation.

DINNER WAS anticlimactic. Vampires didn't need human food for sustenance, though they'd occasionally consumed enough to learn how to cook. It explained the small platter of chicken, bread, and water waiting for Remy, who'd bathed and dressed in the interim and was still getting used to walking about barefoot in the palace like the rest did, a Qing-ye custom rather than a kindred one. The wines in their larder were heavily spiced with blood, and it was the first time he'd ever refused an offer to partake in a free drink. The kindred sitting around the table drank their fill and had nothing else. They chattered to one another for the most part in Qing-yen, and Remy made a note to learn more of the language.

The other vampires had quickly thawed to him. A few regaled him with stories of Xiaodan as a child. About the mischief she'd gotten into, sneaking out of the castle and causing a whole village to come after her when she'd taken a rich merchant's prized steed out for a ride without their consent. When she'd helped another town fight off a horde of vampires from the Second Court, only to have them turn on her upon realizing she, too, was one of the undead.

"You're a Reaper, though," Malira said. "Surely you've gotten into worse situations than making off with a bushel of fruit?"

"I wasn't invited to join the Reapers until I was thirteen years old, and I wasn't officially considered one yet even then. I was only a novitiate when—" Remy stumbled to a halt.

"What he means to say," Xiaodan went on easily, "is that I was a bigger handful than even the infamous Reapers. Surely you'd agree that I was worse than other children my age?"

"Right you are," Honfa said with a laugh. "It took all of us taking our turns guarding you, and even then you'd find a way. They say natural-born kindred are far more rambunctious as children—I was turned two hundred and ten years ago, and whatever you say of me now, I was a quiet child before that."

"How old are all of you?" Remy asked, and was answered by a chorus of voices. Two hundred and fifty, one hundred and thirty-seven, three hundred—none older than Malekh, who stood close to a thousand. Even Xiaodan at forty was young by their standards.

"Naji's the baby of our lot," another vampire named Rongyi said cheerfully. "Twenty-five years of age, only five of them turned."

The youth in question sat apart from the rest of them, sulking at a corner table and nursing a small glass of blood wine. "Nothing to age but numbers," he said shortly. "And I'm still older than he is." He jerked his wineglass Remy's way, uncaring as the red liquid sloshed onto his sleeve. "Yet you all fawn over him like he's wise beyond his years."

"Naji," Xiaodan said reproachfully.

"Oh, I won't start a fight with him, dear sister. Watching you all trying to impress the meat has been delightful to watch. See that weapon of his, how he never seems to let it out of his sight? How many of the Fourth Court have he and his father slain with it? How many of us would still be alive today if not for the bastard you've all welcomed in?"

"Naji!"

The boy raised his hand, drained his glass to the last drop, and then slammed it back down on the table. "If you'll excuse me."

"Please pardon him," Malira said apologetically once he'd left. "He's had some recent troubles, and he's been lashing out at everyone as a result. We thought it best to give him his space for now. Best you ignore him, let him come around on his own."

"He has some fairly good reasons to dislike me," Remy said. "I don't know how many of my ancestors actually fought the Fourth Court, but there's a good possibility that they did."

"You are here, Armiger. So many of your fellow Reapers have refused to even listen. That you are willing to, that you dine with us—that is what is promising."

"Hard to find anyone new willing to join the Fourth," a lad with a round face named Weili said mournfully, "when they have other bigger courts to choose from. You're not here to be turned yourself, by any chance?"

"No," Remy said. "I am happy as a human."

"Really? But I thought that Malekh—" Weili ended the sentence with a grunt, because Xiaodan had clearly kicked at him from under the table. "I suppose I was mistaken," he finished feebly. "He's always been picky about who he brings back here, with the court not being what it used to."

"I thought Malekh ruled the Third Court. Why does he stay at Chànggē Shuǐ?"

"With our queen being a little under the weather these last twenty years"—an understatement of the century, and Weili had to fortify himself with a huge swig of wine to go with the white lie—"and with Xiaodan still healing back then, he took charge. Besides, Xiaodan's engaged to him. His own court's well-run enough that it could go on even without him. He's got capable people there, Malekh does."

"I haven't heard much of the Third Court beyond speculation," Remy said, heart racing.

Honfa laughed again. "You'd think that all the kindred courts would have permanent lairs, wouldn't you? Like we've got Chàngge Shuǐ, even as few as we are. The Second Court had Meridian Keep, and the Sixth control the Situ territories in the southeast. But the Third Court—they're nomads. They've got places scattered all over the region, and not even the other courts know of them all. I'd say Maris, farther eastward, in what was once Agathyrsi, is their true nest, but most of the clan's usually traveling for some reason or other."

"To spy on the other courts? Or on Aluria?"

"To travel and live with humans. To learn to coexist peacefully with them," Xiaodan said. "Zidan believes that it's never good for kindred to keep ourselves distant if we want humans to trust us."

"What about the other courts? Have any members of the Night Court ever shown themselves here in Qing-ye?"

A hush fell in the wake of his words. The vampires glanced at one another and shifted uneasily in their seats.

"My apologies, Armiger," Honfa said in a louder, firmer tone. "The Night Court's never thought us enough of a danger to take action within our territories, and we rarely travel outside our own borders as it is. If you mean to hunt down anyone from that accursed court, I'd advise you to put the thought right out of your head. I thank my good fortune that I've never crossed paths with them in my years. They say the Night King's dead now, but that his queen, or some successor to her, still lives. And the last thing you would want is to attract her notice."

HE SPOTTED Malekh after dinner; Naji was with him, looking far more nervous and guilty than the haughty self he'd projected since their arrival, the conversation clearly a serious one. Remy, however, was not above prying, and was still watching when Malekh drew his brother closer into a surprising embrace. And Naji, much to Remy's amazement, began to cry.

Malekh murmured something. The boy rubbed at his eyes, nodded and fled, his older brother gazing after him. Several moments later, the lord spoke. "Did that satisfy your curiosity, Pendergast?"

Remy flushed. "I didn't mean to—"

"He didn't mean it, either. He was distraught. I thought giving him a few weeks to himself would help, but . . ." Malekh lifted a hand, massaging his temple. "Are you here to trade barbs again, Pendergast, or are you simply lost?"

Remy glowered. He had to say it. Malekh already knew, but he wanted the man to hear it from him. There'd been far too many things left unspoken between them since Zelenka. He could still remember the heat of Malekh's mouth against his skin. "I fucked Xiaodan," he said. "At the hot springs. It was only for a few seconds, but—"

"Yes," Malekh said calmly. "And she came to me afterward. You left her wanting."

"You love her. Why let her come to me?"

Malekh was before him in an instant, this time without any aggression. Instead, he took Remy's chin, thumb gliding across his lower lip. "Were you jealous?" he asked. "Of Xiaodan and myself?"

It would have been easier to lie. Easier to pretend that he wanted only Xiaodan.

"No," Remy whispered, distracted by the strong fingers stroking his jaw, willing him into an honesty he'd never wanted to discover. "I was afraid. You both fit so perfectly together. There's nothing I could possibly add to that."

With a gentleness he didn't know the lord possessed, Malekh's hand pressed against his mouth, face now inches away. Remy's eyes drifted shut. The soft, quiet groan the vampire made reverberated down to his bones, making Remy ache.

But Malekh pulled back. "I must return to my laboratory," he said, dropping his hand, and the disappointment Remy felt was tangible. "We can discuss this later with Xiaodan. But Remington—"

"Wh—what?"

"I intend to work you hard regardless."

Remy jerked up, prepared to swear at him again, but the man had already disappeared into the darkness.

Xiaodan was waiting for him in his room, a fresh roll of bandages at the ready.

"It almost never hurts anymore," Remy protested as she tugged his collar down so she could better inspect his neck.

"Proper care is what makes that possible. Malira has a jar of ointment that's effective for treating all kinds of wounds. Zidan invented it."

"That's reason for me not to bother," Remy groused, but stopped arguing when she applied the medicine.

"It's healing nicely, no thanks to you. I won't need to scold you as much tomorrow, the way it's going."

She was so beautiful and so concerned for him. They were sitting in his bedroom. In other similar situations, the answer would have been obvious to Remy. Xiaodan sensed where his thoughts were going, and her gray eyes flashed with open temptation and desire.

He remembered the night before, the soft, unbearable fire of her as she sank down onto him.

But once again, she retreated. "Well," she said, tucking a stray lock of hair behind her ear, "I hope you have a good rest."

"Xiaodan—" He wanted her, and he . . . he wanted . . .

"He pisses me off," he finally said, hating every word. "He does. But I—I wouldn't say no."

"I believe," she said with a radiant smile, "you should be saying all this to Zidan."

"Bloody hell, Xiaodan. You're not going to help me out here, are you?"

"No. Because I want you to dwell on it for as long as you need to, so you can say it without feeling like you need to hide it." She turned away.

"Xiaodan. Malekh said that he would visit—that tonight—"

"Good night, Remy," Xiaodan said sweetly, closing the door after her.

REMY COULDN'T sleep. It wasn't because he was in a strange castle, or even that there were potential killers all around him with good reason to want to kill him, their early rapport notwithstanding. He couldn't sleep because of Malekh and his fucking threats.

He'd been eyeing the locked door for hours in a near panic. He'd been looking at the windows, too, though he'd bolted them all shut earlier. The only other recourse was for the noble to climb down from the fireplace, and Remy had almost considered stuffing up the chute before deciding he was being too paranoid.

He was terrified. He didn't know if he would reject the offer— should it come—or welcome it.

He certainly wanted Xiaodan. He wanted to strip her naked,

kiss her long, beautiful scar, and explore the rest of her properly. He wanted the soft smoke of her again, imagined how her quivering would feel around him for longer than a thrust.

But Malekh, Remy didn't want to think about. How the man would mock him one moment, be coldly aloof in the next, and whisper filth at him afterward. Malekh's occasional frankness about his desires was the only thing Remy liked about the noble.

It all scared the hell out of him. It also aroused him.

And when a key turned and the door finally opened, Remy lay there, frozen. "I don't know how to fucking do this," he'd muttered. "I've never been with two people at a—and I haven't even given my bloody consent, you goddamn bastard—"

"A Pendergast."

Remy sat up. It wasn't Malekh who was standing by the entrance, nor was it Xiaodan.

"Uh," he said, utterly flummoxed. "I . . . Would you like me to bring you to Xiaodan's room?"

"You're a Pendergast," Queen Yingyue said. "I knew you were as soon as I saw that monstrosity upon your back. Only the Pendergasts are so arrogant as to flaunt their killing weapons wherever they go. And I have dealt with many, many Pendergasts in the past. Your ancestors have slain many of those I've sired. You are a hardy breed. A bloodline almost as old as an Ancient such as I. I have need of you. You will come with me."

"Ma'am," Remy said desperately, his head still so full of anticipation of both Malekh and Xiaodan that he hadn't fully changed course, "I have the strongest affections for your daughter. I'm half in love with her at this point. I think you're a very attractive woman, but I have no intentions of accepting whatever, uh, propositions you're about to make—"

Brown eyes stared back at him with none of the confusion and haze he'd witnessed earlier. "What are you yapping on about, you foolish boy?" Queen Yingyue snapped. "I am here because you are a Pendergast. I am bringing you to the heart because my daughter likes you as she likes Zidan, and you will not say another word about refusing."

SHE DRAGGED him past long corridors he hadn't even known existed within the palace, then up four sets of stairs that wound their way into one of its unused wings. Queen Yingyue showed no signs of her previous lethargy, bouncing from step to step with boundless energy. She could carry him up another dozen flights if she wanted to, even with Breaker at his back. His weapon had been the first thing he'd snagged before she shoved him out the room, because while he was an embarrassed fool who'd thought Xiaodan's mother had had other intentions toward him, he wasn't *that* much of a moron.

"Tithe," the woman observed in midstride. "You have that look about you."

"My mother was Tithian."

"A fine, friendly people. Would give you the shirt off their back, when they bothered to wear one. Even their kindred are frustratingly cheerful. A bit like my Xiaodan." She shoved at a moth-eaten sliding screen, the wood slamming back so forcefully it was nearly dislodged from its hinges. "This used to be my . . ." A quick spasm of pain crossed her face. "No matter. We are here for something else."

Their destination turned out to be a small room within the deepest recesses of the palace, and inside . . .

Inside was an altar, some pagan construction made of old stone and bloodstains steeped so deeply into the wood that no scrubbing would ever get it out. There were no other furnishings, save for a small metal box sitting atop it.

"Here," the woman insisted, pulling him closer. With mounting dread, Remy watched as she opened the chest.

Within lay a heart.

It had been embalmed, preserved, and semi-mummified.

"She was an Ancient," Queen Yingyue said. "The Ancestor. The bloodpride of our clan, one of the first vampires to have walked the lands. She was called Lilith the Mother, and also Lilitu the Forbidding. Her name inspired fear. She lived long and well, and she died fighting the Night Court."

"That was long before I was born, ma'am," Remy said, visibly nervous and fingers ready to reach for Breaker, because if she was about to single him out for revenge—or for some obscure human sacrifice, judging by their surroundings—then he would fight her, Xiaodan's mother or no.

But the Fourth Court queen only laughed and tapped him smartly on the shoulder, nearly sending him to his knees. "Even in death, she was strong. Her heart endured when the rest of her body did not, and what the Night King took away, he returned to us a weapon of our own, but with a terrible curse. Lilith was born with the Sunbringer, wielded it like a weapon her whole life. *She who killed with the dawn.* It was why he had determined her extinction. Since then, others have tried to trade in their hearts for hers. They've died horribly. By the good Mother, my daughter did not. Her eyes were brown once, like mine is. But she has Lilith's eyes now; that beautiful gray of the damned. Lilith watches me, watches us all. You claim you hold affection for Xiaodan. So you must guard her heart well."

Remy stared down at the box with rising horror. "You mean this is—"

"My daughter's heart, Pendergast. I told Zidan to guard it well, and now I demand the same of you."

23

EXPLORATION

"It was not fucking funny," Remy growled.

Xiaodan thought it was hilarious. She was still doubled over with her hands on her stomach, laughing loud and long. "You sincerely thought," she gasped out in between wheezes, "that my mother had come to your chambers to seduce you? And you said so, to her face?"

"It was an easier assumption to make than being dragged out of bed in the middle of the night and led all the way through your fortress to view your bloody bleeding heart," Remy said grumpily as he continued to spin Breaker. Malira had delivered a message for him at breakfast, informing him that Malekh had requested his presence at the courtyard. Remy had already given up on sleeping after his encounter with the vampire queen; Honfa had rushed into the room soon after the woman had showed him the embalmed horror, apologizing profusely to Remy even as he carried her away. It was reported in the morning that Queen Yingyue had suffered a relapse and had no memories of what she'd done the night before.

"She did the same thing to Zidan years ago," Xiaodan said thoughtfully.

"Are you not going to explain why the hell she's been keeping your—" Here Remy's mind broke down, trying to process the sheer grotesqueness of it. "She told me a crockload about how your ancestors and mine have been slaying each other for generations, but I'm not sure that's a good enough reason not to at least wait until daylight to show me."

"You were fortunate." Xiaodan gazed down at the ground. "You caught her during one of her lucid moments. The only emotion she's shown me in the last twenty years is either grief or anger."

Remy paused. "I apologize. I didn't mean to—"

"I know. I'm glad you saw her for the woman she used to be instead of the invalid who's spent nearly three decades living more in the past than present. She isn't keeping my heart for insidious reasons. You could cut it up into as many pieces as you'd like, and I wouldn't feel a thing. She keeps it out of guilt. I'm not the first to come into possession of Lilith's heart—just the one who's lasted the longest. Few vampires before me survived the procedure." Xiaodan shuddered. "The pain was worse than anything I've ever felt. Worse than when Etrienne stabbed me."

"When you told me you'd inherited your ancestor's heart, I didn't think you meant it literally."

"Zidan said that the medical terminology for it would be a transplant. A replacement. Not even Mother was certain it would work, but she was desperate for my sake. I don't know how much you know of our history, but Lilith was renowned—and feared—among the kindred."

"She was the original Sunbringer. Your mother mentioned that, too."

"What else do you know of her?"

Remy wracked his brain for a way to make what he was about to say next sound apologetic. "Nothing at all. We didn't pay much attention to anyone beyond the existing court leaders. My father always said it wasn't necessary to humanize vampires with names.

And if this happened several millennia ago, I doubt that we've got any records of it. Aluria's a young kingdom by comparison."

Xiaodan nodded, not at all offended. "Not even we know how Lilith came upon such abilities. They said she'd been cursed by hell itself to bring all the kindred into damnation with her. The Night King hunted her for that reason. No one knew her abilities could be transferred after her death. There were two other vampires before me to successfully undergo the transplant, but when they attempted to use the Sunbringer's power, they . . . they perished anyway."

"And Malekh . . . ?"

"Zidan was the reason I survived. Sauveterre all but ripped my heart out. I remember Zidan, frantic, finding me on the floor with my chest carved up. Every vampire who'd attempted to take up her heart before I did were full kindred. That I am a cambion—Zidan thinks that's one reason it worked. We're not as strong as full kindred, but we endure certain things that they cannot, including sunlight. There aren't enough dhampirs about to prove any of Zidan's theories yet."

She smiled sadly. "Mother begged him to save me with Lilith's heart. She believed that any complications I suffered in the future would be better than dying in the moment." Xiaodan bowed her head. "She regretted it. Many left the Fourth because of me. And I am the reason Mother's been reduced to such a state of—"

"No," Remy said violently, an angry jerk of his shoulders sending the knifechain above him spiraling faster. "You're not to blame for her deteriorating mind."

Xiaodan smiled wanly. "It's not something I like to talk about, which is why I haven't said much thus far. The memories it always brings back—it's about more than just the physical pain."

"Thank you," Remy said, understanding her better now.

"For what?"

Because she'd understood him, too. Once she'd realized he had his own trauma to bear, she'd accepted there were parts of him he wasn't willing to relinquish just yet, shielded him from other people's inquisitiveness. She'd stopped her clanspeople from prying into his past the night before. "You know why."

She smiled. "I suppose I do."

Zidan arrived a few minutes later. Remy knew vampires didn't sleep, though they sometimes took short periods of rest during the day, but all the members of the Fourth Court appeared old enough to withstand sunlight, excluding Naji. And for someone who'd supposedly spent the night working in his laboratory, Malekh looked refreshed and alert, hair neatly tied back from his face with no lock out of place. Naji was with him, having found shade underneath the roof of a nearby pavilion, but the brat was easier to ignore.

After the night Remy had just gone through, knowing he looked haggard in comparison, the sight irked him. "What did you call me here for?"

A few of the other vampires appeared startled by his rudeness, but Malekh ignored it. "I'm here to work you hard, as I promised. Vampires avoid Qing-ye for its abundance of sunlight, but if there is a coven within Fourth Court territory, then you will need to be fighting better than you do. You once told me that if I still considered your skills lacking, you were open to my teaching you."

Breaker slowed, then ground to a halt as Remy lowered it. It was his turn to laugh, bending down and slapping his knee partly in mirth, partly in frustration at his own asininity.

"I fail to see the humor in the situation."

"No," Remy said, still chortling. "It's all me—I'm an arse. Working me hard. Of course. Think I'm up to beating you today, for a change."

"Would you like to put another wager on it?"

Remy didn't hesitate. "If I win, I want you to help me find everything you can about the Night Empress and the First Court.

Where the coven is hiding, where their most recent nest may be, and everything else you can provide."

"You're a fool," Naji said. "They've already warned you against going after her. You'd be dead before you could do them any damage."

"She killed my mother, and I won't rest until I see her staked through, and to hell with how old she is. Just give me the information I need, and I'll do the rest. You told me that the Night King has died and his queen has taken his place. If it was possible to kill him, then why not her?"

The silence was unexpectedly palpable. Even Naji looked nervous. Malekh reacted little to his pronouncement, his features still carefully blank. Oddly enough, so was Xiaodan's, every bit of emotion wiped clean from her normally expressive face.

"If you can't get past me," Malekh said, "then you'll never get close enough to see the Night Empress herself."

"Name your wager, then."

"If I win, then I will carry out tonight what you were so convinced I would."

An even more deliberate silence fell. This time, it was Remy who was doing his damnedest not to turn red, failing miserably. The others watching registered little surprise. Even Naji contented himself with rolling his eyes theatrically.

"Fuck you," Remy said.

Malekh undid his coat, let it fall. "Then it is agreed. Shall we begin?"

AS ALWAYS, Malekh was a man of his word. Remy's skills had improved considerably in the interim since leaving Elouve, but it still took every ounce of strength he had just to parry the man's blows, and his counterattacks remained few and far between.

It didn't help that many of the Fourth Court vampires cheered with every decisive blow the lord made, which happened frequently. Keyed up on arrogance, Remy had insisted on fighting Malekh hand to hand, despite the disadvantages it would bring him, to the visible disappointment of their audience. Whatever their conciliatory views toward him, Breaker had slain their kin. To see Malekh overcoming him with that most feared weapon would be satisfying for them to see.

But Remy was used to being the underdog anyway, and Malekh was far too familiar with fighting Breaker by now to gain much of an advantage. So Remy focused on avoiding blows, on making a point to get up quickly whenever he had his feet swept out from under him.

"Again," he gritted out, for what felt like the hundredth time, righting himself painfully off the courtyard stones. Malekh was much more relentless this time, but he was fighting him like an equal. Remy supposed he should at least thank Malekh for letting him keep his dignity.

He lashed out before he'd even regained his balance, hoping to catch the vampire unaware, but Malekh simply ducked his punches and sidestepped his high kicks with just as much ease, then clipped him hard against the chin.

Remy staggered back, took a few moments to refocus, and sidestepped Malekh's follow-up blow, giving ground reluctantly. He ducked, delivered a glancing blow to the man's stomach, but the noble didn't seem to feel the hit. He grinned instead and walloped Remy hard in the shin. His knees buckled, and he was on the ground for the tenth time that hour alone.

He could feel Xiaodan's eyes on him rather than on her fiancé's. He risked a look, spotted the bright, pleased smile on her face. Either she was glad that Malekh was kicking his arse at this level of frequency, or she approved of his tenacity, though there didn't seem much to commend him regarding the latter.

"Again," he rasped, struggling back to his feet and launching himself at the noble. Malekh blurred out of view and Remy spun, lashing out with his foot at where the vampire had reappeared. The noble grabbed his ankle; without pause, Remy leaped into the air and kicked out with his other boot, managing to hit his opponent's shoulder before Malekh shoved hard at him, sending him flying.

He landed on his feet, turned to face the vampire again, and paused when he saw Malekh's relaxed stance. The noble was already picking up the cloak he'd discarded.

"I'm not done yet," Remy growled.

"We've done enough today," Malekh said. "The fight is over."

"I told you not to fucking patronize me—"

But Malekh was already shrugging his coat on. "I've finished my analysis of Dr. Agenot's serum. It may be of interest to you, what I've discovered. While we are a ways off from eradicating the infection in its entirety, I may have found a way to slow its progression, to keep the Rot dormant long enough to delay the worst of its effects. See me at my laboratory once you've changed into something less"—he wrinkled his nose—"fragrant."

"Did I win?" Remy asked, watching him leave. "What the hell just happened?"

Xiaodan popped up beside him, laughing. "No one has gone this many rounds with Zidan in a spar, Remy. He's just annoyed that he wasn't able to beat you more conclusively."

"I didn't do shit. He knocked me down so many times I wasn't even sure which way was up half the—"

"Milady's right," Alegra said. She nodded at her fellow clanmates, who were eyeing Remy with newfound respect. "I wasn't expecting a Pendergast so young to hold his own against Lord Zidan."

"Zidan took pity on him," Naji said. "I don't understand why you all act like he's done something impressive."

"I still think fighting the Night Empress is tantamount to suicide, Armiger," Honfa said slowly. "But perhaps if Lord Zidan thinks it's possible . . ."

Remy stared at them, then back at Xiaodan. "Did I bloody win?" he asked again.

IT DIDN'T look like much—the small vial was unchanged from when Remy had seen it the last time, the same oddly transparent color it had been when Malekh had set it down before Queen Ophelia. "So what you're telling us," Remy said, trying to wrap the entirety of his brainpower around what Malekh had just told them, "is that you've found a way to prevent the Rot from spreading in someone who's already been exposed to it? Someone who's been bitten but hasn't fully succumbed to his injuries?"

"Exactly. I see you've been paying attention after all." Ignoring Remy's scowl, Malekh picked up an empty syringe. "I'd like to show you how it works. Roll up your arm."

"Why?"

"I'll be needing blood from you, if I may. We need an uninfected human for this demonstration, and you're the only one available." Malekh raised an eyebrow. His smile was back. "Or would you prefer I use a different extraction method?"

Everyone was still refusing to tell him if he'd won or lost their wager. Remy glowered and did as the noble asked.

Malekh took his blood carefully, injected a small amount of it onto a glass display. "We won't need the optic enhancers to observe the results," he said. "This is, of course, what uninfected blood looks like. I've taken another sample, this time from Tal Harveston's corpse, and added in a reactant that would make the changes visible when I do . . . this."

He selected a dropper already filled with the mutated blood, squeezed out a drop into the set he'd taken from Remy. The liquid changed abruptly from its normal scarlet red to a gradually bluish tinge. "This is what the blood of those infected by the Rot would look like," Malekh said. "In two hours, it overwhelms the human immune system completely, killing the host and turning them into the mindless undead. And if I were to analyze this new infected sample again, it will now show two distinct blood types—your blood type, Pendergast, and that of another."

"Tal Harveston's?" Xiaodan asked.

"No, and that's the most fascinating part. Agenot mentioned this before, but my tests make it conclusive. Tal Harveston is of the type A antigen, but the blood type dominant in this sample is of an AB classification—the original progenitor of this mutation."

"How's that possible?"

"A patient zero perhaps, likely the one responsible for the initial outbreak. It shows me one possible breakthrough. I can sequence the genome of the infector's blood, map out its whole structure for me to modify and test as I see fit."

"Are you saying you can change the molecular structure of this sample to showcase any other deviations, the possible mutations that can come from it?" Xiaodan asked, being far more attuned to the conversation than Remy. "And you can alter it to prevent the spread of the contamination to humans who become infected? So if they're treated right away, they won't die from it?"

"As promising as this is, I cannot say with certainty that any humans would be completely rid of the Rot. But we can keep it dormant." Malekh picked up another syringe from his collection, one with a bright-red liquid shine that reminded Remy of bloodwakers. "Anyone infected who receives this within an hour of being bitten, two at the latest, will retain their humanity. It will not completely eradicate the Rot within them, only render it harmless. They may need new infusions of the serum on occasion, but it should give us enough time to research a more permanent cure."

"You're a genius, my love," Xiaodan said delightedly.

"Once I isolated the infected blood cells, it was easy enough to find the solution. I assume the other scientists at the Archives who took over after Agenot will find the answer before long. It was far simpler than even I'd expected."

"How are you so bloody sure it's effective?" Remy asked.

"I tested it out this morning. I was late for our sparring because I was handing out doses to two recent victims in the villages east of here—Laofong and Huixin. One had been bitten an hour previously, the other closer to death at two. Both are alive and recovering, with no observed mutations. Two subjects treated successfully is not conclusive by any means, but it's a promising start. I've replicated more of the serum for their ongoing treatment and distributed them among the other villages, should other incidents occur."

"You used people for your experiments without knowing how effective it is, or what side effects they might suffer from it?" Remy burst out.

"Tell me what I should have done, Pendergast. All medicines require thorough testing. I would not be a proper test subject, as it would be ineffective on me. The only alternative was to allow the Rot to take its course and have Xiaodan burn them afterward— and as I recall, you were even more opposed to that."

"It still isn't right to experiment on people," Remy muttered.

"You're still frowning, love," Xiaodan noted to Malekh. "If this was so simple, wouldn't this be a cause for celebration?"

"We're making headway, yes," he said slowly, "but there are two things that still bother me. There is a deliberate cold-bloodedness about how all this has been engineered. If this is an artificially manufactured disease, then someone out there has a very particular hatred of humanity."

"And the second point?" Remy prompted when the noble appeared lost in his own thoughts.

"The second," Malekh said, "is that this all seems just a little too easy."

"Milord," Honfa said as he and Alegra entered the laboratory. "Malira and Alegra believe they know where the Fifth Court nest is hidden."

Xiaodan spun toward them, wide-eyed. "Where?"

"It's just as you suspected, milady. A mile or so to the southeast, around the Dà Lán. Alegra says she spotted kindred lurking about."

"Not an Elder vampire, strangely enough," Alegra said. "A young man. No more than a few years turned, I'd say, as he was still avoiding the patches of sunlight among the plains. The Dà Lán is particularly notorious for those. Not ageless enough to look the part, either. He tried to fight when we spotted him, realized he couldn't win, and took off."

"Alegra thinks it could be a lure," Honfa said. "Not even the most foolish and the most inexperienced would be wandering aimlessly around here. But a lure to where, we don't know. We don't have enough of us to man Chànggē Shuǐ and search at the same time, and we're worried about whether it's bait to leave the castle undefended, or to ambush us by the lake."

"None of you are to leave Chànggē Shuǐ," Xiaodan said sharply. "Mother's safety takes priority. Zidan and I shall look into the matter."

"I'm coming with you," Remy said.

"You don't know the lands as well as we do. It would be better to keep you here."

"Xiaodan—"

"I'm afraid this is not a request, Remy." Xiaodan's voice softened. "Please."

Remy hated it. He should be out there with them. He hadn't

traveled this far to be shunted off now. Still, he nodded. "Don't be slow about it," he said, and was rewarded with a smile.

HE SAW them off that afternoon and didn't grow bored until an hour later. He wandered into the courtyard, where a few of the vampires offered their own sparring sessions with him. He opted against using Breaker again, grappling with Gideon before going on an exhilarating melee bout with Alegra, who was by far the strongest fighter in the castle besides Malekh and Xiaodan. He'd found better success against them, trouncing Gideon and forcing Alegra into a stalemate, delivering worthier blows than he'd been able to with the Third Court king.

Naji stood at the sidelines and watched them fight. For a moment, Remy thought the youth might challenge him to his own bout as revenge for their last, but the lad merely frowned, still not happy at the thought of him here, and left when the battles were done.

There was something odd at the farthest end of the courtyard that he hadn't noticed during his first visit. It was a black boxlike structure twenty or twenty-five feet high, with a small opening on the side for peering in that could fit no more than three or four fingers. Remy had an uneasy feeling. It looked too similar to the one at the Archives' laboratory to be a coincidence.

"Did Malekh make a vault of his own?"

"I don't know what a vault is," said a pretty vampire named Liufei, "but it's what we built for Lord Zidan in case we needed to contain any of the infected we might encounter in Qing-ye. No such luck yet."

"He told me he had no plans to keep any of those mutations alive long enough to compromise everyone else's safety."

"He spoke true, but you know Lord Zidan—always ready with a contingency. Did you know that Xiaodan's sunbringer ability is the only way to destroy them completely? Even we could be killed by her light if we stand too close. It is easier for her to take down any beasts if they're enclosed, where it wouldn't affect us." Liufei sighed dramatically. "I'm a hundred and seventy years old. I would have thought that my fear of the sun was long behind me."

"If it's worth anything, you don't look a day over eighty."

"Flatterer." Liufei's smile faded. "If I may be so bold, Armiger. I am glad that there is someone outside of Lilith's Court that cares for Lady Song as much as we do. She has not had an easy life. We would not abandon her had she the power of a thousand suns, and I see that you feel the same."

"I only hope to be useful to her."

"I can think of many different ways and at least twenty-four positions by which she would be delighted by your usefulness." Liufei sauntered away, chuckling, as Remy turned red.

Afterward, he had taken to wandering the castle. The hell-hounds were dozing inside the library but stirred to lick him. A lazy half hour of petting passed—once you got used to their tendency to look skeletal at angles, they were rather charming.

They nudged playfully at his legs while he browsed the shelves. He discovered a fair number of medical textbooks and studies on anatomy, which he figured were from Malekh's collection. Wherever the Third Court base truly was, it looked like Malekh had made the Chànggē Shuǐ fortress a second home of sorts.

"Found any of our secrets yet?"

Remy spun, watching Naji plop himself down on an armchair. One of the dogs trotted over to the boy, demanding his share of head pats.

"Why are you even here?" the young vampire asked bluntly. "Are you really a spy for Aluria, or are my brother and his fiancée your main concern?"

Remy bristled. "I want to take down the Night Court."

"With what? That hunk of steel you carry around? We don't

go out of our way to antagonize the First Court. You know about Zidan's past with the Night King by now."

"I don't intend to do anything that could hurt him."

Naji paused, taking in the look on Remy's face. "So you do like Zidan," he said, almost smirking. "Him *and* Xiaodan. You're easy enough to read."

"That's none of your business," Remy said tightly.

"Why aren't you doing anything about it?"

"You've wanted to kick me out of the castle from the moment I stepped foot inside it. Why would you throw me at your brother and his betrothed?"

"If they brought you here, then they trust you. Zidan saved my life. I want to see him happy even more than I dislike you. Anyone else in your place would have jumped at the chance to share their bed by now."

"I'm not anyone else! I don't deserve—" Remy stumbled to a halt. "I don't fucking know why they chose me." He wasn't sure why he was confessing to the one person in Chànggē Shuǐ who'd been the most hostile to him, but saying it was a weight off his shoulders. "I've never had much of a family, and I'm not in the habit of trusting people. I keep expecting them to demand something in exchange, even if my instincts tell me they won't."

"That's a lot of words to admit you've been acting the fool."

Remy scowled at him but had no answer.

The youth looked down. "You know, I never had much of a family, either. Your father like to punch you like mine did?"

"No," Remy said, taken aback.

"I was the sickly sort, and he resented it. Beat me so bad he all but killed me the last time, and it scared the shit out of him. He dumped me on the side of the road, ready to swear it was the work of some rogue vampire. Except the vampire who found me saved me instead. So I went back and showed my father just how strong I was." Naji looked down at the dog, smiling to himself.

"Zidan, Xiaodan, everyone here—they're the first ones to make me feel like I belong. They've asked nothing of me. Everything I do for them is done willingly. It's just . . ." He paused, taking several seconds to inspect the demon dog's fur.

"I was grieving," he said quietly. "I needed a way to forget. To run wild for a moment. And I would have continued to be that imbecile for far longer if you hadn't beaten some sense back into my head. Suppose I should thank you for not killing me that night."

"I'm sorry," Remy said. "I didn't know."

Naji rolled his eyes. "Talk to my brother when he and Xiaodan return. But first, you need to figure out what it is *you* want from *them*, instead of spending all your time second-guessing what *they* want from *you*." Naji pointed toward the door. "And now I'd like to read in peace. Go find Gideon and make yourself useful."

It wasn't until Remy was halfway down the corridor that he realized the conversation had been a peace offering on Naji's part.

He went up by the castle turrets next, insistent on standing guard for a turn while he was there. In a bid to be friendly, one of the other warriors, a stocky lad with a bright smile named Guoyang, showed him the defenses of their isolated city. A minefield of traps lay just outside the fortress, he explained. The solid-looking ground before them hid large pits with sharpened wooden stakes waiting for unlucky attackers. And as he'd been told earlier, most vampires were nervous about moats, especially when Chànggē Shuǐ's flooded down from the waterfall behind them.

"Won't someone attempt to climb down that?" Remy asked.

"The lake the waterfall comes down from goes on for miles, without any dry ground for them to stand on. Not a likely spot for vampire attacks. Jumping from there and landing on the castle walls—and the many spikes we've set up—won't bode well for them either. We put a guard up there every week or so, just to be sure. There's a small shallow pool right on top where the water only reaches your knees. Everywhere else around it is a good thirty,

thirty-five feet deep, and the next tract of solid land is twenty miles away after that. We make wagers on who can make it up the fastest."

Guoyang was teaching him some Qing-yen while they stood guard—naturally, he learned the curses first—when they caught a glimpse of a figure speeding rapidly toward them from a distance, moving far too quickly for it to be anything else but what Remy feared it was.

The vampire stopped before their gates. They were heavily hooded and holding something up in the air for them to see.

It was Xiaodan's cloak, drenched in blood.

By the time Remy made it to the outer gates, the vampire was already surrounded by the rest of the Fourth Court. Both his hands were in the air. "Don't get all your shifts stuck in a twist," he said. "Your beloved Song Xiaodan is alive—for now."

"If you don't bring her to us in the next five minutes," Alegra growled, "it will be your head that is twisted clean off your body. You're only a youngblood. All we need to do is rip that cloak off and shove you into sunlight."

"How rude," the vampire said affably. "I'm only the messenger, milady, and if anything happens to me, your mistress's head will be at stake. Or *on* a stake, as it were. You see this?" He waved the cloak again. "I was told to give this to the bloodling, along with a message."

"The bloodling is here," Remy said, stepping forward. "If you've hurt her—"

The vampire grinned. "If you wish to see both Zidan Malekh and Song Xiaodan alive, then you are to accompany me back to our coven—alone. Vasilik would like to extend his most esteemed regards to you in person. Reject his offer, and he will be deeply sorry to have to deliver both Malekh and Song back to you in very tiny pieces."

24

CAVERNOUS

"Now listen here," Remy said. "You probably don't like me, because I sure as hell don't like you, much less want to climb on your back. But your mistress is in trouble, and I'm going to do everything in my power to bring her back."

Peanut—or was it Cookie?—whinnied happily and did a little three-legged jig before him.

"I can't move as fast as a vampire, which is why I'm going to have to rely on you for speed, old boy." Remy was stalling. Riding a carriage pulled by the helhests was enough of a nightmare. He wasn't sure what a ride on the demon stallion's back would do to his brain.

Peanut-or-Cookie, far from being indignant, lowered its front legs to make it easier for him to clamber on.

"Thanks," Remy muttered.

"You're not good enough to bring them back," Naji said, looking on. "Xiaodan won't forgive you if anything happens to her horses."

"You sound more concerned about this horse than your sister-in-law."

"Because I don't believe the bastard when he says they're in danger. Don't let her frail heart fool you—Xiaodan is very good at taking care of herself. And my brother is with her and won't let her come to any harm. You, on the other hand, are as good as dead."

"Thank you for the kind words. You do know we have no choice? They should have been back hours ago. They would have never had the guts to send a messenger otherwise. If you're wrong, they'll kill both their hostages the instant they see anyone else with me, and we can't risk that."

Now Naji looked uneasy. "What does Vasilik even want with you?"

"Your brother's old lover thinks he and I are together."

"Vasilik's always been a bastard, but the one thing he's good at is knowing when my brother is interested in someone else."

Remy ignored him, swinging up on the helhest's back.

"It's obvious you're important to them both," Naji continued grudgingly. "Get them back safely, or I'll murder you in your sleep."

"You won't have the opportunity to, because I'm not coming back without them."

The boy finally allowed himself a smile. "That, I can respect."

The vampire messenger had been understandably reluctant to have the steed along for the journey, so Remy had issued his own ultimatum. "Your lord expects us to return quickly. If you expect me to go riding around on *your* back—"

"I do find the idea well beneath my dignity," the unwanted guest agreed. "Might I remind you that any attempts to escape will not end well for your companions?"

Remy had brought more than just Peanut-or-Cookie, having pilfered Malekh's laboratory for what he needed, but the messenger didn't need to know that. He hadn't been instructed to come unarmed, so he'd brought Breaker along for the ride, too. The messenger raised an eyebrow at the weapon, looking oddly amused, but otherwise said nothing.

Peanut-or-Cookie was even faster than the vampire. Once Remy had gotten used to feeling like the skin on his face was peeling away, he learned how to nudge the helhest enough to slow down and keep pace with the boy. The ride was much more disorienting than he'd expected; sitting in a carriage, at least, he could retain his sense of balance. On horseback, he had to keep his head low and clutch tightly at the stallion's neck for dear life, hoping he wouldn't slip off and hit the ground at a speed that could break something important.

He should have listened to his gut instincts and insisted on accompanying Xiaodan and Malekh to the Dà Lán. Maybe it wouldn't have helped much, but maybe it would have. Xiaodan was far too strong to have let her guard down, and Malekh would never fall to a cretin like Vasilik. He didn't want to think about the might-have-beens.

It was only several minutes later—though it felt like a lifetime—when the vampire slowed down, the helhest doing the same, and the world stopped being a blur of bright colors. They halted before a large blue lake with wisps of mountains standing off at a distance, wrapped in a shawl of hazy clouds.

"Pretty," Remy said, noting with vicious satisfaction that the messenger was carefully eyeing the faint gleams of sunlight bouncing off the surface of the water with concern, moving to distance himself from them.

To their left, a series of small caves stood clustered together, the largest with an odd dome-shaped top. The ground by the entrance to the nearest one was stained with telltale splashes of blood, a trail leading farther in. There were no bodies.

"You didn't tell me this was where we were going," Remy said, barely outwardly calm. He could feel the blood pounding in his ears. This was not good. He'd already drawn Breaker, finding comfort in its heavy, familiar steel. He needed it, because the last time he'd been inside a cave—

"You can stay out here, if you'd like," the vampire said. "No telling what Vasilik might do to your companions, though. Perhaps you'll hear their screams from here."

Remy wasn't listening. He was staring hard at the cluster of trees on the opposite shore. "Who is that?"

"What—"

But Remy had already goaded the helhest into action. Peanut-or-Cookie took off—his bones were still rattling about from the sudden speed when the stallion reached the edge of the lake moments later with him somehow still on its back.

"Heel!" Remy shouted, and nearly fell off when the steed obeyed. He picked himself back up on shaky legs and scanned the dark woods. This time, nothing moved.

The messenger blurred into form beside him, angry. "If you thought you were going to get away, Pendergast, I assure you that Malekh will pay for—"

Remy turned and grabbed the vampire's hood, wrenching him closer. "Did you think you could pull an ambush on me?" he snarled. "Tell them to come out and face me."

"'Ambush'?" the messenger gasped. "I came alone. There's no one out here but—"

"I saw them. In a scarlet robe and hood, watching us. Tell me who that was or I'm going to enjoy watching you smoke." He put the threat into practice, shoving the vampire toward a stray burst of sun dotting the ground a few feet away.

"I swear, milord, there is no one else! No others were willing to brave the plains with the sun at this intensity."

The clear confusion in the youth's voice was genuine enough to give Remy pause. Whoever it was, lurking in the woods, the boy had no knowledge of them.

Could be he'd imagined it, seen something that wasn't there?

No. His gut called bullshit on that.

They waited, Remy still watching the woods intently, the vampire struggling to angle away from the sunlit ground. "If you're lying," Remy finally said, releasing the boy, "you won't survive the day."

The vampire coughed and sputtered, then rearranged his hood. "Humans," he muttered contemptibly, like he'd never been one himself.

They returned to the caves, and Remy let the helhest graze along the lake's shore. "Stay here until I return," he told it, still reluctant to look away from the woods, hoping to spot the hooded figure again. Peanut-or-Cookie whinnied.

"After you," the vampire said, bowing low to him and gesturing at the bloody entrance.

"Any attempts to bite me once we're inside, and your insides will be decorating the walls."

The vampire laughed. "No attempts. Not from me, anyway. I'll keep you safe until we meet Vasilik."

"He's going through a lot of goddamn trouble just for a chat."

The cave was larger than it first appeared, widening at another hundred or so yards in. The path after that began to twist downward. Several forks marred their way as they went, and Remy tried his best to map the way back out while the vampire guided him through the first entryway, then another, and then several more.

He shoved his free hand into his coat pocket, not wanting the messenger to see it was trembling. He hated caves. Too much terrible shit happened in caves. At one point he thought he heard a scream ring out, and his head jerked up, Breaker's edge slamming into the side of the wall as panic threatened to overwhelm. The passage was too narrow to use his knifechain this time, he thought wildly. He couldn't beat them all back with just his scythes. They were coming after him—they were—

It wasn't until the messenger made a curious, questioning sound at him that Remy realized he'd only imagined the scream. He was covered in sweat, gripping Breaker so hard he wondered how he didn't dent the silver, and forced himself to relax. *These aren't the same caves*, he told himself, *and it's been ten years.*

"Don't like small spaces, do you?" his companion asked, grinning maliciously.

"They make me nervous enough that my hand just might slip," Remy said, shaking Breaker a little harder for emphasis, and the man shrunk back at the solid thunk of steel hitting the wall. "You'd be surprised at how much damage I can still do with this, mate. Let's forgo the scenic route and head straight to Vasilik. I haven't got all day to waste."

"East is your best bet. There are air currents here, and the wind always blows in that direction."

"What?"

"On the rare chance you might lose your way. Keep heading east. I believe it's where the underground rivers flow in these parts."

"And you're telling me that out of the goodness of your heart."

The messenger shrugged. "Don't know if there's enough goodness in me to claim any. Just some friendly advice. Few humans would brave these caves for the sake of kindred. I find it . . . refreshing."

The path eventually led to a much larger chamber, lit by a few torches mounted on the walls, and the wider space helped to ease Remy's nerves. Unfortunately, it was also large enough for him to see Vasilik Preobrazhensky. The vampire sat on a chair carved from one of many rock formations littering the area, lounging with one leg draped over a makeshift stone armrest, elevated so he could survey the rest of the room with a smug air.

There were, at a quick estimate, sixty to seventy vampires in the cavern with them. Remy had been expecting a well-sized coven, but their actual numbers were more than he'd anticipated. That had likely caught Xiaodan and Malekh unawares, too.

"Surprised?" Vasilik drawled. He was almost unchanged from their last fight, with the same jackarsed hair and the same jackarsed clothes and the same jackarsed smirk on his jackarsed face. The only discernible difference was a thin scar now running vertically through his eye, ending halfway down his cheek. "Thought you blinded me permanently, didn't you?"

"Sorry to see that I haven't."

"That fabled Pendergast silver. And that's not my only gripe with you and the Third and Fourth Courts. It doesn't feel fair, does it? Dozens of my loyal followers slumming in these caves, while the Lady Song has run of a castle with barely enough clansmen to occupy it."

"Sounds like a *you* problem," Remy said evenly. There was no sign of Xiaodan or Malekh anywhere, and several vampires were already moving to block the entrance he'd stepped through. Not good. "Tell me where they are."

"An excellent question," Vasilik said. "I seem to have misplaced them as well. The passageway of caverns around us is such that exploring them all can take years if they've a mind to stay hidden. My people have blocked all the exits, but it might be easier to flush them out if they know I have one of Malekh's little bloodling lovers as a hostage."

"I'm not anyone's accursed bloodling lover, and I'd like for everyone to stop saying that," Remy said, secretly relieved. Vasilik had lied about the Third and Fourth Court couple's situation. There was a chance that one of them was injured—Xiaodan might have attempted her Sunbringing powers—or maybe they'd already escaped to the surface even as they spoke, no matter how many minions Vasilik thought he was throwing at them. He was the one in far greater peril at this point.

"I will find them sooner or later. Oddly enough, I had other reasons to call this meeting of ours, Lord Pendergast." Vasilik set an elbow against his seat, braced a hand under his chin, and inclined his head Remy's way, smiling. "I would like to propose an alliance."

"And why in the hell would I ever agree to that?"

"Because we have a shared goal, milord. We have a mutual ally, a benefactor that wishes for peaceful relations between you and me. I know something of you Pendergasts beyond that frightful bludgeon you carry about. You want to annihilate the First Court and the Night Empress. So do I."

Remy hesitated.

"It is an open secret, the Pendergasts' hatred toward that ancient clan. I, too, have had some unfortunate skirmishes with them in the past. It would be easier, I think, to accomplish our objectives by joining forces."

"I don't need your help."

"Oh? Did both Lady Song and Zidan volunteer to help you against the Night Court?" Vasilik's eyes gleamed brightly in the dim light. "Did they pledge to tell you more about the Night Empress?"

"They know as little about her as I do."

Vasilik burst into laughter. "And you believed them? You believed Zidan, who has lived for several hundred years at the First King's court himself? Did you think that he would tell you the truth, or that he would assist you in fighting his former clan? Zidan Malekh was sired by the First Court, you fool. And yet he tells you that he knows nothing?"

"He's cut ties with them since," Remy said, but he'd paused for too long, and Vasilik pounced on his hesitation.

"Good old Zidan. Withholding the truth doesn't count as a lie in his book. Ask him yourself. Scream out the question into one of these passages, and perhaps the echoes of it shall reach his ears. Mayhap he might even answer." Vasilik stood and stretched. "Malekh is a lying, cheating whoreson who will use you to further his own ends. The Lady Song is far too vapid and naive, and he prefers his lovers that way. You are made of the same cloth as she. Once he no longer has use of you, he will chew you up and spit you out, leave you to the wolves."

"He cares for Xiaodan. He would never have fought for the Fourth Court otherwise."

"Are you so in love with him that you would defend his treatment of his own betrothed?" Vasilik's lip curled in disgust. "Do you know how the Night King died? You will find very few who speak of it." He rose from his stone throne. "In the beginning, the Night Court was the only court in existence. It was one of decadence and cruelty, where all lived and died according to the king's whims. He murdered more vampires over the centuries than any of you humans ever could. Many grew restless under his rule, unwilling to be the next casualty. The Night King had a unique ability of his own, you see. He could compel others to do his bidding, even those with no desire to do so. Malekh would know more than I. He used to be the king's most favored pet, after all. His favorite whore."

He laughed at the look on Remy's face. "He was not always the high and mighty Third Court king he would like you to believe. He could whine and grovel as well as any other." Vasilik leaped gracefully to the ground, his subordinates parting so he could approach Remy.

"Lilith was the first to oppose their court," Vasilik continued. "Yes, the Songs' ancestress. She, too, carried within her a great and terrible power. The Night King wanted her dead because of it." He grinned. "Malekh betrayed his liege. When the revolt happened, it was he and Lilith who faced the Night King, and only he emerged from that fight alive."

He circled Remy, who willed himself to stay put. "It was Lilith's final wish to have her heart preserved, Malekh said—but who really knows for sure, when no one else can confirm or deny his claims? Perhaps he killed her himself, hoping to claim her powers for his own. You say he is protective of the Lady Song? He was always uninterested in her until she acquired Lilith's heart."

"And what makes working with you any different from working with him?"

"You know what you're getting with me."

"You laid waste to the village of Brushfen. Attempted the same to Zelenka."

"Yes, I did. Regrettable, but it had to be done. They are not all innocent, you know. My boys all came from abusive homesteads, unwelcoming villages. I offered them a home and hope. Humans are just as cruel."

Something locked into place in Remy's head. "Brushfen was an experiment. You were testing the effects of the Rot, to gauge your control over the infected."

"Oh, a clever guess. But I am not responsible for creating those mutations. I did not transform them into the grotesque things you saw. I simply took advantage of the situation as I saw fit. The Rot can be controlled, in a sense. Its bearers can be directed to carry out orders. I placed Jorgr in charge of Zelenka, but unfortunately, he wasted the opportunity to do more with my army, as you saw firsthand. I believe you've already met."

"He neglected to provide us with a name, but yes."

"I owe you for killing him. It would have been a waste of time to come and find him myself."

"And how are you able to control the infected?"

Vasilik waved a finger playfully. "Ah-ah-ah. Why give everything away?"

"You know who caused this plague on our kingdom," Remy said heatedly, "and you're working with them."

"Does it escape you, Pendergast? Are you so disastrously idealistic? We will need *more* than even the strongest kindred if we are to defeat the Night Queen. We can now control the Rot. Do you not understand that we will be unstoppable with it once we find the right formula to make these creatures invulnerable? We could even save the humans you so admire if you'd like. I will help you chip away at the First Court until its queen is dead if you will but join us. See? That's what honesty sounds like."

Vasilik seemed to shift and fade as he spoke, first reemerging at one end of the cavern, then several feet away in the next second, shifting randomly from one place to another until he was finally before Remy, lifting the latter's chin up with a finger so Remy could meet his gaze. "And as a sign of my goodwill, I shall tell you more of what I know about the First Court and its queen. There is, however, something you must provide in exchange."

"And what would that be?"

"Renounce your ties to Zidan Malekh. Step aside and allow me to kill him, as he deserves. You owe him no allegiance for all the lies he's told you. I promise to spare his betrothed. I may even go so far as to withdraw my claim on the Fourth's keep and leave them in peace. All I want is Zidan's head, and his heart, in my hands." Vasilik's voice was a whisper in his ear. "You owe him nothing. Just say the word, Pendergast. A yes, a nod, a quick shake—and we shall have our deal."

Remy would have been lying if he'd said he hadn't thought about it. The information he desired about the Night Empress right within his grasp, and someone finally willing to tell him.

"For all your talk of honesty," he said instead, "you've lied about taking Xiaodan and Malekh prisoner, and you've lied about the villages. You never bargain. Attacking Zelenka wasn't just to test your control of the Rot—it was to lure us there, to see how many of them it would take to overcome us. It was you who sent those mutations after us in the woods of Wurkenbacht. You do not intend an alliance—you would never do so with anyone you consider Malekh's consort."

Vasilik's face changed. He hissed, long fangs bared. "I've changed my mind," he said.

Remy was ready. He parried the vampire leader's strike with Breaker's scythe. He angled the knifechain upward, the slash catching his opponent by surprise. Blood spurted out from his cheek where the blade had sliced, and he snarled, rearing back.

The other vampires dashed for Remy. There was only a quick glint of silver as a warning, and then half a dozen vampires were down, Remy cutting right through them.

He slammed his scythe into the throat of another blocking the path out of the cavern; before the vampire's body even hit the ground, Remy had fled through the opening. The messenger who'd guided him in had already disappeared—smarter than his fellows, to sense when the tide had turned.

There would be more guarding the passageways. In this confined space, there was no real way for Remy to weaponize his knifechain effectively, and if he could only rely on his daggers and scythes, it was just a matter of time before their sheer numbers overwhelmed him. He took a sharp detour, choosing a more isolated path despite not knowing where it led.

There were more forks and corridors the farther he progressed, and he could understand why Vasilik had been unable to find Xiaodan and Malekh. Remy briefly worried about getting lost inside the caves forever; at the worst, he could always leave a trail for one of the vampires to find, then threaten him for the way out.

Hypotheticals were the only thing keeping him from going into another panic. The walls closed uncomfortably around him, but he did not stop moving.

He tucked himself into an unused corridor to wait, decided that the coast was clear after he judged a half an hour had passed. Cautiously he retraced his steps, trying to remember whether he'd gone left or right at a particular fork, or if he needed to keep to the larger tunnels. He could hear a faint *drip drip* from somewhere nearby, which was heartening. If there was water, then he might be closer to an exit leading back to the Dà Lán.

He stuck to the eastern paths. The vampire messenger had been honest about that, at least—his fellows were staying clear of this area, and he saw few of them. But he had yet to see either Xiaodan or Malekh, which was worrying, given all the ruckus he'd started.

A shadow filled his vision up ahead, and he froze.

It was not one of Vasilik's untried coven. A large shape loomed, blocking what little light there was. It smelled of decay and death. It shuffled, a gargle rattling out from its throat.

Remy had seen that shape before. He was a child at three and ten again, and trembling, Breaker a new, untested weight in his hands.

The frenzied shuffled like that, too, and rattled the same way—

He couldn't—he *couldn't*—

He ran. He'd had no choice ten years ago, trapped and surrounded on all sides. But there were multiple forks in the path now, and he tore down one with undue speed until the sounds died behind him. He crouched into a half-hidden crevice and waited, breath stuttering, to see if it would return.

It did not.

In that time, Remy broke down, then forced back the sudden rush of tears and did his best to pull himself together. His feet had moved without his consent upon seeing the beast. He hadn't even stood his ground to fight, instead had simply run like a coward. He'd been braver as a novice.

It wasn't real. He'd survived those caves. He'd survive *these*. Xiaodan, Malekh—he just had to find them.

"The fuck are you doing, Pendergast," he growled at himself, slapped at his cheek with one hand, and stood.

He didn't know how long he'd spent wandering, stumbling, still running. Another half an hour? Two hours? He'd encountered more vampires along the way, but they'd either been alone or in pairs and were easy to dispatch, Remy hiding their bodies from view easily and efficiently. Finding them in ones and twos was good. He didn't need to think about the ceiling above him, the tons of rock that could crush him before he even realized the danger. He didn't want to think about that dark shape or whether it had all been a figment of his imagination. The echoes of sound traveling up and down the corridors, the screams of—

No. He wasn't going down that road again.

Faint noises to his right. It was coming behind one section of wall and sounded like voices. Remy pressed his ear against the stone, straining to hear.

The words were faint but distinct, and it took some more concentration for him to realize that he didn't understand the words because they weren't speaking Alurian. It sounded like . . . yes. Qing-yen. Guoyang's hasty tutoring had come in handy.

He may not have known what they were talking about, but he did recognize Malekh's timbre, stern and unyielding.

Remy rapped at the cave walls with Breaker, hoping they could hear it. A swift, illogical terror swept through him. His actions might bring down an avalanche or that—that *thing* might hear him.

"Nà shì shénme?" Now he could hear Xiaodan.

"Děngdài." Malekh's voice rose, startled. "Pendergast?"

"How the hell did you know?"

"I can smell you through the stone." Malekh's voice was low, pleased. "I'd recognize your scent anywhere."

Remy took in a shaky breath. "Fuck off."

A chuckle through the wall. "It's him."

"Remy?" Xiaodan cried. "I told you to stay at the castle!"

"I would have, but one of Vasilik's vampires paid us a visit with your bloody clothing as a gift," Remy growled through the wall. "They insisted I come along. Light's sake, Xiaodan—I was scared to fucking death that he really hurt you—"

"You'll need to come to us," Malekh broke in abruptly. "I'm familiar enough with the passages here that I believe I know your position, but I don't know if I can leave Xiaodan on her own."

"I'll be all right by myself," Xiaodan interjected. "It doesn't even hurt anymore."

"Your heartbeat tells me otherwise."

"I can try and break down the wall," Remy offered.

"You will do nothing of the sort. That will alert them to our presence and could compromise the structure of these caves. Are you at a corridor with three forks in the path leading south?"

Remy was. "Do you have the whole map to this place laid out in your fucking—"

"Stop getting distracted, Pendergast. You are to take the right fork and follow it until you come to another split, this time with four branches. The leftmost one will lead you to another chamber. From there, follow the passage again, and take the right, and then the middle route. You'll know you've reached us when you see a large rock formation shaped like a skull, and an underground lake beyond it. Do you understand?"

"I got it," Remy said. "Right, follow the route, left, chamber, right, middle, up and down, upstairs and downstairs, in my ladies' chamber."

"Pendergast—"

"I'm only jesting, Malekh. Fuck if I've never been so glad to hear the sound of your goddamn voice before." And Remy meant it. He exhaled noisily, then stepped toward the three forked paths. "Be there soon."

Malekh's directions were easy to follow, at first. Remy duly took a left turn, promptly dispatched a vampire who'd been skulking around a curved path, and then took out two more who'd been intending to ambush him from behind and found the chamber the noble had mentioned. From there he paused, because he now found himself looking at a split in the path that had the two passages Malekh directed him toward—except the one on the right he'd been instructed to enter was completely obstructed by stones.

Sometime after Malekh and Xiaodan had entered, he surmised, a small cave-in must have occurred. Brilliant.

"Fuck," Remy said, and went down the other path. It was a longer walk, but the path seemed to curve toward the right, and he hoped there would be another opening up ahead that would bring him to the original passageway he was supposed to take.

He stumbled into another cavern, smaller than the one Vasilik and most of his coven occupied, larger than the one he had just went through. There were numerous rock formations here, too, though he couldn't make out any that remotely resembled a skull, nor was there any body of water in sight.

There was another opening ahead. Remy figured, what the hell, and started toward it.

It was a dead end. Remy explored the walls, hoping a secret opening lay within, but had to give up and return.

He felt the prickle at the back of his neck as soon as he stepped back into the wider cavern, and turned just in time. His knifechain went flying through the air, cleanly beheading a vampire that had tried to leap out at him from behind a large outcropping, and killed another. More were climbing out from behind the rock formations, darker shadows than the rest of the cave, silent but for the hissing noises they made, fangs bared as they converged. Remy swore and raised Breaker.

Something bothered him about these vampires. They were smaller than he'd expected, many of them skinnier than he'd first thought, almost like Vasilik had gotten his hands on a group of extremely short people, or—

He stumbled back. "No," he whispered, fear twisting wildly in his gut. A closer look at the ones he'd already killed confirmed his worst fears.

"Do you like our latest additions to the Fifth Court, Reaper?" Vasilik stood across the stone chamber, leering.

"You goddamn sadist." He couldn't kill them. The one part of him that was still idealistic hoped that they could be spared, that Malekh's serum could somehow revive them, but the cynical pragmatism he'd built up from hopeless battles and bloodshed meant he knew better. "I'm going to fucking kill you and feed what's left of you to the hounds at Chànggē Shuǐ. I'll slice you from throat to cock—"

"I see dirty talk is one of your more noteworthy skills," the vampire purred. "We would have been wonderful allies, darling. I'm a far better lover than he ever was." He leaned forward. "Let me change your mind, sweet bloodling. There's still time to turn your back on him, to come to my side."

"I'd rather eat acid."

Vasilik laughed. "Fortunately for you, you won't have to. You'll be food for my lovely sons and daughters if you're lucky enough, and one of my rabid, ravening infected if you're not. Did you really think I didn't know about your past? You've held up longer than I thought you would, which is a shame. I had hoped it'd break you earlier. Play with your food for as long as you like, my little dears."

He disappeared, and the infected children, panting and snarling, fell on him.

Remy swung his scythe before him in a half circle, trying to ward them off. *I can't*, he thought desperately. *I can't*, and his mind flashed back to ten years ago, when he'd stood in a cave very much like this one, only this time he was losing. He was going to die.

They reached out for him, eyes glowing, mouths parted to reveal fangs. Just as bloodthirsty as their adult counterparts, the children reached for his throat.

25

HEALING

Remy was dimly aware of arms around him, of the sudden rush of air as he was hauled out from the midst of the ravening pack of children that had descended upon him. "Stay quiet, and don't move," a voice grated by his ear, and Remy obeyed not because he wanted to, but because he was too weak not to.

He experienced a dizzying sensation, the world at times tilting around him, and realized he had been thrown over someone else's shoulder, which was why he was viewing everything upside down and at dizzying speeds, the ground flying above his line of vision. He closed his eyes, but trying to get his bearings from inside his head only made everything worse. He felt cold; his teeth were chattering despite the heavy moisture that lingered everywhere.

He was burning up, and it was painful. He wanted to thrash from the pain, to roll over on the ground and douse all the imaginary flames that were consuming his body. He felt like he was in a furnace. He wanted to die.

All he could manage was a soft croak.

"We're almost there. Hold on."

It was getting hard to think, so all he could do was nod dumbly, even if he was the only one who could see himself agree. "Fuck you, Malekh," he mumbled, no longer thinking. It seemed only heartbeats later that everything came to an abrupt stop. It felt worse than when it was all still spinning. Someone had laid him down on the ground so that he was looking up at the ceiling. Two faces blurred into view.

"Remy," Xiaodan said, stricken.

A strange bubble of laughter threatened at his throat. "No tiles," Remy mumbled, staring at the dark stone above him. "Can't count the tiles here."

A debate seemed to be raging above his head. "I don't know how many times he was bitten," Malekh was saying urgently, face strangely drawn and pale. For once, he looked like shit, but Remy was in no frame of mind to gloat. The noble was removing his coat; seconds later, Remy felt the blessed weight of it on his chest. His teeth continued to rattle from the cold. "We need to keep him warm. Help me locate all the places he's been injured."

"How many were there? He couldn't have been overwhelmed unless Vasilik had sicced the whole coven on him at once—"

"They were children, Xiaodan," Malekh's voice was like sharpened whetstone grinding down on diamond. "Vasilik sent children after him. He hesitated, and they swarmed him."

"No . . . oh no."

"Missing children," Remy interjected, already halfway into a delirium but singling out the words he remembered and grabbing on to them like a lifeline. "Missing children. All over Aluria. Couldn't figure out where they'd gone, and now I've found them. Found them. Can't bring them back, but I've found—"

"I should have brought some of the serum with us," Malekh said, snarling in his frustration. "I can try to make it past them again, see if there's another way out, but I can't leave you—"

"You have to. If we stay here any longer, he won't make it."

Xiaodan sounded near tears. "We can't lose him, Zidan. He'll succumb to the Rot, and then we'll have to—I can't do it—"

"Pocket," Remy mumbled incoherently. "Pocket."

"They have all the exits blocked. The only reason Pendergast managed to get close enough to us is because there aren't any paths going back to the surface in this part of the caves, and they're less guarded."

"Pocket," Remy said, louder this time.

"Snap out of it, Pendergast," Malekh barked, ragged and angry. "You're going to fight this, and you're going to beat it. We didn't drag your damnable ass from Elouve all the way to Chànggē Shuǐ only to have you die on us now."

"Zidan, wait. I think he's trying to tell us something." A rustling of clothes—Remy didn't feel any of it—then Xiaodan's triumphant cry. "Here!"

Zidan drew in a breath. "He's not always as foolish as he makes himself out to be."

More indeterminate noises. Remy felt something cool and silver and sharp prick at his skin. "You're going to be all right, Pendergast," Malekh said, and then life flooded back into him.

Remy groaned weakly. The burning sensation was starting to ease, becoming much more tolerable than before, but now he was unbelievably thirsty. A different kind of heat was moving in, causing him to twitch uncontrollably.

"Is it working?" Xiaodan's voice, anxious.

"Give it time to. Now we need to staunch his wounds. He's still bleeding." Several sharp, tearing noises. "I'm going to tie a tourniquet around his thigh. Wash these and wrap them around his arm."

Something was pulled tight around one of his legs, and Remy gritted his teeth from the sudden pressure. A flint was struck. And then something white-hot and agonizing was applied somewhere on his skin, and he cried out.

"Bite, Pendergast." Something was shoved unceremoniously into his mouth. Remy clamped his teeth down hard onto it, screaming for all he was worth into the cloth. Hours must have passed before the pain receded, back to quick, throbbing stabs that were endurable compared to what he'd just been subjected to.

"Don't let go just yet," Malekh instructed, sounding even grimmer. "There's more to cauterize."

It was an agonizing, excruciating process, and it took a very long time. By the end of it, Remy was limp and unmoving, hoping that if he pretended to actually be dead, everything else would stop hurting.

"He's still lost far too much blood."

"What can we do?" Remy could hear Xiaodan's heart go *baduthump-baduthump-badubadubaduthump*. "Can we replenish what he's lost?"

He somehow felt Malekh hesitate. "You know his thoughts about familiars and taking blood from vampires. He said he'd rather die than—"

"Fuck what I said," Remy muttered, recovering both a few moments of lucidity and some of his old fire. "Do what you have to do to get us out of here."

"Pendergast." Every inch of Remy was either in pain or a worrying numbness, and Malekh's voice by his ear could still get him so goddamn aroused even in this condition. "You understand that there could be consequences."

"Give us permission." Xiaodan was by his other ear, soft and breathless, and his desire only tripled. "Please. We don't want to overstep—"

"I'm dying," Remy said faintly. "Fucking fuck me if that's what it takes."

He felt his head being tilted up, his neck exposed. He still had that old wound from Zelenka there, though it was healing quick, and he wasn't sure if they were both going to work their way around that injury or just—

And then his mind stopped functioning entirely as a different kind of agony hit him, the most painfully pleasurable one Remy had ever experienced.

It was Malekh's fangs sinking down on the base of his neck just above where it met his shoulder, to his right. And then Xiaodan's on his left, the sudden sharp prick still gentler than her betrothed's.

And then he was lost.

This was why there had been no lack of demand to become a vampire's familiar before the ban. Why so many had tried to keep their conditions a secret even afterward, until the Reapers had made it clear that they would be punished with extreme prejudice. It was as good as sex. Remy could feel the heady rush, the sudden surge of euphoria overcoming, overriding his senses until he blanked out, nothing existing within his little bubble of the universe but the intense, arousing pleasure that washed over him again and again.

Finally, they withdrew. Remy laid where he was, panting, wanting more.

"Your turn, Pendergast." Malekh's voice was a husky growl, just as hungry. He felt something press against his lips and recognized it as the man's wrist, which had been slit open. Blood poured into his mouth, and it was the most exquisite experience he'd ever had.

Malekh's and Xiaodan's fangs biting into him had been the sweetrum, and this was the lime. It tasted like the finest wine, like the ambrosia of the gods, and Remy continued drinking greedily, yearning for the next mouthful before he was finished with the last gulp. And then the noble was pushing him gently away because it was Xiaodan's turn, her blood with that delicious hint of smoked cider. Just as sweet, just as addictive, the unbelievable flavor bursting in his mouth.

Remy feasted. He drank long and deeply, and whined when he was finally denied another drop. A new heat had suffused his body, heavy and sensual. He was no longer hurting. All he knew was hunger.

"Please," he could hear himself begging. "Please, please . . ."

He heard whispers; Xiaodan's tormented, aching voice. "We can't leave him like this."

He felt more rustling as his breeches were undone, watched as Xiaodan lowered herself to his lips, her gray eyes wondrous. And then she was kissing him hungrily, their tongues dancing. She abandoned his mouth to move lower, laying sweet kisses on his chest and stomach, following the trail down.

Someone turned his chin sideways, where he beheld Zidan Malekh this time, the noble's golden eyes afire. "Answer me before I forget again," Remy said, his own tongue still thick from the memory of Xiaodan's. "Did I win the fucking wager, or didn't I?"

That brought out a low chuckle from his now-lover. "You won, Remington," Zidan murmured. "You do always seem to win."

And then the man's mouth was on him, more forceful and demanding than Xiaodan's yielding softness, just as the Fourth Court heiress's mouth pressed against his stomach.

"Have you ever been with a man, Pendergast?" Malekh murmured.

"No." It came out a whimper, but Remy was too far gone to be horrified by his subservience, his easy capitulation.

A chuckle, then a tongue drawing lines across his skin, at his neck where Malekh had taken his fill. "A virgin."

But not too subservient. "I am not a fucking—"

Remy was mollified quickly by Xiaodan kissing his navel, biting him just a little. "Have you ever been with anyone else that you hadn't been compelled to for favors, Remy?" The vibrant purr of her voice sent small shocks up his body.

"N—no," Remy stammered, as her hand quested lower, found her prize.

Her giggles floated toward him. "Then you're a virgin," Xiaodan said, and shifted down.

They were torturing him, they truly were. Remy had no idea how protracted and lingering bliss could be, drawn out and quartered until he was certain he was incapable of enduring more, only for them to prove him wrong. His conspirators switched frequently, one drawing him further with mouth and beguiling tongue, while the other feasted at him lower, and all Remy could do was groan and fist his hand at their hair, while urging the other deeper, harder, *faster*, with his hips.

Until finally—finally, finally, *finally*—they took pity on him, gave him the release he needed. And in an underground cave somewhere at the Dà Lán, among the boundless lands of Qing-ye, ruled by the Fourth Court, Remington Pendergast shattered for the first time.

"FUCK," REMY said, still prone on the floor, still half-naked and wonderfully dazed. He was exhausted beyond measure; not from the familiar aches that came with fighting, at nearly losing his life, but from the languid sense of completion that only an extraordinarily good tup could achieve. He felt boneless, adrift in the afterglow.

It wasn't even *sex*. Or at least what he was accustomed to when he thought of sex. They had only taken him into their hands and mouths. If they were more than capable of wrecking him with nothing but those . . . then exactly how sublime would it be if they actually . . .

"Are you all right?" Xiaodan asked gently, cheeks still pink.

"I'm more than all right," Remy said. "I feel bloody fantastic."

Gingerly, he peeled himself off the floor for the first time since being brought in, on his own volition no less, and examined himself. Xiaodan had bandaged him with what remained of his tattered shirt, and without poking underneath the strips, he could sense that his wounds should have been more grievous than was normal. He felt the pain when he moved, but nothing as agonizing as when he'd first been bitten. He looked down wonderingly at his leg, where Malekh had cut part of his breeches away to administer his tourniquet. He flexed experimentally. It stung. Nothing he couldn't handle.

"How?" Humans who chose to be familiars were always in it for the pleasure. None of them acquired the regenerative qualities of the vampires who fed on them.

"It's not information I tell anyone else, for good reason," Xiaodan said. "Feeding off me has a few perks beyond the usual aphrodisiacs. Sometimes being a sunbringer can work in my favor."

"You made me stronger?"

"It's nothing permanent. It'll wane as time passes, but you should be good for another few hours."

Remy looked at Malekh.

"I modified my blood for Xiaodan's sake, as you know," came the wry response. "Her constant feeding on me has also imbued my blood with similar properties. I've never tested it on a human before, but I suspected it was possible."

"You really need to stop using your own body as a fucking testing specimen," Remy said.

"Is that concern for me I detect, Pendergast?"

Remy ignored that. "I was bitten," he said, remembering the infected children. They had been unschooled and not as strong as their older counterparts, but he had taken pause, which had been his mistake. Vasilik had known he would. The faint terror lingered, remnants of his past rearing back up, but the fears that had nearly overwhelmed him were now somehow muted in his mind, like drinking the couple's blood had helped him put up the mental barriers he needed not to dwell on them too much.

"You were. I'd like to monitor you closely once we return, ensure you suffer no other side effects. Just as with the Laofong and Huixin villagers, your blood will test positive for the Rot, but it shall lie dormant and harmless."

"It's too late for them, isn't it?" Remy asked stiffly.

"I'm sorry, Remy," Xiaodan said. "The serum cannot work for those who have already died from it."

"Fortunate that you brought the reactant I synthesized here with you." Malekh was back to his grim, expressionless self, like he hadn't just done gloriously unspeakable things to Remy in the past hour. "You cast doubt about the effectiveness of the serum enough times that I wasn't expecting you to bring it along as a fail-safe."

"I still think you're a bastard for testing it out on people without finding some other ethical means first," Remy said sourly, the affection he'd felt toward Malekh quickly evaporating.

"Then why bring it?"

"I may not like your methods," Remy said gruffly, "but I suppose I trust you."

"You—you trust me." Remy wasn't sure why there was a sudden stutter in between the words. Malekh's eyes were slightly dilated, though the rest of him was still infuriatingly stoic. "You even wrapped the syringe exactly as I instructed. I didn't think you were listening."

"I'm not as moronic as you think I am," Remy said. "I can pay attention and follow orders. I even asked Alegra for your carrying case—the steel one you're so fond of, since I noticed you prefer it for more fragile equipment, though it's a shame your ego's too big to fit."

Malekh's breathing seemed to grow more rapid at the teasing jab.

"Zidan," Xiaodan admonished, but there was an equally lustful expression on her face as she looked back at Remy. "He'll need some time to recover before anything else."

They'd given him his release, Remy had realized, but he hadn't done the same. And now they were watching him like they couldn't wait for a second round once they returned to Chànggē Shuǐ, like they could barely keep themselves under control.

And Remy was going to let them—wasn't he?

But the moment was gone; Malekh was already scanning the entrance to their underground lake. "They know we're here," he said with dark satisfaction. "But Vasilik's boys know better than to approach us."

Remy tugged his own coat back on and noticed for the first time that the place was awash in sunlight. The ceiling curved outward, and several shafts of light streamed in through the small openings there.

"I overexerted myself," Xiaodan admitted, wincing. "There were far more in Vasilik's coven than I expected . . . too many. His plan was to overwhelm us with numbers, and the narrowness of these caves makes it difficult to fight them all at once. He knew it would tire me out."

"You've been exceptionally resourceful, bloodling. I was certain you were dead already or had taken up membership among my infant horde."

Vasilik loitered by the entrance, though he too did not venture closer to the light. His minions filled the path behind him, most taking fearful glances at the bright rays filtering in.

"Took you long enough to find me, Vasilik," Malekh said calmly. "Would you like to end things here for good, or shall you skulk away again with your tail between your legs?"

"A fine thing to say, Zidan—you, who had started your kindred life as a moxie of the First Court, drooling at the First King's feet."

Vasilik's gaze shifted to Remy. "And you call *me* the liar, Pendergast," the man said, mocking. "Here—let Malekh tell the tale himself. Before he was the powerful, omnipotent Zidan Malekh, king of the Third Court, he was a sniveling little toy for the First Court to play with."

"Step into the sunlight and face me yourself, Vasilik," Malekh said, undeterred by the insults and still as composed as ever. "Or have you forgotten how I rescued you from the literal sewers to stand with the Third Court? Even the First couldn't be bothered to look at you—"

And that was all it took for Vasilik, who came hurtling toward Malekh with such preternatural speed Remy was surprised he could track the vampire's movements. Malekh avoided the man's claws as he turned and lashed out with his foot, catching Vasilik squarely in the stomach. The younger vampire skidded several feet away to a halt, a hand pressed against his midsection.

"You're still several centuries too slow for me," Malekh said.

"Not even you can fight off my whole army."

"On the contrary," Xiaodan said calmly, rising to her full height. "You caught me off guard, but with the fresh sunlight here and your minions' obvious fear, I doubt that you'd have the same advantage in numbers as the last time. I can take on as many of your followers as you wish, and I promise you I won't need to stop."

Some of Vasilik's minions moved threateningly toward them, but Remy blocked their path, the metallic scrape of his scythe blades snapping loudly into place, the sound echoing against the cavern walls. "You heard the lady," he said. "Take another step forward, and you won't be leaving here."

Vasilik moved again, and this time made a better fight of it, matching Malekh stroke for stroke, parrying whenever the other noble countered with his own attack. Their battle was a master class in combat, movements quick and graceful, jabs and follow-throughs brutal and powerful. Remy watched it all, amazed by how newly heightened his senses were that he could watch them in motion.

But it was clear that in a battle of endurance, Vasilik would come out on the losing end; he was slowing down, his strikes half a second slower than they ought to be, and Malekh caught him a second time with a stunning blow to the head that had the vampire stumbling back.

Malekh was toying with him. Remy could count at least four other instances where the man could have delivered a killing blow to end things the way he'd promised, but always the noble stopped and gave his opponent the chance to recover. "What is he waiting for?" he asked Xiaodan.

But Xiaodan watched with sympathy, eyes tearing up. "As horrible as Vasilik has turned out to be," she said, "Zidan sired him some hundred years ago. Court law frowns on masters killing their subordinates."

"Even after Vasilik's been doing his damnedest to kill him?"

"Vasilik isn't trying to kill him. He's trying to kill me, and possibly you as well. But not Zidan. They were together for a long time."

"You are far too forgiving when it comes to Malekh and his past fucks."

She grinned weakly. "Maybe it's that empathy that makes me much more compatible with him."

Vasilik had given up on attacking directly, instead resorting to moving around Malekh in circles, fading in and out of focus as he sped up, hoping to catch the man in a vulnerable spot. Malekh merely folded his arms and waited, once more the bored noble. "All you're doing is wasting my time," he said.

"Maybe your time, Zidan. But I've always put mine to good use."

Remy felt the shift in the air, his senses on full alert long before Vasilik blurred into view before him instead of attacking Malekh.

But instead of shielding himself with Breaker, as he'd often done in the past with vampires far quicker than him, he spun to the left so that Vasilik's slash missed entirely, then whipped Breaker up like a bat to hit the vampire fully in the face.

The man disappeared, reappeared back at the cavern entrance, clasping at the side of his face with one hand. "You fucking bastard," he rasped.

"That's for sticking me into a pit full of infected children, you dandified sot," Remy snarled, pleased by his unexpectedly improved reflexes. "Malekh might spare you because you have shared history. But I won't, and I'm going to pummel you out of existence if you don't let us leave."

There was an audible snap as Vasilik clicked his jaw back into place. "He will betray you," he said. "He will lie to you, and he will leave you at the mercies of the very Night Empress you fear. Still you choose to stay by his side?"

Remy didn't reply; he had no good answer to give.

With a frustrated snarl, Vasilik turned his back on them. "This isn't over," he said, and disappeared once more into the passageway, his followers retreating with him.

"I wouldn't advise following him through that route," Xiaodan said. "He's likely to leave more traps, despite what he says."

"It's the only way out," Remy groused. "What else do you propose?"

"There's an opening above that should be large enough for us to get through," Malekh said. "I intended to bring Xiaodan through it, but she was far too weak earlier to be moved. It was good that we waited, or else we wouldn't have found you in time. Can you climb up on your own, Xiaodan?"

"I can." Xiaodan licked her lips. "Perhaps it's Remy's blood, but I feel much more invigorated now. I can last until the castle, at least."

"Oh, fuck no," Remy said. "You're not about to carry me through the damn ceiling."

"It's either that or through the underground lake that leads to the Dà Lán, but I'm not sure you can hold your breath for that long," responded Malekh. "You're still not as strong as you think you are."

"I'm not going up there on your back," Remy said stubbornly. "And you can't bloody make me."

"FUCKING HELL," Remy said not five minutes later, clinging on to Malekh's back for dear life.

26

RESOLVE

The vampires at Chànggē Shuǐ had seen them arriving from several miles off and were already gathered at the courtyard to hurry them past the gates, welcoming their return with cheers. No one in Elouve had ever been this happy to see Remy alive and well, and it was an unaccustomed, albeit pleasant, sight to come home to.

Home. Three days in Qing-ye and he was already putting down roots. He'd never realized how lonely his life had been, or how much he had relied on Elke to assuage that, until today.

Could be that he was still suffering from the ill-effects of being Xiaodan and Malekh's—he couldn't bring himself to say the word *familiar* just yet, so *temporarily under their enthrallment* was as good a description as any—and that his newfound affection for the fortress and its people would wane with a good night's sleep? Malekh insisted on him resting, and Remy was thankful it was Alegra (stone-faced, as always, in her delight at seeing him again) who slung him across her back and carried him upstairs, back to his chambers, saving him from the embarrassment of having the Third Court noble once more do the honors.

And then he slept like the dead.

He was starving when he awoke hours later—still daylight, from what he could see of the rays of sun spilling down in between the dark clouds through his window. It had been difficult to tell time inside the caves, but he estimated that they had arrived back at the castle a little before dawn. Vasilik hadn't sent anyone after them in pursuit.

Someone had dressed him in fresh clothes while he was asleep, even changed his bandages. Remy hoped fervently it had been Alegra—the woman talked of him being dinner so frequently that he knew she wasn't interested in him at all. Remy sat up slowly, wincing, and inspected his wounds. The bites and lacerations were still apparent, but they'd healed at a far more rapid rate than the neck wound he'd received at Zelenka, which was already gone.

His hands traveled higher up his throat, moving to either side where he could feel the faint sting of both Xiaodan's and Malekh's bites. Those weren't healing as quickly, but that was as intended.

It had always been the quickest way of proving whether someone was a vampire's familiar, a way for Reapers to catch those who'd broken Alurian law. And now he had not one, but two transgressions to show for the sorts of accusations he'd received his entire life.

There had to be further ramifications. Familiars became familiars for the pleasure of the act, for love or worse. Vampires would be warier of taking in humans if the latter could gain their abilities through bloodsharing.

But these weren't normal vampires. Xiaodan's blood was an extremely powerful counteractant. And Malekh might be an arsehole and an unethical scientist, but his experimentations on himself were almost as potent.

People would kill for such a prize. Remy knew his father would have.

The vampires had been kind enough to provide him with a bathtub of his own, so Remy washed, scrubbed, and found a clean set of clothes to put on. Then he headed out in search of Malekh.

Vampires didn't require sleep, but this time of the day appeared to be a favorite for retiring before supper. Remy could only find two vampires on duty, plus Alegra, whom he had never seen at rest. The woman was hard at work in the courtyard, sharpening numerous weapons retrieved from the palace armory.

"If you're looking for Lord Zidan or Lady Xiaodan," she said without bothering to turn her head, "they've retired to their private quarters. They will be glad to see you there."

"Uh," Remy said. "I don't—I really don't want to trespass—"

"On the contrary. They've been hoping for a visit from you once you were awake, so you'd best not keep them waiting."

"But I'm not—" Remy stopped. "You know, don't you?"

"Everyone with eyes in the castle can see how things stand between you and our lieges. It is especially easy to see with Lord Zidan. He has never been good at hiding his emotions." And without another word, Alegra picked up a heavy battle-axe to whet.

Remy delayed. He attempted to explore the kitchen but was immediately chased out by Malira, who scolded him about overexerting himself so soon. Honfa rejected his offer to take up guard duty, citing the same thing. The bearded vampire did rise in Remy's estimation, though, by opening a bottle of finely aged rum for him—"we keep a few unspiced, just for the flavor"—along with a cheerful reminder that while he'd need some time to heal, this might aid tremendously in his recuperation.

Remy accepted the rum but not the suggestion that he rest longer, and soon found himself walking around the castle's extensive gardens instead, occasionally taking a swig from the bottle. It was a relief to see trees thriving beautifully without being forced into animal-shaped hedges. And the constant hum of the water-fall behind Chànggē Shuǐ was an oddly comforting sound.

A small graveyard lay at the end of the garden. It felt strange to Remy to see one here, given the circumstances.

Remy crouched down to read some of the markers. They provided no other details beyond the names of the fallen.

Genovese. Teophani. Gandura. Mikkels. Anastacia—

Remy tensed as a voice behind him said, "Don't touch her."

Naji didn't attack. Remy moved farther away, and the boy took his place, staring down at the tombstone. He didn't ask Remy to leave, but he didn't seem willing to explain himself further.

Remy could make a guess. The look on Naji's face as he stared down at the grave was an expression he knew all too well. "It's a pretty spot," he said. "Reminds me of where we buried my mother."

"If you're here to interrogate me," Naji said, "I've already told my brother everything. Those vampires were a pack I ran with for only a few nights—not long enough to know them well, and certainly not long enough to commit any sort of atrocities with them. I don't know which clan they belonged to. Likely they were Vasilik's, but I had no idea then. I spoke of Lady Daneira out of bravado. As I told you then, we did nothing to her."

"They were freshly turned youths bored with their human lives, convinced to join Vasilik's coven and cause us no end of headaches," Remy disagreed. "Given time, they would have done more. That vampire I ashed—he was likely Vasilik's subordinate, tasked to oversee the pack in his stead. Likely thought you were another runaway-turned-undead."

"We did have every intention of killing you, if you must know."

"Thought you said you weren't with them long enough to commit any atrocities."

"We didn't consider the death of a Reaper to be a crime. Not then."

"And it's different now?"

Naji continued to kneel, ignoring him.

"Has anyone told you that my mother was killed by the Night Court?"

"They told me, yes," the youth said shortly.

"They also tell you I was still inside her belly when she was attacked?" He could sense Naji's hesitation before the youth slowly shook his head. "Not something I like to talk about often, but I've found it gets easier. It's the kind of burden you carry for the rest of your life, even if you never asked for it."

"That's different. You didn't know your mother, not really. Not like—" Naji balled his hands into fists. "It isn't fair."

Wordlessly, Remy passed him the bottle. The boy took two long swigs, coughed a little.

"The Night Court killed your mother," the youth said. "But I killed Anastacia. She was my sweetheart. My human sweetheart. I wanted to turn her. She wanted to be turned. But then . . ."

Remy understood. "She didn't survive the frenzy."

"We knew the risks, but we never thought it would happen to us." Naji stared unblinking at the ground before him. "And now, instead of everything that I promised her, I have nothing to give her but dirt and shade. She would have been better off finding a mortal husband." His voice broke slightly. "I would have liked to see her grow old, even if it wasn't with me."

"And then you tried to drown your sorrows by joining up with a pack of miscreants roaming Alurian forests."

"As I said, I did nothing to that lady you were hunting," Naji said. "I was . . . angry. I'm not anymore."

"Just grieving. I can sympathize with that."

"I don't need your sympathy."

"And that's the problem. Understanding what you went through isn't a weakness. You need someone to listen—someone you can't just push away. Malekh's worried about you, but he hasn't been human for centuries. I don't think he knows how to give you the space you need to mourn."

"And what do you know about grief?"

"I know it's an unwanted rat up my arse," Remy said. "I also know what it's like to be the youngest in the group, so desperate to prove yourself that you wind up doing the opposite and getting into a whole world of trouble. Being human doesn't mean things are any easier for us. The only difference is that vampires get to hold on to those grudges for much longer."

Another pause before the young vampire nodded. He knelt and traced the engraved letters on Anastacia's grave with his hand.

"She loved you, mate," Remy said. "I know you already know that, but it's worth saying out loud."

"I know," Naji said. "And it's hard, knowing she's gone. Was that why you were so angry at me when I mocked the Lady Daneira? Did you love her, too?"

"Not in the manner you think, no."

"Zidan nearly killed you, and you didn't even love the woman you almost died for?"

Remy chuckled, suddenly feeling much better. Galling that it was Naji, out of everyone, to make things simpler for him. "When you say it that way, it puts some things I've been struggling with into perspective."

"If it's anything," Naji said grudgingly, "you likely saved both their lives. I wasn't expecting much from you at first—I thought Vasilik would flay you alive and wear you like a cape—but I'm impressed. I've never seen them so terrified as when they brought you back."

"Thanks for that." Remy handed him the bottle for keeps and stood.

"Where are you going?"

Remy took a deep breath and focused on the palace above them, majestic against the waterfall behind it. A rainbow arched its way over its many roofs, disappearing into some clouds. "Probably to try and get laid."

Naji didn't protest, merely looked him over and sniffed, almost approvingly despite his next words. "Zidan has good taste in women," he said, "but not much else. His clothes look nice enough on you, though."

REMY WRESTLED with his better instincts all the way up to Xiaodan and Malekh's quarters. The pair must be just as tired as he was, undead or not, after their narrow escape from the caves, and likely needed private time to talk. Alegra could have been screwing with him, as she was wont to do. But if there was even a fraction of truth to what Vasilik had said . . .

Still, he didn't have to confront them in their own quarters. He didn't want to stick his nose where he wasn't welcome.

The devil part of his brain suggested that perhaps it wasn't his nose that had led him here. Remy told it silently to fuck off.

The conflict in his head continued even as he came to a halt before the door to the vampires' chambers, lifting his hand to knock, only to change his mind halfway through, lower it again, then change his mind in the other direction and lift it back up—

The door swung open. "Were you planning on standing here the whole day?" came Malekh's low, husky tone.

Remy stared. Malekh must have just returned from his laboratory, because he was still wearing the overly long frock he favored when he was busy there. This time it was unbuttoned down to his waist, exposing far more skin than the conversation Remy had planned to have with him required.

Behind the vampire, he could see Xiaodan sprawled artlessly on their bed in a loosely wrapped turquoise robe, one pale shoulder peeking out from beneath the folds. Her preference for riding breeches and thin pants weren't in evidence here; he could see her long, limber legs stretched out, naked as almost the rest of her.

He was nervous. They were both studying him with a particular . . . craving, that he was by now accustomed to seeing; at the unabashed desire on Xiaodan's face and the shuttered, wooden expression on Malekh's that belied his heated bright eyes.

They'd tended to his needs right after saving his life, but Remy hadn't had the opportunity to compensate them.

"I've bloody forgotten what I was supposed to say," he blurted out.

A smile lingered at the edges of Zidan's mouth. "If you are here because you believe you owe us for saving your life even though you disobeyed Xiaodan's orders, then—"

"First of all," Remy interrupted, because it didn't take much for the man to piss him off, even now, "I didn't fucking disobey anyone. We all thought Vasilik had captured you, and Honfa verified that the blood on the cloak they'd brought back was Xiaodan's. And second of all—" He paused, decided he was yelling at Malekh already so why the hell not, and forged on: "Yes, I do owe you both for saving my life. But I'm not here to offer myself as repayment. I'm here because—" And then he had to stop again, but his pride refused to let him quit and flee while he still had the opportunity.

"I'm here because I want to be," he finally said, defiant. "It's not because I owe you anything. It's because I know what I want now."

"Remy." Xiaodan had moved off the bed and toward him halfway through his rant. Her warm hands reached out to take one of his own. "What are you saying?" she asked softly.

She knew. They both did. But it was as important to Remy to say it out loud as it was for them to hear it from him. So he said, "I want you. Both of you. I still don't know why you actually want me back, but I'm here, and I'm all I've got."

Both vampires regarded him seriously, and Remy was beginning to think that he'd somehow botched the whole thing when Xiaodan smiled widely, her grip on his hand tightening.

"You think far too little of yourself," she said, "but for now, this is good enough," and pulled him inside.

"AHH," REMY panted into the pillows much, much later. "Aaaah, *fuck*. Ah, shit."

Time was an enigma to him. He was sure the little sun there'd been in the sky had disappeared hours ago, that it was now the dead of night, but that was the extent of it. Xiaodan was curled up beside him, sated, contented, just as naked but not as sweaty as he was, and all but plastered to his chest. Malekh was equally bare, though he'd abandoned the bed and had crossed the floor toward the windows, looking out at the darkness.

"I thought you would have more endurance than this, Pendergast," he said.

"It was three times, you bastard," Remy said languidly. "I've never done it this way before."

"And you think we have?" Xiaodan asked from somewhere between his shoulder and left clavicle.

"Maybe you've got a point, but Malekh's got centuries on me." Remy felt pleasantly sore. Only minutes ago, he'd hovered over Xiaodan, feeling Malekh's warmth behind him, groaning as Xiaodan wrapped her ankles around his back, encouraging him deeper, deeper, deeper, into her while Malekh did the same to him.

Two vampires. *Two* goddamn vampires, and at the same bloody time. He deserved some kind of award, and also a drink. If this was what Vasilik had had before Malekh had rejected him, then Remy wasn't surprised he'd been throwing tantrums ever since.

They had asked much of him. And he had submitted, just as they had wanted.

Malekh returned to the bed, lazily crawling his way toward them—sleek with broad shoulders that took up the rest of the room from where he lay—and offered Remy a magnificent view of pectorals, abdominals, all his seductive -als. Xiaodan turned with a satisfied sigh, presenting her round, beautiful bottom to them both.

"You'll need practice," Malekh said, sitting back and letting his eyes travel down him, searing wherever they lay on Remy's form. "As with the sparring, you'll measure up in no time."

"If you have a problem with my performance—" Remy sputtered, itching to be insulted.

"No. I am more than pleased, Armiger, as is Xiaodan." Malekh laid a hand on the curve of Xiaodan's leg, his fingers traveling up. "Don't tell me you didn't enjoy the show afterward, even after you pleaded for rest."

"Ummm," his fiancée moaned, eyelashes fluttering as Malekh traced circles on her skin, the movements slow and erotic. "Mmm, Remy. I know you did."

Remy had. When he'd reached his limits and tumbled into the covers, exhausted worse than from any physical training he'd ever gone through, he'd watched Malekh take Xiaodan. Like the time they'd spent at the woods before heading toward Zelenka, Remy had watched them move effortlessly, fiercely, Xiaodan's soft, sweet cries filling the air.

He knew they loved each other. And he didn't know what his place was with them, but if he had even a tenth of that affection, it would be more than he'd ever had in his life. It made him feel lonelier, but also a little less alone.

Xiaodan snuggled closer and pressed kisses onto his neck. "None of that self-doubting, Remy. Not in our bed."

"I'm just not sure why you chose me," Remy asked, staring at the wall across the room. "I was an absolute cock when I first met each of you."

"I don't know," Xiaodan said, repeating the movements her betrothed was making on her on Remy's chest, and the light touch was doing unsettlingly ridiculous things to him. "I was attracted to you from the start. Perhaps it was the ease in the way you talked to me, like I was someone worth knowing rather than a vampire to be feared, as many in Aluria still do, or a source of intrigue the way the Elouvian demimonde delighted at. You were selfless, even then. When you were so candid about your relationship with Lady Delacroix, I was jealous that she could take up so much of your attention, get you to bend to her whims even when it was clear you weren't as invested in her as she was in you."

"And how did you think I felt when you introduced Malekh as your fiancé that day at the gardens?" Remy grumbled.

She laughed. "I never thought about it that way. I already knew Zidan had similar feelings about you. We made up our minds shortly after."

Remy nearly sat up, but the soft, pleasant ache in his muscles made him lie back down. "As early as then?"

"He'd returned mad as hell a few nights before, saying he'd had to extricate Naji from some trouble. I knew he couldn't get the Pendergast Reaper out of his head since."

"I said nothing of that sort," Malekh said drolly.

"No, but you were thinking it. After the Astonbury gala, it was you who insisted I handle Remy's situation while you investigated the lord high steward's death. You frightened Feiron into freeing Remy when he was arrested. It was what started those rumors in Elouve about him being our familiar, remember?"

Remy's gaze flew to Malekh, incredulous.

"You agreed it was the right choice," Malekh reminded her. "All I did was suggest that you seize the initiative to free him yourself."

"All I was focused on then was shoving one of my daggers into your guts," Remy said, bewildered.

Malekh met his gaze directly without a trace of humor. "And all I noticed was that you were in top physical shape, able to not only fight off multiple vampires and survive, but to kill nearly all of them in the process. It crossed my mind that you would be a good test subject for certain experiments of mine."

Remy paused to see whether he was serious or if it was an innuendo. Only his fiancée's grin exposed it as the latter. "Xiaodan, was Alegra by any chance one of his wards?"

"He trained her, and she might have picked up on some of his quirks, yes. Why?"

"Nothing. Tells me everything I need to know."

"Was that all you really felt?" Malekh asked. "The urge to stake me through the heart?"

"Yes," Remy lied. "I didn't have much on my mind beyond trying to stave your face in."

Both vampires moved in unison, beyond the need for words to come to the same conclusion. Remy was flat on his back again, Xiaodan straddling him with a wicked smile that lit up his nerves. Malekh's hands had captured his wrists, pressing them down against the bedsheets.

"I truly believe that, of the three of us, Armiger Remington," Xiaodan teased, bringing her face close to his, her long hair falling to tickle at the swell of his shoulders, "it is you who finds it hardest to express your feelings, always hiding behind a veil of self-deprecation. If we are to continue these relations, then I expect you to give as much as we do and be sincere. Your body is honest, even when you are not. Perhaps we shall start our training from there."

"Training?" Remy asked, breathless in yearning and already hard again. His previous pleadings of exhaustion were forgotten.

"Three is a paltry number, love. You'll improve over time."

"Three times is *paltry*?"

"Proper training requires the constant, vigorous testing of our subject," Malekh's voice was a soft, luxurious velvet, and somewhere on Remy's neck, he felt a tiny bite with the promise of more to come. "And we are nothing, Pendergast, but constant and vigorous."

AGAIN

The days that followed were heaven—or, in a way, hell.

"Again," Remy snarled, as he was wont to do most mornings as of late, after being thrown to the ground for the eighteenth time in the last three-quarters of an hour. Malekh always said nothing in response, merely waited for him to stagger back up and try to rush him one more time. It was almost always futile on Remy's part; the noble would dodge most of his blows and successfully counter with more of his own that hit flesh. Remy lasted longer with every spar, but he was human. All Malekh needed was to tire him out, then yank his feet from under him with some new and unfair vampire maneuver to end the fight, half of which he couldn't even see and the other half he could, only because they were still sharing blood.

"Again." Remy remained mostly uninjured, give or take several bruises and minor cuts. The objective of their fighting was not for Remy to win, Malekh had said. The objective was for Remy to *survive*, and so far he was doing a fabulous job.

Another hard hit sent Remy stumbling, though this time he

didn't fall. He wiped at his mouth, noted that there wasn't any blood on his sleeve this time, and grinned. "Again," he said, and charged.

"AGAIN," REMY groaned much later, his hands making fists against the ground, bringing up soil.

"Patience," Malekh whispered, his hands firm on Remy's hips, keeping him from moving. The noble was proper and restrained for the most part, but Remy was quick to learn that a good hard tupping in the dirt, often at the more isolated parts of the castle grounds, brought out all the animal instincts in Malekh that Remy would rather die than admit to liking.

A small container of oil lay opened nearby. The vampire lord had made it a habit of carrying it wherever he went, on the off chance he could catch Remy unawares to put it to good use. He remained unapologetic, even when Remy accused him of premeditation.

"It's all your fault," the noble murmured. "You know what it does to me when you're wearing my clothes."

"I know fuck all about that," Remy said, who had filched at least one of Malekh's clean shirts per day for his personal use and secretly enjoyed the consequences of his thieving. There was nothing else to grip for leverage but the loose dirt around them, but he hung on for life all the same. Malekh was fond of keeping him on the edge, drawing the pleasure out until he couldn't take it anymore, and then giving it to him rough when he least expected it. The whole of Chàngge Shuǐ probably knew every time he was being buggered by their liege, from the sound of his hollering. At this point, Remy no longer cared if they did.

"Again, you coxswabbed bastard," he swore, "because if you keep me hanging for an hour like the last time, I swear I'm going to shove *my* hand up *your*—"

Malekh rutted into him, and Remy's desperate howls carried across the garden.

"Now you're ready for me," the man murmured throatily, and from the way his other hand gripped his thighs, spread them even wider, Remy knew he was in for it now.

"Again," he still managed to say. "Again, a—"

"AGAIN," REMY moaned, gripping at Xiaodan's hair as she knelt before him. She hummed, and he was ready to burst from that alone, the worry that he would spend in her mouth too soon the only thing reining him in.

"One more time, Xiaodan," he grunted, his hips moving of their own accord, but Xiaodan was more than accommodating, taking him in easily despite his size. "Fuck, Xiaodan," he moaned again. "I love your mouth. Ahhh, fuck, again—"

"AGAIN," XIAODAN squealed, her hands wrapped around his neck as he plunged furiously into her, slamming them both against the wall. Her legs locked around him, his strength the only thing holding her up. The vampire heiress was just as ornery as her fiancé in that outdoor sex, too, turned her on.

This had not been their intention on this outing. She had offered to show him a closer look at the waterfalls behind the fortress. It was an hour's ride that the helhests had accomplished within minutes, and there was a lovely grotto-like structure carved out in the waterfalls' cliff that was dry enough to give them protection.

That no longer mattered. Their clothes were wet. Remy had all but ripped her shift free, and then his breeches, and was taking her hard while the water poured down around them, she riding him for all he was worth.

I love her, Remy thought, surprised by the realization, insignificant amid everything else. *Her and Malekh.*

"Don't stop," Xiaodan pleaded against his ear, as he resumed his quick, punishing, hard thrusts. "Again—"

"AGAIN," MALEKH said, and Remy winced at the telltale prick of the syringe against his skin, the vampire slowly drawing more blood. The noble had probably taken more out of him than any other undead creatures combined had ever managed, and Remy was *willingly* letting him do it.

"Do you really need this much from me?" he growled, rubbing at his arm around the small wound Malekh had pressed a piece of gauze against.

"These are safety precautions made for your protection, so it's best not to complain about it." Malekh transferred the blood to a glass vial, setting it down on a small sliding display and shutting the compartment closed. "I need to keep track of any new mutations the Rot might create in your system, assess how many doses you need to keep the infection at bay. My current estimate is that you should only require one dose every seven days. That's the result with the other test subjects in Huixin and Laofong, but I need more data from your blood to be sure that the same holds for you."

"And what happens if I don't take the doses?"

"There's a likelihood the Rot will return, with the devastating effects I'm sure you are familiar with. It will require more testing for me to be certain. I've since had to reassess my initial hypothesis on how the Rot mutates and affects its victims. You may be right, Pendergast. The infected are not *completely* mindless. There are certain impulses within them that can be guided with the right triggers. That much is clear with the colossi, and with Lady Daneira's visits to her mother while under its influence—they can act on strong emotions that do not require thought. This may be how they can be controlled by other outside forces."

Malekh paused. "The mutations are showing up even less with your results than with the villagers'. It is possible that Xiaodan and I possess antibodies of our own that are helping you fight the disease. It could clear completely on its own, and if it does, you will no longer need the doses."

It was nice to know that the fresh bites the two made on his neck every day weren't just for fun. "Are you going to try out more experimental serums on those villagers?"

"Upon your suggestion, I've opted to use other means that I believe would be much more in keeping with your ethics. Certain livestock react in a similar manner to humans, but pig carcasses are more than enough for an initial testing to determine any severe side effects."

Malekh had listened to him, actually acceded to his request. Remy was shocked. "You can always use me for any new tests," he said, hiding his reaction. "I always seem to recover, no matter what the—"

He wasn't prepared for the sudden anger in Malekh's dark eyes, the way he leaned forward at him, the corners of his mouth turned down. "The ethical considerations for my experiments were done on *your* behalf. If I am choosing not to test the villagers to ensure that they suffer no ill effects, what makes you believe I would put you at an even greater risk?"

It was the most pronounced display of affection Malekh had ever made, discounting all the swiving they'd done. The only thing preventing Remy from moving up the table toward him was because this laboratory was the only place where Malekh strove not to be particularly lustful toward him and Xiaodan, lest his experiments be contaminated.

"You know, they had to cut me out of her long after she stopped breathing." Remy wasn't sure why he'd decided to keep talking instead of simply apologizing, retreating from the laboratory, and leaving Malekh to find a cure for the Rot, then world hunger. "They weren't even sure if I was still alive, if they'd found her in time. They cut open her stomach, pulled out what they thought was a lifeless baby. Then one of the Reapers got to work on me, and just when she was about ready to give up, I started bawling."

Malekh slowly turned back to him, still unreadable save for a hint of curiosity in his eyes. He didn't ask about the abrupt change in subject. "It must have been a harrowing experience," he said instead.

"I wouldn't know," Remy said. "I don't remember any of it, obviously. But it's the story I grew up with—how I'd been cut out of my mother's corpse after she'd been attacked by some great vampire of the First Court as payback for my father's victories. How he had rejected me at first, claimed that I was no son of his to have been born in this manner. He accused my mother of infidelity, and it didn't help that I grew up in her likeness and had very few of his features. He ignored me until I was seven, when he decided that if he had to acknowledge me as his sole legitimate heir, then I may as well be his weapon against those who'd disrespected him by murdering his wife. So you see, I've been a test subject all my life. It's the one thing I know how to do, even if that doesn't always come with bottles and syringes."

"And you have been carrying out your father's will ever since," Malekh said, with none of his usual censure. "I can understand how, even after his mistreatment of you, you feel like you owe him your allegiance, but certainly there are limits to such obedience."

"He's the only family I've ever known," Remy said. "The only one who shares my blood. He wasn't much of a father, but he sired me all the same. I—I owe him. For many other things. I imagine it's similar to your court customs. We're tied by blood, but in a different way."

He saw the noble's shoulders stiffen and decided he'd gone a little too far.

"If you're done with me, I'll head out. I shouldn't be distracting you from your experiments."

He was about to step through the doors when Malekh spoke again.

"You're right," the man said. "I was sired by the Night Court king. Like you and your father, it was not an easy relationship. The Night King has been dead for a very long time. I have severed all my connections with what remains of his court, but it was many more centuries before I could completely break my allegiances with them.

"I know nothing about the current incarnation of the First Court and of its whereabouts, and even less of its current ruler. When I told you I had little information to give, I was not being dishonest, no matter what Vasilik told you. I know nothing about this new Night Empress or where their lairs are. But occasionally . . ." And Malekh hesitated.

"Occasionally," he said, "I received warnings. Human bodies for the most part, left for me to find. All of them carved with the Night Court sigil. A reminder that they have not forgotten my role in the Night King's demise."

"What?" Remy asked, horrified.

"If this troubles you, know that I have not received any such threats for over two decades. The last victim was . . ." Another pause. "It does not matter. I had hoped the last of them had died out or given up. Their sudden silence coincided with Xiaodan coming into her sunbringing abilities, and I have always wondered if there was a connection.

"I am sorry that I cannot tell you more. But if there is anything you wish to know about the former First Court king, if only to talk and share stories of how we have each survived the schemings of our sires despite the odds, then neither my laboratory nor the chambers I share with Xiaodan will ever be barred to you."

Remy felt warm. "Thank you. I appreciate that."

"No thank-yous necessary. It is important to you, and that's all that matters." And Malekh turned back toward one of the other vials waiting for him to test, like he hadn't just told Remy a most remarkable thing.

"AGAIN," XIAODAN said, spreading her arms wide, the wind whistling through her raven-black hair. "One day, I'd like to have the castle teeming with dozens of clansmates again. Hundreds. Chànggē Shuǐ is equipped to comfortably hold more than two thousand strong."

They were atop the castle turrets, and seeing Xiaodan's lands in all their entirety was breathtaking. Remy could spot the Dà Lán from a distance, that gleaming lake of deep cerulean, and the streaks of sunlight that peeked out from the otherwise dark clouds overhead, blanketing the landscape in a soft yellow glow.

"But I can't focus on that yet," Xiaodan said. "I need to deal with Vasilik, and I do want to help you with finding more of the Night Court. I know that Zidan has been reluctant because it brings back so many awful memories for him, but I know he wants to help. I'm sorry you haven't found the answers you were looking for, Remy. If only Mother wasn't so sick . . ."

There had been no change so far to Queen Yingyue's condition. Remy knew it saddened Xiaodan, though she tried her best not to let it show.

"We've made it possible here in Qing-ye," she said. "The villagers here—they understand that we are just as good and as bad as humans. If we can do it here, then we can do it in Aluria."

He didn't doubt her enthusiasm or determination. She'd brought him to Huixin only the day before, accompanying Malekh while he served as the village physician, checking up on the survivor who'd been infected by the Rot. He had watched her play with the children, skipping garter and laughing with them when she'd gotten entangled in the rope. He'd seen how she had looked when she had looked at them. She would make a good mother, he'd thought.

Remy gazed across the horizon. "When I was thirteen," he said, "there were intelligence reports circulating, detailing a large-scale vampire raid that was about to hit Darenkirk, just ten miles north of Elouve."

Xiaodan's eyes widened. "Darenkirk. I think I remember. A Fifth Court offshoot. But it wasn't land that coven wanted, it was . . ."

"We know what they wanted now, but we didn't back then. We never knew for certain which vampire court we were fighting, only that they were out for blood. Astonbury needed as many Reapers as he could get his hands on and wound up roping the rest of us novices in to bolster his ranks. I was only three and ten then—about fifteen of us young recruits, all eager for our first mission, wanting to prove ourselves. My father was taking part in the defense under His Majesty's orders—King Beluske, Queen Ophelia's father—rather than put himself under Astonbury's command. Every Reaper worth their salt was itching to join in, but informants said it was First Court vampires who would be attacking Darenkirk, not the Fifth."

Xiaodan had fallen silent, watching him.

"What we weren't told, and what Astonbury didn't know, was that the intel he'd received was faulty, and this had all been a trap specifically to target the Reapers and leave Elouve defenseless.

They fell on us before we'd even reached the town. Half the Reapers died that day. The vampires divided us easily enough, to pick us off faster. Astonbury gave the order to retreat—to bring back as many hunters as we could to the capital and bolster our defenses there, leaving any who couldn't follow."

A quick indrawn breath from Xiaodan. "And you were one of those they left behind? But surely your father would have searched for you."

"He was the first to withdraw, intending to make it to Elouve before Astonbury did."

Xiaodan's mouth thinned. Remy's eyes wandered to the stone buttresses that lined the castle walls below them.

"Breaker saved my life. Father had opted to use his battle-axe and lent me the weapon—I was still green about the gills, he said, and my training abysmal so far. Using Breaker was the only guarantee I'd get out still breathing, because it was the only thing I was halfway competent at. And he was right. I took refuge inside the first cave I stumbled into, hoping they wouldn't be able to come at me all at once." Remy reached back behind him and drew out his scythes, tilting it in his hands so what little sunlight there was could catch off the twin silvers.

"This is a heavy piece of shit, you know? I couldn't lift it the first time I tried. Father didn't even give me the chance to get used to the weight, just came out strong at me during the first sparring session I ever had. Said I wasn't going to make it as a Reaper if I couldn't lift the one thing that was going to save my life. Half of my scars are from him, including this one," he said, gesturing to a long mark down his arm. Every day without fail, I'd stand for an hour in the morning at Blackstone Manor and spin it above me as a warm-up, trying to get it fast enough to weave a defense around me."

"Oh," Xiaodan said in sudden understanding, a hand over her mouth.

"And that's what I did, inside that cave. It was wide enough for Breaker to fit through, for me to spin it. Wide enough that the knifechain and the scythes could handle everything that came through the passageway. But they didn't let up. I think they knew who I was, recognized the weapon, and they were even more eager to get at me. But I didn't let up either. I just kept Breaker spinning, hour after hour, terrified that if I stopped, they would kill me or turn me. The worst part . . . the worst part was when they'd taken my fellow novitiates, turned them intentionally, and sent them after me while they were still in the throes of a frenzy."

"The children at the caves," Xiaodan said softly.

Remy couldn't meet her eyes. "Only after Elouve was secured did Astonbury and my father set out to find any survivors. They found me there, still spinning, with all the dead vampires piled up around me, some of them recruits I'd trained with. I couldn't stop, even after they said it was over. I just kept spinning and spinning and spinning. It was Father who finally broke through and wrestled me to the ground.

"And I—I hurt him." Fingers clenched against the stone. "I lashed out with my scythe, still thinking he was one of them. He was hit badly, nearly bled out. His leg was heavily mangled when they brought him back, and it was a wonder they'd managed to save it. But he couldn't walk right after that. Needed a chair. It was hard on him. The great Duke of Valenbonne, taken out by his own flesh and blood. The papers had a good news day with that one.

"I didn't know what I'd done. I passed out once they'd finally wrested Breaker from me. Slept for two days."

Remy ran his hands through the hidden groove where his daggers were secreted. "This is what I owe him," he said. "I fight because I'm the reason he no longer can. The Reapers used to hunt in their own groups and answered to their own leaders. The raid exposed that weakness. There was no order, no one person in charge to direct the battle using all the resources we had.

"It was determined afterward that one hunter would be in charge of the Reapers, form one official dræfendgemot overseen by a lord high steward. Astonbury got the position. He'd handled the raid badly, but they all agreed that he was still the most experienced. Father was another among those considered. He'd been instrumental in defending Elouve . . . but many found the idea of someone who could so easily abandon his only heir, ascending to such a position, distasteful. And then there was the added burden of his infirmity, the humiliation of being laid low by his own young child. He still resents me for it. He has good reason to."

"Remy." Hands circled his waist. Xiaodan stepped closer, her head pressed against his chest. "Remy," she said again, her voice filled with the unshed tears he could no longer summon for himself. "You braved the caves a second time for Zidan and me. You've been through so much. Stay in Chànggē Shuǐ with us. You've never been happy in Elouve. Ask Elke to join us if she'd like. If there is anything here that gives you even a modicum of happiness, please stay. We will cherish you, each and every one of us."

Remy held her close, but his eyes stole back at the sunset, in the direction of where Elouve lay. "I want to," he admitted hoarsely. "Believe me, Xiaodan. I wish I had the choice."

ALONE IN his quarters, he examined himself in the mirror.

The rest of his other injuries had long been healed. All that was left were the previous scars he'd suffered from years of hunting, plus the daily marks Xiaodan and Malekh put on his neck and chest. Remy touched one gingerly, but it gave him no pain. If he allowed them long enough, he knew those marks would become permanent.

It had to end. He had responsibilities. Allies or not, they would likely terminate his position as a Reaper for warming the vampires' bed. Worse, they could try him at court, even execute him. They had been wanting an excuse for years.

A finger pressed down on another love bite that bloomed against his dark skin; he recalled, with pleasure and with pain, how it had come to be there, and who had inflicted it on him.

He could not linger here forever. One day, these too would disappear, and there would be nothing left of them on him.

It hurt to think that he could have a place here, that he might belong somewhere. And it hurt, so unbearably, to find a seed of hope that he could.

"AGAIN," REMY rasped, his hands filled with Xiaodan.

"You're greedy, Pendergast," Malekh rumbled from behind his fiancée, moving in deep, deliberate motions. His lips lingered by her neck, brushing against her fevered skin. "Good," he whispered.

Xiaodan was atop Remy, eyes closed and mouth parted, as Third Court king and hunter thrust in rhythm into her. Candlelight flickered somewhere above them, illuminating first her face thrown in relief, ecstasy, and desire—and then Malekh's, his mouth a sensual, hungry line, eyes full of need for her, full of need for him.

Remy wasn't greedy. He just wanted to reach out and find them both, take in as much as he could of them now, to bring with him as he grieved in the colder, longer nights ahead.

Because he couldn't stay. He *couldn't*.

"Again," he said in response, bringing Xiaodan's head down for him to kiss and then raising his own to meet Malekh's, furious and sweet.

28

BLOOD

It wasn't meant to last forever, this peaceful idyll. Remy had never been lucky enough for that.

It started with an abrupt change in weather two weeks into his stay—a roll of thick, dark clouds that enveloped the sky, extinguishing the pockets of sunlight that he was used to seeing on Fourth Court lands. Now thunder loomed from a distance, growing louder with every passing hour.

"We've got a trying few days before us," Honfa reported gloomily. "There's a heavy monsoon coming in from farther east. Judging from its size, I doubt we'll be getting much sun for the next forty-eight hours at the least."

"Is this a normal occurrence around these parts?" Remy asked.

"It is not," Malekh said, voice terse. "This is court magic."

Remy tensed. "They can control the bloody skies?"

"Ancients can. But Vasilik is not strong enough for this."

"Put out as many torches as you can and shroud the castle in darkness," Xiaodan ordered. "Best not to make us the only light for them to see by."

Remy took a deep breath. "And you think they're going to mount an attack?"

"The patches of sun were all that was stopping them from staging a frontal assault on us. Double the guards on duty. I don't want anything near our walls without my knowing."

The first day passed with little issue, though everyone was keyed up from waiting. Remy accustomed himself to quick catnaps to make up for the shorter bouts of sleep once night came, to store up his strength. He still had an ample supply of bloodwakers at his disposal, and they were all that was stopping him from returning to either Xiaodan or Malekh; he'd grown accustomed to feeding off them, albeit normally as foreplay rather than to enhance his strength. This new threat was enough to snap him out of his indulgences. Their blood was potent and addictive, and it was time he cut back.

So he downed his less-tasty bloodwakers, kept Breaker sharp and ready, and waited for the axe to fall.

On the second morning, he ambled into Malekh's laboratory for his daily checkup, but the noble wasn't at his usual position by the medical sequencer, nor by his fragile display of vials where he inspected blood and other more questionable liquids under glass. Instead, the man sat on a chair by the wall, head in his hands.

This was alarming to Remy. Malekh took pains to never show feelings, and certainly never to this degree of desolateness. "Something the matter?" he asked, resuming his usual perch by the sterile counter. "Couldn't cure leprosy today?"

Muffled, stricken laughter erupted from somewhere between Malekh's fingers. "Something the matter?" the noble echoed, raising his head. His eyes were bloodshot, stress straining at the sides of his eyes. His hair looked tussled and unkempt for the first time since Remy had known him—not even the fashionably mussed variety the man often sported, but a genuine rat's nest that some-how still didn't detract from his good looks.

And he looked murderous. Absolutely murderous.

"I've finished analyzing the various blood strains taken from the corpses at the Ministry of the Archives," he said, "to confirm the same blood type present in them all."

"Right. The one whose blood started all this."

"It's your blood, Remington." Malekh was staring at him with cold, furious anger. "It's *your* blood in all these samples."

Remy did his own share of staring right back, still half-certain this was another one of the man's unconventional jests. "What the fuck are you talking about? I've never infected anyone, if you don't count my dry wit—"

And then the breath was knocked out of him in a heavy whoosh. He was shoved back several feet, Malekh still on him, and Remy hit the wall hard, ears ringing from the force.

The noble kept his arm pressed against Remy's throat, letting him do little more than breathe shallowly. This was nearly a repeat of their first encounter, but this time there was no glint of desire in Malekh's eyes, only rage at a perceived betrayal.

"Who put you up to this? Edgar Pendergast? Matthew Aston-bury? Was this companionship a ruse to gain our confidence, to lay the Rot's blame on Xiaodan and I?"

Malekh's grip was starting to surpass being tolerably painful. "Let go of me," Remy gasped out. "I didn't do whatever the bloody fuck you think I did."

"Zidan!" Xiaodan's voice rang out. "What are you doing?"

Malekh stepped back, and Remy sank down to the floor, thank-ful the man hadn't crushed his windpipe.

"Pendergast's blood is in all these infected humans," the Third Court king snarled out. "He's the Rot's carrier."

Xiaodan shook her head, as bowdlerized as Remy felt. "Surely it must be someone else who shares the same blood type he does. I can't imagine how—"

"I've perfected the process to identify a specific person through the unique properties in their blood, using the sequencer Ophelia gifted us. I am not mistaken in this. It's Pendergast's."

"What's my blood doing in them?" Remy wheezed out.

"That is exactly the question I intend to ask you," Malekh snarled. "When we fought Vasilik at the caves, he said that you were involved. That you and the Alurians had orchestrated the whole thing, that you carried the Rot in your veins. I'd dismissed it as nothing more than an attempt to strain the ties between us, but now . . . Are you working with Vasilik, Pendergast? Did you do all this just to bring yourself more firmly into our confidence? Straight from his bed to ours?"

"Zidan!" Xiaodan gasped.

"How else would Vasilik have known what I would find? How else could your blood have gotten into the most virulent plague in these lands? You've acted as your father's weapon for years. Did *he* send you here to spy on us? Or did Astonbury use the rivalry with your father as a cover, order you to earn our trust? Is this all a plan to weaken Aluria long enough to seize power from Ophelia? You've fucked people for information before, so what makes this any different—"

And this time it was Remy's turn to fly at Malekh. For all his anger, the noble didn't move to defend himself, and his punch landed solidly against the noble's jaw.

"Stop it!" Xiaodan threw herself in between them, wrenching Remy away before he could deliver a second blow. "Zidan, do you really believe that Remy could have done this?"

"I couldn't have!" Remy shouted. "My father's a bastard through and through, but not even he would betray Aluria."

"Other humans have risked more for lesser rewards."

"Well, Remy isn't just any other human." Xiaodan raised her hands, pleading. "Are you telling me he's capable of manufacturing everything that's happened here? He was genuinely infected back at the Dà Lán. He could have died."

"I planned *nothing!*" Remy exploded. "I've bled halfway to Elouve and back these last several years. It shouldn't be hard for someone to find samples of my blood!"

Malekh set a different vial down on the table. "It took a much more thorough analysis to realize you already had the necessary antibodies to fight off the Rot. You had been exposed to it long before you ever left Elouve. You would have survived being bitten at the caves, and my serum would not have been necessary on you. I assumed that the swiftness of your recovery compared to those in Huixin and Laofong was due to your physical conditioning. But once I took a closer look—"

"Zidan—" Xiaodan began again.

"Give me one good explanation how this could have been done without him being a willing participant, Xiaodan."

Xiaodan hesitated. "I can't," she whispered. "But there must be a reason. There has to be. Remy?"

"I don't have it," Remy said, desperate. "I don't know what's going on. The Reapers at the Archives often drew our blood to test for vampire bites and other sicknesses, given our line of work. I can't tell you anything else, only that . . ." A spurt of insight. "They started drawing more blood from me over the years. Packets of it, said it was some new health protocol. They told me Astonbury had wanted more of my blood in particular. If it's been Astonbury who was experimenting on these mutations, then that's how he would have gotten mine."

"Even if that is true, and we are to believe you when you say you have never worked with Vasilik, you cannot say the same about never having worked for your father, however you dislike him. From the moment we left Elouve, you have not been shy about demanding what my role within the Night Court was. Did *he* order you to seduce us for information?"

Remy couldn't move. "He did," he whispered, because he couldn't lie to them. "But I never came to your chambers because of it. I—I wouldn't—"

He watched Xiaodan's face fall, her confidence in him finally wavering. The fury on Malekh's was still plain to see, but so was his pain. "It was a mistake to bring you here," he rasped. "It was a mistake to let you close to Xiaodan."

"My lady!" Honfa burst through the door. "There's a vampire at the—" He stuttered to a halt, noticing the tension. "Err," he began again. "Milady. There's an injured vampire at our gates."

"One of Vasilik's coven?"

"No. She claims to be of the Fifth Court—a *former* member of the Fifth Court, not this new coven of bo lan jiao hiding out at the Dà Lán—and she's asking for sanctuary. Said she was ambushed by a large pack, which she claims is heading our way. Calls herself Lady Whittaker?"

"Elke?" Remy shouted, alarmed. "She was supposed to stay in Elouve!"

"Is this another trick, Pendergast?" Malekh demanded.

"I don't even know why she's here!"

"She said your father was attacked, Armiger," Honfa said meekly, "and that she was faster than any carrier pigeon or messenger Aluria could think to send."

Remy felt his knees wobble. "My father was attacked? Is he—?"

"Alegra scouted the perimeters and reported nothing else amiss, so unless they're very well-hidden, I doubt she's come here with an army of her own."

"No sudden moves," Malekh said, tone harsh. "Reach for that Breaker of yours, and I won't hesitate to kill you where you stand. Do I make myself clear?"

Remy looked at him. It was as if the last couple of weeks hadn't happened at all. "I understand," he said quietly, because there was nothing else left to say.

ELKE WAS bleeding in the courtyard, her fire lance beside her. She was cradled in Alegra's lap. Far from looking injured or in pain, she was looking up at the muscular woman with an expression bordering on infatuation. "I'm not sure I've ever met your acquaintance before," she said.

"You arrived here only a few minutes ago," Alegra said.

"Did I? How impolite of me."

"Bloody hell, Elke," Remy said, kneeling beside her. "If you wanted to visit, you should have sent word beforehand."

"And spoil the surprise?" Relief lit up Elke's face momentarily, though it eventually gave way to worry. "Remy, someone tried to kill your father at Loxley House last night. They think it might be the same person—people—who murdered Astonbury."

"Is he—"

"He's alive and unharmed. That great butler of his managed to chase the would-be assassin off, but I'm told that your father's in shock. It can't be good for his health. I set out here as soon as I learned everything I could. It would take a good three days for a competent pigeon to reach Qing-ye, and I figured I'd be faster."

"You're too good to me, Elke." There was a dull ache in Remy's chest. Edgar Pendergast wasn't much of a father, but he was the only family he had left. "I need to return to Elouve."

"I didn't run all the way here just to drag you back. Something strange is going on with the Alurian court, and I believe your father is not the only target. If you return to Elouve, I'm convinced that there could be an attempt on your life, too."

"Do you have proof of that?"

Slowly, Elke shook her head. "No. I have nothing to go by save for my instincts, though they've saved me too many times in the past for me not to listen. But you all have an even bigger problem at the moment. I believe Lady Song has a few hundred or so vampires squatting on her lands."

"Oh, we very much do know about it," Xiaodan muttered, but then promptly followed with, "Did you say a *few* hundred?"

"Maybe closer to two-thirds of a thousand, give or take. I saw a whole mess of them. Believe me, it's not something you'd ever want to see when you're traveling alone. I've never seen a horde of vampires standing so silently before. I'm fairly quick on my feet, but—" She gestured at her injuries. "One of them tried to help me before the others were alerted to my presence. Said I should keep going north if I knew what was good for me, because they'd commandeered everywhere else for miles. Took his advice because I didn't have much choice, but it did bring me here."

"A vampire?" Remy asked. "Nondescript face; shaggy, wheat-yellow hair; and brown eyes?"

"You are acquainted?"

"You could say that." The messenger who'd brought him to the caves had survived and was as helpful as always.

Malekh gestured, and Honfa hurried forward with a map in his hands. "Show me where you encountered them."

"Lower down this gorge behind your castle. I've never seen so many in a coven in one place before that weren't court vampires. Most of them didn't even look like kindred. They were . . . odd." Elke scrutinized the chart carefully, then pointed her finger, running it across the bottom of the large cliff behind Chànggē Shuǐ. "This area," she said. "I recognize the woods they were milling around at."

"We're defending the wrong side," Malekh affirmed grimly. "They intend to scale up the waterfall from the opposite end and attack us from behind."

"There's nothing up there but the lake!" Xiaodan exclaimed. "They would have to swim through it, then jump off the falls to reach us! Newly turned vampires won't have the endurance for such a—"

"If Vasilik has nearly a thousand forces at his command, then he wouldn't care about the losses. Particularly if many of his followers are the Rot-infected who would not protest traveling twenty miles underwater just to strike at our weakest point. He had reason to be so smug—he has far more vampires than he was willing to reveal. Not even a dozen of us, against that army. Gideon, Alegra, we need to shore up the rear immediately."

"How could he have hidden nearly a thousand vampires and infected?" Xiaodan was visibly shaken.

"Vasilik?" Elke sat up, true fear now on her face. "He's still alive? You haven't killed him yet?"

"Yes," Malekh said curtly. "And if you're lying to us, Whittaker—"

"She isn't," Xiaodan said. "She hated Vasilik even when the Fifth Court was thriving. She would never ally herself with him."

"Like bloody hell I would," Elke said with a shudder.

"I want two people keeping an eye on the forests in the north. Everyone else get out the pitches and line them along the rear of the castle. We'll burn the falls if we have to. The more we can take out with them, the less we'll have to fight."

"Lady Whittaker," Malekh said brusquely. "If you intend to leave before they attack, I would suggest doing so now. I've asked Malira to prepare the helhests and a carriage to send you back to Elouve. It may take longer than your journey to the palace had, but it would give you ample time to recuperate. You will not want to be here when they come."

"My wounds are not so severe as that, milord."

"Even so, you would find it strenuous to bring Pendergast with you on foot. The ride should take four days, six if you stop at night.

There is a farmstead two miles from Elouve that we use to stable the stallions. They should be in good hands there."

The other vampires shifted uncomfortably. "Remy's leaving?" Honfa asked, turning to Xiaodan. But the woman only bit her lip, bowed her head.

"But why?" Naji demanded. "If we're about to be attacked, he could help our defenses with—"

"You've wanted him to leave since the day he arrived at Chànggē Shuǐ," Malekh said coolly. "Why change your mind now?"

Naji looked chastened. "I simply don't understand why you're making such a hasty decision."

"There is nothing to question. His sire is ill."

"What exactly are you saying?" Remy snapped.

Malekh turned to him then. The cold rage hadn't left the noble, but what was new was the suspicion in his eyes, the look of mistrust that hit Remy like a stab to the gut. "I think it would be best if you returned to your father and see to his whims as you've always done, Pendergast. You've outlived your welcome here."

"YOU THREE were on much better terms when you'd left the capital," Elke said as the carriage sped on. "Care to enlighten me?"

Remy stared out the window. "It's nothing," he said shortly.

"Lady Song had to fight to convince Queen Ophelia to let you accompany them back to Qing-ye, and now she lets you leave without another word? Did you at least find something new regarding the First Court?"

"Not quite."

"Then what are you doing?"

"I'm heading back to Elouve because Father is unwell. Wasn't that why you came all the way here to warn me?"

"I came because I was worried that you might want to return without my convincing you otherwise. There are strange whisperings in Elouve. The Reapers tried to quash the preachers calling for hell's damnation, but it only makes those unhinged sots the victims in the people's eyes. I didn't want to say so in the others' presence, but there's a growing resentment against the Queen's court for the alliance with the kindred. The priests were spinning the deaths at the Archives as a new conspiracy. Saying Lady Song and Lord Malekh had created the undead plague, forcibly turning people to fight in their war. But even without all that, the Remy I know would have stayed to fight with the Fourth Court."

Remy kept silent. The rain came down harder.

"Lady Song and Lord Malekh need us. Your father is unharmed, and he's no sicker than he was when you left. It's not like you're a doctor specializing in whatever he has, that your constant presence is required at his bedside. Look."

Elke fished out a newly reworked knifechain. "I made it tougher and more durable, added six more feet to the links because you said you wanted more range. I replaced the thinner blades with the round spikes you wanted. I would have thought you'd prefer to test it out here first. I'd even brought my fire lance, with some of the new and improved adjustments to the lightning specifications you're so admiring of, to help."

"Thank you, but that's no longer my choice to make," Remy said bitterly, accepting the gift. "As you said, it's not like they asked me to stay. They think I'm responsible for the Rot."

"What? How?"

"It's a long story."

"Seems like we've got a lot of time for that."

Remy turned his head and stared back in the direction of Chànggē Shuǐ; at the speed they were going, it had already disappeared into the distance. "They're going to die," he said. Perhaps not Malekh, because the bastard always came out on top.

But Xiaodan could not handle so many of those vampires without it putting a strain on her heart. And then there was Alegra and Gideon and Naji and everyone else.

It wasn't like he could fight a thousand vampires all by himself, either. His presence wouldn't be enough to stem the flow of that particular tide. If Malekh was right in his findings, and the arse always was, then his small consolation was that he would be safe from the Rot. . . .

"What are you doing?" Elke gasped, when Remy stuck his head out of the carriage, heedless of their speed.

"Hey!" Remy yelled at the galloping helhests. "Peanut! Biscuit! No, wait—Caramel? Scone? Cookie! Peanut and Cookie! Heel!"

The helhests were ignoring him, so Remy gritted his teeth and shoved himself out of the window, clinging to the roof of the carriage for dear life as he angled forward and braced his body against the edges. He slid forward, nearly slipped from the wetness and missed the perch, righted himself up in time, and grabbed at the reins. One good tug sent the horses into a startled halt, though it also nearly sent him flying forward over their heads.

The undead stallions nickered, then looked curiously back at him.

"We're not going to Elouve," Remy told them, more certain now with every word he said. "We're going back to the eastern palace, and then we're going to help your family fight, and I don't give a shit what Malekh thinks about that."

The horses whinnied and were compliant as Remy turned them around. "Do you remember what those vampires you'd seen looked like?" he asked Elke.

The vampire frowned. "Others seemed far too young to have been vampires for long. The rest moved sluggishly. Are they mutations? They still looked remarkably humanlike. I don't expect any vampires under Vasilik to be particularly stimulating at conversation, but most of them were just . . . standing around. They weren't even talking, just gazing blankly at nothing. The coven youngbloods were the noisy ones. I didn't have time to think much about it because they spotted me soon after that." Elke's mouth fell open. "Ah, were they infected? Then how are they being controlled?"

"That's a question someone smarter than me is going to have to answer. But right now . . ." Remy gave a quick flick at the reins, and the horses began to move again, this time back to Chànggē Shuǐ. "I'm going to help them. You're right, Elke. I shouldn't have left in the first place."

The helhests were back to full speed. "I still could have reined them in myself, you know." Elke said. "That was far too risky of you to do."

"You're injured."

"I've got some scrapes and bruises, but nothing that would immobilize me. I was just hamming it up back at the palace. Otherwise that gorgeous warrior with the frown and the pretty hair would never have given me the time of day. And, meaning no offense—as capable as you are, you were never this nimble before you left Elouve."

"Being their familiar has given me some unexpected attributes."

"And when were you planning on telling me this?" Elke's eyes narrowed dangerously. "Is it Lady Song? Or . . . Lord Malekh?"

Remy cleared his throat, pushed the horses to go faster so he could pretend to ignore Elke's gleeful shout.

"You tupped them *both*? Remington Adrian Pendergast, you sly dog!"

29

THE SIEGE

The attack had begun soon after he and Elke had left. As Malekh had predicted, Vasilik had not attacked Chànggē Shuǐ head-on, where the numerous obstacles and hidden traps would have taken out a good number of his followers. He was hitting them from the rear, using his minions' lack of fear of running water to his advantage. And the raging storm still in progress was doing the defenders no favors, because it was diminishing the fires the Fourth Court had started around their moat.

Guoyang had told him that few vampires would think of leaping off the waterfall, despite their enhanced abilities, but neither of them realized then how easily the infected could be compelled to climb tens of thousands of feet up the opposite end of the cliff, swim through miles of water, and then make the dizzying jump from there to the fortress.

The barricades should have been more than enough. There were sharpened stakes in rows along the outer walls facing the waterfalls, where any average vampire would have immediately found themselves impaled after leaping down from such heights, but with the infected these were no real obstacles.

With mounting horror, Remy watched several wriggling atop the poles. Some lay inert; others revived almost instantly, pulling themselves away with a bloody, moist, wrenching sound, and then continuing their descent down toward the battlements, wounds already regenerating, their previously human-shaped bodies morphing into more repugnant forms.

The stakes were triggering their extended mutations. They were growing stronger with every resurrection.

"You're going to help me climb up that waterfall because I can't do that on my own," Remy said. The helhests seemed to be aware of the obstacles as well, detouring around the fortress and bypassing the front gates. "We won't get past the main walls—far too many traps, not enough time to go through them slowly."

"Armiger Remington!" Honfa was peering over the battlements at them, startled. Remy saw Naji behind him, looking surprised and pleased. "I thought you were heading back west to Aluria!"

"Change of plans. Any chance you can haul us up?"

"Hold on, let me find something!" Honfa cut down a vampire who had tried to come up behind him unawares; a few minutes later, a rope ladder was dropped down. "Think you can get up on your own with this?"

By the time Remy and Elke had both hauled themselves up over the walls, Honfa and Naji were already engaging another four vampires—three obviously infected, from their blank stares and single-mindedness, and the last, one of Vasilik's youngbloods. Elke pounced on the latter as soon as she landed, swinging with her fire lance. The vampire paused, mouth agape as a deep red slash appeared on his throat. With a spinning kick, Elke sent him over the wall they'd just climbed up from.

"Another modification?" Remy asked, observing the retractable blade that now jutted out from the end of the barrel, a compliment to the regular sword already built into the other side.

"What can I say? Watching you with Breaker has always been inspiring."

"Knew you couldn't stay away," Naji said, slicing an infected cleanly through. Once Honfa had taken down the other two, the youth produced a small syringe, drew out liquid from a small vial inside a pouch at his waist. He took out another bottle and tossed it at Remy, followed by two more needles. "Take these. It'll immobilize any of the Rot-infected we've killed, prevents them from reviving."

"We're planning to head up the waterfall," Remy said. "Is there a way up from here?"

"You're gonna have to run up the eastern palace's highest tower, then make the jump from there. That's how we do it. Should be easy enough for you, if you've been sucking on my brother and his fiancée's blood the last few days."

"I haven't, matter of fact."

"You'll need to talk to them for replenishments, then. They're fighting on top of the falls as we speak."

"What? Why?"

"There'd be more of these bastards down here if it weren't for them up there. They ordered us to stay put and fight off anything that gets past them, but since they didn't expect you to come back like you did, I suppose they won't be mad if I send you up to them. They toss the infected our way, we run around and inoculate as many as we can with my brother's serum."

A mutated figure landed hard on the ground ten feet away from them, a lifeless blob of flesh and blisters.

"See?" Naji said.

"Will the rest of you be all right?"

Honfa gestured at a stack of barrels lined up along the battlements. "We've got enough pitch here to fry up a kingdom if it gets down to it, but the rain's putting a literal damper on our plans. Still, Lady Xiaodan and Lord Zidan's keeping the influx of vampires here to a trickle, so we're managing well."

"You want to climb up?" Elke echoed blankly, staring petrified at the gushing cascade of water above them. "You do know there's a reason they built the castle against the waterfall side of the cliffs, right? We *hate* moving water. We sink like deadweight."

"Vasilik's able to get them up there because the infected don't think enough to be afraid. That's where we ought to be."

Elke sighed and squared her shoulders. "The things I do for love."

"I'll take you on my back, Armiger," Naji said, grinning. "I can tie a sash around you like a newborn babe, if you're afraid of falling."

Remy did so reluctantly, forgoing the sash to keep a death grip on Naji while he clambered easily up the rocks, trying not to look down at the emptiness below them.

Elke often said that she was the nimblest vampire in the Fifth Court, and it was no false claim. She jumped from rock to stone formation to overhang with the surety of a mountain goat and the gracefulness of a dancer though she'd never made the ascent before, and soon they were all standing atop the falls.

Atop the falls in a spot roughly twenty yards wide where the water only went up to Remy's thighs, and nothing else that could pass for land for miles around them.

Xiaodan and Malekh were there. So were the infected, who were slowly pulling themselves up from the deeper portions of the lake and into the shallows with them. Some had already mutated, massive enough that their clothes had been replaced by oversized tumors all over their bodies, larger than even their heads. Their eyeballs were straining, bulging from the inner pressure of muscles expanding beyond what their skins could withstand.

"Remy!" Xiaodan cried out. She and her betrothed were throwing off almost as many of the mutations who had successfully climbed up to face them, but more were rising up from beneath the lake's surface.

"You're not going to be able to fight them off this way," Remy grated.

"Do you have a better idea, Pendergast?" Malekh ripped one infected's head from the rest of its body out of sheer strength, kicking the carcasses off the falls.

"I always have a fucking better idea. You killed Vasilik yet?"

"The coward has yet to show his face."

"Then maybe this will help get his attention. I want you all off this rock."

"What exactly are you planning to do?" Xiaodan didn't look winded yet, the short breaks in between infected staggering out of the water, giving her time to rest.

"Can you all make a leap from here back to Chàngge Shuǐ?"

"Of course," Xiaodan said. "We know a method to land safely past the spikes. I can assist Lady Whittaker if need be."

"In that case—Elke, I have need of your fire lance."

"Words I never thought you would say," Elke said, grinning, lifting the weapon onto her shoulder. "I can guess at what you intend to do, but you forget that we're standing in water. The shock will kill us just as much as it will kill them. Probably even worse."

"That's why I don't want anyone else here when I do it."

"And then what? Have us return to retrieve your burnt corpse?" Xiaodan bisected another vampire, then scowled at him. "I've handled fire lances before. I can do it."

"My idea, my finger on the trigger."

"*My* weapon," Elke said. "*My* lightning. Xiaodan isn't familiar with the new changes I've made to this lovely little jewel."

"Lightning?" Naji asked. "That lance possesses lightning inside of it?"

"Lightning," Malekh said, eyes gleaming. "A clean shot will be enough to incapacitate everything in these waters. Prevent them from reviving quickly, long enough for us to properly dispose of them."

"That was the plan," Elke admitted. "Not quite Reaper regulations, decidedly. Shall we?"

"Let's do it," the noble decided, and the redhead charged up the fire lance, the barrel sparking merrily.

"Wait," Naji said uncertainly. "What are they doing?"

The Rot-infected who had already emerged from the water were staring at Remy. They drew closer.

"Don't come near me, you bastards."

Much to his surprise, the mutations obeyed, slowly shuffling to a stop.

"How are you doing this?" Xiaodan asked.

"I do *not* fucking know," Remy said. "Don't move. None of you fucking move."

And then he felt it. A sluggishness in his head, a rumbling of indistinct voices crowding into his mind growing louder by the second.

"Don't move!" he shouted, and the murmurings in his head ceased abruptly.

None of the creatures moved. Experimentally, Remy took a step toward them, and artlessly took off one of their heads. It sank into the lake, bobbed up briefly, and sailed merrily down the falls, and still the rest of the infected didn't blink.

"They were made with infusions of your blood," Malekh said. "It may be all that's necessary to establish a connection. Why didn't it happen earlier, with others we've faced?"

"Hell should I know," Remy growled. "I'm not deliberately controlling them, if that's what you're implying. I just yelled at them to stop. Think I can make them dance?"

And then a large beefy hand rose up from the water and latched on to a small rock bordering the shallows, gripping it with enough force that bits of the stone crumbled underneath its grip. With a sickening, lurching sound, like something wet and hairy was sliding grossly over the slimy moss, a colossus lifted itself up from the cliff's edge.

"Oh no," Xiaodan said.

It stepped toward them, its great eyes devoid of intelligence. It had a face that was familiarly blank, and yet animated, twitching with a repugnant, grasping hunger. It looked like it was made of the rock itself, its skin gray and hard. It was at least nine feet tall, its fists like boulders.

"What is that?" Elke gasped.

"The final form of what Vasilik wants his infected vampires to be," Xiaodan said grimly. "Invulnerable, capable of controlling a small army of its own, and completely loyal to him."

"Listen to me, ugly," Remy ordered. "Stab yourself."

The colossus ignored him.

"Either it's not my blood powering that hideous body, or its head's too dense to take in any more commands."

"Are we ready, Lady Whittaker?" Malekh grunted.

"Give me another minute. The lightning rods take a while to reach the required strength necessary."

"I'm not sure we have a minute to spare." Xiaodan was before the hulking brute in an instant, battering at its chest and torso. Remy could see the colossus take in the blows with little effort, unrelenting even as its stomach twisted and deformed from the force of her assault. It reached out to grab at her, but Xiaodan ducked out of the way and kept up the attack at a new angle, focusing on its back and forcing it to turn away from them to engage with her.

"Lady Whittaker," Malekh said tersely.

"We're ready!" Elke shouted.

It was the Summer Lord's turn to move in close and hammer at the colossus. His punches weren't as strong as Xiaodan's, but it did the trick. The colossus shuffled back around, and Xiaodan made a flying leap, using the creature's head as a stepping-stone to return to her fiancé's side.

"Now!" Remy shouted.

Malekh grabbed him and jumped with the others, just as Elke

leveled her fire lance on the waters beside the colossus, shooting just as she leaped. Remy could feel the sizzle as lightning slammed through every infected atop the falls. Some floated to the surface, lifeless; others fell, plummeting down into the rapids.

But the colossus was made of sturdier stock. Its gigantic body jolted from the powerful thunderbolt, shuddering uncontrollably as the deadly light crackled through it, ricocheted into the shallows, gained second life when it sizzled in the surrounding waters, and then rebounded back into its hideous form.

It made one last leap for them, would have snatched Elke had Remy not thrown Breaker at the monster at the last moment. The base of it hit the creature fully in the face, pushing it a few steps back, far enough for its fingers to claw at air instead of the redhead.

Remy was too busy watching the colossus, even as the grotesque mutation receded from his view while they plummeted down the falls, to realize the danger they were still in until his left side began to throb. He heard Malekh throw out a curse and veer sharply to the right.

And then something painful slammed into Remy, and then he was somersaulting without Malekh, free-falling down toward the palace below.

This was bad. Remy was good at what he did, but no amount of training in the world could prepare a very human body with very fragile bones to hit the ground at this velocity. There was nothing to hold on to, and the next closest thing to grasp was still a few hundred or so feet below.

His hand dug into his coat pocket and felt the familiar, cool touch of silver. "Thank you, Elke," Remy whispered, fishing out his new knifechain. "Thank you, thank you, thank you."

It was nerve-racking to time his attempt, with the ground rushing eagerly up to him, but he pulled it off. He threw the links like a grappling hook once he'd drawn close enough to the highest of Chànggē Shuǐ's towers, the chain wrapping securely around a protruding beam. After that, all Remy had to do was hold on tightly while he let momentum do the rest of the work, swinging him forward so he could tumble safely onto the parapets, Xiaodan on hand to catch him before anything else could break his fall. Another quick tug shook the links free, clattering beside him.

Remy staggered up and turned to see Vasilik and Malekh now fighting, leaping from lattice to rooftop to turret. There was a heavy gash across Malekh's shoulder; the noble had taken the blow meant for him.

There was a fresh desperation to Vasilik's movements, as if he was only realizing he was losing despite starting out with the bigger army. The vampire coven leader wielded a broadsword, and Malekh was countering his attacks with his own curved saber.

They both blurred back into view at the palace courtyard, breathing heavily.

"It shouldn't have gone this far," Vasilik snarled. "We could have ruled the world together, Zidan, if you hadn't let that simpering Fourth Court woman and her infatuation with humans sway you."

"The world is changing, and the old ways have been rendered obsolete with the old Ancients, Vasilik." Malekh dodged, and his sword sang a counterpoint, catching the other man on the leg. "We must adapt, or you will follow them into irrelevance soon enough."

"Never!" Vasilik shouted. "We were like gods, Zidan! Even as the First's whore, you lived like a king! We could have had the humans bowing before us, fearing us, worshipping us, while we eradicated what remained of the other courts! And here you are, bowing before them like a dog? Taking a hunter into your bed? It is good that King Ishkibal did not live to see you fallen so low."

"Ishkibal died on his hands and knees, begging for a mercy he did not deserve, Vasilik. I do not want to live as a king. I am content to be a man."

Vasilik wiped at his mouth. "Then it is all the more fitting to see you reprise your sire's last moments," he said. "See how cruel you are, Zidan, to the people you claim to want."

"Tell me who brought the storms, Vasilik. However you may boast, it is not you who leads this attack."

The vampire only grinned and blurred to a new position. "Wouldn't you like to know the powerful Ancients who have allied with me?"

Remy heard Elke gasp and saw another heavier, larger figure land on the courtyard, hitting with enough force that the stones actually shattered from its weight.

He stared at the colossus, which rose to its full height.

In its great meaty hands, it clasped Remy's Breaker.

"Well," Xiaodan said, imitating Remy's exact tone of voice whenever he said the same thing. "Fuck."

"How did it recover?" Elke asked, stunned, and then retreated hastily when the colossus lumbered forward, swinging his new weapon indiscriminately.

"Stay away from him, Elke! That one won't feel any pain!" Remy leaped out of the way himself as Breaker swiped dangerously close. He had no other weapon on hand save for his knifechain, so he began spinning that, trying to keep the hulking brute at bay. Whatever it lacked in intellect it was nonetheless quick to adapt, reaching out to grab the links. Its massive strength sent Remy skidding forward, struggling to retain the chain even as the monster swung his own scythes back at him.

"No!" Xiaodan drew close enough to score a deep gash across the beast's back, and the monster redirected its attentions to her, sensing the bigger threat. "You're fighting *me!* Jiàn nǚ rén."

Whatever she said, the colossus took offense. It let go of the knifechain, and it was Remy who staggered backward this time. "You've fought these damn things before," he gasped out. "It's evolved for endurance. You can't keep this up for long."

"It has to have a weakness," Xiaodan insisted. "Everything does, even something this monstrous. Honfa!"

"Milady!" The bearded vampire bellowed from across the courtyard.

"How long will it take for the tar to be ready?"

"Ten, perhaps fifteen minutes, milady. It will need the temperatures that Lord Zidan calculated for it to be of any use—"

"Bring it now, and position it over the enclave as we discussed."

There weren't as many youngbloods scampering up the walls through the front, and their numbers were much more manageable given that most of the Rot-infected had been indefinitely indisposed, judging from the bodies that were still going over the waterfall. Remy kept an eye on Xiaodan even as he used his knifechain to slice through a few more of the coven kindred who'd refused to admit defeat, spinning it effortlessly above his head to wreak havoc. Occasionally they would grab at it, trying to make him weaponless just as the colossus had, but he had a couple more daggers waiting inside his sleeves to throw, and they relinquished their grip permanently soon enough.

Two minutes. Five minutes. Seven minutes. Xiaodan was still as agile as ever, attacking the colossus seemingly in all directions at once, probing for a weak point.

The battle between Malekh and Vasilik was still raging, neither prepared to admit defeat. Malekh's injury was more severe than he had let on, his movements slower than Remy was used to seeing from him. The Third Court noble was also distracted, gaze constantly flicking toward Xiaodan's fight. He avoided a debilitating blow from Vasilik that scored a light slash across his torso, one that would've been deeper if he hadn't shifted in time.

"You're not as spry as you once were, old man," Vasilik taunted. "Don't worry—once my warrior finishes off your girl, I'll make sure you join her right away."

Malekh didn't even condescend to reply, and a quick jab from him sent a deeper, uglier slash across Vasilik's chest. The man snarled and redoubled his attack.

Ten minutes. The weariness beginning to shadow Xiaodan's face told Remy all he needed to know. She'd been fighting atop the waterfall for much longer than this.

"Where are you going?" Elke asked, staking a vampire quickly so she could glare at Remy.

"I want my weapon back." He hurled his chain at the colossus again. The creature was slower to react this time around, and the links wrapped securely around Breaker, catching just underneath the joints where his twin scythes were attached to the bludgeon. He tugged hard, but the monster was unyielding; it jerked back, yanking him forward a few feet. Remy gritted his teeth and dug in, refusing to let go.

"Remy?" Xiaodan asked. She was already breathing hard, her face pained.

"Catch your breath and let me handle this." His feet began to skid along the ground, forcing him inexorably toward the colossus, who was dragging him in link by link. "Let me try. Give Breaker back to me, you—" What was that Qing-ye word for fucker again? "—căonímă!"

The colossus's arms shot forward, and Remy scampered out of the way. He nearly had a fist to the face but dodged just in time, and the glancing blow he took on his side as a result all but sent him to his knees. Remy rolled, narrowly avoiding the hulk's foot stomping him dead into the stonework. The colossus brought Breaker down again, and Remy sidestepped, grabbed at his weapon, and suddenly found himself face-to-face with the giant, who was even uglier and more malodorous up close.

The colossus yanked Breaker out of his grip and prepared to deliver a final fatal blow, but Remy hadn't gotten this near to the demonspawn to come out the loser. Instead, his fingers jerked over to his sleeve and came back out with his last knife.

The colossus didn't howl when the dagger plunged into its left eye. It didn't cry out in pain or even let go of Breaker. It did step back, as if puzzled by the sudden change in its vision, leaving Remy scrambling for safety.

"Milady!" The cry that came from above sounded a lot like Honfa. "I'm ready!"

"Thank you, Honfa." Some of the color had returned to Xiaodan's face. She rose to her feet, strength renewed. "Over here, you bastard!"

The colossus's head whipped back toward her. Xiaodan had picked up Remy's knifechain, which he and the creature had both lost in the scuffle. She copied his movements, spinning it in a circle over her head. Her wrist flicked forward, and the knives scored long, dark slashes against the colossus's chest. If Remy had made that attempt, it would have done no more than a glancing blow.

Ignoring the dagger still sticking out of its eye, the colossus stalked her. Xiaodan lashed out again even as she continued to retreat, raining fresh wounds on its sides and face. She was luring it away from them into the inner courtyard.

Deprived of his usual weapons, Remy snatched up a sword from one of the fallen vampires and followed. As the colossus shuffled past an overhang, a black viscous substance poured down on it from above, drenching it completely.

"Milady!" Honfa shouted; he was holding a barrel over his head, its contents now emptied onto the brute. Beside him was the grim-faced Alegra, who raised a crossbow, in which an arrow already lit on fire had been nocked, and aimed it at the colossus. With a twang, she set it loose.

The monster caught fire. It paused, its gigantic body aflame, and painstakingly continued its pursuit of Xiaodan, albeit decidedly slower this time.

"How is it still standing?" Honfa roared, amazed.

"Because it's going to take more than hell to end its cursed half-life," Xiaodan replied. Still swinging the chain, she nodded at the special compartment Liufei had shown Remy days before, the one similar in build to the Archives' vault underneath Elouve. "Open it."

"Milady, you can't! If you're trapped in there with it, you could—"

"Open the container, Honfa. That's an order."

Something sharp, circular, and spinning moved through the air, cutting deeply into the colossus's shins. The creature sank down on one knee, momentarily incapacitated.

Queen Yingyue marched forward. No longer the small and frail figure Remy had last seen in her quarters, she was now dressed in armor, breastplate gleaming. A beautifully crafted helmet with hammered steel wings were forged onto either side of the head-piece. She caught the weapon again as it came spinning back toward her—it appeared to Remy like a circular saw, with handles attached for gripping.

"Mother!" Xiaodan cried out.

"Where are my other soldiers?" the queen demanded. "Who is it this time? Montague? Gorgona? Have our men and women grown so lax as to allow our castle walls to be breached? Must I do everything myself?"

"Mother, please be careful!"

"I have fought far greater beasts than this, my child. Surely one of Etrienne's experiments, by the looks of it, though none he has wrought has ever gotten the better of me. What have I told you about brutes of such sizes, Xiaodan?" The queen aimed for the colossus's legs again, and the hulk sagged down a second time. "It doesn't matter how big they are if they bow down before you in the end." A coven vampire made for her, but the queen dispatched it easily, even as she turned to face three more.

The colossus climbed back to its feet with greater effort, its steps slower, limping. "Get him inside the vault," Xiaodan said.

"You're too exhausted for this!" Remy barked.

"I won't need to use as much effort in an enclosed space. Shut the door as soon as I give the word." Xiaodan backed into the container, the monster trudging in after her.

Remy rushed toward the vault. Through the opening he spied her crouching down in the farthest corner of the enclosed room, waiting, the whole of her tense and ready. The colossus filled up the cramped compartment and reached for her with one ham fist.

"Now!" Xiaodan shouted.

Honfa was already slamming the door shut with clear finality, and then fled from the vault with his eyes closed. The other Fourth Court vampires were covering their faces, too, or running away as fast as they could.

Helplessly, Remy watched as Xiaodan held out her hands, a bright light glowing around her.

"Eat shit, you foddle-swapped coxcomb," she said before the sun's fury blasted from her fingers.

The explosion sent Remy to the ground, the walls of the vault expanding from the concussive force as the brightest light he'd ever seen filled the room. As the dust settled and the gloom returned, acrid black smoke began to drift from inside the small opening.

Remy scrambled to the door, then yelped with pain at finding its handle too hot to touch. He shook off his coat, wrapped it around his hands, and forced the vault open, fearing the worst.

Xiaodan stood in the middle of the blackened room, smiling. Remy saw the charred carcass on the floor, much smaller in size than the creature that had entered only seconds before.

"Oh," Elke said as she reached his side, blinking rapidly after not having completely shielded her eyes in time. "Well, there was something I never expected to see again."

"Again?" Remy echoed.

"How did you think she killed Etrienne Sauveterre and most of the Fifth Court? If I hadn't fled, I would've been ashes myself."

Honfa sidled close to Remy. "Cào nǐ mā," he said helpfully. "Not cǎonímǎ. That's an alpaca."

"Xiaodan's frustration with certain aspects of the Alurian language is clearer to me now," Remy said.

There was a low moan. Queen Yingyue sank to her knees, staring blankly at the vault and the dead colossus within.

"Mother?" Xiaodan sounded exhausted. She looked ready to collapse but forced herself to walk toward the queen. "Are you—?"

"Stay away from me," the older woman hissed, shrinking from her touch. "Stay far away from me."

"Mother—"

"I said stay away!" The cutting saw was back in the older woman's hand, aimed at Xiaodan's throat. "You are no daughter of mine. Monster! Sunwielder! You will be the death of us all! You have caused the ruin of the Fourth Court. They will kill us like they killed Lilith!"

Xiaodan began to tremble. Remy took the initiative, pulling her into his arms and away from Yingyue. "I think someone else should attend to your mother," he said gently.

"I'll take care of her, milady," Honfa promised.

Xiaodan could only nod and allow Remy to carry her away, Elke following closely behind.

The battle between Malekh and Vasilik had come to a halt. The Fifth Court leader was on his knees, hand pulling at his hair as if in agony. Malekh stood a few feet away, wary and on guard, but not pushing his advantage.

"You killed my prized warrior!" Vasilik shrieked at Xiaodan. "Impossible!"

"As my love always says," Xiaodan said, grinning weakly but defiantly, "improbable, but never impossible."

"He dropped to the ground without my brother ever touching him," Naji whispered. The youth had been watching the fight, hands trembling like he itched to join in. "When you killed that hulk, it caused him pain."

"It's over, Vasilik," Malekh said wearily. "Your army has been defeated, your colossus no use to you other than compost. This is your last chance to leave with your head still attached to your shoulders before I change my mind. Surrender, and I will be lenient."

"After everything he's done, you're going to let him go?" Remy exploded.

Vasilik laughed weakly. "Your little bloodling lover has the right idea, Malekh. Are you going to let me escape, knowing I might return another day with an even bigger army of colossi?"

"These are my terms, Vasilik," Malekh said coldly. "Make your choice."

"You seek to build a reputation of strength and power, Zidan, but in truth, you are just as soft-hearted as your cursed little fiancée here. You said I wasn't the only one involved in this enterprise, and you are right. The storm around us is not my doing. It's not over. There will be more armies. The Rot shall continue to spread and overwhelm human lands."

"What are you talking about?" Remy snapped, stepping forward. "Who are you working with?"

Vasilik smiled, and blood dripped down from inside his mouth. "This is all *your* fault, bloodling. You shouldn't have been here. You should have been on your way back to Aluria by now. My kindred would have overwhelmed Chànggē Shuǐ, brought about the deaths of Queen Yingyue and her daughter. But you shall lose this war yet. Already another army marches for Elouve. You'll be surprised to find who leads it, Zidan."

"That holds little interest to me."

"It should. I promised your bloodling here that I would turn my back on the First Court, tell him everything he needed to know about the empress if he only joined forces with me. And still he chose you." His nails raked at the ground, his face twisted in despair. "Always, *always* they choose you, Zidan. Why? You throw them away, and still they come crawling back."

Suddenly he was moving, and this time his target wasn't Malekh. "This one won't be able to crawl back to you," he snarled.

Remy saw him approach but could do little with Xiaodan half-conscious in his arms, so on instinct, he did the only thing he could—turn to use his body to shield hers from the incoming sword.

There was a heavy, sickeningly wet sound.

Vasilik gurgled, black blood pouring from his mouth. A blade had sprouted from the center of his chest, and the hands that had once attempted to kill Remy could do nothing more than to grasp at his shoulder as he sank down, no longer able to bear his own weight. The vampire's eyes were still trained on Remy, lips moving soundlessly.

From behind him, Malekh wrenched his saber free.

"Mahlk," Vasilik guttered, clasping at Remy's wrist with his other hand, though his grip was limp. "Mahlk kulg."

Elke gently took Xiaodan away. Remy gripped the other man's hand, guiding him down as the vampire's fingers, still on his shoulder, slackened.

"Zidan," Vasilik whispered, taking in another, final breath, so low that Remy thought he had only imagined the words. "Zidan killed your mother."

And then he sighed, and his body shriveled up, turning into dust that quickly dissipated before it touched the ground.

30

FORGIVENESS

It was far more difficult to clean up the corpses than it had been to kill them. Remy grunted as he lifted a body onto the wagon Honfa had brought, loaded up half a dozen more, then paused to glare at the stack they'd accumulated. "How many does that make so far?"

"Six hundred and fifty-three," Alegra said. While Remy had to pause every now and then to rest his aching muscles, the woman showed no such weakness, tossing twelve corpses into the wagon for every three that he managed.

It was tempting to leave all the bodies in the lake, but Alegra pointed out that they would likely contaminate the waters, attract other unwanted creatures, and eventually pop back up onto the surface anyway, bloated and engorged. Most of the Rotted corpses had deteriorated enough that identifying their remains was nearly impossible. Vasilik had targeted entire villages. There would be very few left alive to mourn them.

After that came the children, the hardest by far.

Remy had insisted on accompanying Alegra and the others to the Dà Lán. Honfa was as familiar with the caves as Malekh had been, and among the five of them, they'd found more of the unfortunate infected and put them out of their misery. Remy focused on bringing them out instead of the cave walls threatening to close in on him once more. It was easier this time.

There was still enough of Malekh's serum to ensure that none of the corpses would rise again. Lady Song would handle the burnings once she felt better, Liufei had said. Just not today.

One more mystery remained unsolved. After Vasilik's death, the skies had cleared, the sunlight returning in waves past the clouds. At least one other vampire had gotten away from the siege at Chànggē Shuǐ. A powerful one.

Remy hated loose ends.

"Xiaodan said you were injured here," Malira said as she carried out several of the small, broken bodies with as much gentleness as she could, as they all were trying to do.

Remy looked down at the young raven-haired girl he was holding, her eyes staring out at nothing. "Had my guard down," he said gruffly, laying the child on the wagon. "Was trapped in a cave myself when I was younger."

"A wonder you'd even found a way to both her ladyship and Lord Zidan, knowing how deep these caverns can go. More surprised to see how many Rotters are in here. You'd think the humans would have missed them."

"They were taken over the course of many years. Runaways, mostly." He should have known. How many reports had he sifted through of these children? How many times had he persisted even in the face of his old man's dismissiveness? Should he have done more? "Others were taken from outside Aluria, in kingdoms like Bergroves and Falaci farther away."

"Where I suppose the loss of villagers isn't considered as important." Malina sighed. "You didn't need to accompany us for this, Armiger. You require sleep. Lady Xiaodan's still unconscious, according to Liufei, and Lord Zidan's not in the best shape either, though no one really knows how to stop him when he insists on shutting himself in the laboratory like this."

"I'll drag him out. Beat some sense into him."

The girl smiled. "You like him, don't you? Lord Zidan. And Lady Xiaodan, too. Never seen them so happy the last couple of days, attack notwithstanding."

Remy wasn't too sure about that. *Zidan killed your mother*, Vasilik had said. Would he have used his dying breath to lie, to sow more discord between them?

Yes. The dead vampire had promised him all he knew of the Night Empress, and yet the chances were higher that he'd been working with her all along. And his threat that an army led by the Night Court would soon descend on Aluria—maybe he'd been lying about that as well. After all, Vasilik had told Malekh that Remy had willfully infected the villagers, and Remy knew fuck all about that. No, it was best not to dwell too much on the man's last words when he'd been false about so many other things.

The words dug into his back all the same, a burr he couldn't shake free.

Malekh hadn't heard the words. The noble had stumbled back and stared down at the ashes of his former lover in wordless shock, as if he hadn't been the one to land the killing blow. He had closed himself off at the palace laboratory ever since, leaving only to attend to Xiaodan, who was still asleep. It wasn't the right time to demand answers, and Remy, all too aware of the man's grief, had chosen to give him the space he needed.

He at least owed him that. He'd been rightfully pissed that Zidan had thought him capable of creating the Rot when half the time he couldn't even figure out the vampire lord's simplified explanations of his own experiments—and Remy would be a damn hypocrite if he jumped to conclusions about the man in the same way.

He was too soft, like his father had said. Must have gotten it from his mother. And then he wondered if his mother had only been soft because she'd loved his father. Like kindness had ever been a sin.

Once Remy returned to the capital, inquiries were in order. There was always the hope that Astonbury's successor wouldn't hate him as the former lord high steward had, but Remy had never been known for his optimism.

His hunt for the First Court had barely progressed. Malekh said he knew nothing that had taken place there since he'd left, and Remy believed him. But if there were kindred armies out there with plans to attack Aluria, then he needed to report to Her Majesty immediately.

They kept the corpses near the waterfalls inside a small narrow cave. Honfa sealed it temporarily with a pile of rocks—"You never know, eh?"—to safeguard them until Xiaodan woke. There was no need for a burial, but Malira felt like they owed the infected some measure of dignity and recited a poem for them in melodic Qing-yen.

"May they return to us as seeds in the wind," she translated for him when he asked, "so that we may enjoy their beauty after they grow where they land, and may we rest in their shade. May their souls know peace."

"It's beautiful," he said.

"It gives me comfort, and I hope it does the same to their spirits. Would you like to contribute something from Aluria to the eulogy?"

"Well . . . it's not Alurian," Remy said, and his mother's song sprang to his lips. He felt self-conscious now that he had a larger audience than was the norm, but Honfa leaned back against a tree, closing his eyes, and Malira nodded along to the melody with a smile on her face.

Something in the foliage around the nearby woods shifted with a sudden flash of color halfway through the song. He broke off.

"What's the matter?" Malira asked curiously, but Remy gestured at her and the others to be silent.

Again. Another flash of brown and dark red.

Remy ran toward it, pausing once he'd reached the forest's edge, because he knew better than to plunge through without support. For a moment, he found himself staring at a strange sight—a figure in a thick hood, wrapped in a cloak of dark scarlet; its features were unseen, but he thought it was gazing back at him.

It was the same one he'd spotted at the Dà Lán.

Remy blinked, and it was gone.

He watched and waited, not trusting himself to breathe until he was certain, but whoever it was did not reappear. Honfa, Malira, and Liufei scoured the forests thereafter, but in the end, they said they had found nothing.

XIAODAN SLEPT for two days straight, and Malekh was in his laboratory for nearly as long, emerging only periodically and very briefly to ask for any updates regarding Xiaodan's health, when he wasn't visiting her himself. After the whole grisly business dealing with the dead bodies was over and done with, Remy scrubbed himself clean and raw, then spent what time he could dozing off at an armchair by Xiaodan's bed to make up for her betrothed's lapse.

He spun Breaker, trained and sparred with the other kindred in the mornings. He ate copious amounts of food because it was hard to say no to Elke, who had taken over the kitchens at her insistence. As a vampire who had lived among humans for many years now, she had pointed out, *and* Remy's closest friend to boot, it was natural to want to see to *his* health while he concentrated on Xiaodan's.

"You never cooked this much for me at Kinaiya," Remy complained.

"That's because you rarely told me in advance how long you were staying at Elouve, so I could never prepare well enough beforehand. You seem much more settled here. Besides," she added with a mischievous glint in her eye that told him she was up to some new trouble, "I'm doing this as a favor for someone else."

When she wasn't trying to woo Alegra into the temporary quarters she'd been provided with by Honfa—the stone-faced vampire warrior appeared strangely resistant to her flirtations, which the former Fifth Court vampire took as a challenge—Elke told Remy of what he'd missed at Elouve while he was away. "I wanted to warn you about the assault on your father, of course," she said, "but there is more. The Marquess of Riones has been investigating Astonbury's death. He knows of our friendship and asked me to convey the few details he could reveal about the murder. It all circles back to the suspect the butler had mentioned seeing, entering his study."

"Yes, the one that Feiron initially claimed was me. But the butler wasn't really the butler, was he?"

"Well, Feiron hasn't learned that at all—he's still calling you the culprit. He's realized that Her Majesty has no plans to appoint him for lord high stewardship, and he's been ticked ever since. He's echoing the rising vampire hysteria the preachers are spreading and blaming you, Lady Song, and Lord Malekh for it. The Marquess of Riones has been doing his best to deny his accusations, but logic has little sway in Elouve right now. Do you think he's working with whoever it is using your blood for the Rot?"

"I suspect every one of Astonbury's lackeys at this point. This isn't a coincidence. Someone's taking great pains to frame me not just for his murder, but for the Rot, and they've been using the doctors to bleed me dry for months."

"I can try to find out more when I return."

"When *you* return?"

"I came here because I couldn't trust anyone else to tell you. The queen doesn't want to let it get out that your father was targeted, in fear that it might inspire similar attacks against other Reapers. Feiron isn't the only minister from the opposition capitalizing on the preachers' sermons—they're claiming it's a plan from the Third and Fourth Courts to politically bend Aluria to their will. Lord Malekh and Lady Song are no longer welcome in the capital. And I don't think you will be, either."

QUEEN YINGYUE had reverted back to listlessness, rousing only once to ask Naji politely where her husband was. Remy received the news with sadness, knowing Xiaodan would be heartbroken.

Malekh continued to annoy him with his absence. Couldn't the noble spare an hour to be by her side, should she wake earlier than expected? The vampire also refused to let anyone else see to the wounds he'd sustained during the fight with Vasilik. Remy wasn't even sure the man had slept since.

Remy had tried to make that point once when he'd caught Malekh visiting Xiaodan, only to be informed politely, coldly, that he was not the one in the room with medical experience, and that Malekh could handle himself just fine. Later that day, Remy decided his patience had human limits.

"What are you doing in here?" Malekh barked without looking up when Remy marched into the laboratory unannounced. As always, some medical apparatus was on the table, and the vampire was looking through it at some new speck of blood or whatever bullshit he was occupying himself with instead of his fiancée.

"Nothing." Remy perched at his usual spot by the table, leaned forward on his elbows with his hands tucked comfortably under his chin, and watched the man work.

Ten minutes ticked by. Fifteen minutes. Twenty.

Malekh lifted his head, removed the eyepiece he wore for inspecting the stained blips on his glass slides. Then he took off his gloves and threw them angrily down on the table with a faint smack. "What do you want, Pendergast?"

"Like I said, nothing," Remy said. "I've been sitting here, doing absolutely nothing at all. Just like when you say your wounds are nothing, that nothing is messing with your head so badly that you need to hide out here at all hours despite needing some bloody rest yourself, that there's nothing to worry about. Nothing. Doing absolutely fucking goddamn nothing."

"There is little you can do for me. I am a vampire; my wounds will heal."

"They'll heal slowly, is what's going to happen. As you're fond of pointing out, there are a good amount of things I don't understand. I need them explained to me with simple drawings and hand puppets. I could be the tip of a blade and not be its sharpest point. But once I do catch on, I don't forget. And what I remember is that you and Xiaodan have been together for so long, having been each other's meals, that it's her blood that heals you the fastest. She's currently in no shape to make good on that, and you haven't consumed anything else. I've seen Naji lug in a jarful of blood for you to take, then lug it back out, still untouched and clotted. Feeding heals you. You're not feeding. What hypothesis would you bloody make from that observation?"

"Has it occurred to you that I'm simply not hungry?"

"Because you had to kill someone you once cared about?"

Malekh glared at him.

"Remember the first time you beat my arse after I wiped out your youngbloods in the forest?"

"They weren't my youngbloods."

"At least one of those youngbloods was yours. The rest stuck themselves to your younger brother like leeches. I was pissed off long before you ever showed up, and it was also because I had to kill someone I cared about. Not in the same way—I'd met her only a handful of times before, but she was always kind to me when everyone else wasn't, so . . . Ah hell, maybe that wasn't a good analogy—"

"It's a sound analogy," Malekh said. "You grow attached to anyone who's been kind to you for longer than five minutes. I understand."

It was Remy's turn to scowl, but that slid off his face when he noticed the faint smile on the noble's. It occurred to him just then, that perhaps Zidan Malekh had finally made a passable joke, even if it was at his expense.

"I took blood samples of some of the infected children and what little remains of the colossus. The dominant blood group therein isn't yours. Likely it's Vasilik's. It explains why they didn't respond to your attempts to control them. This is how the mutations can be commanded." Malekh pressed a thumb and middle finger against the bridge of his nose, rubbing carefully.

"Xiaodan would have told you by now," he said, "but there is a . . . bond between sire and subordinate that is difficult to break. Such is the case between Vasilik and I. It is instinct to recoil at the thought of killing him. While it causes no physical pain, there is a certain amount of . . . mental duress involved afterward. I have already done it before. I did not wish to do so again."

He was talking about the Night King. Remy could tell by the way the noble's hand trembled, so slightly that he'd almost missed it, as he slotted a glass display back into place. He opened his mouth to tell the man he didn't need to say anything to him to justify his actions, but Malekh shook his head and continued.

"I have not sired many kindred. Many consider our long lives a boon, a gift that must be shared as indiscriminately as possible. I do not share in that sentiment. Eternity should be given only to those who can hold themselves responsible for it. Those I've begotten were often close to death, with little choice left but to turn them. Naji was the last.

"I was reviled for killing King Ishkibal, though his death brought freedom to the other courts. There is a shame in the act that many cannot see past."

Malekh's fingers traced paths on the table, making circles on its surface. "It is why I cautioned you against going to war against what remains of their court, wherever that may be. They are ruthless. They will bait you for years as they have done to me, send you corpses, pieces, to taunt you into making another mistake for them to exploit. The Night King could compel minds, his vassals to a lesser extent. As I said before, under their control I have . . . done things that I have since regretted."

He was opening up to Remy, but he was struggling, still unwilling to reveal parts of his history that had broken him. "I'm not asking you to relive your worst memories," Remy said quietly. It wasn't worth the man's pain. "You don't need to tell me those stories for me to believe you. I am in no shape to be going after the First Court, even if I want to. And however it sounded at first, I have no intentions of dying at the Night Empress's hands. I do still intend to find a way, but if you tell me going against her *now* is a futile effort, I trust your judgment."

Malekh smiled grimly. "I wonder if you should. I erred in my estimation of Vasilik, but I did not relish bringing about his death. I am worried about Xiaodan. But I do not want my current state of mind to be the first thing that preoccupies her when she wakes."

Remy sat back and stared at him. "You know," he said, "I always thought that Xiaodan had strong-armed you into rescuing her helhests and her hound dogs from death. Now I'm thinking it was *you* who'd suggested it to begin with."

"If this is your attempt to put me in better spirits, then it isn't working."

"If I wanted to put you in better spirits, I would have asked Malira for your favorite bottle of wine with blood from yours truly mixed in for spice." Remy cleared his throat. "And if you don't happen to like wine at the moment, just know that I am otherwise still here, doing nothing, with a body full of fresh blood that I believe you've acquired a preference for."

He'd been nervous about this. Offering himself as a balm to ease the noble's obvious distress at having killed his former lover while also worrying about his current one struck him as arrogant. But the man had to drink something to get his health up, and he'd never turned Remy down before. If Vasilik hadn't been lying about the dangers regarding Elouve, or if there were other armies lying in wait, then Remy needed both Malekh and Xiaodan at peak strength, because he wouldn't be able to do it on his own.

And it was a perfectly logical reason for a quick, satisfactory shag.

"Are you offering yourself to me, Pendergast?" A flicker of lust was back in Malekh's gaze, liquid in its heat. It was a relief to see the noble exhibiting something beyond the desire to bury himself in his work. It was also worrying, given that most of the trysts between them ended in deliciously violent ways, and there was quite a bit of fragile equipment inside the laboratory that Remy would no doubt be blamed for later.

"I—am I?"

"I was waiting for Xiaodan to wake before making any overtures toward you. Whenever she goes into this deep a hibernation, she later wakes up with a ravenous, unquenchable hunger that has little to do with drinking blood—a hunger that doesn't only require feeding. From the hours you've spent by her bedside, there was a very good chance you would have discovered that on your own."

Remy tried not to gulp. "Is that why you haven't been by her bedside longer than required?"

"Yes. The last time it happened, we took from morning until nightfall the next day to pacify her urges." Malekh's smile this time was like one who'd just paid for the choicest meat at the butcher's at an immeasurably low price. "If you thought she was insatiable before, Pendergast . . ."

He let that linger, enjoying watching Remy squirm before taking pity on him, his gaze falling back to his glass vials. "My time here was not wasted. I've had time to think about my previous accusations and realize that I have been unfair to you. I am not always familiar with Alurian politics, and I suspect someone has been using you and your blood as a pawn in their schemes. The attempt on your father's life tells me that you are just as much a victim in this as anyone. Astonbury could likely be the culprit; the Reapers could have used the blood they drew from you in their experiments. I want to apologize. To find a way to make up for my error. I . . . do not trust others easily. It is a fault of mine, rather than yours."

Remy was stunned. "You're apologizing? To me? Have I too fallen asleep beside Xiaodan's bedside?"

"Is it hard to imagine that I would express sincere regret after coming to the wrong conclusions?"

"No, it's that I'm so used to you being so confoundingly right that I started second-guessing myself, even knowing I was innocent."

Remy hadn't been expecting his own confession to serve as an aphrodisiac, but the vampire's eyes widened, then narrowed with more newfound lust. "W—wait," he stuttered, as the man slowly rose from his seat. "Wh—what I meant was that you're so goddamn hard to read. You always look at me like you don't know if you want to fight me or—"

"Or?" Malekh prompted. His hand came up, and his thumb grazed Remy's chin, pressing against his lower mouth. "Or what, Pendergast?"

Remy licked his lips, aware that Malekh's eyes were following the movement. "Don't know if you want to fight me," he said, nearly a whisper, "or fuck me."

"It's both, Pendergast." The noble's free hand was fisted on the table, elbow lowered and body tense like he was about to leap for him, and Remy was already bracing himself for the impact they would make before he'd thought it through. "It's always been both."

It was his chance to ask about Vasilik's dying words, now that Malekh was in a livelier mood. Likely Remy'd get yelled at again, for taking a liar's words at their value. If Malekh had his way, he was going to get yelled at anyway for breaking the breakables. Remy wet his lips again. "There's something I—"

"Lord Zidan!" The knock sounded at the door, Liufei's voice both joyous and apprehensive. "She's finally up, milord! Ah— we've taken the usual precautions, but I think it would be very helpful if you come up to see her immediately. She's asking for you. Uh—and you, Armiger Remington."

"Looks like your wish is about to be granted," Malekh said, the hunger in his eyes dimming not one whit. "Perhaps we'll both be enough to tame her this time."

XIAODAN WAS alone, already sitting up in bed when they entered. She'd unbuttoned the front of her dressing gown, though she hadn't taken it off completely. Her cheeks were flushed red, her eyes glowing bright. "It's about time," she said with a low purr. One of her hands had disappeared underneath her covers, and she was writhing slightly. She paused briefly when she saw Malekh.

"You haven't been eating," she accused, though she resumed her slow, lazy undulating, and Remy felt himself harden, knowing full well what she was doing. "You're going to be very exhausted by the time we're done, my love."

"I have help this time around," Malekh said, with a slow, sensual smile of his own, as he tugged his collar loose, hands running down his buttons to undo them. "He's plumped with blood from the meals Lady Whittaker has been making, and should be more than adequate for us both. Enough not to tire him unreasonably."

"How did you know about the—" Hell. Elke and her cooking. Her sly admission that she was doing it as a favor. "You planned this?"

"Are you fine with that, Remy?" Xiaodan whispered, visibly struggling to keep herself in check. "We won't do anything that you're uncomfortable with. Zidan gets a little carried away, and he's accustomed to me falling in with his plans, so he might not always make concessions with you in mind—"

"For once, you and your affianced are injured and I'm the one healthy," Remy said, no longer bothering to hide the happiness and desire he was sure was radiating off him. This wasn't just a tryst, or a bartering, or an affair. With them, with this, he would always be given a choice. "I suppose it's my duty to provide you with some"—he tapped at the side of his throat for emphasis—"wine this time, so you don't only have to rely on each other while you're both weak."

"Duty?" Malekh said, accepting the challenge. "You consider this a duty?"

"How else should I bloody well consider it? I'm the reason you had to kill Vasilik. Xiaodan risked her life to exterminate the colossus. I owe you. Do with me as you'd like. I'll lie back and think of Aluria. Heard that helps get through most objectionable of encounters."

There was silence from both of his lovers before Xiaodan let out a giggle. She moved toward him with a litheness not in keeping with one who'd only just risen from a two-day coma, shrugging out of the rest of her dress en route. She grabbed at Remy's collar and tugged him onto the bed, Malekh joining them seconds later.

"You're jesting with us," she groaned into his ear, as her hands reached down for him, "but what you'll find out soon enough, my Remy, is that in matters of play, we never do."

XIAODAN'S HANDS on his hips. Soft. Caressing.

Malekh's laid over hers on him. Firm. Insistent.

Both keeping him in place between them, where he belonged.

"Look at him. Oh, Zidan, look at how exquisitely he takes us both."

Caught in the throes of them, Remy could not have said, in that moment, what the hell Aluria even was.

31

GRIMESWORTHY

"For the last time, Elke, it's not a horse," Remy grunted, staring balefully up at the helhest who, despite the hunter's usually abominable behavior toward it and its brother, always responded with a happy flip of its tail in his direction, followed by cheerful neighing. It wasn't that Remy disliked Peanut or Chocolate or whatever name this hell stallion in front of him answered to. It was just that his body was very sore at the moment, and he hadn't even climbed atop the steed for the painful ride ahead.

"And to think I was actually worried about you," Elke said, her grin unabashedly lewd.

"I would like for you to stop talking, Elke."

"Give me the details." She stared appreciatively at Remy's neck. The wound he'd sustained at Zelenka had healed well enough that there was no scarring at all, but what Elke was looking at were the faint, red love bites dotting his collarbone. Both vampires had forgotten his previous plea to bite lower, where the marks wouldn't show. *He'd* forgotten, for that matter.

"How far down do those go?"

"Elke."

"Do you really want to return? Seems like you're enjoying yourself so nicely here. And with the head of not just the Fourth Court but also the Third? If only I had such conquests."

So her attempted seduction of Alegra hadn't worked. If anyone would have been successful, it would have been Elke, but Alegra was, unsurprisingly, Alegra. "Why are you so worried about me heading back to Elouve? The people's dislike of me isn't anything new."

"Why are you so eager to return?" Elke frowned. "I know you're concerned about your father, Remy, but . . ." She grimaced. "I know I have nothing substantial to go on. But it's not normal for me to not know what's going on in Elouve, and I'm worried."

"The answers we need regarding the Rot are calling me back to Aluria, so that's where I need to be. Someone's trying to frame me, and it's someone within the Alurian court still loyal to Astonbury's schemes. I'm betting on Aglaice—Feiron's too incompetent to manage this without getting caught. And if there's another army about to mobilize and attack Elouve, then we need to warn the queen." Remy paused. "You're certain Father's doing well?"

He still had so many questions. Why his father had been attacked. How much Astonbury had been involved with creating the Rot. How many Reapers were compromised in this—he wondered if Riones had any suspicions. And then Vasilik's admission that Malekh had killed his mother. He'd been too exhausted to ask about it the night before, and it was too late now, when they were on the cusp of leaving. Perhaps in Elouve, once he was brought back up to speed on everything else.

"As I said, his manservant was able to raise the alarm before any harm was done. At least they can't accuse you of that, though Feiron's still all het up on thinking it's you. It's not your description this time—just someone in a hood and cloak. But both crimes must be connected somehow."

"No carriage this time," Xiaodan said with a grin, popping up from behind them. "We should be entering Elouve a little before dusk today. I feel more than well enough to travel without."

"There are two horses and four of us," Remy pointed out warily. "I'm not used to riding with anyone. And the last time I was on one of these beasts, I nearly threw up."

"You wanted speed, didn't you? I don't think you want to wait another three days with the carriage, and I'm not sure you'll appreciate Zidan carrying you all the way to Aluria."

Remy shook his head defiantly at the thought. "You're right."

"Fortunately, there are more than two helhests in our stable." Much to his horror, Zidan had arrived with two other great beasts in tow, just as black and as bestial-looking as the first.

"How many undead horses have you two actually rescued?"

"A whole barn of them, if you must know."

"Bloody hell."

"Did you really take Remy's maidenhead, milord?" Elke asked impishly. "He's been sore all morning."

"Elke!"

"I'm not comfortable with discussing such intimate matters with acquaintances," Lord Malekh said, to Remy's relief, but then murdered his hopes with, "but as you are good friends with him and considerate of his health—it was Xiaodan who did the honors, some weeks ago."

"I hate you all," Remy muttered, giving up and climbing on his helhest.

THE RIDE back to Elouve was a mere ten hours. Remy's bones rattled in his frame for most of the way back, his grip on Peanut's mane so strong that Elke had to pry his arms off the horse's neck every time they stopped for a rest to keep his sanity. To his credit, Remy had stopped screaming after only the first hour.

By the time they brought their mounts to the helpful farmstead near the city limits and approached Elouve's gates, night had fallen, the city burning as brightly as it always had. Elke took her leave before they departed from the stables. Remy had expected as much; to keep her identity hidden, she could not be seen with the rest of them.

And a good thing it was, because there were Reapers waiting just outside the Elouvian gates, grim-faced as usual, but with weapons at hand. Very few of the hunters had ever been his friends, but even so, this seemed excessive.

At their head was the Marquess of Riones, still as apologetic as the last time Remy had seen him. With him was Dorst Aglaice, smug as always. "Pendergast," the lickfinger said. "We expected your arrival days ago."

"And you arranged a welcome party on my behalf. I'm flattered."

"Quite the opposite. We're here to take you in for questioning."

Remy heard Xiaodan let out a muffled gasp and could sense the tension radiating off Malekh, who was ready to do violence. He held up his hand to stop them. "If they need to take me in," he said, "then they'll have to take me in."

There were sounds of surprise, from the hunters this time, when Xiaodan took off her hood, ignoring Remy. "I am Lady Song," she said. "And I demand to speak to the queen before you arrest anyone."

"I'm sorry, milady," Riones said unhappily. "But there's discontent in Elouve right now, and I can't allow you or Lord Malekh to enter the city, much less see Her Majesty. It's for your own protection as well as the citizens', as your presence may likely incite a riot."

Remy accepted the inevitable. "I'll find you both again after this is done."

"They have no reason to arrest you," Xiaodan protested.

"I think they do." Riones was his only ally amid the Reaper crowd, so Remy addressed him instead of Aglaice. "Was it because Feiron had been accusing me again of murdering Astonbury while I was away?"

Riones coughed. "That investigation is still ongoing. But Dr. Panlai has continued Dr. Agenot's experiments regarding the Rot, sans anymore corpses. Previous samples taken from the infected contain traces of blood that she has since verified as belonging to you."

"So they discovered that, too," Remy heard Malekh mutter.

"I didn't kill or infect anyone, and I decidedly would not be fool enough to put any of my own blood where it could be traced back to me, if I'd even had such inclinations," Remy said. "We have more problems to worry about, Anthony. There may be an army approaching Elouve soon, and we need Astonbury's successor to confirm—"

"An army of what, Pendergast?" Judaea Hathorn, one of Astonbury's cronies, jeered at him. "Of infected vampires that carry your blood within them, under your control?"

"Hathorn!" Riones barked.

"But it's true, isn't it? That's what they've been whispering about in the villages to the east. The cambion burned down Brushfen and tried to do the same at Zelenka."

"That's not true," Xiaodan spat out. "We were all there. We were too late for Brushfen, but we fought off the attack at Zelenka and killed the vampire responsible. Or are you calling me a liar, Hunter?"

"What I'm calling you, you wretched undead bitch, is a suncursed whore—"

Remy supposed that Malekh had moved, even if he hadn't seen

him do so. The noble had plucked Hathorn out from among the hunters and was immediately by Remy's side with his saber already poised between the hostile Reaper's eyes, his other hand a claw against the man's throat.

There were the sounds of several fire lances charging up in unison.

"Zidan," Xiaodan said, "let him go."

At the same time Riones said, "At ease, all of you. They're not here to fight, and neither are we."

Without changing expression, Malekh divested Hathorn of his own lance, then tossed him at the ground between them and the other hunters. The man came up spitting dirt, enraged. "Are you going to let them do this, Aglaice?" he snarled.

The man hesitated, eyes flicking nervously back at the vampire couple. Aglaice had not bootlicked his way up the ranks without understanding how badly it would go for him to offend two powerful vampire clans, even if they were unwelcome in Aluria at the moment.

Riones took the initiative. "This was your own fault, Hathorn. I would have boxed you along the ears myself if Lord Malekh here hadn't responded first." He turned to the other Reapers. "Are there more insights any of you would like to share with the lord and his lady? Anyone else volunteering for a drubbing?"

No one responded, a few glancing uneasily at Malekh.

The marquess rubbed at the back of his neck. "The ability to trace blood to any specific person was a recent medical breakthrough, or so Dr. Panlai tells me. Logically, neither you nor anyone else would have realized that such a thing would have been possible to begin with, enough to have covered it up beforehand." He sighed. "I am sorry, Remy, but he is correct. The orders come from Her Majesty herself. It was the queen who asked me to take charge of these proceedings, and I promised her I would find a way to convince you without needing to bring in the other Reapers.

Unfortunately, Lord Aglaice here thought differently. No bindings or ropes if you come with us without any more protest."

"Will you tell the queen about the army, Anthony?"

"I swear I will, Remy. Once we have this sorted out, she'll want to hear more."

Remy nodded. He should have known. Elke had warned him, but he'd always been stubborn to a fault.

"Lead the way," he said, "and I'll come quietly."

HE'D BEEN released from the gaols at Xiaodan's insistence a mere few weeks ago, had fought vampires all over Aluria and beyond since then, had traveled to a vampire stronghold and back, only to be stuck in the same cell all over again, the bars Xiaodan had destroyed already replaced.

At least there were more considerations for him this time around—a tray of actually edible food brought out at mealtimes, frequently changed chamber pots to piss in, a pail of clean water for other basic toiletries. The Three of the Light still beamed happily across the room at him. But Remy disliked the waiting, not sure what fresh intrigues were brewing on the other side of his cell door. Xiaodan, Malekh, and Elke didn't—or couldn't—visit. Things appeared far more serious than Riones had suggested.

There was a lock on the cell door this time. At least they'd been making improvements while he was away.

Finally, the door opened, and the marquess himself stepped in.

With him was his father's valet, Grimesworthy—not the savior he'd been anticipating.

"What the hell is he doing here?" Remy growled.

"You're being released on your father's recognizance," Riones said, "and gladly. I'd prefer you at Loxley House rather than here.

You may not be on good terms with your father, but at least you'll have better food and a bed to sleep in."

"Surely you know I'm being framed for this."

"Likely so, but a lot of the other brainless fools at the council have other thoughts on the matter, and I cannot let my own biases rule in this. My duty is to ensure you're well protected until they see reason. It's all been bad business since you left, Remy. Could be some of Astonbury's associates still wanting their revenge, could be someone else. Your father's gone out and hired private soldiers of his own, in case there's another attempt on his life, so your safety is guaranteed with him. But you're not to leave Elouve till we figure out what's what. It's either Loxley House or Kinaiya Lodge for you—Lady Song's with Queen Ophelia right now, and she's no doubt pleading on your behalf, since the queen has already agreed to those concessions. They've been mum about the meeting, of course. Don't want the queen compromised."

"Thank you," Remy said, meaning it. "I know I'm not a favorite in the dræfendgemot, Anthony, but I appreciate you doing your best looking out for me."

"No thanks necessary—it's the principle of the thing. Partly my fault, anyway."

"What do you mean?"

"I was in charge of the Astonbury case. I was the one to insist that every speck of blood found in his study be tested. That's how we found samples that matched yours. Not that I actually think you did it, Pendergast, but—"

"You were only doing your job. You'll find the proof that exonerates me as well."

"Any inkling as to how your blood's even there to begin with?"

"Riones, how much blood do the doctors at the Reaper training hall draw from you in your physical assessments?"

"Not much. Perhaps a vial's worth. Why?"

"They were taking enough blood from me to fill at least fifty.

Vampires have pulled less out of me. They told me it was a new standard measure, but . . ."

Riones nodded, troubled. "And you think Astonbury's minions might have planted your blood at both the crime scene and in those mutations?"

"Not so much planted as continued to use my blood to create the Rot, if Astonbury's the one responsible for all this."

"I agree; this sounds extremely suspicious. Let me run up to the hall and get the truth from them after I send you off." The smile the other Reaper shot his way remained tense, worried. "Just a warning before you go—things have changed in the short bit you'd been away, so don't take a lot of what they say to heart, yeah? Once this gets resolved, I'm sure they'll put it out of their heads."

Remy didn't quite understand what Riones meant by that until they'd emerged from the building to find a crowd waiting for him outside.

"There he is!" he heard someone shout, and then he was confronted by a sea of faces yelling absurdities at him, followed by a foul stench when the mob began pelting refuse and rotten vegetables their way.

"Vile abomination!" Another preacher was on hand, eyes burning with triumph as he pointed at him. "The reckoning is coming! Only when you are hanged by the noose and purified by fire will this foul curse lift from us all!"

Riones strode angrily toward the priest, threatening him with arrest as more constables crowded around Remy, keeping him away from the crowd long enough to guide him into a waiting carriage. Dazed by the unexpected deluge, Remy didn't process what had happened until he was within the safety of the hansom.

Outside his window, a boy selling tabloids had taken advantage of the crowd to call attention to the *Wayward Post* headlines he was gleefully waving about.

VALENBONNE'S SON ROT-TEN TO THE CORE! it read, PENDER-GAST BLOOD SOURCE OF INFECTION!

And then Riones slapped at the sides of the carriage, yelling out more orders, and it took off immediately, carrying Remy away from the enraged mob.

"WHAT DOES Father want with me now?" Remy asked after a few minutes. "Not like him to bail me out of trouble."

His companion didn't respond.

"Don't know where Elke is, by any chance? Father's been keeping an eye on her, hasn't he?"

Still more silence. Remy stared out the window.

He'd seen a few more newspapers along the way, several more headline variations regarding his blood and its connection to the infected. Someone had even gone all the way to Zelenka to report on the battle that had taken place there. The headline caught his eye as they had rolled past a corner. SURVIVOR'S ACCOUNT! it proclaimed. ZELENKA MASSACRE! VALENBONNE'S SON, AIDED BY VAMPIRES?

Fair, honest reporting would have cleared his name, but in Elouve that was too much to ask for.

Loxley House was surrounded by soldiers, and the intimidation worked. There were no mobs in sight when the carriage wheeled past the gates and into the large compound. Stone-faced soldiers lined every path, saluting Remy on his way to the front door.

His father waited for him in the drawing room rather than at his chambers. There was a pleased smile on Edgar Pendergast's face. Given everything that had happened, Remy found it disconcerting.

"Finally back in one piece, aren't you?" He chuckled as Grimesworthy closed the door behind them. He looked much better than at their last meeting, with a touch more color to his face and in a far better mood. "I thought word of the attack would finally reach you. Was it that young redheaded girl who told you?"

"Why is my blood inside these infected, Father?" Remy asked bluntly.

"What, no concern about the attempt on your father's life?" The elder Pendergast was still smiling. It was not a good sign. "It was fortunate that Grimesworthy was there to head the killer off—and a very good idea I have of who it is, too. I shall make my formal report to the queen—"

"Why the hell is my blood inside those mutations, Father?" Remy was at the end of his patience. The arrest, the gaols, the people who now so openly detested him; but the worst, the *worst* of them all, sat right in front of him. He'd told Riones his suspicions of Astonbury to point the Reaper down a different path, because he knew—he *knew*. "You may not be able to move about as you once did, but don't throw that bullshit on me. You know far more about things that happen in Aluria than even the queen herself. I know you have something to do with this."

"And what gave me away, Son?" His father didn't even bother defending himself or even feigning innocence. Instead, he watched Remy like an instructor gauging a student's aptitude for an upcoming exam.

"I had my suspicions as soon as I learned what those samples contained. My first thought was that someone in the Archives had stolen what blood they'd kept of mine there. It wasn't until later that I remembered you. Your illnesses required blood transfusions of a similar type. I've given enough to you over the years that you could have used it for other means instead."

There was a long silence. His father's expression was unreadable. No longer wanting to back down, to accede to his father's whims, Remy stared stonily back.

And then the Duke of Valenbonne burst into laughter—a stronger, heartier burst then the wheezes and gasps he could manage in the past. "Innovation is a two-edged sword, isn't it? The things you can do with science, and the things you never expected science could do to disrupt your plans. Grimesworthy."

The man had already brought out his father's wheelchair, transferred the old man to it. "Where are we going?" Remy demanded, as the manservant began to wheel the elder Pendergast down the hallway.

"All in good time, my boy." They were entering the man's library, one of the few places Remy was barred from entering. Grimesworthy produced a small silver key from his pocket and, with great effort, pushed against one of the bookshelves against the wall. It slid back to reveal a small keyhole, a barely perceptible one at first glance. The valet fumbled with the key, pushed it in, and twisted. There was a click.

A portion of wall slid back.

"Bloody hell."

"Why did you think I was fine with you taking up residence at your Kinaiya Lodge? And you were only too eager to jump at the chance."

A long ramp led downward in lieu of stairs. Grimesworthy guided the old man down the incline, and Remy followed, at a loss to say anything else.

A door sat at the bottom; behind it, a laboratory. Inside, Dr. Yost coughed loudly and grinned at Remy, rubbing at his overly large spectacles with a handkerchief. "Oh, is it about time we let the young man know about our experiments, Your Grace?"

"Can't be helped now. The pressure is on him, and it's to his benefit and ours that he understands what we're doing. I'd have been more remiss about letting him in on it, but he figured out some of it on his own." There was a faint note of pride in his father's voice; rare enough in itself, rarer still to be directed his way. "Come, Remington. Let us see what fresh discoveries lie in wait."

The room had been set up to resemble the laboratory in the Archives, though there was far larger machinery occupying space here. A small room beyond served as a morgue. Two walls were lined with long shelves displaying hundreds of containers of varying sizes, all filled with blood and clamped into place to prevent dislodgement.

"Nearly every vampire I've ever slain," the duke chortled, anticipating his question. "Managed to bleed most of the lot before I reduced them to ashes. It's been very useful. My laboratory is better funded than even Astonbury's. The fool had to balance his budget with other requirements demanded by the Crown. I have no such restrictions, and more money to spend."

"What is all this, Father?"

"Science, Remington. A golden age of science that we shall usher into Aluria."

"You're just in time, Your Grace," Dr. Yost said. "I've just gotten my hands on another very lovely test subject for me to work on." He led them toward one of the gurneys, where a heavy piece of cloth had been draped over an unmoving figure lying on top of it. He took off the sheet with a flourish, and Remy saw a dead man, fairly young, naked. There was a peculiar tattoo on his left chest—a familiar one.

"This is one of the vampires at the Dà Lán," he said. "One of the ones who tried to attack Chànggē Shuǐ."

"A sound specimen, too," Yost enthused. "And still a youngblood, perhaps only two years turned, only taken in yesterday. Perfect for what I had planned."

Remy turned to his father, wracked with rage. Malekh had killed Vasilik only a few days ago, yet one of Vasilik's boys was here, a thousand miles away. "Which vampire are you in league with? Who was the spy you sent to watch over me?"

"Why so surprised?" The duke was unnervingly calm. "It is

normal for a father to look out for his son, especially when the latter frequently involves himself in dangerous situations that, I may add, he himself endeavored to take regardless of any opposition I would have made."

"There is nothing normal about any of this!" Remy shouted. "Who was your spy, Father?"

"You don't have to be so loud," another voice spoke up from a dark corner of the room. "You humans must look out for your blood pressure. It is a small wonder why many of you die so easily."

A vampire stepped out from the shadows, grinning.

Remy whipped out his Breaker. "*You.*"

"You should have taken me up on my advice." The youth chuckled—the vampire messenger who'd brought him to the caves. "You're far more devoted to your vampire friends than I thought. Did you sleep with them? I know that Zidan Malekh has quite the reputation—but then again, so do you."

Remy advanced, but the vampire shifted out of view, reappearing on the other side of the room. "Still the same temper," he said chidingly. "I did try to help, you know."

"We wiped out Vasilik's coven," Remy said.

"Did you see me fall at the Qing-ye palace? Even without the infected, Vasilik had a substantial number of followers that he'd turned. Fortunately, I was not one of them, merely a hanger-on he'd accepted into his coven." The vampire shrugged. "Did you really think you'd gotten us all?"

"You're a traitor."

"Is it really a betrayal if I'm siding with your father, Lord Remington? I acted in his best interests at the Dà Lán, and in yours, however you might feel about it. You may not have survived the caves if you'd stumbled onto the other traps Vasilik had laid out there. And I did my best to point your beautiful redheaded friend in the direction of Chàngge Shuǐ so she could spirit you out of trouble faster." The man bowed low to the Duke of Valenbonne. "The body, as promised. Have I performed to your satisfaction, Your Grace?"

"Barely," Remy's father said. "You should have found a way to get him back to Aluria quicker."

"It's difficult enough for you, his flesh and blood, to force him into doing your will. I am but a simple youngblood, off to make his own way in this new world."

"What has my father promised you?" Remy demanded.

"Nothing beyond coins, young Armiger. The rest is of my own choosing. I am tired of the court machinations that plague my kindred, and your father wishes to see them all destroyed. It would please me greatly to see them wiped out, for us to start anew. Very satisfying to see Vasilik defeated—may the rest share his fate. Your father did give me a lovely gift for my assistance." From within the depths of his cloak, the vampire messenger produced a zweihänder. "I think it suits me very much."

Astonbury's weapon. The heavy sword that had gone missing from the Archives' armory. The weapon the man had been slain with.

"If you will pardon me," the vampire said, bowing, and was gone.

"Arrogant little brat," the old man huffed.

"You were working with Vasilik," Remy said weakly. It explained why the vampire had offered to join forces. He'd hinted that they had a mutual benefactor, that they shared the Night Empress as a common enemy. He'd been angry to find Remy still in Chànggē Shuǐ when his coven attacked. Remy's father had wanted him gone from the palace by then.

"A necessary evil. I had the ability to give him the army he craved, and he kept Her Majesty and her Reapers busy long enough for Dr. Yost to perfect his formula. You were never in any real danger from the Rot, Remington. Your blood called to them. They would never have harmed you."

"Not all of those monsters thought that," Remy said grimly.

"Ah, the colossus Vasilik wielded? And those young children . . . I draw the line at using those so young for experimentation, but it appeared he had no such qualms, used his own blood, and went against my instructions. I knew he would eventually turn on me. I had every faith that Zidan Malekh would exterminate him."

"You gave him his army. You allied yourself with the offshoots of the Fifth Court."

"I merely gave Vasilik a limited supply of Yost's serum and acceded to adding his blood to it in place of yours as a sign of my good faith. Good for a colossus and a few dozen mutations, all of which he wasted. He always did resent that I was the real power in our alliance, not him. His was a flimsy control, at best. For one who's lived for ages, Vasilik was weak. Pathetic." His father turned back to the gurney. "Show my son what you've done, Doctor."

"Nothing you haven't seen before—an improvement, really." Yost carefully extracted blood from the dead vampire with a syringe and deposited a few drops of it into a large beaker that sat at his worktable.

"This wonderful little elixir," the doctor explained, "is what I'd call the fountain of youth. A wonderful serum, carefully sequenced so its healing properties benefit only the person whose blood it has been synthesized with. Your father's blood is slightly too weak to be used for such experiments, but you, Lord Pendergast, made the perfect donor for my initial studies. Why do you think that my bloodwakers have been so effective on you, even moreso than what the Reapers use? The more ancient the blood, the better, of course, but those have been quite hard to come by. The younger ones work well enough for now."

"Why use *my* blood?" Remy asked. "Why cause such an infection?"

"You don't understand, my boy," his father said calmly, like he wasn't responsible for hundreds of deaths and a kingdom-wide panic. "Neither the doctor nor I caused this infection to spread all over Aluria. That fool Astonbury did. He knew I was up to something, the old cockwhafe. Not even the poor sods he calls geniuses at the Archives could replicate Yost's brilliance."

"Worked for the Archives once, I did," Yost said. "Wanted to do more than the little fripperies Her Majesty wanted. It was I who invented the sângelui, you see. I created a magnificent splicing apparatus that would break blood down into its most basic structures for faster results. My life's work was within those walls.

"But Her Majesty only wanted safety for her Reapers. She had not liked the necessary additives I added into the wakers, what with Parnon going insane from overimbibing. But safety doesn't cut it in medicine, milord. If Her Majesty wasn't to risk her Reapers' lives with my medicines, I said, best to just take some random fellow off the streets and fiddle with them for a bit. She wouldn't have any of that, either, Queen Ophelia. Turned me out with nothing but the clothes on my back, not even severance pay. Astonbury took credit for my bloodwakers—serves him right, dying like that."

"No. She was right," Remy said. "You can't just kidnap innocent people and subject them to your mad experiments."

"They were scum," his father said dismissively. "Thieves, smugglers, criminals. I was doing the kingdom a favor."

"You unleashed a horde of infected corpses onto Aluria!"

"As I said, my dear boy, *Astonbury* did. He stole one of my corpses while I was transferring it to an isolated site outside the city. The body reanimated, killed his guards, and escaped. Naturally, I covered it up. Matthew knew he would be blamed, should the truth come out—I have more than ample proof and was willing to bring him down with me—and so did the same thing."

Two old men who hated each other, forced into a shared secret for fear of either being exposed. Remy would have laughed at the irony in some other lifetime. "Did you kill him?"

"Do I look like I am physically capable of such an act? Of course not, Remington." The duke leaned back against his wheelchair, a pleasant smile on his face. "I merely sat back and watched."

Yost extracted another syringeful of the serum and approached Remy's father. Grimesworthy, who had been so quiet that Remy had nearly forgotten he was there, returned to his master from the corner he'd been lurking in and was already rolling up the old man's sleeve.

"Matthew Delacroix was always a coward," the elder Pendergast said. "His ineptitude stopped him from killing the infections he released, and he was desperate. He asked me to come to his study in secret and threatened to confess all to the queen. I had to take steps to ensure his silence."

"Your vampire servant killed him off, then?"

His father only smiled.

"And you left my blood at the crime scene, to implicate me."

"I did nothing of the sort. It was an accident. I didn't know then that the science could be advanced to identify blood with such accuracy. Neither did Astonbury's sycophants. They tried to murder me, to pretend that Astonbury's murderer was also my killer. Their would-be assassin is dead, properly disposed of, though I claimed he escaped."

"You can't do this, Father," Remy whispered. "You can't just commit murder and think you can get away with it."

"Oh? And who'll tell on me, boy? You? Might I remind you that *you* are a suspect, that the ire of the city is against *you*. Only I can provide the protection you need. Take that away, and you will be stripped of your status and gaoled like a commoner. I wouldn't be surprised if they consigned you to the gallows."

"Innocents have *died* because of you!"

"Are you still bemoaning Tennyfair's pretty daughter? I thought you'd have gotten over it by now, given your closeness with the Lady Song." Remy's father allowed himself a slow, predatory smile as Yost swabbed at his wrinkled skin with a piece of clean cotton. "Did Vasilik ever tell you that it was Zidan Malekh who killed your mother?"

"That's a lie," Remy whispered hoarsely.

"Are you so besotted with the man that you would turn against Ligaya now?" The needle, long and thin, plunged into his arm, but his father didn't even blink, still watching Remy. "He admitted as much early in his alliance with Aluria, and independent research I have made since has supported his claim. I wondered if you would find out in the course of your travels with them, if you might behead Zidan yourself.

"You forget that you owe me, boy. It was *you* who put me into this chair. It was you who ended my career, my influence. My reputation suffered because you couldn't handle Breaker. The one thing I've asked of you is to find your mother's killers and end their miserable undead lives. Your blood is the least you could have given me. Will you stand there and tell me that you will hand your poor father over to the authorities, Remington? You would betray your only kin, the one you crippled and humiliated, before all of Aluria?"

"You need to confess, Father."

"You have guts, Remington, to say such a thing to my face. I will say that much. But does it ease your conscience to know that my arrest will trigger a fresh wave of infections within the city? That I have installed a private army at Loxley grounds to protect myself from more than just the living?"

Remy stared helplessly back at him. "You wouldn't," he whispered. "You wouldn't fucking dare."

"Oh, but I would, my boy. I will take this accursed, ungrateful city down with me if I must, to protect Aluria. Say one word of this to your vampire lovers, and there may be no Elouve to ally with. Never doubt me on that."

There was a long silence before Yost took the needle away.

"I thought so," his father said, satisfied. "You wouldn't want any current anti-vampire sentiments to spill over into fresh violence now, would you? Think of all the lives that would affect. Your lovely redheaded friend, the Lady Whittaker, would not look so pretty tied to a stake, burning into the wind."

He knew about Elke. Remy's fear rose. "If you harm her, I swear—"

"I will do nothing. The Reapers and an Alurian mob would not be so kind, however. But even then, it should not matter, Remy. See what power we could have, with our own army of the undead? We can protect the city. We can protect the kingdom. They shall never mock the Valenbonne name again."

"No one should have this kind of power."

"But why not? Are you afraid of other colossi running amuck? Already Yost is improving on his antivenin. We shall fully control the Rot before long, boy. Vasilik's colossus was simply a weaker, watered-down version of the original."

"The original?"

"But who else? I have very little blood to spare, but what there is of it has been put into a masterpiece. A loyal servant of my own. Come forward, Grimesworthy."

The manservant lumbered forward.

Remy froze.

"A shining specimen. Absolute obedience. Absolute deference. Could Vasilik boast this of his infected? An offspring of the Rot who follows me without question, a pure weapon disguised as the perfect valet? A mutation so thoroughly controlled that it could pass for human? Look closely, Son. Would they even believe you?"

Grimesworthy turned to Remy, and he saw the blank face, the

wooden expression that Vasilik's colossus had worn too, and now he realized why it had looked so familiar.

"It is time for the Pendergasts to rise again and take back what we have lost." The Duke of Valenbonne clasped his hands on either side of his chair and slowly pulled himself up. Remy watched, open-mouthed, as his father, an invalid for most of Remy's life, stood on uncertain feet. The old man took a step forward, and then another, his gait surer with every movement.

"See, Remington?" the duke said. "Behold the miracle your blood has given me."

32

FALL APART

"You are an absolute wretch, my Remy."

It took awhile for Remy to see through the haze clouding his eyes and deduce that there was someone else in the room, and that they were speaking to him. He groaned, tried to walk, and discovered he was unable to on account of having planted himself face-first into the chaise he was sprawled on. That explained the darkness.

He'd forgotten that he had arms, so he groaned again and rolled over instead, landing with an ungraceful thump on the floor. He was in a room that looked slightly familiar. The fog was making everything indistinct, like he'd been underwater and couldn't see which way was up. "Ah," he told the ceiling, then realized he didn't know how many tiles were up there, and was faintly pleased that he wasn't in Giselle's bedchamber.

A new face swam into view above his. Straight black hair in harsh fringes around a soft face, lovely bow-red lips, penetrating gray eyes. Of course Remy knew who it was. "Miss Grissell," he said. "How am I down here and you all the way up there?"

"Remy," Miss Grissell said, not sounding at all like his old nanny. "You're very drunk."

"I am not drunk," Remy said, quite drunkenly. "I just haven't decided to be sober yet. It is too late at night for anyone to be this sober."

"It's six in the morning, you lout. I didn't come all the way here and risk getting seen by your lovely Alurian mobs just to find you sloshed and giving up."

Remy stood. Or rather, someone hauled him back to his feet without needing any assistance on his end. Light, but Miss Grissell was strong for someone he just remembered had been dead for over a decade.

He stood for a moment, swaying slightly, and then was lifted up again and thrown over a shoulder, the rest of the room tilting on its axis as he was marched out of it and into another. He heard the sounds of splashing water, and his whole world was promptly upended as he was somersaulted.

His face hit cold liquid. He gagged briefly as a good lungful of it shot up his nose, and then he was dragged back up so he could noisily gulp down more air. Xiaodan stared at him only inches away, with annoyed, though nonetheless worried eyes. "Was that enough," she asked, "or shall we get another good dunking in? I am unfamiliar with human resuscitation, but I was told in the past that this is the best way to sober drunkards up."

"Are you trying to get me into bed again because no one else will?" Remy slurred, and promptly had his head shoved back under.

"All right," he gargled as he came up a second time. "I'm fucking thinking again. Stop trying to drown me, Lightdamnit," and then promptly threw up.

To her credit, Xiaodan didn't turn a hair, simply helped hold him as he emptied whatever it was he'd drunk the night before into an empty washbasin. Remy dunked his whole head back into the tub after that, willingly this time, and felt a little more human when he raised it up again for the third time.

"Why are you here?" he asked weakly. "They're threatening to hang every vampire they find in Elouve."

"I have my ways of avoiding detection. As far as the humans are concerned, Zidan and I have successfully been chased away. I thought you were at Loxley House. Why would you come all the way here, alone?"

"Put on a suitable enough disguise. Done it a few times before. Had to get away from my father's supervision for a bit. Rather brave the tar-and-feather crowd than another hour with him." He was trying to go back and deduce the progression of thoughts that had brought him from his father's detestable manor to here, though his tongue was threatening to detach from his mouth at a moment's notice. "I got out and saw everything they've been saying. Everything. Getting wasted felt like the better idea at the time. Got any drinking water, by chance?"

Xiaodan manhandled him out of the washroom and settled him in an armchair that didn't smell too strongly of whiskey, because everything else seemed to. Judging from the overturned bottles on the floor, he supposed that it was the only thing that wasn't drenched in it.

"I'm dragging you back into your chambers and will attempt to find you a decent beverage," Xiaodan said sternly, having reached the same conclusion. "I will not clean this mess up like I did the last time. That is your problem to handle, once you are no longer—I believe the Alurian term for it is *soused*?"

She was true to her word; she found water for him to drink, then had him up into his room in almost no time at all, a steaming mug of what smelled like strong coffee by his elbow. She tugged back the curtains to let the dim light in, and even that made him wince. "Now that that's done," she said, sitting cross-legged on his bed beside him, "tell me again why you decided to go and drink yourself into insensibility."

Remy stared at the smoke rising out from his cup. He couldn't tell her. She would encourage him to tell the queen, or perhaps tell Her Majesty herself, and then everything would go to shit.

She might only tell Malekh. Remy wanted to trust the noble, but his father's words kept echoing in his mind over and over again.

Edgar Pendergast never bluffed. Not like this. He had much more intel than he had let on, if he had already known about Elke. He might even have spies in Queen Ophelia's court. If the Duke of Valenbonne could unleash hell at anyone learning of his involvement with the Rot, hobbling off on his bad leg to throw open the gates of damnation himself, Remy couldn't chance that yet.

No. Not a bad leg, not anymore. He'd used the knowledge he'd gleaned from the Rot to heal himself. Fuck.

He knew now why his father had been so nonchalant when Remy had informed him of his decision to travel with the two Court vampires. It was enough for him to want to drink himself insensible all over again.

"Do you know if Elke's all right?"

Xiaodan eyed him curiously. "To my knowledge, yes. It doesn't appear that she was discovered reentering the city. She's worried about you. The Marquess of Riones was kind enough to tell us what's been happening, but he also told me you were safe and sound at your father's."

Remy said the only thing he could tell her. "Father told me it was Zidan who killed my mother."

The look of shock on Xiaodan's face was genuine. Remy felt a rush of relief. "What? Zidan would never have done that."

"Vasilik told me the same thing when he died. Challenged me to ask Malekh. I didn't believe him then." The coffee was bringing him back to life, but it was also making him angry. "Even if he had reason to, however absurd it would be, how could he have done that and never tell me? That he would—that we would *fuck* and still never say anything?"

"How certain are you of this?"

—*with a Valenbonne?* Paolo had asked Malekh. *You have done that family a great injustice . . .*

"Ask him, then," he said. "He can lie to me, but I doubt that he would ever do so to you. I need another drink."

Fingers closed around his. "No," Xiaodan said firmly. "I'm staying with you for as long as you need me to. You're in no condition to be on your own. I don't know why your father believes Zidan killed his wife, but there isn't a—"

She broke off abruptly, eyes going wide. "Oh," she said. "Oh."

Dread stirred within him. "So he did kill her."

"No," Xiaodan said faintly. "We didn't know who killed her."

"Xiaodan, if you know anything about my mother's death—"

"The war with the Fifth. In one of the skirmishes with them, long before Etrienne nearly killed me." The pain in her voice was fresh, her hand once more pressed against the valley between her breasts like the wound was new. "We found one of their nests near Qing-ye, by the mountains. She must have been the one with them."

Remy stared. "What?"

"We thought she was a prisoner. There were dungeons within their lair, full of people they'd intended to keep as food during long sieges. But she was not in those underground caverns. We only realized she was human in the aftermath, after finding her body with the other Fifth kindred. She—"

Xiaodan paused, frowning. "I don't know if it was Zidan who killed her. There were other Third Court vampires with us. But it was he who found her." She looked suddenly stricken. "I could have killed her. I hadn't even thought about who she was. There were so many of them."

"She was in the wrong place at the wrong time." His father had implied that the murder had been deliberate. Remy was willing to consider that he might be wrong about that, simply because he believed Xiaodan more than he ever would his father. But why had his mother been in a Fifth Court lair to begin with? Had she been kidnapped, carried off for food or for experiments, and found herself caught in the line of fire? "Was she a familiar?"

"Perhaps. There were bite marks on her, but that could have just as easily meant she was being used as a blood source."

Remy closed his eyes. "And what makes you think she was my mother?"

"I didn't recognize her at first from her portrait because she looked so different. But in hindsight, she was wearing a robe and cloak much like the one the Fifth Court vampires wore, but her hair was cut shorter and her face smudged with dirt. She was heavily pregnant. We thought the babe—you—had died with her. You said she had the mark of the First Court on her. I didn't observe any of that on her body. Zidan never told me."

Remy set his now-empty mug on the table beside him and stared out the window. "He would have seen it," he said emotionlessly.

"The Night King's lords, back when they were still alive—they used to taunt him that way. They would kill humans and weaker vampires, carve their court's seal into their flesh, dump them where Zidan could find the bodies. A reminder that they did not forget his betrayal, that they would do worse to him. If he'd seen that mark on your mother, it would have shaken him. He wouldn't have told me because he wouldn't have wanted me to worry."

Xiaodan closed her eyes. "I didn't understand why he was so unsettled back then. I'd thought he'd been horrified that she'd been killed by one of us in the raid. But now . . ."

"What did he do after that?"

"Nothing. Etrienne had already escaped, but some of his high nobles were slower than he. We caught up to them outside, at the Barun hills, and slaughtered them all."

"Father said that they found my mother cozying up to vampires at one of their strongholds," Remy said. "She'd been missing for weeks, and they thought she'd been abducted. She was too heavy with child to have traveled alone." He tried to laugh, but it came out choked. "So my encounter with him a few weeks ago wasn't the first time we met."

"Once Sauveterre's minions were killed, Malekh wanted to return and see if anything could be done for your mother, but the Reapers had already arrived. We had no treaty with Aluria then, and they would have challenged us to a fight. We left. We never knew what happened to her." Xiaodan looked down. "I'm so sorry, Remy."

"He may not have killed her, but he knew who she was." The look in Malekh's eyes when Remy had knelt before his mother's grave, the quick, indrawn breath the noble had made when Remy had talked about her death, about the First Court insignia that marked her shoulder. "And he kept it from me. Everything I would have wanted to know about my mother that even my father never knew, something that would have helped give me some measure of closure—he withheld that chance from me."

"If he's kept anything from you, it was out of guilt," Xiaodan pleaded. "He thought it was his past returning to hunt him down. It's why he's been reluctant to tell you about the Night Court. You have to go talk to him."

"I don't—I don't know!" Remy leaned forward, grasping at his hair with his hands. "You're telling me the truth, right?" he asked, with the desperation of one who was close to breaking.

"I swear I am. I always will."

"Everyone else thinks I'm lying. I thought I could handle merely being tolerated in Elouve. But now it's different. People shout at me to my face what they used to whisper behind my back. They're accusing me of engineering this Rot, of murdering Astonbury. Of conspiring to overthrow the queen and install myself as the new king, of planning to have my father murdered so I could come into his wealth and titles." He'd seen the headlines plastered all over the city, from respectable newssheets to the most ludicrous tabloids: REMINGTON PENDERGAST, MARQUESS OF APHELION: POSSIBLE MURDERER? He'd heard everyone talk about nothing but him while he had spent an eternity walking back to Kinaiya Lodge, trying not to see, trying not to feel. The gravity of his situation had hit him halfway there; he saw nothing but revulsion, anger, fear.

He had changed course abruptly and made his way to Astonbury Manor.

"I went to visit Giselle," he said.

He knew that Xiaodan wouldn't like it; she'd already frozen when he'd mentioned the other woman. "Oh?" she asked, trying to sound like she was taking it in stride, but he knew her far better than that by now.

He hadn't been planning to ask Giselle to resume their relationship. All he had wanted was some reassurance, some promise that she didn't believe what they were saying, after all their time together.

Her butler had met him at the door, disappeared to consult his mistress, then returned with his profuse apologies. Her Grace is busy, he'd said, and would not be taking any visitors at the moment.

"It's not that I wanted her to take me back," he said. "But her tacit association with me was what helped me keep my status. She was the reason the ton still welcomed me, even if it was just as a source of gossip for them. And I thought that, even with the . . . unconventionality of our arrangement, that she would at least offer me some kindness, some words of support. That she would wish me well. But she wouldn't even see me."

He sensed her softening, always so easy to forgive, felt her arms encircle him. "Come back with us," she said. "If you feel that there is no longer a place for you here, then make my home yours. I know you have some resentment toward Zidan, but given everything we've been through, isn't a conversation with him worth having first?"

"There is nothing for me here, but I can't leave yet." He had to find a way to kill Grimesworthy, at least, even if he couldn't turn his father in. To look back at that blank, wooden expression and realize that he was not a taciturn valet who had chosen loyalty to his father, but a mindless undead who had been masquerading as Edgar Pendergast's devoted servant . . .

He could trust Xiaodan. But he couldn't tell her, not yet. Not until they were out of Elouve. His father never bluffed. Xiaodan would try to find a way to help him—her successful attempts at getting him out of the gaols the first time was proof of that—and her actions might tip off someone in his father's pay. He couldn't risk it. He'd risked far too much already.

"If you're worried about the army that Vasilik mentioned," Xiaodan persisted, "I've told Ophelia, and she has heeded my words."

"I can't leave Father here." More than what Remy owed the duke, more than the guilt, he couldn't let the Duke of Valenbonne carry out his plans. He couldn't bring himself to turn his own father in, but surely there was a way to foil his schemes without seeing the old man imprisoned. "I don't want him here alone. *I* don't want to be alone."

"You're not alone," Xiaodan said quietly.

Remy kissed her; he couldn't help himself. It wasn't just that he needed comfort as his life fell to pieces around him. He needed her, the only person besides Elke who'd never lied to him, never abandoned him, even when he was at his shittiest. And if he lost her, too, he was certain he would break.

Clothes rustled as she slipped out of hers; bedcovers shifted. The fierce need to dominate, to be dominated, desires that highlighted the numerous times they'd been together—those were no longer the priority. She didn't feed off him; nor he her. He didn't need the prolonged pleasure, that addictive high bloodsharing always brought them. Now, he only wanted her.

And she him. It filled him with wonder that she could accept him still, drunken and lost as he was.

"I love you," Xiaodan whispered as she settled on top of him, her hips moving gently, languidly, against his. "I love you so much."

"You love Malekh," Remy said; even in this intimate moment, unable to believe she could be telling the truth.

"I love Zidan and I love you. After Etrienne ripped my heart out, I learned how great my capacity was to give love, to accept it. I've never regretted Zidan. I've never regretted you." Xiaodan bent down and left soft kisses along his jaw. "And I know you love me too," she whispered, "and I know you love Zidan, and you don't need to ever say it. Just show me. Every day, for the rest of our lives, please show me."

Remy raised himself on his elbows, brought her mouth down to meet his, and rolled her over until it was she clinging to the headboard, gasping out her want for him, meeting his every greedy thrust with one of her own.

Shunned by society, betrayed by his own father, reviled once more as a cambion—and yet, it was the best morning of his life.

HE SUPPOSED it was late afternoon by the time he roused. His head still throbbed from overimbibing the night before, but Remy felt refreshingly at peace. He stretched and yawned, then discovered he was alone in bed.

There was a letter, carefully folded in half, lying by his night table. Remy rubbed his eyes and reached across the tousled sheets to take it.

It was written in a lovely, if slightly archaic-looking, cursive.

Off for a few errands but will be back soon. You look so adorable sleeping, I was almost tempted to wake you up.

The note was unsigned, but Remy smiled and flopped back onto the pillow. He wasn't entirely sure what errands Xiaodan could be running, especially in a human city that was wary of all things undead at the moment, but he was sure she had her reasons.

He was considering falling asleep again just so she could have another go at waking him, when he became aware of shouts outside, louder with every second. Instinct kicked in, and he leaped from the bed, throwing on whatever clothing lay in reach, which were the rumpled shirt and breeches he'd discarded earlier.

Another look out his window confirmed his worst fears.

There was a mob outside. And unless they were angry at one of his neighbors, of which he had none, the possibility was good that they were here for *him*.

Remy took a few minutes to grab Breaker and head out of the house through the back door, away from the irate crowd. He opened it . . . to find himself staring down the sharp tip of a fire lance.

"Knew you'd scuttle out back like the coward you are," said a familiar, satisfied voice. The Reaper on the other end of the weapon—Hathorn, he remembered, the degenerate who'd insulted Xiaodan at the gates to Elouve—was smiling smugly, with two more lackeys from the Ministry behind him.

"You'd best come quietly this time," Hathorn said. "No more mouth on you."

"I have permission to stay here from Her Majesty herself," Remy said. "You have nothing to arrest me for. You lot already did that to me yesterday, and it seems a waste of Reaper resources if you're to keep trying every day after this."

"Oh, but this is for a different matter entirely," the Reaper said with a smirk. "And the way I see it, you're just about to violate her instructions by sneaking out of the city, so my arrest now has merit."

"I'll come quietly," Remy said wearily. "Riones won't be glad to see me again, after just having sorted out all this bollocks on my behalf."

"You need not worry, for he won't ever have to again." Hathorn grabbed Remy forcefully by the arms, forcing them behind him. Remy winced but put up no resistance. "Almost a shame," the Reaper gloated, as his subordinates secured Remy's wrists with rope. "You would have made an excellent hunter if not for your father and for your own penchant to cavort with those bloodsuckers. They say you've been sleeping with them, supplying them with information about Alurian defenses."

"I suppose you fuckers can get at least one thing right," Remy said through gritted teeth as they took Breaker away.

Hathorn made a sound of revulsion, spat. "Then you're the traitor everyone says you are."

"I meant them fucking me, you absolute git. How the hell would I know what the kingdom's defenses are? You lot won't even let me into the dræfendgemot."

"But you've also been sleeping with Giselle Delacroix, and she's passed information to you before, hasn't she? Never liked that bitch. Always looked down on me just because my father was a butcher." A strange smile appeared on Hathorn's lips. "She won't be looking down on anyone else now."

Remy had expected another night spent at the gaol. But the man dragged him back to the front of Kinaiya Lodge and grinned at the angry crowd still gathered there.

There were far more than Remy had first thought, and they were armed. There were rudimentary weapons, and some less rudimentary. There were torches.

"Turns out news has spread about a strange army amassing to the south," Hathorn said. "The queen had sent a few men out, and they were killing their horses returning to the palace, describing the undead hordes. Victims of the Rot reanimated, they said, spread out for miles around and aiming straight for Elouve. Some of these good citizens got it into their heads that killing the vampire responsible for the infections would kill the rest of them as well, and unfortunately for you, you're the vampire they've decided to blame."

"You know that's not how it works," Remy growled. "You know I'm not a bloody vampire."

"Be that as it may, there's no going back now. The people of Elouve are in a frenzy of their own, and it's far more dangerous than a berserking bloodsucker's. They've been dragging out everyone even remotely connected to you Pendergasts, or those suspected of aiding vampires, or even of being one. There shall be bonfires raging across the city before the day's out. The other Reapers have ridden out with Her Majesty, who's been evacuated from the capital for her protection. No one can save you now."

Hathorn leaned closer. "This is payback for Astonbury," he snarled in Remy's ear. "You and the old man were responsible for his murder, I know it. Edgar Pendergast should have been the one to die. We could have spared you, if you hadn't stuck up for the father you'd maimed with your own incompetence. But I won't be needing to show evidence now, where you're going."

He turned back to the crowd. "Look who I found hiding like a coward behind his lodgings," he shouted, to the sound of cheers. "You're welcome, ladies and gentlemen!" and then shoved Remy forward into the mob.

Someone punched Remy across the face, and he sank down to one knee. Another kicked him from behind and sent him sprawling into the dirt. He grunted when a boot was planted into his lower back, and then couldn't help but snarl when something thick and sharp slammed into his leg, sending red hot pain up his body.

"Don't kill the vampire just yet!" he heard someone shout. "Wait till the gallows, give 'em a show!"

The boisterous laughter around him sounded like agreement. Remy was hauled back to his feet, then dragged, the blows still raining down on him from all sides. Through the haze of blood, he realized dimly that they were leading him into the town square.

"Take a look at that, dhampir." One of the men forcing him forward crowed. "Soon you'll be joining their ranks, decorating them like fancy curtains."

A row of scaffolds had been set up at the plaza. Figures dangled from the end of the ropes, proof that the townspeople's purging had started long before they'd come for Remy. Horrified, his gaze moved from one corpse to the next, not recognizing any of them until he'd settled on two at the very end.

"No!" he shouted, starting forward, but a mass of bodies pressed down on him, keeping him immobile as he kept screaming. "No! No! Please, no!"

Her hair had fallen down from its usual intricate knots, covering her face, but Remy recognized Giselle Delacroix's dainty feet, dangling motionlessly, and the scarlet dressing gown she was fond of wearing when she rose from bed. Beside her was Elke, her long hair flowing and her face pale as she hung lifeless.

He was still screaming when they pushed him toward the wooden steps, up a makeshift crate, where another noose waited. Remy struggled, even managing to push some of the weight off him, fighting madly despite his bound hands, kicking frantically, only for more pain to bloom at his shoulder as someone stabbed at him again. "Stop struggling. You'll be with them soon enough!" another shouted as they looped the noose around his neck, then punched him hard one last time. "We'll stake and burn you all afterward to be sure!"

His vision blurred, Remy looked out into the sea of faces before him and saw nothing but fury and hatred.

"Long live Aluria!" a man shouted, and the crowd roared.

The crate was kicked out from underneath his feet, sending him hurtling down, and Remy prepared to die.

ESCAPE

*S*hit happened all at once.

Elke's eyes shot open. She grabbed at the rope above her and swung with her legs, the momentum quickly sending her forward, close enough to swipe at the noose that bound Remy, slicing through.

Remy fell, and then kept on falling, tumbling onto the wooden floor with a grunt. Above them, the scaffolding splintered abruptly, the wooden beam cleaving in two, and the whole structure began to collapse. Elke slashed at her own noose and freed herself, then crouched down to grab Remy and run just as the gallows tipped over and went crashing into the crowd, inciting a stampede. Panic had taken the place of glee, and soon people were scattering.

Remy had stopped feeling pain the instant he'd dropped. Elke had thrown him over her shoulder and was racing through the streets unhampered. Remy could only focus on the way her hair was whipping behind her like it was caught in a great gust of wind, occasionally slapping at his face. *Elke's alive*, he thought dumbly. *He* was alive.

"Is he all right?" he heard someone ask when the redhead finally slowed, and it was Zidan's voice, quiet and concerned.

"I don't know yet."

"Neither of you are safe here."

They were moving again. Remy closed his eyes.

When he opened them again, there was an unfamiliar ceiling. It was made of stone, devoid of any finishings, and looked like it hadn't been dusted for a hundred years, given the thick cobwebs gathering across the bulwark. Remy stared up at it, uncomprehending, for a very long time.

Eventually, he turned his head and realized he was on a small wooden bed. On his right was Xiaodan, her arms lying on the covers and her head on top of them, sound asleep. One of her fingers lay over his own, and her touch was warm, comforting.

He sensed another presence to his left, and Remy turned to see Malekh sitting at a nearby chair, leaning back against the wall with his arms folded over his chest and his eyes closed. The man rarely ever slept, even after sex, so this was an unusual sight. Remy stared at him, too.

"Feeling better, Pendergast?" Brown eyes slid open, the noble looking back at him. "You had everyone worried."

"Sorry. Shoulder hurts."

"Getting knifed tends to do that. And one more across your lower joint, two above your knee. Minor enough not to cause any permanent injuries, but I don't want you moving around yet."

"Sorry." It was coming back to him in ugly splashes of memory. The mob at his doorstep. Hathorn handing him over to them. The gallows.

Oh, Light. Elke. And Giselle.

Remy bolted up from the bed and lurched over to one side, waking Xiaodan up. Malekh was on his feet, reaching out to him, but Remy shoved him aside so he could fall to his knees before an empty wash bucket. "Sorry," Remy said again, and then proceeded to relieve his stomach of everything. He'd eaten little before all this, so his efforts amounted mostly to dry heaving, hacking great big gasps of air into the pail.

He could feel both Malekh and Xiaodan behind him, both holding him steady, and he had no energy to push them away. Once he was done, Remy sagged, forehead resting against the cool metal, though it did nothing to alleviate the new fever sweeping through him. "Giselle," he said, and it came out a sob. "They killed Giselle. I—I killed . . ."

He wept like she'd been a cherished lover, threw up again, and wept some more until there was nothing else to give. He heard the murmurs between Xiaodan and Malekh but couldn't decipher any of their words.

When he was done, he felt someone lift him up and carry him back to the bed. "Don't touch me," he gasped, pushing in vain against Malekh's chest. "Don't touch me. Everyone I touch, every-one I care for—they die. Don't . . ."

He fell asleep mid-sentence and woke up to a new morning. Malekh and Xiaodan were still there, the latter still holding on to his hand. They watched him sit up.

"I feel like shit," Remy said by way of greeting, with none of his previous hysteria.

"Elke should be along with breakfast," Xiaodan said.

Elke. They'd hung her with the—no. She had rescued him. They all had. His eyes felt sore and crusted over. "And she's well?"

"More than fine."

"Where are we?"

"Miss Mari's farmstead. Both Alegra and Naji are here. We need all the help we can—what are you doing?"

Remy swung his legs over the bed and attempted to stand.

"We're still in Aluria," he said, the words tumbling out of his mouth before he could stop himself. "We're still too close to Elouve. They'll find us here. They'll burn down her farm, kill everyone else. I can't take that chance. We have to leave now before they harm her like they've harmed—!"

He didn't realize he was hollering until the sound of his own panicked voice reached his ears. Xiaodan and Malekh solved the matter for him, the former by wrapping her arms around his waist to keep him from getting up again, and the latter by laying a hand on his shoulder, the grip firm enough to let him know he wouldn't be.

"You don't understand." The breaths were leaving him rapidly, too quickly for his heart to keep up. "They killed Giselle. They were going to kill Elke. My father is safe only because he has an army of private soldiers loyal to his money." He paused, struck by another terrifying thought. "Where is Father?" It had been a large mob, but he hadn't seen Edgar Pendergast among the bodies they had hung.

A fresh wave of dizziness hit. Remy wanted to be sick again, but there was nothing left in him to hurl, and despair was sticking to his gut.

"Your father's safe," Xiaodan said urgently, taking both his hands and clasping them against her own. "Not even they would dare. It's not easy to forget that he saved them many times before."

"But easy to forget everything I've done for them, right?" Remy asked bitterly.

"Remy. This is my fault. If I hadn't left you alone . . . I should have listened to the rumblings. I shouldn't have left you when they were this volatile."

"We were escorting Queen Ophelia to another Alurian stronghold in Belamy," Malekh said, his hand still burning a hole into Remy's shoulder, "while some of the Reapers were dispatched to guard the perimeters around Elouve, to give the signal should they sight an army approaching. We were foolish to have left you alone in the city."

"I made that choice," Remy said, weary. "Not your fault. I should have known better. There were zealots on every street corner talking about the doom coming to Aluria. Newspapers encouraging people to defend themselves by any means necessary. There were glimpses of that before I left Elouve the first time, and I should have realized it would only have grown worse. But I never thought they would . . . if I'd acted earlier, maybe she would have been—"

Xiaodan hugged him, and Remy let her. The hand on his shoulder squeezed.

"You are not to return to Elouve without us," Malekh said brusquely. "I'm tempted to leave the Alurians to their own devices. With Ophelia out of the capital, I doubt any of the other stewards she left in charge would accept our assistance, even if we volunteered."

"You'd leave Elouve undefended?" Remy asked.

Malekh turned his shoulder so Remy could face him—and only then did he see that the noble was furious. "They tried to kill you," Malekh said harshly, every word a thunderstorm, "and you still think to help them? I promised Ophelia that I would protect her, but not even she would expect me to stay and do the same to her citizens when they've tried to hang my consort."

"But your ongoing alliance—"

"Do I look like I care about a damned alliance at the moment?" Malekh bent closer, breath rasping against Remy's. "You nearly *died*, Pendergast. You nearly well fucking died, and your first thought when you regained consciousness was not about how close you'd come to certain death, but about an old lover who'd used you for most of your relationship and worry for the people who murdered her? I am sorry that she is dead, and that we were unable to save her. But had I been in your place, I would not have given another thought to the mob responsible for causing her death."

Remy gaped at him. "You're jealous," he said, poleaxed.

Malekh drew his head back, face wiped clean of emotion in an instant. "I was simply worried for you, as you seem incapable of doing for yourself."

"Oh, he's *quite* jealous," Xiaodan said, not without some amusement. "You should have seen him fret over you while you were asleep."

"Xiaodan," Malekh warned.

His fiancée ignored him. "I agree with him. You are not to step foot within the capital. There is only so much I could threaten them with."

"Threaten?" Remy asked blankly.

"The mob who tried to take your life." Her humor faded, and Xiaodan's expression grew dark. "Malekh destroyed their scaffolding and Elke carried you off, but I stayed behind. I told them all, in no uncertain terms, that if they so much as looked at you the wrong way again, or at anyone else they believe to be aiding vampires, then I would turn their city into nothing but ruins and the ghost of a memory."

"But—"

"It doesn't matter. Malekh and I discussed it. Things are far too contentious at the moment for a lasting friendship with Aluria. Queen Ophelia and I remain on good terms, and I have promised to defend any of their borders alongside Qing-ye's. But there will no longer be an official concord. If the humans are so determined to defend their kingdom without our help, then I wish them good fortune. We will wait for as long as we have to for another opportunity."

"But this was important to you." Xiaodan had talked wistfully of coexistence. He had watched the delight on her face when the local children had played with her, heard the pride in her voice when she talked of her work helping the human villages near Chànggē Shuǐ.

"Yes, it was." Xiaodan reached out and lovingly brushed a stray lock of hair from his forehead. "But I have found that there is someone else much more important to me than the treaty. I will find another way to seek peace between my kindred and yours. But you, Remy—I almost lost you. I cannot forgive them for it."

"Aha, it seems the hero has finally awakened." Elke had pushed the door open, a tray holding a bowl of soup and some cornbread in her hands.

Remy glared at her. "I thought you were dead!"

"I already am, love. What they say about a mob being only as bright as its most foolish member holds true. Staking is the weapon of choice for suspected vampires, not a hanging. I knew there was a chance they would come for you next—that's all they were braying about after stringing me up—so I shammed until you were within reach." Elke's face fell. "Ah. I didn't mean to be so blasé, Remy. I'm so sorry."

"None of this is your doing." Giselle's death would weigh on him for the rest of his life. Like Lady Daneira's. Like all of those who'd been infected with the Rot because of his blood. Because of his father. "You saved me. But what are you going to do now? You can't return to Elouve."

"What's one city when there are many more to choose from? To be honest, even if they had never discovered my secret, I would've left eventually. Especially after how they treated you. I tolerated them because staying in Elouve was part of your duties. I didn't want you alone there." She looked at him, green eyes worried. "You'll leave the capital for good, too, won't you?"

"There's still that rumored army. I know I have no reason to stay and fight for them, but . . ." Remy lifted his hands helplessly. "It could be an army sent by the Night Court, Elke. And if there are any infected within those ranks, if they can be controlled by the Night Empress—"

The warmth by his shoulder fell away. Malekh rose to his feet.

"I will need to inspect the serums I brought from Chànggē Shuǐ, to see them safely stored," he said coldly. "Xiaodan, find me once you've finished discussing these matters."

"Was it something I said?" Remy asked feebly, after the noble departed.

"As I said," Xiaodan said, "jealousy."

"I haven't mentioned anyone—"

"The Alurians tried to fight him while you and Elke were escaping the city. They knew he was of the Third Court, and still they came after you and him and Elke with knives and swords and fire and anything else they could use for weapons. He was so enraged when he saw what they'd done to you, how close they'd come to succeeding. I kept the cooler head of the two of us, and you have no idea how surprising it is to be in that position when it is so often the reverse."

"Speak for yourself," Elke said. "Channeling the sun out of every inch of your body while you swore that you would burn them all to a crisp if they took another step is not what I might call keeping the cooler head."

"It worked, didn't it? And I didn't have to kill a single soul. You don't understand, Remy—Zidan never gets angry like this. With other kindred, he would have simply shrugged and slain them without a thought. But he never laid a hand on any of the Alurians. Said you were such a damn ass that even if he had good reason to, you would never have forgiven him."

Remy had nearly stopped breathing. "I—"

"He thought at first that Elke hadn't gotten to you in time, that your neck had snapped in the fall," Xiaodan barreled on. "He didn't know for sure until you were safely out of Elouve. And when you did wake, all you could think about was defending the city. He's not jealous of anyone else. He's angry that you value so many others over yourself. And yes, he does think that you care for him only because he comes with me in this relationship."

Remy stared down at his bowl of soup. "I don't know what he's thinking half the time," he said gruffly.

"I want you to know, because he's even more stubborn than you are about not needing reassurance." Xiaodan smiled as Elke sat on the bed beside him. "Give him a little more patience. He'll come around eventually."

"I've almost single-handedly broken the treaty you two have worked so hard to maintain," Remy said. "How can you all still be so kind?"

"Remy," Elke said gently, laying her hand against his shoulder; a comforting gesture, though not as heated as Malekh's had been. "Has it ever occurred to you that perhaps you are worth saving? That you are worth the time to be kind to? Do you really want to stay to defend a city that has treated you so terribly?"

Remy picked up his bowl, consuming the soup greedily in almost one go. "It's never been about them," he said. "It's never been about whether they treated me well. It's about whether I think they deserve to die. I don't care if they never think I'm respectable enough. I don't deserve being kind to, if I walk away now. It's not about them. It's about me."

And then, for emphasis, he belched loudly.

Xiaodan and Elke looked at each other. Then Xiaodan leaned over and placed her head on his shoulder.

"This," she said with a sigh, "is why we love you. We should all best begin the preparations. Alegra tells me that the storm headed this way is bigger than expected, and we'll need to be ready before it hits."

MISS MARI, the human owner of the farmstead, served Remy a fresh batch of biscuits in chicken gravy to quell his still-growling stomach. She was grateful to Malekh and Xiaodan for saving her home when it was nearly beset by vampires years ago, she'd told him while he greedily worked his way through the stack. She'd shown no alarm at court vampires using her residence for both a makeshift stable and a temporary base. Their arrangement, it seemed, had lasted for some years now.

"I cannot thank you enough, Lady Mari."

"Oh, think nothing of it. And a simple Mari will do, Armiger Remy. I have never once been a noble, and I would prefer it that way."

"Call me Remy, then. The way things are going, I'm afraid I will no longer merit a title myself."

The woman set a glass of fresh milk down beside him. "Lord Malekh and Lady Song are the kindest people I have ever met. Lady Song would often stay and help me in the kitchens. Lord Malekh would clean out my barn, feed some of my pigs, even see to the repairs on the roof whenever it leaked. I tried to persuade him that it wasn't necessary, but he always insisted."

"Zidan Malekh feeds your pigs?" The thought of Malekh slogging it out knee-deep in a dirty sty, dumping slop onto the hogs' troughs, brightened Remy's mood considerably.

"He's rather good at it." Mari set a cup of tea by his elbow next, the steam rising from it fragrant and soothing. "He might be an aristocrat," she said, "and maybe it's just little old me speculating, but I think very early in that long life of his, Lord Malekh learned all too well what it was to be just like the rest of us."

Remy ate until he'd had his fill, thanked Mari profusely for the meal, and wandered out in search of Malekh, only to find his younger brother waiting.

"About time you came out," Naji grunted. He'd been standing by the entrance to the stables with his arms folded across his chest. The farmstead was carefully camouflaged behind several thick groves of trees. There was nothing to guard over there, which meant the youth was just as protective of his brother as Malekh was of him.

"Is he still acting the grouch?" Remy asked.

The boy shrugged. "Whatever goes on between you two goes on between you two, and it's nothing I need knowing about. I employ that tactic with Xiaodan, and it has worked well for me so far."

"You didn't have to come all this way from Chànggē Shuǐ to babysit him."

"Tough talk for someone who was nearly hanged." Naji glared at him. "Aren't you supposed to be resting? Just because you've gotten a tenth of their strength from bloodsharing doesn't mean the other nine-tenths can keep up."

"Thank you, Naji," Remy said sincerely. "For everything."

The boy grinned. "Speak to him already. Patch things up. You won't believe how long he can sulk when he's of a mind to. Longer than even I can."

Mari had said that Malekh occasionally helped her with the pigs. Much to his disappointment, Remy found the noble leaning against a gate leading into an empty stall instead, tossing small cubes to his undead horses across from him, the stallions nickering gleefully as they chomped down on their treats.

"Thought you didn't want them eating sugar," Remy observed.

"It is of no nutritional value to helhests," Malekh said. "Nor is it a substitute for blood. But occasionally I will indulge them."

Remy fell back into silence and waited. He seemed to be more successful at getting Malekh to speak when he himself was shutting up.

"I didn't realize she was your mother until much later." Malekh never looked his way, his eyes only focused on his steeds. "Only when you brought us to her grave and mentioned how she'd died. When you talked of the court crest that was carved onto her shoulder."

"Why didn't you tell me as soon as you knew?"

"I didn't *know* what to tell you. Had I killed her? Had someone else? I have done many terrible things, but her death was a mystery I never found the answer to. The First Court insignia on her—it was all I could focus on. I thought she was another warning for me to find. I may not have killed her, but I might have caused her death."

"I don't think you did."

"I didn't know until you were well on your way to leaving with us. You would have thought the worst if I told you then. And afterward, you would have thought worse of us still. I had no real answers to give you, so I thought saying nothing would be the most pragmatic option. I wish now that I'd done the opposite. Will you forgive me for my lapse in judgment?"

"I do," Remy said, startled by the quickness of his response.

"So easily?"

"I'm not happy that you didn't tell me all this sooner. But I believe you when you say you never intended my mother harm, and that you did what you could in the moment. I . . ." Remy scowled at the ground.

"I trust you," he said through gritted teeth, like it was killing him to say that out loud. "I trust that you don't tell me things because you're worried about hurting me, even though I think it's a fucking bloody misguided thing to do and you really should stop it. What I'm tired of is being jerked around like a puppet by my father. And . . . my mother's dead. I'm not, and it's about time I started building my life around that." Wise man, that Paolo. "I've been thinking about things since returning to Elouve. I want to be more than just my mother's avenger. I don't want to have to feel guilty over something that happened before I was born. I don't want anyone to have that kind of power over my life anymore. And maybe I'm allowed to feel deserving of kindness, as Xiaodan and Elke like to point out frequently, even if I don't always feel I do." Remy allowed himself a quick smile. "You wanted me to come along that badly?"

"Xiaodan believed that you would be in danger if you were left to fend for yourself in Elouve, and I believed her. As it turned out, she was right. It did not help that she was already enamored of you by then."

And so were you, you bastard. Remy's smile grew. "Any reason why my mother would have the First Court's mark on her?"

"There are many. A court could claim a human as one of their familiars. Or keep them as livestock. But most wouldn't bother, given the . . . transience of such an arrangement. And as I said, there was a chance that the survivors of the old Night Court wanted to get to me. I have been susceptible to the Night King's compulsions in the past. If any of the First Court Ancients survived, they could have put your mother under a thrall and then killed her as a warning to me."

"But why would they choose her? Have you crossed paths before?"

"No. I'd never laid eyes on her until then. The First Court would have used any human they came upon, knowing that I had been working toward a mutual peace with them. Perhaps it was also meant as a warning to your father."

"Was that why you began conducting experiments on yourself?" Remy asked in a rare flash of insight into Malekh's mind. "To stop yourself from falling under their compulsion again? Decided that if anyone had to fuck around with your head, then it might as well be you?"

A ghost of a smile settled onto Malekh's mouth. "I have fought other high-ranking members of the First Court since the king's death and have held my own against their attempts. But I have never met the Night Empress, nor do I know what her previous affiliation to the king was. I don't know if I would be able to fight her off. But if you are so determined to confront her, then we must at least discuss a sounder strategy than you single-handedly fighting your way through her court like you imagine so grandiosely."

Malekh loved him. The arsehole really fucking did love him, just as much as Xiaodan did. As much as Remy loved them. He was wholly tempted to go back and grab Xiaodan, slam them both into the unused stall the noble was resting against, but his wounded shoulder and legs and exhaustion screamed otherwise. Additionally, he didn't want to traumatize the horses. But—

"You better," he said. "Everything I touch seems to wind up dying on me, and I'd like to improve those odds somewhat."

The smile on Malekh's face was clearer to see. "Fortunately for you, I am already dead."

Remy considered asking Malekh for some blood, then going off to find Xiaodan to ask for hers, preferably all three of them together, so they could do the happy work of healing Remy completely and getting his bollocks off at the same time, when Malekh froze, slowly peeling himself away from the gate. The horses sensed his unease, their playful whinnies turning into worried braying.

Absently, Malekh reached out and stroked Cookie's mane, calming it down. "Something's happened. We need to return to the others."

Xiaodan was already standing outside the farmstead, staring grimly into the horizon. Remy followed her gaze and saw a dark storm approaching, the flashes of lightning visible and the roll of thunder clear even at this distance. "That isn't natural," she said as Remy and Malekh joined her.

"It's not." Malekh was breathing heavily. His fingers were twitching as if flexing to break something. "I recognize this."

So did Remy. The area surrounding Elouve was always a miasma of fog and depression, but thunderstorms of this scale were not common, nor did they appear like this without warning. These were the same kind of clouds Vasilik had brought with him to Chànggē Shuĭ.

"You may have just gotten your wish, Remy," Xiaodan said softly. "There's an army coming, and if it's anything like what Vasilik brought, then the Alurians are going to have a problem on their hands."

34

THE STORM

"Figured you might need this," Elke said, handing Remy his Breaker. "Xiaodan paid Hathorn a visit to demand it back. She also let him know, in no uncertain terms, that she was not pleased with his choice to turn you over to the mob instead of bringing you safely to the Marquess of Riones."

"She didn't do any permanent damage, did she?" Remy tested his weapon, pleased to see it was in the same condition he'd left it.

"Knocked him around a bit, the way she tells it. Didn't kill him, more's the pity. Are you certain you're well enough to fight? Your wounds could take another day or so to heal."

"I can manage." The Reapers had returned to Elouve and were hard at work bolstering up fortifications there. Elke had seen a few more scouts from the city ride on to investigate the storm, suspicious about its nature as they had been—only to ride frantically back to the capital at breakneck speed, with only half the number they started out with. The activity in Elouve had increased after that, groups of Reapers and workers alike busily digging up ditches and erecting silver barricades around the capital.

Neither Xiaodan, Malekh, nor Elke had proposed leaving the Alurians to fend on their own again, to Remy's relief.

"Best if you take another drink of this." Elke set down a decanter of wine and an empty glass at the table. The alcohol had been mixed with both Xiaodan and Malekh's blood; Remy had already consumed several glasses in the hours since, and his shoulder was almost fully healed, the wound reduced to only a sliver.

Remy sighed.

"You're usually more enthusiastic about good liquor."

"It's not that. I'm accustomed to drinking it in a different manner."

Elke smiled. "You really do care for them, don't you?"

"For as long as they'll allow me, yes." Remy drained the glass. "Any other news?"

"Xiaodan thinks that the fortifications in Elouve will hold— barely. They've endured sieges in the city before, so the Reapers should be experienced enough to know what to do. Mari's farmstead is far enough from the main road and in the other direction that Xiaodan doesn't think any vampires will be headed our way, but that's only if Elouve *doesn't* fall. She's tasked me with getting Mari out safely, should the worst happen. And here's the part you might not want to hear—she wants us to wait until the army is at Elouve's gates. Easier to gauge their plan of attack once they're fighting in full force, she said. Incidentally, Alegra's here, if you didn't already know."

"You don't sound as happy as I expected you to be."

"She's been ignoring me." Elke shrugged, trying to hide her disappointment. "There's nothing else I can do. I know when I'm not wanted, and I've acted enough of a buffoon, throwing myself at her for this long."

"Ah. If you need any—"

"Not now, Remington."

"Fair. So we're not going to fight?"

"Engaging them out in the open field would be a disadvantage, given there's only five of you and a hell's load of them. Xiaodan strikes me as an able tactician. She proposes staging our assault when they're a hundred percent committed to attacking Elouve's walls. Hit them from behind."

Slowly, Remy nodded. "I can go with that."

"You're not to jump into the fray until her say-so, though. She prefers that you stay behind but knows you well enough not to suggest it. She also realizes that having you around might be to our advantage. If there's any more of those infected with your blood swimming through their veins, then there's a chance you could stop them in their tracks."

"I can try," Remy said, not looking forward to it.

"She and Lord Malekh are waiting for you outside. I'm to stay in and keep guard over Miss Mari, just in case." Elke shuddered. "I much prefer this arrangement. Battles still turn my stomach. I'd rather not have to watch them from a distance before I have to fight them up close. Stay safe, Remy. I've nearly lost you far too many times in this week alone."

"Always, love." Remy pressed down on a switch, and Breaker's scythes flared up with a satisfying swish. "Always."

THEY TRAVELED through the forest's edge bordering the south of Elouve, keeping out of sight. The storm was nearly upon the city. The thunder was loud, lightning bright against the dim.

"You're not to fight them until Xiaodan gives the word," Malekh said. "You are not to leave my sight even then."

"You're not my fucking father, Malekh," Remy growled. "And not even he cares all this much."

Malekh smiled, wide enough to reveal the points of his fangs. "You're still human, Pendergast. You're the most vulnerable of us, and also the most hotheaded in a fight. I already thought you dead once—let us not make it a habit."

"I know you're saying that because you're worried about me, and I appreciate it," Remy said. "But the way you express this shit still pisses me off."

"Will both of you scallops please condescend not to talk for the next hour or so that it will take the army to arrive?" Xiaodan snapped.

"*Scalawags*, not scallops. We still need to work on your vocabulary of insults."

"I don't care. Don't make me spank both of you."

Malekh frowned at Remy, who glared back. Both lapsed into a silent compromise.

It was a tense wait. As darker clouds rolled across the skies above Elouve, the Reapers and soldiers continued to build their defenses. Remy could see cannons being loaded, catapults being wheeled before the gates, torches that indicated they'd planned on using pitch and other incendiaries. Trenches around the city had been dug in nearly record time, and he had no doubt that there would be sharpened stakes waiting at the bottom.

"Too much light," Remy muttered. "They need to cut down on some of their fires. They'll be too much of a target."

"The darkness could induce them to panic. Your citizens always seemed to me to be very much afraid of the night," Xiaodan whispered. "They're doing well for such a short time to plan. But they should have slicked the walls with oil they could burn later, to slow them down. I could scale that in a heartbeat, even with the trenches they've prepared beneath."

It didn't take long for them to see the approaching army, just as the rains grew harder.

The incoming horde was preternaturally silent. It was an unnerving sight, to see the gaunt, shuffling figures steal over the plain, drawing closer and closer to the waiting city. Many of the vampires wore tattered clothes, dirt and worse still staining their bodies. Remy could smell their foul odor even from where he lay hidden.

"Rot," Malekh said, confirming his fears.

"The First Court and their compulsion," Xiaodan murmured. "Easier to control them if they had their minds robbed of them to begin with."

Slowly, the mass of moving infected came to a stop before the trenches and took no steps farther. Nor did they retreat. They simply stood, bodies stirring slightly against the strong winds, but otherwise they made no other sound or movement.

There were far too many of them. Ten times what Vasilik had brought to Chànggē Shuǐ, and that was a conservative estimate.

"Almost like they're waiting for something," Remy heard Xiaodan muse. "But what? I don't understand."

And then the vampires came. They were much more disciplined than Vasilik's coven, swooping into view with steady formations, lining themselves up neatly behind their infected companions. They all wore long, flowing dark hoods, the crimson color nearly black against the night. Like the mutations, they made no other sound; like them, they simply waited.

From within the city came streaks of fire shooting up into the sky—burning tar and pitch from catapults. They bore down with unerring accuracy at the unmoving front line, crashing into the infected. They toppled into the trenches, their bodies burning. More flames came over the high city walls, taking out scores of the Rot.

And yet the army didn't move. Not the infected, not those who were still on their feet and burning, and not the vampire coven at the rear.

Next came the burning arrows; arching down, falling faster than the rain. More of the mutations fell, and their vampire brethren sidestepped the incoming hail. Remy saw a few reaching out and snatching at the arrows with their bare hands, snuffing out the flames with a flick of their fingers before tossing them back to the ground. But they did nothing to retaliate, content simply to stand where they were.

And then the screams began—from inside Elouve.

"What?" Xiaodan cried out. "Have they gotten in? How—"

Her question was answered when the ground around the capital began to move. Shadows broke through the soil, pulled themselves upright, and that was the unspoken signal the rest of the coven was waiting for. The vampire army surged forward; the infected sluggish, the court kindred moving with dangerous grace; both scaled the city walls. More arrows streamed down; Remy saw some of the coven fall, but that was not enough to stem the tide of undead.

Remy was running, but he was the slowest of the lot. Malekh was already gone from view. Seconds later, the noble was a dark figure on the castle walls, launching himself at one of the vampires who had very nearly made it to the top. His opponent had no time to react, no time to even realize Malekh was there until the noble had already struck; the body hit the ground first, followed by the head and other disjointed parts.

Xiaodan had joined him, whipping from one opponent to the next, leaving a trail of bodies behind her, still far too quick for Remy to see more of her than a blurring of air and the arc of falling corpses by their unseen foe.

"Thanks for letting me know we were bloody ready," Remy groused, mostly to himself, once he'd reached the intersection of battlefield where soldiers, coven, and infected were colliding.

"Stay close, Armiger!" Alegra was vicious. She carried the battle-axe she'd scoured back at Qing-ye and was laying waste to all before her. Naji, who fought more defensively, was racking up kills with his own sword, longer than Malekh's preference.

Unlike his companions, Remy had stuck to the original plan

and attacked from the rear. He focused on the dark hoods, the ones he knew marked them as coven and uncorrupted by the Rot, and felled three with Breaker before they realized another enemy had joined the fracas. The silver of his knifechain, now longer in range and forged with Elke's deadlier maces, made a singing sound as they whipped through the air, systematically cutting the undead in two or more bloody sections.

But the hooded vampires were far more skilled than both the mutations and the youths who had run with Vasilik. More than once, Remy found himself on the defensive, taking his share of cuts from barely dodged strikes as the vampires came at him in fours and fives—for every one he took down, another immediately filled their place. After several minutes, he was finally able to put enough distance between him and his opponents to swing his knifechain around like a shield again, which proved much more effective. His double scythes kept them at bay, picking off the ones he wanted to engage first while the maces did their work, giving ground whenever he had to, then gaining it back in the next attack and generally destroying everything the chain came into contact with. Malekh was single-handedly preventing a good portion of the vampires, both coven and mutation, from leaping over the wall, and some of the Reapers and soldiers inside Elouve were finally fighting back with greater success since the initial fire attack. They were pouring boiling oil and pitch over the walls, burning anyone unlucky enough to be underneath. Malekh moved out of the way, reappearing near Remy to take out the vampires who'd started to converge around him.

"You weren't supposed to be fighting out here alone," the noble grated.

"It's not like you or Xiaodan gave me a choice."

Xiaodan had also returned, and now all three were fighting, backs to one another, guarding against ambush even as more of the coven leaped at them. Remy beheaded one with his scythe, stuck his knifechain into another and pulled out guts when it tried to gun for Xiaodan. "The hell's happening?"

"I believe there's someone in this army with control over not just the infected, but also the undead." Xiaodan killed two vampires who'd been aiming for Remy's unprotected side. "From the Reaper talk I overheard, it sounds like corpses that were buried inside the city came back to life. Among them the Reapers killed at the Archives."

Craggart, Pyalia, and Kibold. "Shit. Even the ones not infected by the Rot?"

"Too early to know if they were buried with it undetected. Not all of the dead, but enough to cause concern. There's someone else here with a far more unnatural power over the mutations than can be done with your blood." Malekh's voice was tight with anger and something else. The noble sounded almost . . . afraid. "I know of only one person who was able to enthrall the dead this way."

"The First King? So this really is the First Court?" It was Remy's turn to be gripped by fear, anticipation coiled alongside it. He'd fought so long for this. "Where?"

"Whoever is responsible, you need to stay away from them, Remy. This isn't Vasilik."

"Then who will face them? You?"

"Yes," Malekh said.

"The fuck you are. Not without me, and not without Xiaodan."

The city gates swung open without warning, and a cavalry of soldiers, many of them armed Reapers, came thundering out.

"About bloody time," Remy muttered, and killed another vampire, inching himself closer to the walls.

"Where are you going?"

"Seems like whatever undead sprung up inside the city, the hunters have sorted out; they wouldn't be sending troops if they still had a mess on their hands inside. And they've sent some of their best—I see Riones leading the charge—so they'll make short work of these bastards. But there's still thousands of these damn infected, and we can't kill them all without losing more of our own, so it's time to put one of your theories into practice, Malekh."

"You are not going to—"

"I can, and I will. Elke said I was one of your contingency plans, and this is about as contingent as it can get. Let me. Just watch my back while I try."

The vampire nodded reluctantly. "If anything goes wrong, we're bringing you out of here."

"Pendergast!" Riones greeted, looking relieved to see Remy as he fought his way over to them. His fire lance was a bright beacon; the other vampires hesitated at drawing nearer, and he took advantage of that, setting several dead on fire with his first shot. "I was told Lady Whittaker managed to spirit you out, but I was worried."

"Still alive and breathing, but thank you for the concern."

"I was escorting Her Majesty with the Lady Song when word reached us; I didn't have her speed, so I only made it back in time to stop them from completely torching your residence."

Remy's spirits lifted. "Kinaiya Lodge didn't burn?"

"Part of it did, but most of your possessions have been recovered. The Lady Whittaker—she's a vampire?"

"And one of the best people I've ever known. You think you can help Lord Malekh watch my back while I do something that will make the Alurians really hate me?"

Riones didn't understand but nodded anyway, being the good sort of chap Remy had once hoped more of the Reapers would have been. "Won't let them get within a hair's breadth of you, Pendergast. We brought some of the serum the lord left behind, manufactured enough to spread the good cheer around. Loaded all our arrows up with it, so it's unlikely these bastards will be getting up afterward. Good evening, Lord Malekh. Apologies for the abruptness at our last meeting."

"No offense taken."

Remy didn't know what to do, exactly. The last time he'd controlled the Rot, he'd had no idea he was doing it. He focused on the nearest infected within stabbing distance, one whose clothes were already burning. "Look at me!" he shouted, feeling rather ridiculous.

Not only did the creature not heed his order, but it continued to shuffle straight toward the trench lying before it. More fell willingly into the pit. There were so many impaled within, that some of the stakes had actually broken off from the weight; but they must have been slicked up with Zidan's serum too, because they weren't moving or mutating further. Those lucky enough to avoid the sharp poles shuffled along the bottom, attempting to climb out the other end. Many more faltered and sank down whenever the archers landed a hit.

"Look at me!" Remy said, louder now. "Hey, shithead, look at me!"

"What is he doing?" Riones asked, bewildered even as he continued to cut through his attackers.

"What he can," Malekh responded, slaying another vampire with a flick of his blade, the body sagging and spurting black blood on the way down.

"Look at me!" Remy shouted. "Look at—"

And then he'd fallen in without realizing it, that familiar thick fog in his head, the sluggish presence of outside minds—

No; they weren't minds. Minds required thought, and there was none of those in the bodies that surrounded him, devoid of anything but a desire to obey.

The burning vampire shifted its head and turned to look at him. All around them, the other infected did the same, pausing in mid-step to swivel their charred, ruined faces at him.

"Fuck," Remy said. All well and good that they were looking out their eye sockets at him now, but getting them to attack their leader was another thing entirely. He hadn't been successful at getting them to do more than stop and gawk the last time, but if Malekh had said it was possible . . .

He trusted Malekh.

The brainless things he'd let into his head couldn't drown out his thoughts by virtue of having none of their own, but the weight of them pressed down heavily into his mind, almost like the bastards were sitting on his chest, making it hard to breathe—and in fact, his lungs felt like they were on fire in a very physical way. Remy worked to keep from hurling them out, screaming silently for them to do what he was bloody well damn ordering them to o.

"Is he keeping them from attacking us?" he heard Riones ask, shocked, and Malekh's response: "Don't worry about that. Focus on the coven. They're in First Court colors. Take them down first—they're much more dangerous."

Lord Anthony Castellblanc was used to taking orders. He deprived two hooded vampires of their innards, still sticking close to Remy, while Malekh worked his way back into the thick of the battlefield, slaying through another swathe.

As more vampires poured in, Remy saw another hooded figure standing just beyond where the swarm was at its densest—a figure in hooded scarlet, standing alone.

Malekh was fighting his way through the horde to reach it.

Something shifted in the shadows that made up that strange, robed face. It turned his way, and Remy felt the pressure in his head increase, his ears ringing. He'd seen this person before, in the woods by the caves near the Dà Lán.

He felt the infected stir, their bodies beginning to move again in response to the silent call from their cloaked master, away from his control.

"No." He was back on the ground above with Breaker beside him, fingers digging into the dirt because it was the only way he could stop himself from clawing at his own face at the agony that keeping the infected immobile was now causing him. But Remy had endured pain before, and to Light's hell and back if he would let it win again.

"No!" he shouted, voice rising over the din of steel and rendering flesh as he pushed with all his might—at the infected vampires, at the coven, at the strange, hooded figure.

And the Rot obeyed. Without another sound, they turned on the nearest kindred, fangs and hands sinking into them before the latter could realize their betrayal. Remy saw some of the First Court vampires shifting strategy, fighting off the infected, giving Malekh the distraction he needed.

The noble only had eyes for what Remy deduced was the army's leader, and he was killing every vampire in his path to reach the scarlet-robed figure. A swipe, a parry, and the pair were soon engaged in battle.

Remy swore. Staggering to his feet, he began to fight his way toward them.

They were evenly matched. Remy only saw a series of blurs that shifted back into Malekh every time his saber struck and found resistance, the figure needing no more than its hand to block even his finely sharpened blade.

The infected Remy now commanded were following him, forming ranks like he was leading them into battle. They were taking down every vampire who drew too close and leaving most of the Reapers unmolested, much to their confusion. Some had even started mimicking his movements, swiping at the air just as he did, lifting unseen weapons whenever he hefted Breaker. It was the most jarring, horrifying, ridiculous thing Remy had ever seen.

"Stop attacking the bloody space around you and start with this git, you useless sods," he growled, not quite believing that they would take him up on his word, and then was somehow stunned when they did, the whole lot of them bearing down on Malekh's opponent.

The figure disappeared and reappeared behind Malekh. The

noble turned and looked straight into the hood; a stunned look crossed his face, as he stared at whoever it was within. He staggered backward, gasping, hands coming up to the sides of his head.

From behind that dark, shadowed robe, came a soft whisper. "Kneel, Zidan Malekh."

Malekh knelt, fighting every step of the way down. His right knee sank to the ground, and with great effort, his left followed suit. "Can't," Malekh panted, battling with himself to stand, even as the hooded figure approached. "You . . . can't."

The First Court's specialty was enthrallment, Malekh had told him. His one fear, the reason he had avoided confronting the First Court directly, was that they could compel him like the Night King had.

Remy's knifechain whipped through, the triple maces aimed at the hooded figure's heart.

It wrapped around Malekh's fist instead. The noble yanked hard. Remy would have stumbled straight into the waiting saber had he not spun in time, releasing the catch to sever the links.

Malekh let the chains drop to the ground. His face was carefully blank when he turned to face Remy again, and he raised his blade, assuming a guarded stance.

"Fuck no, Malekh," Remy said, leveling his scythes at him. "Get a bloody hold of yourself!"

Malekh did not get ahold of himself. Instead, he made a running leap for Remy.

He dodged out of the way—only for Malekh to materialize at his rear. Remy avoided the slash of the man's blade, jumped back when another sliced at his shirt, barely missing skin. The lessons he'd learned from sparring with the Summer Lord were saving his life, though the hypnotized man was doing his best to undermine his own instructions.

The infected approached Malekh, too, but none of them were

a match for his skill. He slashed his way through the bodies to reach Remy. Even with the mutations on his side, Remy knew how this was going to end. Eventually he would tire, and then Malekh really would kill him.

"Zidan!" A swipe of Xiaodan's hand sent the saber out of Malekh's. Even then, her fiancé didn't pause, lashing out at her, barefisted this time. Xiaodan dodged his blows easily but did not counter. "Get out of here!" she shouted to Remy.

Remy disobeyed. Seemed to him that the hooded figure in red was responsible for all this, and taking it out would help the other vampire snap out of it.

Easier said than done. He was going to try anyway.

He grabbed the knifechain Malekh had relinquished, spun it above his head, and launched it at the figure, spikes pointing straight at it.

It reached out and snatched the links easily out of the air, but Remy had a follow-through, his scythes already swinging.

Unlike its fight with Malekh, the figure did nothing to avoid him. The blade sank into its chest with a horrifying sound, but the figure did not fall. It didn't even move. It remained standing, looking at him with the hood still obscuring its face, and Remy somehow had a feeling it was smiling at him.

Behind him, he heard a stuttered gasp from Malekh as he retreated, lucidly aware again, though severely weakened from fighting his enthrallment. "Zidan," came the relieved cry from Xiaodan, who sounded just as exhausted.

Remy wrenched his scythe free and felt the vampire's blood splash back on him—on his arms, on his face, on his clothes. So much blood. This should have been enough to kill it.

Instead, it laid a hand—a very gentle, soft hand—on the side of his face, the blood dripping from its fingers and smearing his cheeks with even more scarlet.

The hood lifted.

He saw a woman's face, beautiful and smooth-skinned. He saw gently sloping eyebrows, dark eyes the color of moonless skies. High, noble cheekbones, a generous mouth, tumbles of black hair framing her pale features.

It was a lovely face.

A familiar face.

He had seen it too many times, looking down and smiling at him from the mantelpiece at Kinaiya Lodge, for him not to recognize her.

"My darling boy," his mother said softly, "why do you fight with my murderers against me?"

And then she opened her mouth, fangs gleaming and pearl white.

35

SINGING

There was a song in his head. Somebody was singing to him. It was a song he'd heard often enough in childhood, and yet it sounded different somehow. His nanny, Miss Grissell, had sung it often, taught him to sing it in turn when he was still so young. She'd said that Remy's own mother sang it for him while he'd been in her womb, a lullaby she'd brought with her to Aluria from the small island of Tithe where she'd been born.

Miss Grissell had sung it, and then he had sung it, until his father had heard the melody and sent his nanny away as punishment for teaching him. Remy had kept the song locked away in his heart since then, bringing it out only during moonlit hunts, where his father would never hear.

But Miss Grissell wasn't the one singing. Another woman was, her voice soft and sweet, and Remy could think of nothing but to listen.

He was moving, but he wasn't thinking about that, either. He was sinking his scythe into something else, possibly someone else, but he wasn't thinking. He was spinning Breaker again, that constant, comforting motion he'd always done since he'd been abandoned at a cave at the mercy of vampires, and he found easy solace in the motions, even when he wasn't thinking about anything at all.

He was hitting things. This was good. He was supposed to be hitting things. He was in a fight, and others were trying to hit him in kind. His scythe met some resistance when it sank down on something fleshy, but Remy ignored that. All he wanted was to keep listening to the song, the one thing that had promised him some measure of solace his whole life, though it had not always been good at living up to that promise.

She was singing, and it was beautiful.

Something else was happening—another woman was shouting. Remy didn't like the noise. All he wanted, all he needed, was to listen to the song forever. This unexpected voice sullied it somehow, and he didn't like that. He shut his ears out and closed his eyes, straining to hear more of the lullaby, trying to block out everything else.

"Remy!" The voice cried, louder now and more insistent. "Remy, please stop!"

It was a familiar voice, too. He should know it from somewhere. The song wore a lovely voice, but this new one, this was a *beloved* voice. There was a difference. There would always be a difference.

A great part of him struggled, wanting to forget everything but the melody. Another part of him listened to the shouting.

"Remy!" Xiaodan—it was Xiaodan!—was pleading. He was holding a dagger, and it was aimed between her eyes, a hair's breadth from plunging into her forehead. Xiaodan wasn't defending herself. She was simply there, risking injury to wait for him to come to his senses. The sight of her gray eyes, still trusting despite everything else—trusting him to stop, not to attack her—and the song in his head grew sour and ugly, cacophonous now when it had once been sweet at the shock of what he had almost done.

"Come back to me, Remy," Xiaodan said. "Please, come back to us."

Remy came back to her. He stared at his suddenly bloody hands. His Breaker was gone, but Xiaodan had a grip on his wrists, so strong that she could have easily broken them if she wanted to.

He lifted his eyes to her terrified gaze, dazed. "Xiaodan?" he asked, like he'd just been woken from a deep sleep.

"You're back," Xiaodan said, relief mixed in with the horror still clear in her voice, as was the pain. Memories came swimming back into his head. The fight. Malekh and the hooded figure. Himself, looking into the latter's face and seeing—

—seeing—

He turned.

Naji was lying on the ground, his eyes open and sightless, looking up at the storm clouds. Malekh was cradling him in his arms, his face a ruin of misery. Remy's Breaker lay beside the younger vampire, its scythes drenched in blood.

"I didn't—" Remy stumbled back a step, flashes of remembrance lancing into him like lightning. His Breaker. His attack on Malekh. His intent to kill.

Riones, intercepting, but getting knocked away. Malekh, defending himself but refusing to return the blows, still recovering from his enthrallment. Naji, leaping in front of his wounded brother before Remy could administer the kill. The impact. The sound it had made.

"I didn't—"

"It wasn't you," Xiaodan said urgently. "Remember that, Remy. This was not your doing."

No. It was his mother's, who—

His mother.

The hooded figure remained where Remy last remembered it, motionless against the turbulent winds ripping through the plains, the rain. Its face was once more hidden, yet he knew it was watching. The infected that he'd gained hold over were strewn across the ground. When Xiaodan had broken through to him, had they suffered from the backlash? Had Xiaodan killed them, or had he turned on them himself? It was difficult to remember more, beyond the horror of what he'd already done.

His mother. This person wore his mother's face. Knew his mother's song.

"Riones," Xiaodan said. "Watch over him."

She let go of his hands, replaced by the marquess's on his arm. His grip wasn't as strong as Xiaodan's, but it was enough to keep him steady. "Easy now, Pendergast," the Reaper said. "You've done enough for one day."

Fourth Court heiress and First Court empress circled each other; gauging, waiting for the opportunity to strike. It was Xiaodan who made the first move, and Remy only saw the attack after the fact, when she was already skidding away, her assault deflected. It was the latter's turn next, moving at the same invisible speed, but Xiaodan met it head-on. The ground around them rocked, broke apart from the savagery of both attack and defense.

Numbly, Remy watched. The figure was just as evenly matched as Xiaodan in both quickness and strength, which was to Xiaodan's disadvantage. How long had she been fighting already? Ten minutes? Fifteen? It had felt longer to him, and though strain was beginning to appear on her face, she showed no signs of letting up or acquiescing.

She couldn't last long in these conditions, and Malekh was in no shape to help.

Xiaodan perhaps realized that; her gray eyes shone in defiance. And then the rest of her started to glow as well.

Remy knew what she intended to do. He wanted to rush forward to her, but Riones wasn't letting him take another step. The hooded figure must have realized the implications of that shine; its efforts redoubled, distracting Xiaodan enough so she focused on protecting herself from its attacks instead of preparing to release that deadly brightness.

Remy looked down at the dagger by his right boot. Elke had insisted on outfitting him with more; her insistence protected him, though not in the way he'd wanted. He must have removed several and tried to stab people on the field with them during his thrall.

He was still thankfully numb, his mind working frantically to compartmentalize his pain and guilt and shock, shoving it somewhere more distant.

The hand on his arm tightened. "Don't even think about it, Pendergast."

"I'm fine," Remy said. "I don't want to be, but I am. Xiaodan's strong, but she's not going to defeat a First Court vampire with her heart condition. And if she loses, we're all going to die out here. Stab me if I start berserking again, but let me do what I need to do to help her."

A pause, and Riones released him.

And then Remy was running straight toward the pair, dagger balanced in each of his hands. He threw the one on his left as hard as he could at the figure.

It turned and caught the knife effortlessly in its fingers.

"Mother!" Remy cried out.

The figure shifted so that it faced him a second time, leaving Xiaodan still panting for breath, winded and close to her breaking point.

"They told me you were dead," Remy said. "Father said you were dead."

My poor boy, it said, and he felt the strains of the lullaby once more playing in his head, her crooning voice once more soft and sweet. This time, he shut it out.

"No!" he shouted. "Who are you?"

My poor boy. He could almost believe that the sorrow he heard from within the hood was genuine. He could not bring himself to look closely again, to see if it truly was his mother's face looking back at him, or if it was an illusion and something else had taken her place. *I am alive. I am eternal. Why do you hunt with my murderers?*

She raised her finger to point at Malekh. *Why have you gone with them? The one who brings the sun and her Ancient lover. Why do you not avenge me?*

"I am avenging you," Remy said desperately. "No—you're not her. She's dead. She couldn't have—"

An arrow came whistling through the air. Just as before, the figure caught it in its hands. Remy turned to stare at the newcomer, who pulled back his own hood.

"Get away from my son, you undead bitch," Edgar Pendergast said.

His features were grim, stronger than the frail old man Remy had known. Gone were the unfocused eyes glazed over by white film, the frail arms and liver spots, and even the shriveled leg. Now his gaze was sharp. While leaner still than what Remy had remembered of him, his father had regained some of his muscular physique and walked with the step of one who was fifty years younger, crossbow in one hand and leveled at the First Court vampiress. The other wielded an immense shield forged completely of silver. He now walked unaided but still carried his mahogany cane, tucked into a heavy belt.

A hiss rose from behind the hood.

"Yes," Remy's father said. "I knew it would attract you, the taste of your own son's blood. There was no way to take back what Astonbury had already unleashed, so I started seeding the vampires from here to the farthermost regions of Aluria, hoping you would take the bait, Ligaya. I knew you would be curious. That it would bring you out of hiding. You have never been clever. You were an imbecile when you ran away from me, and you're an imbecile now, with this pretense of a First Court."

The figure rushed him without another sound, and Valenbonne

only barely managed to deflect the blow, bringing the heavy shield in between them before she could do damage. It was for naught; she disappeared to move behind his father, seizing him by the throat. The crossbow dropped from his hand.

"No!" Remy cried out.

I am the Night Empress, the being said, fangs inches away from the old man's neck, *and I will destroy you.*

"I don't think so," Xiaodan said. She was an incandescent ball of sun, shining so brightly that her face was nearly obscured by the light. Her hands were raised, pointed at the Night Empress. "Eat shit, you scum-sucking cuntrabbit!" she yelled, and fired.

Edgar Pendergast's hand dipped down and seized his cane. A deft twist sent a sharp blade shooting out of its base, which he thrust at his former wife.

Remy was still running, reaching his father just in time—only for Malekh to have gotten there half a second ahead of him. The noble grabbed at Remy, then at the elder Pendergast, and flung them both down and away from the incoming attack just as the Night Empress released him to face the new threat.

She was too late.

The ensuing blaze enveloped her, consumed her whole, even as Remy crashed down to the ground beside his father, safely out of range. For the briefest moment, he could have sworn he saw the woman disappear just before the light reached her; then there was nothing else but sun.

The whole battlefield lit up from the blinding display, the dark sky brightening as a second sun seemed to rise alongside the moon, turning night into day in an instant. A groan rose up as what remained of the First Court turned and fled from the sight until there was no one left but the sounds of those already dying, the silent dead, and the survivors, Reapers and soldiers alike who, though exhausted and confused, cheered nonetheless at the sight of their enemy retreating.

The light faded. His mother was gone.

Remy scrambled over to where Xiaodan lay prone, Malekh already beside her. The woman's eyes had fluttered closed, but the faint grin at her lips was on prominent display. "I know I'm not supposed to be so reckless," she said feebly, "but considering everything else . . ."

She was going to be all right. Remy's hopes lifted. But she had severely overtaxed herself again. "Stay still," he said.

Malekh looked at him, a strange look on his face. It wasn't an expression Remy had ever seen him wear before, until he remembered.

"I—Zidan," the words were raw in Remy's throat. "I'm sorry. I wasn't myself—I didn't know—"

"I know," Malekh said. "You didn't know what you were doing." He squeezed Xiaodan's hand, his face changing as he looked down at her with fresh, tender concern. "Attend to her. I have to see after—see after Naji." There was a brief break in his voice, a catch of the throat, but his face had returned to its careful stoicism. With a heavy heart, Remy watched him return to his fallen brother.

"There was nothing you could have done, and he knows that," Xiaodan murmured, already on her way to falling asleep, as Remy cut himself shallowly along the side of his arm to bring it up to Xiaodan's dry, parched lips.

"There's always something I could have done," Remy whispered as she took in his blood hungrily, slipping into unconsciousness soon after. He had grown to like the youth and Malekh cared deeply for his brother. Naji had died saving him, and by Remy's hand.

"I was correct." The Duke of Valenbonne was watching him, a faint sneer on his face. He wiped his blade, examining the speckles of blood there. "You have become the familiar of not just one vampire, but two."

Remy said nothing. The shock of seeing his father fighting was only just less than the shock of seeing his mother, alive and yet nothing like he had pictured. "You weren't surprised it was her," he said dully.

"I suspected." The duke retrieved his shield next, frowning at the faint nicks there. "The little whore you call your mother had run off to be with her lover. A vampire from the First Court, as I've always said. Why else do you think they found her in a coven's nest, boy? Your mother betrayed me to become a familiar, and all while pregnant with you." He looked from Remy to Xiaodan. "And you've taken after her, like I thought you would."

"Only an insouciant would insult his own child after he was instrumental in saving your life," Malekh said evenly, rising to his feet with Naji in his arms. The boy's face was bloodied, but he looked peaceful. The sight of him hurt.

The elder Pendergast scoffed. "An observation, nothing more. He is my only son, after all. Whatever her faults, his mother never pretended he was anything but mine, whatever the rumors say."

His father gazed out over the ruins, at the bodies still smoking from the fires Xiaodan had sent forth, the smell of burnt flesh still permeating the air. "Seems like Elouve has you to thank, Lord Malekh. I have very little love for its citizens myself, at this point, for nearly subjecting my son to the hangman's noose."

"Easy to express your disdain when you were safely hidden away at Loxley House with an army to protect you," Remy snapped, unable to hide his anger any longer.

"You thought I would do nothing? I had my own people stationed at the plaza, bows aimed at your rope and batons ready for dispersal, except it was that redheaded vampire who'd retrieved you first. And when Lord Malekh destroyed the rest of the scaffolding, I thought it more prudent not to reveal my hand yet. Did you seriously believe I would let my own flesh and blood, my only heir, perish? I didn't train you to be a survivor for this long only to watch you die, my boy."

"You've always had an ulterior motive to explain your concern for my well-being," Remy said. "You told my mo—the Night—*her* that you used my blood as a lure to draw her out. You didn't care that her wrath could have destroyed Aluria, or that I would have been blamed for it."

"You benefit only from hindsight. I took a gamble. If she or her vampire lover were alive, then they would have recognized your blood. It would have pulled them out of hiding. And I was right. Astonbury had nothing on the First Court, refused to even look for it, knowing how badly I wanted the information. Not even your vampire friends had any inkling of where she'd gone."

"I don't know how long ago Ligaya came to control the First Court, liar that she always was. Her vampire consort must have been much more powerful than I'd thought. But as long as she remained alive, she would be a constant danger to the kingdom. And now?" Remy's father stretched out his arms, lifting them toward the capital. "Now they know that the Night Empress is a real threat. Now we can finally mobilize against their Court, using all of Aluria's resources, as it should have been. And finally—*finally*—we shall annihilate the First Court."

"I wanted to avenge my mother," Remy choked, "not have her die again."

"Are you blind, boy? The Ligaya I knew died years ago. This wasn't your mother anymore—only some vengeful kindred bitch that we had to destroy." Edgar turned back to Malekh. "We have not always been on cordial terms, Lord Malekh. We've had our own brief skirmishes in the past, haven't we? Aluria has proven wanting in its treaty with you. Perhaps you would be more interested in one with me instead."

"And what do you have to offer?" the noble asked.

"The tide of politics is changing here, even as we speak, and it turns in my favor. It is very likely that I will rise to a position of much higher prominence soon and shall therefore be in a better place to render assistance. For as long as you pledge to fight with us against the First Court, you will have the alliance your betrothed very dearly wishes for." The Duke of Valenbonne's eyes gleamed. "In fact, as surety, I would be more than willing to offer my son to you as a . . . well, *hostage* would be too harsh a word, so let us say he would be a guest, a ward for as long as our agreement holds. Though I suspect you and the Lady Song would not be against the idea. Neither, I believe, will my son."

"I will think about it," Malekh said shortly.

"Not for long, I hope. I shall tell the Reapers to form a guard for you when you return to Elouve, Remington. Once word spreads of what has transpired here, and of your efforts to save the capital—you make me proud, Remington. You make me very proud. You need not be concerned for Reapers like Feiron or Hathorn. I have already seen to their punishment."

"And who's going to see to yours?"

His father's laugh was far too loud and far too offensive in the wake of the destruction still burning about them. "You, too, will be welcomed in Elouve, Lord Malekh—you and your powerful little Sunbringer here."

Remy didn't even look at his father when he departed; all his attention was concentrated on the sleeping woman in his arms. He was exhausted beyond measure. He wanted to weep, to lie down and close his eyes beside her and perhaps never need wake up.

"I'm sorry," he said again, because it was the only thing left he could do.

"So am I, Pendergast." Malekh didn't even sound angry. He didn't lash out at him the way he had back at Chànggē Shuǐ when he had accused him of spying for his father. He only sounded as weary as he was, and somehow that made the guilt that much heavier.

"Alegra," Malekh added when the other woman materialized

beside him, her normally stoic expression tinged now with a look of bewildered sorrow as she beheld the fallen vampire in his arms. "Help Pendergast with Xiaodan. Take them back to Mari's. I need to . . ." He looked down at Naji, and a spasm of pain flashed across his face.

Remy swallowed. "Malekh."

"Leave him be," Alegra cautioned softly.

For a moment, Malekh remained, looking down at his beloved sibling's tranquil face, holding him closely in his arms. The next, he was gone.

"He needs some time alone," the woman said, still uncharacteristically gentle. "What do you intend to do now?"

"I don't know." Remy closed his eyes and held Xiaodan tighter. "I don't bloody know anymore."

36

REGRETS

The fanfare that had received him when he'd finally steeled himself to return to the city two days ago had been muted. It was not quite the raucous welcome that his father had said he would receive, but at least it was neither hostile nor homicidal. Reports from the battlefield had reached the masses quickly enough, announced by a reluctant Feiron. Riones had kept Remy's secret, possibly browbeaten other Reapers who might have witnessed it. No gossip spread of his ability to control the infected, which was almost laughable, as it was the only rumor about him that had ever been true.

But their fear of him remained.

Remy never went outside if he could help it. On the rare instances he had to leave Kinaiya Lodge—mainly because parts of it needed repairs and rebuilding, though Riones had been truthful when he'd said he'd saved enough for it to remain habitable—people avoided him.

A few from the ton had the stomach to greet him—nervously, warily, like he might attack them mid-conversation—but most took the coward's way out. They scurried away when the opportunity presented itself, crossed the street and ignored him entirely, or managed barely perceptible nods in his direction before turning their backs.

The rest of the commonfolk were even less polite, crowds parting before him with every step he took in their direction. His father had demanded public retaliation; some of the more vocal, the most violent of the mob, had been consigned to the gallows themselves. He had not even known until the newssheets had printed the one regarding Hathorn's execution, an unusual punishment for a Reaper. But the man, after all, had only been the son of a butcher.

It was all against Remy's wishes. But he had no power now to change things in Elouve. He wasn't even sure if he'd ever had it to begin with.

Neither Xiaodan nor Malekh had sent word to him since he'd returned to the city.

Elke was gone. Her varied businesses in the city had been settled, handed over to trusted staff or, in many cases, the deeds ceded over to them entirely. She had been so careful in everything but her friendship with him, and the guilt gnawed him up even further, that that was all it had taken for her to give up everything.

He had found her apartments boarded up and bare of furnishings, with nothing but a mahogany box and a note waiting for him. *It should not take very long to find myself a more comfortable situation*, she had written, *and once I do, I shall send word. In the meantime, here is a gift for you—let it not be said that I do not keep my promises.*

He opened the box, peeled away the delicate wrapping paper to reveal its contents. Twin sapphire eggs, he saw, nestled underneath a perfectly carved golden—

Despite himself, or perhaps because of it, Remy began to laugh.

HE COULD not attend Giselle's funeral without causing a commotion, but he visited her grave afterward with a bouquet of her favorite roses. She had been buried beside her husband, the inscriptions nothing but praise and prayers for them both, with no mention of their eventual fates.

She would hate it here, Remy thought, lying forever in repose beside Matthew Astonbury. If he'd had his way, he would have buried her in her beloved gardens, or perhaps on a cliff that overlooked the sea, where she would have a stunning view of the waters. Not here, with a man she had despised.

The only true power within Elouve, it seemed, lay with old men who should long ago have been relegated to obscurity. Change only occurred when they allowed it, according to what they considered proper, never for those most affected by it.

He had knelt by her tombstone and stayed there for a long time. Another victim, another in a long list of people he couldn't save.

He hoped that Malekh had buried Naji where the boy would have preferred. Maybe beside his young lover back at Chànggē Shuĭ.

The pain grew.

It took longer to travel, to reach his mother's grave. Remy had a different purpose in mind this time. He stared at the mound before him, shovel in hand, at the gravestone that marked where her body lay.

He didn't hate Malekh for finding her body. He didn't hate her for being what she had become. *It is what it is.*

He began to dig.

LIGAYA BASCOM PENDERGAST, the headstone read.

The sun rarely broke through the clouds over Elouve, but for the hour it took him to uncover the grave it did, splaying across the ground around him like the light, too, knew that there was a secret waiting to be uncovered. Sweat poured down his face, bathed his back, and still he didn't stop until his spade hit something hard beneath him with a hollow thud.

LIGAYA BASCOM PENDERGAST.

With his hands he swept the dirt off the wooden casket. Another rough jab with his shovel broke through the lid.

Breathing rapidly, his shirt drenched, Remy stared at the disturbed soil and dirt, at the empty coffin below him.

BELOVED WIFE AND MOTHER.

Queen Ophelia summoned him not long after.

THIS WAS only Remy's second meeting with Her Majesty Queen Ophelia, ruler of Aluria, and he presumed she was already tired of him. Their first meeting had not been to commend him for his valor or for his impeccable service as a Reaper, and neither was this one. The queen appeared neither happy nor angry to see him. Considering that he had almost single-handedly upended the kingdom she so dearly loved, it was the best he could have hoped for.

Instead, the intelligent green eyes that studied him now were almost inquisitive, the way Malekh looked sometimes when engrossed in some new experiment. Remy endured her quiet scrutiny and tried not to think about him or Xiaodan.

"It is clear to me," Queen Ophelia finally said, "that I have you to thank for saving my city. Perhaps even for saving Aluria. It could also be said that you are to blame for much of the havoc that had occurred in the first place."

Remy said nothing in his defense. Everything he'd have wanted to say, she would have heard from somewhere else by now.

"The dead who'd risen from within Elouve were the dormant infected, or so my scientists tell me, buried without anyone ever knowing they had the Rot. Planted by those who work for the

Night Court, culprits unknown. Astonbury, too, lied to me. Some of his subordinates, under Aglaice's questioning, had confessed to witnessing the duke carrying out experiments on these beasts, his incompetence accidentally setting them loose on my lands. It appears his ire for you emboldened him to use your blood in these accursed studies."

Remy was silent.

"I have asked you here to inform you, personally, that I have elected your father to the vacant position of lord high steward."

His head snapped up. He stared at her.

"While I do not condone him sponsoring Yost's experiments and serving as his benefactor after the doctor's disgrace and expulsion from my court, I cannot deny that the antidotes the man has created are nearly miraculous in their benefits. That the Duke of Valenbonne himself has regained much of his health in spite of his having been in poor form for years now . . . even my finest royal physicians cannot explain his rapid recovery. These new serums have proven to be better even than bloodwakers. Lesser side effects, lesser withdrawal symptoms . . ."

She shook her head. "The duke has also confessed to me, quite candidly and without prompting, that he was aware of Astonbury's schemes for some time, hence his employment of Dr. Yost as a countermeasure. I would have punished him myself, duke or no, had he not admitted it to me without prompting, but he was contrite besides. His zeal to see to the protection of Aluria is admirable, though I do not appreciate being left in the dark about these matters. He has gone so far as to turn down the position I've offered as part of his penance."

Of course he has, Remy thought. *But.*

"But he is also the most competent man we have left to lead the Ministry of the Archives, and so I insisted. We do not believe we have seen the last of the Night Court, and he is the only one knowledgeable enough to defend our kingdom from them. We have also decided to put Yost under probation, with scientists of our choosing on hand to keep an eye on any new . . . developments of his."

"I don't think you should be trusting my father all this much," Remy said. Edgar Pendergast had planned everything far too well. Astonbury's downfall and murder; luring the Night Court out of hiding for his revenge; his rise to lord high steward; creating the Rot, then claiming credit for its defeat. And Remy—no one would believe him now. Even if they did, his father had already wormed his way into a position that made him indispensable to the kingdom.

"I know. Your father is a far, far cleverer man than anyone thought, Remington. It is in Aluria's benefit to put that brilliance to work for us. For now. Which brings me to you."

"I don't want it." The words fell out of his mouth even before she could pose the question. "I wish to continue serving you, Your Majesty, but I have no desire to find a role for myself at your court. I have no head for politics, and my skills are better equipped on the field than at your bureaus."

"Xiaodan told me that you would refuse our offer," the queen said, smiling now. "But I thought to make it all the same. You would be invaluable to the Archives. We had hoped that you would be more enthusiastic about being offered now what Astonbury denied you in the past. You and your father are right; the First Court poses more of a danger than we thought they would, and the longer we allow them to continue to hide and thrive in the darkness, the more powerful they will be when they try again. We want you to lead the charge against them. Will you at least consider it?"

He would once have leaped at the chance. It was all he'd ever wanted. Strange how much had changed in just a few short weeks. "It was my father's desire to see me join the Reapers, and I did so to please him. But to command the army is to garner trust among my soldiers, and I—I do not have that privilege yet among the Alurians. I would rather be on my own terms than remain beholden to what my superiors might dictate for me within the Archives, Her Majesty being the only exception."

"In other words, you do not wish to work under your father regardless of any rank I bestow upon you," the queen said, though her look was one of understanding. "I have another proposal you may be more willing to accept. Things remain fraught between Aluria and the Third and Fourth Courts, and I need someone to serve as an unofficial liaison for my kingdom while Lord Malekh returns to his own coven to solicit support among the other vampire clans against the Night Empress. Most of the kindred have remained neutral in the years since the First has lain in hiding, but he believes they can be persuaded to act now that the Night Empress has shown her claws. To everyone else, you will be taking a voluntary leave of absence from Elouve to continue your search for the Night Empress farther east."

"Xiaodan killed her."

"Lord Malekh doesn't think so, and I'm inclined to believe him. Even First Court vampires left ashes behind after their deaths, he said. He found no such evidence on the battlefield."

Remy's breath caught. "Malekh's leaving, then?"

"He and Lady Song. With the Rot expected to be fully neutralized in the coming months, Xiaodan believes that Qing-ye will no longer be under immediate threat, the First Court notwithstanding. She has, as always, petitioned for you to accompany them on their behalf."

Remy hadn't spoken to either court vampire since returning to Elouve. He had resigned himself to the idea that they had both chosen to permanently break off all contact. "I am not sure Lord Malekh will be eager for me to be his companion."

"On the contrary, he adds his request to hers." Queen Ophelia's expression became grave. "It will not be an easy task, Remington. You will be entering the heart of their territories, a lion's den. You will be considered Xiaodan and Zidan's familiar, in every sense of the word. You must be strong enough to defend yourself if they cannot do so in your stead. There are many court vampires who consider humans beneath them."

"But familiars are forbidden in—"

"I will issue a special, secret dispensation if you believe it necessary," Queen Ophelia said with a faint grin. "I am aware of your relationship. It is one that I do not wish to inquire about, nor do I wish to judge. But it puts you in a position to work for Alurian interests. Your father is a capable statesman, but it is you that I trust." The smile disappeared. "Remington. There is something about Xiaodan that I don't believe you know yet."

"Is she all right?"

"Yes, and no. After the fight she had with the Night Empress, she tells me that she can no longer call on her sunbringing abilities."

"What do you mean?" Remy had unconsciously taken a few steps closer to the queen before realizing the faux pas. "Is she hurt? Are you—"

The queen raised a hand to stop him. "Do you love her?"

"I love them both," he responded promptly, with none of the embarrassment of their first meeting.

"She is fine. She is as strong and as quick as she ever was. She is also distraught, though trying her best not to show it. Though there is a stigma among her kind for having such powers, I believe it's been a part of her for so long that she mourns it most keenly."

"I need to go to her."

"I've cautioned them against stepping foot inside Elouve for now. I have imprisoned the preachers and those attempting to incite chaos, but I would much rather not have two vampires in the capital so soon after such a battle. You are to meet them tomorrow morning outside the gates—with a private guard of your own to see you off safely."

Remy thought about the kingdom he would have gladly given

his life to save. Elke was right. He always seemed to give more than what he was ever given back.

"Many Alurians already view me as something inhuman," he said. "Something less than themselves. If anything, it's been good practice. Please inform Lady Song and Lord Malekh that I will be ready to depart with them at their convenience."

"I'M NOT surprised," the Duke of Valenbonne said, his rapier making short work of the target before him. His speed and agility had noticeably improved, and he moved with almost the same skill and nimbleness that Remy remembered from his youth. "Your infatuation with these vampires will be the death of you, if you take no precautions."

"And yet I don't see you asking me to change my mind, to stay and work in the Ministry alongside you."

"You're as stubborn as I am. Tell you to do one thing, and you'll bring down hell and high water to do the opposite. Surprisingly enough, I agree with your assessment. No matter what Her Majesty thinks, you'll be wasted in the Archives. Imagine that, Remington—after all Astonbury had tried to do to sabotage you, including his attempts to drain you of blood to weaken you in your hunts." He glanced back at Remy, grinned at the look on his face. "Oh, you didn't know? Aren't you grateful now for Yost's fortifying bloodwakers despite Astonbury's attempts to murder you? Light, the money I would part with to have watched him convicted at Her Majesty's court!" His father made another practiced lunge. "You've never been exalted for intelligence, Remington. But skill, strength, bloody instinct besides—those are where you excel."

"You never told Queen Ophelia that the Night Empress was my mother," Remy said. "She wouldn't have offered you the position of lord high steward, had she known."

"After all the trouble I went through pretending to turn it down? Don't act so high and mighty with me, boy. Surely you've told her yourself, then?"

Remy didn't answer.

"You're as much a hypocrite as I am. Your vampire friends, too, keeping their silence. They know things will be worse for you, should that get out. Make no mistake, Remy—Queen Ophelia couches it in delicate, honorable terms, but you are to be a spy for Aluria within their vampire strongholds. I will make arrangements for you to send word to us of their plans, their targets, whatever weaknesses of the First Court they know of—and whatever weaknesses *they* have, to use against them. Ophelia has forgiven me for not telling her about the Rot, you know. I've convinced her that Astonbury had been responsible for creating it. She understands as well as I the possibilities of using the dead as an army. Her distaste for it holds her back, but she will give in eventually. They often do when it's their lives at stake. Let us both prove our loyalties first in an official capacity, before she need learn of Ligaya.

"Perhaps you are soft-hearted enough to forgive Malekh for killing the mother you claim to love, but we have many more questions now that require answers. I want to know how she ascended to become the Night Empress, find who was responsible for turning her into the nightmare she became. You must bring her the true peace she needs, boy. Do you understand?"

Slowly, Remy nodded.

"Good. Stay alive and return, Remington. I am too old to sire new heirs, and I have invested too much in you for you to fail me again." His father steadied his rapier and attacked again. The sword's tip sank deeply into Grimesworthy's shoulder, but the undead man stood silently without protest.

"I, of course, have not told Her Majesty about our other experiments," Valenbonne said. "She may have promoted me into this enviable position, but that doesn't mean she trusts me, only that she knows I can handle Aluria's defense, when Astonbury never could. Grimesworthy must be a secret for now. You understand that I do all this for her and this kingdom, Remington? We need armies of our own to fight the First Court. An army of infected under our control will save the lives of soldiers and citizens alike. What they do not know, they cannot fear, even if what they fear is what will save us all. I will persuade her of the necessity of our experiments. We will see this through, my boy. And we shall be honored for it. They will never besmirch the Pendergasts or the Dukes of Valenbonne ever again."

He was right. And that was the problem with Edgar Pendergast. In the end, he always came out on top.

"Father," Remy said before he left, not willing to see his father puncture more holes into the unmoving Grimesworthy. "Did you know that Mother was the Night Empress before this?"

A pause. The duke smiled. "Aglaice tells me that someone recently dug up her grave. Was that you, trying to make sure?"

"Did you know, Father?"

"No, Remington. I didn't. I had no idea it would be that bitch's face looking back at me when she compelled you to start killing the rest of those vampires. Sometimes I'd see her—or think I had—in the forests, in places I've hunted, sometimes even in the thick of the crowd. That damn scarlet hood. Her face staring at me, only to disappear. Thought it was my imagination, until I realized it wasn't.

"But you weren't the first person to dig up her grave, Remington. I was the first to realize the whore's tomb was empty. She'd escaped me once and thought she'd find a way to do it again, even in death. I presumed she was hiding out in the Night Court, not that she *was* the Night Court. But now I have two of her own clans and the whole of Aluria against the First Court. It will fall soon enough."

"Did you ever even love her?" Remy asked bitterly.

His father met his gaze. "Of course I did, Son," he said calmly. "I wouldn't hate her so much if I hadn't." He turned back to Grimesworthy and readied his blade. "Take Breaker when you go, Remington. You'll be needing it."

HE'D LEFT a note for the Marquess of Riones, a letter of thanks for everything he'd done. The man had been awarded the position Remy had turned down, and he was pleased for the Reaper's sake, a well-deserved reward. That would make at least two competent people in the new administration, though only one that he liked.

It was better not to meet Riones again before he'd left—the marquess had a more important reputation to lose now.

It had been painful to do, but Remy had put Kinaiya Lodge up on the market—immediately, once the repairs were done. It was no longer the sanctuary he had wished it to be.

What possessions he couldn't take with him had been entrusted to lawyers for safekeeping, along with the handling of the lodge's sale—not the high-priced attorneys that the Dukes of Valenbonne had always retained, but the small, capable firm Elke used for her businesses. Remy did not trust his father not to come snooping while he was away. He'd left no other instructions, save a stipulation that the new owners, upon purchase of the lodge, were to continue feeding the stray cats that wandered into the garden.

The items that had survived the fire included the portrait of his mother and the books on Tithe he'd collected over the years. Remy had spent his last night by the painting, staring wordlessly up at her, unable to find answers there.

Nobody in Aluria had the answers he sought. But the courts might.

And somewhere among those kindred, his mother would be

waiting. Because Remy somehow knew that she hadn't died in the fight against Xiaodan. If there was one thing they had in common, it was that neither of them would perish so easily.

"Forgive me," Remy told his mother, and slowly drew the sheet over her painted, smiling face.

You're too kind for this. You'll always leave pieces of your heart behind, whether you want to or not.

"I know, Elke," Remy sighed quietly to his best friend, now so far away because of him. "I know."

THEY WERE waiting for him. Xiaodan still pale, not quite recovered. Malekh silent as usual, face unreadable, though his eyes looked hard.

Remy wanted to wrap his arms around Xiaodan. To demand that they postpone the trip until she was healthier, to yell at Malekh for pushing her, as he'd done many times in the past. But things had changed. The group of stern-looking Reapers flanking him, for instance, ostensibly for his protection. Even without an audience, he was no longer sure if the couple would ever show him the same affection as those days at Chàngge Shuǐ when he'd lived with them, bedded them, loved them.

Things had changed. Xiaodan was vulnerable. Remy had killed Naji, and it was not in Malekh's nature to easily forgive.

"The laws of the kindred will be different from the laws of Aluria," Malekh said coldly. "There will be fewer accommodations for humans there. The instant we set foot in the heart of court territory, you will be a familiar. You are to obey both Xiaodan and I at all costs. It will be difficult, but it will be to protect you."

He paused. Silence fell. Remy wished he could ask where he had buried Naji's body so he could pay his respects. But he didn't.

"You would have done better to turn us down instead," the

noble added harshly. "The disdain and intolerance for you here in Aluria will be nothing compared to what you will face with us at the courts."

Xiaodan and Alegra had once told Remy that it was easy to see through Malekh, a statement Remy had met with confusion since statues changed expressions more frequently than the Third Court king. But now he understood. It was a bleak morning, the sky grayer than usual and a light drizzle starting to set in, but Remy felt warmer than he had back at his hearth.

"Remy," Xiaodan said softly, still so wan, but her eyes just as beautiful in the soft brown they were now as they had been when they were the color of mist.

No, he thought. Things may have changed for them where it concerned him, but it changed nothing for him where it concerned *them*.

He set his shoulders and lifted his head, proud as ever. Whatever might come, he'd be by their side, and that was better than being without them.

You're too kind for this.

Like bloody fuck I am, Elke, Remy thought, doubling down. "Let's get going, then, before the Alurians change their mind and try to hang me one last time as a goodbye present."

CACKNOWLEDGMENTS

As always—to my agent Rebecca Podos for nearly a decade of support and trust. From the highest of peaks to rock bottom and back again—thank you for always being there.

My endless gratitude and appreciation to Joe Monti and to my editor, Amara Hoshijo, for being stalwart champions of this oddball story about a boy who, vampires aside, just wanted to be loved. I wrote this book during one of the lowest points of my life, but it was they who brought it out into the sun. Thank you, Joe, for always believing. Thank you, Amara, for making everything shine.

To everyone else at Gallery and Saga who worked hard to make this a reality: my dedicated publicist, Kayleigh Webb; Caroline Pallotta, Sherry Wasserman, Kaitlyn Snowden, and Michelle Marchese for their production and design savvy; Stacey Sakal, Laura Jarrett, and M.L. Liu for their sharp eyes; and Jennifer Bergstrom, Jennifer Long, and Paul O'Halloran for helping this find its readership the world over. This book would be a mess if it wasn't for all of you.

To all my family and friends who've been there since day one, especially to Andy Guzman, Laurel Monsanto, and Abby Macaraig. You are the strongest heroes I have ever been blessed to know; I am so proud to be friends with all of you and I try not to be angry anymore even though nothing about this was fair, because none of you would have wanted that. I wish you three could have read this book. Especially you, Abby. You love *Castlevania* and Alucard more than anyone else I've ever met. Let's all meet up again one day.

For the trash writers gang who has stuck by me all these years— Sam, Pippa, Lee, Bernie, and Jessie, who've encouraged me ever since our cringe fanfiction-writing days when we should have known better. I hope this made you all happy to read.

And finally, to Les—who has spent many a night and day manning the fort and being my personal comforter while I worked on deadlines and tried not to self-combust. I'm not sure I would have made it without you and the kids and I am so happy to be here.